Shiver

The Unbreakable Bonds Series

By Jocelynn Drake and Rinda Elliott

Praise for *Shiver*

"I love it when a new to you author leaves you wanting more! I really enjoyed this first book in the Unbreakable Bonds series and can't wait to see where it goes next."

—Prism Book Alliance

"Shiver was everything I hoped for and more. I didn't want to put it down. I loved these characters. It is an alpha-male hot mess (I mean that in the best possible ways). In m/f romance, a caveman mentality is a big turn off, but if you pair that up with another caveman alpha-male…fireworks!"

—I Smell Sheep

"I just flat out enjoyed this. The relationships, suspense, mystery, and hot smexy times…it all boils down to fun. I had fun while reading this and look forward to a continuation of the series."

—Gay Book Reviews

"I thought Drake and Rinda Elliott did a good job putting me in the headspace of these damaged men. I believed in their emotional ties and in the growing romance between Lucas and Andrei. The sex is hot. The pacing is good. And I liked the overall story… I would recommend for fans of m/m romantic suspense. I am curious to see what the authors have in store for the next installment."

—Red Hot Books

"This book was filled with angst, excitement, action and a whole lot of emotion. I loved how Lucas and Andrei slowly grew together, and Andrei discovers his true sexuality. How Lucas realizes he's let in Andrei without him noticing and without a whole lot of effort. The amount of feelings that these two authors have managed to write into and action filled book is amazing."

—Love Bytes

Also by Jocelynn Drake

The Dark Days Series

Bound to Me

The Dead, the Damned and the Forgotten

Nightwalker

Dayhunter

Dawnbreaker

Pray for Dawn

Wait for Dusk

Burn the Night

The Asylum Tales

The Asylum Interviews: Bronx

The Asylum Interviews: Trixie

Angel's Ink

Dead Man's Deal

Demon's Vengeance

Also by Rinda Elliott

Beri O'Dell Series

Dweller on the Threshold

Blood of an Ancient

The Brothers Bernaux

Raisonne Curse

Sisters of Fate

Foretold

Forecast

Foresworn

Also by Rinda Elliott Writing as Dani Worth

The Kithran Regenesis Series

Kithra

Replicant

Catalyst

Origin

Crux Survivors Series

After the Crux

Sole Survivors

Copyright

This book is a work of fiction. Names, characters, places, and incidents are products of the author's imagination or are used factiously and are not to be construed as real. Any resemblance to actual events, locales, or organizations, or persons, living or dead, is entirely coincidental.

SHIVER. Copyright ©2015 Jocelynn Drake and Rinda Elliott. All rights reserved under International and Pan-American Copyright Conventions. By payment of the required fees, you have been granted the nonexclusive, nontransferable right to access and read the text of this e-book onscreen. No part of this text may be reproduced, transmitted, introduced into any information storage and retrieval system, in any form or by any means, whether electronic or mechanical, now know or hereinafter invented, without the express written permission of Jocelynn Drake and Rinda Elliott.

Cover art by Stephen Drake of Design by Drake.

To Rachel

Acknowledgements

Writing a book isn't supposed to be this much fun. I've written quite a few books now and I'm sure I must have just done this one wrong, because it really isn't supposed to be this much fun. Thank you, Rinda, for making *Shiver* such a great experience. I love brainstorming with you. I love that you're my No. 1 bad influence. I love that you called me out when I did it wrong and cheered when I finally got it right. I loved falling in love with our boys with you and creating this amazing world. Thank you, and I'm ready to do it wrong all over again with the next book.

As always, thank you to my amazing husband for giving me the space and time to get lost in a book. You get me and I do realize just how rare that is in this world. And a big thank you to my family for always supporting my writing, no matter where it might lead me. I've tackled vampires and warlocks. I thought it was time to give love a shot.

Jocelynn Drake

First up, I'm thanking Jocelynn for jumping into this new adventure with me. Working with her has been a blast! She puts up with my sentence nitpicking so unbelievably well. And my late night emails. And my "oh crap" emails. LOL. In other words, she's incredibly patient. We found a lot of things in common while working on this book and became good friends. I'm excited about us working on the next. And the next…

Also, a big thank you to Rachel Vincent, who helped jump-start this for us. Jocelynn and I had talked about working together and Rachel gave us that last nudge. She also helped brainstorm titles and more!

I had such fun with them both at RT in Texas!

Thanks to Christy Jenkins for the last minute beta read and line edits.

A big thanks to the Deadline Dames for always being my biggest cheering section!

And as always, a huge thanks to my husband and children for putting up with my long, long hours and the stress of book deadlines, releases, and the publishing business overall. I love you guys so much.

Rinda Elliott

Chapter 1

Shiver was alive.

Lucas Vallois leaned over the waist-high wall and surveyed the first floor of his favorite club, pride sending a welcome stream of warmth through him. People were crammed into every available space, gyrating to the music the guest DJ played while six bartenders expertly crafted unique drinks and cracked open beers with speed and finesse. Low and intimate lighting created secluded areas for stolen moments.

He smirked. Maybe not low and intimate enough because he could see bare skin from here—not that he minded. But it was surprising considering the temperature in those corners.

A different world existed on the second floor.

Lucas turned and settled across from his assistant on the supple black leather sofas. They were cool to the touch thanks to the steady stream of frigid air being pumped in from the air conditioning vents. Fall had settled into Cincinnati and the surrounding river valley, but the crisp, evening temperatures outside couldn't cut the body heat that tried to lift the temperature inside the building toward triple digits. But even without that, Lucas demanded that the air remain cool and sharp inside the nightclub.

How could you expect anything less at a place called Shiver?

Lucas leaned forward and picked up one of the glasses. Taking a sip of water, he kept his eyes locked on the petite blond with the wide blue eyes seated across from him. She'd begun adding smart, matching coats to her business suits when they'd started meeting here more. Though heat rose, the upstairs couldn't compete with the amount of grinding, crowded bodies below. Candace's hands flew before her as she signed a list of updates regarding business contracts, negotiations, and other interests he had brewing. He nodded, making mental notes of where he would need to follow up the next day.

When the music changed, a swift jab of annoyance made him frown. Candace's fingers instantly halted, but Lucas shook his head once, indicating that his frown wasn't due to anything she had signed.

God, he hated trance. It all sounded the fucking same. Clean, sterile, lifeless, and digital. What happened to the days of Trent Reznor's raw voice and screaming guitar hammering against the walls? Nine Inch Nails, KMFDM, Thrill Kill Kult, Skinny Puppy, and Front 242 echoed through some of his more pleasant memories, but it seemed as if they didn't have a place now. Of course, whenever he brought it up to one of his friends, they would snicker and mock him about being old.

Restless, he returned his glass to the table, pushed to his feet, then motioned for Candace to halt before he walked back to the half wall. Shiver had been open for more than a year and it was still packed every night it was open. Of the three nightclubs he owned, it was the most popular and his most successful. Bodies writhed in dance and alcohol flowed in a constant stream of lovely profit. Guest DJs fought for spots on his calendar and celebrities made regular appearances. It was *the* place to see and be seen in Cincinnati.

But Shiver would probably be closing in a year. If he was lucky, maybe two. People followed trends like lemmings scurrying for the cliffs. And what was hot now, wouldn't be hot in a few years. Nightclubs—the truly profitable ones—never stayed on top for more than a few years at best. Lucas had learned to close his clubs as sales started to dip, timing it so that a newer, more exclusive one was opening up at the same time.

Shiver was his favorite. The sleek, modern atmosphere made an impact and Lucas loved making an impact.

Candace rose and stepped up to the wall in his peripheral vision, but she waited for him to turn toward her. Lucas let her stand there as his gaze slipped over the two bars and dance floor that were visible. Shiver wasn't at capacity yet, but it was close.

He turned his gaze on his assistant and she immediately started signing, her long, delicate fingers flying through the air. The sleeves of her slim, red coat flapped around her wrists.

"Table service is booked for tonight and all weekend," she reported. "The whiskey distributor has agreed to our terms. We will have the new contract on Monday."

Lucas nodded and she immediately stepped back, indicating that she had nothing else to say. Some of the tension eased from his shoulders. It had taken him six tries to find an assistant who could keep up with him, and Candace had come with an added bonus: she knew sign language. It proved to be an excellent opportunity to pick up fluency in a fourth language. Three nights a week, Lucas surveyed each of his clubs and he refused to shout instructions over the pounding music until he was hoarse. He also would not be shouted at in his own club. Of course, most of the bar staff wrongly believed he was deaf, but that was fine. It kept him unapproachable.

With his eyes back on the crowd, the horde below grew more scantily clad as the night wore on. The club scene was incredibly predictable and boring normally. As a form of entertainment, it was useless. But he loved it for the money it brought in. And he still felt a fierce sense of pride that he'd been right about the concept here—even when some of his friends insisted a cold club would keep women out.

Skin sliding against skin always brought heat.

He started back for his water when a tall man turned away from the bar, carrying a drink in each hand. Lucas couldn't clearly see his face, but something about the way his dark suit hugged his broad shoulders and wide chest caught Lucas's attention. The man deftly weaved through the crowd without spilling his drinks until he reached a woman chatting and laughing with some friends. She accepted the drink without looking up, continuing to talk uninterrupted. Lucas nearly smiled when the man shook his head in irritation and half turned away to take a large gulp of his drink. Looked like he needed the alcohol to get him through the night.

Lucas had an alternative in mind for him.

He waited, impatience coiling in his stomach, willing the man to look up at the second floor overhang. The area was cast in heavy shadows. Lucas knew he was invisible to anyone on the lower floor. He wanted to see the man's face, hoping it turned out to be as great as that body. It was by sheer luck that a light passed over his face when he finally lifted his eyes. A strong jaw shaped his oval face and almost too large eyes stood out under a dark brow.

Yeah, maybe this one could do something to liven up Lucas's evening.

Motioning for Candace to join him again, Lucas pointed before signing. "Can you find out who he is?"

She stared at the stranger for several seconds before nodding.

"Just want his name." Lucas wouldn't give her a reason. He didn't really care what she took from his request. A man hadn't captured his attention in over a month, his focus locked almost completely on work and his newest project. And partially on a woman he'd been seeing—though that relationship had already gone beyond a place he liked. Stephanie had lied one too many times to stay in his good graces. He merely had to find time in his schedule to let her know he was ready to move on.

He narrowed his eyes on those broad shoulders. This one would be a good distraction for a night.

Candace started to step away as if she were intending to begin her quest for the stranger's identity when she lurched back, her eyes wide and alarmed. Lucas followed her pointing finger and his stomach clenched. Hard.

Snow.

Lucas watched the white-streaked head of his oldest friend as he cut a fierce swath through the crowd. Ashton Frost had started prematurely graying in his early twenties and never bothered coloring it. He didn't need to. The white made the startling blue of his eyes even sharper, gave his olive skin a sharp contrast. It was why he'd picked up the nickname when they'd been in the service.

Even though the man never uttered a word, people rushed to get out of his way. Snow was a formidable figure, standing well over six feet with broad shoulders that made him like a Mack truck plowing down a pasture of sheep.

The doctor's grim expression drew Lucas's gaze. While Snow had never been an outwardly emotional child, he'd grown even more reserved and cold to the world after years in the army and even more years working as a trauma surgeon at the University of Cincinnati Hospital. The man showed little emotion beyond biting, cold indifference—unless pushed. Then, sometimes...came violent rage.

And based on the predatory way he was moving, Lucas was willing to bet that Snow was on the verge of violent rage. Seemed Candace had been around long enough to see it as well.

He took a deep, calming breath—the last before the storm—and turned to Candace, giving her some final instructions to continue to the other two clubs without him. Ever efficient, she took notes and seemed relieved to beat a hasty retreat. He didn't blame her. Snow could be...well, Snow.

Lucas paused to send one quick text to Rowe.

Snow storm at Shiver.

Slipping his phone in the breast pocket of his tailor-made charcoal suit jacket, Lucas picked up his glass and the bottle of imported water before moving to the enclosed private room at the back of the second floor.

Their mutual friend, Rowe, was one of the few who could make Snow laugh. And it didn't always require alcohol, though booze helped. Lucas pulled out his favorite bourbon and got glasses ready. Snow and Lucas had met Rowe after Army basic training and the three men had been stuck together ever since. Rowe could be silly and ridiculous, and while usually quick to lose his temper, Snow couldn't rile him. No matter how hard he tried at times.

Lucas sank into the worn, brown leather sofa and checked his phone to see Rowe's one word reply.

Fuck.

Lucas didn't doubt that he was on his way.

Snow stalked in, slamming the door closed as Lucas tucked his phone back in his pocket. The room was painfully silent, the soundproofing blocking out the annoying trance music. Lucas could have conducted his business in here, but he preferred to keep an eye on things. This room was for his private use, not business.

"I need a favor." Snow's voice came gruff and low like he'd been yelling all day at the hospital.

Lucas merely lifted one eyebrow to indicate he was listening.

"Help me find a screamer tonight."

Lucas didn't flinch at the request—though it was hard. It certainly wasn't the first time he'd heard those words from Snow. When his best friend was in a bad place, he needed rough sex with a man who could tolerate being manhandled. *No, a man who liked it.* While Lucas liked both women and men in his bed, Snow liked men and men only. The tougher, the better.

After taking a sip of water, Lucas placed his glass on a small end table before rising to his feet. He kept every movement smooth and precise; made sure his expression didn't show worry or anything else. "I'm not a pimp."

Snow's lips curved into something close to a sneer. "No, but you're a man who knows how to find things. Knows all the hot spots. I've been busy and out of the loop."

"Right. Like I believe that." Lucas ground his teeth, but refused to rise to the bait. Snow knew good and well that Lucas didn't engage in illegal activities in business. No, his friend was in one of his foulest moods and if he couldn't fuck his anger away, Snow would bait him until Lucas would beat sense into him. And Lucas wasn't willing to oblige him. That had never been a long-term solution.

Damn Snow and his bruised soul.

Lucas would give all of his wealth to find a way to erase the pain of Snow's past. And the hardship his wall-wrapped bleeding heart caused him daily in that hospital. But after all their years together, Lucas hadn't found the answer to that particular dilemma.

"Yes, I can get things." Lucas frowned. "But not everything. Not that."

"You have the clubs, the connections." Snow's smile was cold. "Come on, find me a screamer."

"It's a stupid request and you know it." Lucas paused, his heart starting to beat a painful rhythm against his ribs. "Will you accept a substitute?"

Snow's shoulders stiffened, his icy, pale blue eyes narrowing.

"Will you take me again?" Lucas asked, the words little more than a whisper.

Pain slashed through Snow's eyes before he jerked away, his body cringing against the question as if Lucas had struck him. "Fuck you." Snow's low voice, ragged and raw, broke. He stabbed his finger at Lucas as his entire body trembled with rage and maybe even pain at the memory that Lucas had called up.

It had been years ago. Snow had been teetering on the black edge of complete self-destruction, demanding a screamer. But Lucas had been unwilling to let Snow prowl the bar scene. It was too dangerous. Lucas couldn't let Snow risk everything he'd been working his life to achieve. So, he'd offered himself. He'd pushed his friend, knowing exactly how to manipulate him until Snow finally cracked.

The experience hadn't been completely unpleasant and had in fact, left Lucas with a better understanding of why men were drawn back to his rough friend. But that wasn't really Lucas's scene and he'd been left battered enough that it had taken a few days to recover so Rowe could see him without raising too many questions.

It hadn't really bothered Lucas—he'd been bruised in rough sex before—but the abject horror and pain in Snow's eyes after it was all over had burned a hole into Lucas's soul. Their friendship almost hadn't recovered, but Lucas would never, ever, let Snow leave him. His love for his friend was fierce and solid and unbreakable. He'd mowed down every obstacle Snow had put up, reinforced a friendship forged in mutual childhood pain.

Snow snarled and prowled the room, stomping to the small bar. Gripping the edge with both hands, he stepped back and stretched his long, lean body into a taut bow. His black slacks and white shirt molded to his frame, accentuating hard muscles he seemed to keep despite his hectic schedule. He hung his head low, his ragged breathing the only sound in the room.

Heart aching, Lucas flashed back to the blond seven-year-old friend with the bruised face and lonely eyes. Snow's intense expression had let Lucas know he'd be in for a fight if he gave in and joined the other boys in their taunts. Lucas had seen something of himself in Snow— even that far back. Something he had never felt completely comfortable with. And that was before he'd learned about the even hotter hell Snow faced when he went home to his family.

He briefly closed his eyes. That memory always brought him back to the present and reminded him that Snow wasn't always right about what he needed. But handling him sometimes took more than kid gloves.

Lucas grabbed his water off the table and walked over to the bar. He set the glass down before wrapping his other hand firmly around the back of Snow's warm neck. "Drink."

"Fuck you," Snow growled but some of the heat had left his voice.

Lucas continued to rub rigid muscles, his long fingers sliding through cool, silken hair, working away days of stress. Tension hummed through Snow's frame, making him vibrate.

"Drink it."

Snow sucked in a deep, steadying breath, his body growing still as if he were deciding whether to punch Lucas or drink the water. Lucas waited, having learned many years before that patience won out over anything else with his friend. His muscles tightened though, as he waited to see if Snow would shatter. When the doctor released a ragged breath and reached for the glass with a shaking hand, Lucas barely managed to hold back his sigh of relief. Snow took two long swallows and put the nearly empty glass back on the bar with a loud thunk.

His body still shook as he continued to stand stretched out like a man waiting for his forty lashes.

Lucas stepped closer, crowding him, letting his presence soothe him as he continued to rub his neck.

"What happened?"

"Ten year old. Three shots to the chest. He was drowning in his own fucking blood when he got to me." His rough voice was a steadily growing rumble like a wall of snow and ice charging down the mountain.

"Dead?"

Snow gave a jerky shake of his head. "He was alive when I closed him, but it'll be touch and go for a couple of weeks. He's been sent on to Children's."

Lucas squeezed his fingers in Snow's side. "He's alive now. Focus on that."

"Motherfucking bastards!" Snow's shout was a good thing, his emotions finally getting a release instead of slowly suffocating under his skin until they bled through in violent actions he couldn't take back. "Why can't they just kill each other off and be fucking done with it? Every day there are more. And the victims are getting younger and younger."

Gang violence had been bad during the past few years and Lucas had passed more than one night helping Snow after he patched up the innocent bystanders bleeding to death on his table. Lucas bit back the same words he longed to say every time he saw Snow suffering. *Walk away. Find something else. Just walk away.* But he said nothing because Snow would never stop. Under the layers of cold indifference he shared with most of the world, laid the most tender, battered heart Lucas had ever known.

"I should just quit. Let them burn themselves and everyone around them out." Snow shoved away from the bar.

Lucas caught the wild, pained look in his friend's eyes. Snow was desperate and lost, hurting more than he could process. Catching him behind the neck again, Lucas jerked Snow into his arms, holding him tight. The doctor stiffened, his arms out. Lucas waited for him to thrust him away before slugging him. To his shock, Snow wrapped his arms tightly around him, laying his forehead on Lucas's shoulder.

"I'm so tired, Luc," Snow whispered.

Closing his eyes, Lucas leaned his head against his friend's, swallowing hard against the lump of frustration and pain clogging his throat. "I know."

Despite his angry words and utter lack of people skills, Snow would never quit. Never walk away from someone who needed him. It wasn't who he was. Being the man's friend filled Lucas with pride, but it killed him to see the unrelenting wear on Snow. Lucas knew how to keep Snow moving, to keep him from completely self-destructing, but it was only a temporary fix. Snow needed something else—but Lucas hadn't a clue as to what it was.

They stood, holding each other, as minutes ticked by. The busy nightclub and the rest of the world slipped away. It had always been that way for Lucas and Snow—from that first day when Lucas had expected a fight and instead earned a life-long friend. They knew each other's secrets, fears, regrets, and dreams. As disappointment, betrayal, and heartache tried to tear them down, they'd remained strong—solid all these years.

A blast of music and cold air poured into the room as a shorter, stockier figure with a shock of auburn hair and shining green eyes strolled in. Lucas kept his hand on Snow's shoulder even as Snow pulled away from him. Lucas needed the reassurance of closeness more.

"What's up, guys?" Rowe's mischievous grin changed his face as it always did into something more akin to wicked imp. He was rough and ready gorgeous with his coloring and his sturdy, muscled frame, but that smile gave him a sort of pretty edge he hated. Lucas personally loved it—Rowe had his own field of energy that made him stand out. Mostly when he whipped out that lethal grin.

"Melissa let you out?" Lucas gave Snow's neck one last squeeze before he walked behind the bar. Grabbing another tumbler, he set it next to the other two and reached for his bottle of bourbon.

Rowe snorted. "More like kicked me out. She was tired of listening to me shout at the game. Damned bullshit."

Lucas said nothing as he poured the amber liquid into each glass. Hell, the man was a horrible liar and Snow had to see through that blatant attempt like it was made of glass. Yet, Snow's shoulders relaxed slightly. More than likely, Rowe's wife was praying that Lucas or their other friend Ian would accompany Rowe and Snow on their drinking binge in hopes of keeping her husband out of trouble. Snow might like to rough people up during sex, but Rowe had a love of bar fights. He always said he liked to start fights when he was drinking—just because he could.

The man did fight like a gladiator. A volunteer gladiator.

And what kind of fucked up person would be like that?

"Lucas is going to get me laid," Snow announced as he picked up one of the tumblers. The half-grin that tugged up one side of his mouth had a wicked bent.

Lucas watched him closely, liking that he sounded more composed and controlled than he had been before. There was still an edginess to his frame, but at least he wasn't demanding a screamer now. It could be less wear and tear on both their souls.

"Come on, Frosty," Rowe teased, using the one nickname that Snow despised. "We both know if you'd smile once in a while, you wouldn't need help getting a piece of ass."

Snow let a smile loose—a cold predatory thing that sent shivers through lesser men. "My smiles haven't gotten me into your ass."

"That's because Melissa doesn't want my ass destroyed, you psychopath." Rowe chuckled as he joined Snow at the bar. He picked up the remaining tumbler and clinked it against his friends' before draining its contents.

Lucas sipped his bourbon, savoring the slow burn down his throat and chest. A reluctant smile pulled at the corners of his mouth as he watched his companions. Between Lucas's hands-on style and Rowe's relentless teasing, Snow already seemed more at ease. Rowe had a gift. He could disarm you with his charm in seconds and have you spilling your life story before the end of the night. He was all bright colors and loyal heart, a fiery sunrise that could, and likely would, punch its way through a cold, blustery day.

"So. Do we want to grab Ian and make a night of it?" Rowe reached across the bar and snagged the bourbon. He replenished his glass and Snow's.

"No," Lucas replied before taking another sip. "Rialto opens to the public tomorrow. I don't want him going through that with a hangover."

Two years of cajoling, badgering, and persuading were about to pay off. Ian had taken the leap and was set to run his own restaurant. Of course, after Ian finally agreed, it had taken him two years to settle on a location, theme and menu. Lucas had been happy to front him the money. The young man was a genius in the kitchen and the investment would easily pay off. So tomorrow night needed to go perfectly for their friend.

"Shit." Rowe cringed. "I totally forgot. Ian promised Melissa and me a table at eight."

Lucas swirled the remaining bourbon in his glass, watching the amber liquid dance in the light. "Try to dig up a tie and a jacket."

"Fuck you."

Lucas smirked. Clothes had been a long time subject of argument between him and Rowe…and Ian. It took great effort to get Rowe out of his jeans and T-shirts.

"Ian's out then," Snow interjected, heading off their bickering before it could spiral out of control.

"We could hit O'Malley's," Rowe suggested.

Snow let loose one of his rare, loud laughs, bringing a full smile to Lucas's lips as the weight of worry lifted from his chest.

"I said I wanted to get laid, you idiot. I'm not going to find any ass at a fucking sports bar."

"You could." Rowe kept his eyes on the glass he held with both hands. "But you'd actually have to work for it. Put in some effort."

"Snow prefers when they buy him drinks and parade in front of him like beauty pageant contestants," Lucas teased.

"Hey now. I work hard to be this beautiful. They should work hard to get a piece of me." Snow grinned.

Rowe reached over and roughly grabbed Snow's jaw with one hand, shaking his head. "Exactly. Look at this face. You know it makes you want to suck his cock."

Snow shoved him away with a curse and Lucas laughed. It was hard to be serious around Rowe. The man had ridiculous down to an art form.

"So then, we hit the Laundry Room or Fortune," Lucas suggested.

Rowe's shoulders slumped and his compact body sunk into an exaggerated sulk. "Really? I hate being the only straight guy in those places. I have to send back all those damned drinks."

Snow's brow furrowed. "Don't you have to do that when women buy you drinks?"

"Nah. Melissa is usually with me and I split them with her."

Lucas hid his smile behind his glass as he finished his drink. Both locations were not only nightclubs that catered to gay men, but they were utter meat markets. People there had one goal: A quick hook up. If Snow truly wanted only to get laid, then they'd be there for less than thirty minutes. But Lucas had a feeling that Snow would stretch things out to make Rowe suffer. Rowe had no problem with the fact that his best friends were gay or bisexual. He just tended to squirm when man after man hit on him at the bars they liked to frequent. His solid, muscled form and that startling smile drew men like ants to honey. So did the shock of dark, auburn waves on his head.

"Laundry Room, it is." Snow paused long enough to finish his drink before leading the way out of the private room.

Rowe met Lucas's gaze, his own laughing façade melting away to reveal his underlying worry. "He okay?"

"Wanted a screamer," Lucas murmured, putting the bourbon back under the bar. Rowe, like him, knew that demand came rarely, thank goodness, but it usually came on the heels of some of Snow's darker periods.

Rowe cursed softly, shaking his head.

Lucas stepped around the bar, motioning for Rowe to precede him. "He's better. Keep him laughing."

The shorter man shot him a look as if to say "if only it were that easy." But he clapped Lucas on the shoulder, squeezing it for a second as he headed back into the club. Rowe knew the role Lucas played and Lucas could guess that Rowe would prefer to never switch with him. They did what they had to in order to keep Snow from unraveling.

Stepping back into the blaring music, Lucas could feel the protective wall go back up around him. Snow, Rowe, and Ian were the only ones who could reach inside him, make him feel vulnerable. But in this world of his making, he was untouchable and always in control.

He followed Rowe as the man bulldozed through the crowd, probably grumbling about crappy music and goofy drinks as he went. Lucas loved Rowe but he didn't understand his taste for flat beer, chicken wings, and things covered in chili while watching sports and listening to country music. In their little group, Rowe was always the odd man out with his taste in food, clothes, and entertainment. Plus, he was all the way straight and happily married to an amazing woman.

But he fit with them. Always had.

As his friend dodged a woman carrying drinks, he roughly shoulder-checked a man. Lucas caught the stranger by the upper arms as he started to stumble to the side. Lucas's pulse jolted a second. It was the same man who'd captured his attention earlier. He wasn't as handsome as Lucas had first thought—his features less refined and a little more blunted, but still not bad. And there was no missing the hot flush on his cheeks or the widening of his eyes when their gazes locked.

Lucas smiled slowly, taking the man's hard swallow as a good sign. "Excuse my friend." He leaned so close his lips nearly brushed the man's ear. Subtle, earthy cologne wafted to his nose and it was hard not to draw in a deep breath.

"No-no problem," he stammered.

Lucas slid his hands down to the other man's elbows, feeling strong muscles under his jacket, before releasing him. "Have a good night." Lucas felt that hot gaze on him as he walked away.

Rowe waited outside the entrance, smirking. "Did you find yourself a piece of ass already?"

"Considering it."

Snow stepped behind Rowe, one eyebrow raised. "Luc likes to be coy."

"Yeah, both you pricks make it look so damned easy." Rowe scowled, shoving his hands into his pockets.

"But you've hit the jackpot with Melissa." Lucas motioned to where his driver had parked his black Mercedes.

"And I'd never give up Mel. For anything." Rowe released a happy sigh, his dark look melting away with the first mention of his wife. "Still, sometimes hanging out with you single bastards makes a man miss the chase."

Lucas had to smile. The thrill of the hunt was addictive.

Chapter 2

Lucas shivered when he stepped out of the Laundry Room at just after two in the morning. Cold gripped the city, sending the temperature down to the forties. It whispered of frigid nights in the near future. Leaning against the wall, he roughly rubbed his hand over his face as he let the crisp night air help clear his head. Why he'd let Snow talk him into those shots he'd never know.

Rowe had left an hour earlier after receiving a frantic call about a terrorist mouse. Both Snow and Lucas heard Melissa's screams coupled with barking dogs. Rowe had two Rottweilers and a German shepherd. If they were attempting to chase down the mouse, the house was getting trashed in the process—which had to be why Rowe's wife screamed. Lucas couldn't see that woman felled by a mouse. Three huge dogs bent on destruction? Oh yeah.

Both Lucas and Snow were wiping away tears, gasping for air between laughing fits, while Rowe scurried out of the club, cursing his friends, the dogs, too many drinks, and Mickey Mouse.

Apparently, Snow had mostly needed the calming influence of his friends because he seemed content to drink and relax most of the night. Man after man hit on him, but he stayed put, talking to Lucas about nothing important. Lucas had been sure that Snow would be crashing in his guest room until a tall, muscular man with a crooked grin finally caught the surgeon's attention.

Lucas had been left with the tab. He'd had his share of flirts while seated with Rowe and Snow, but brushed them off. A nice, hard fuck would have been nice and if Snow hadn't stormed into Shiver, he might have been in the mood to try harder with the man on the dance floor. But Snow's mental state proved effective at killing his libido—and it hadn't been the first time that had happened.

Pushing away from the wall, he cursed himself for releasing his driver after they were dropped at the bar. Drinking with Rowe and Snow was always a late affair and grabbing a cab hadn't seemed like such a hassle. But now that he walked alone on the sidewalk, exhausted and buzzed, he wished he could slide into his own car and confidently doze in the backseat as someone else drove.

Lucas paused while reaching for his cell phone when he noticed a large man in a dark hoodie walking toward him. His lowered head hid his face, but something in his gait sent alarm bells off in Lucas's head. Flexing his hands at his side, Lucas tried to relax his body when he heard two more sets of footsteps approaching him from behind. He started to turn but it was already too late.

The two behind him swept in from either side, hooking their arms through his while the first man stepped up and delivered a hard shovel hook to Lucas's solar plexus. All the air left his lungs in a rush as his feet came off the ground. A flash of pain radiated through his chest and Lucas gasped for breath as the two men grasping his arms dragged him into a nearby alley.

They slammed him against the rough brick wall, pinning his shoulders while the first man stepped in front of him. His face was hidden in shadow. The smell of beer and stale cigarettes buffeted to him, momentarily overwhelming the odor of rotten garbage that filled the narrow alley.

"You should have stayed out of Price Hill," the man drawled in a thick southern accent. "Now I don't know if you'll have a chance to sell it and save your ass."

A chill bit Lucas, pushing aside confusion and the last tendrils of his buzz. This hillbilly had been sent by the same asshole who'd threatened him two weeks earlier over a plot of land he'd purchased on the outskirts of downtown. So much for it being a simple mugging. No, these fuckers were out for blood, if not more.

Survival instincts kicked in and years of close-quarter-combat training took over. Pressing his weight against the wall, Lucas gritted his teeth and kicked out, aiming for the man's knee. His howl was loud enough to hear over the music pouring from the club. He barely had time to stagger back before Lucas kicked again. This time, hitting his chest and knocking him to the ground.

Lucas brought his right foot down hard on the instep of the man on his right. The assailant grunted and released Lucas's arm, stumbling backward. Spinning to the left, Lucas slammed an elbow across the bridge of the third guy's nose. Bone broke, blood sprayed, and the man screamed and cursed as his head banged against the wall.

Immediately backpedaling, Lucas was careful to keep all three men in front of him. His heart raced. He needed to incapacitate each man as quickly as possible or he didn't stand a fucking chance. The man with the injured instep bounced back first. In a traditional boxer's south paw stance, his lead hook caught Lucas clean on the jaw, jerking his head to the side. Lucas dropped back, putting a little more space between them. Pain seared the side of his face. He sidestepped the attacker's cross and passed the next punch, putting him in the perfect position to land a side kick to the man's knee. A pained cry echoed through the night as he crumbled to the broken wet pavement. Lucas delivered a final brutal overhead punch to the man's temple, knocking him out cold.

The hillbilly stumbled forward, keeping his weight off his injured knee. Lucas attempted to put some space between himself and the unconscious man. A quick glance revealed that the guy with the broken nose was still on the ground, wiping tears and blood from his face.

Lucas's only choice here was quick and dirty, or he was going to be back to having the odds out of his favor. The ache in his jaw was forgotten, his attention trained completely on his opponent.

But the hillbilly's stance gave him pause. The man's fists were up and turned outward while his body was open and facing him. This wasn't a fucking boxer's stance but that of someone trained in Muay Thai. He'd seen it often enough with Rowe's men as they trained.

Fuck.

As if to prove Lucas's assessment, Hillbilly led with a hard kick to the outside of his thigh. Lucas shuffled a couple of quick steps backward, trying to shake the sore muscles loose after the impact. The man grinned at him, as if taunting him, then followed with a cross jab that Lucas knocked aside before sliding past the second. The next rear leg round kick caught Lucas just above the left knee, staggering him. A sharp hiss of pain slipped between clenched teeth as he was spun slightly to the side. The attacker took the opening to deliver an elbow. Lucas turned his head at the last second so that it was little more than a grazing blow, but it was still enough to split him open just above his left eye.

Hillbilly chuckled, a low evil sound, as if to say that he'd been holding back. But that was over now. He came at Lucas with a flurry of punches that Lucas barely managed to sweep aside and block as blood leaked into the corner of his eye. Lucas regulated his breathing and watched for an opening. The other man wheezed already. He might have had Muay Thai training, but fat and muscle weighed down the rest of his body. He wasn't accustomed to an extended fight and he was wearing out fast.

A sloppy punch created the opportunity Lucas had been banking on. Pivoting to the left, Lucas smashed his fist right behind the man's ear. As his head dropped, Lucas threw his knee up in his face, breaking his cheekbone and knocking him onto his back. His head hit the concrete and he was out cold.

Lucas drew in a pained breath. His body trembled in aching exertion. It had been far too long since he'd last been in a fight for his life and even then he'd had the benefit of a weapon or two. He started to turn toward the third remaining man, but he was too slow. Broken Nose launched himself at Lucas low, grabbing his left leg at the thigh and twisting. Lucas instinctively threw out his arms to break his fall, but he didn't act fast enough to tuck his chin. The back of his head bounced off the pavement twice. For a second, the dimly lit alley went completely black and Lucas gasped, fighting to surface and remain conscious as pain swamped him.

Broken Nose was immediately positioned on his left, pounding his left knee hard into his ribs, weakening them so that Lucas was now struggling to catch his breath through the pain. The man was lightning fast, cursing the entire time he moved. An elbow slammed down on his right side, catching his floating rib. Lucas struggled to get his hands up as a final elbow slammed down on the already open gash above his left eye, widening it.

Pushing through the pain, Lucas caught Broken Nose's arm with both hands. Bringing up his left knee while holding the man's wrist and elbow, Lucas twisted, pulling him up and over until his back slammed onto the pavement.

Lucas instantly rolled, throwing his right leg over the man's neck and shoulder and tucking his foot under his own left knee. Locking in the hold, Lucas applied pressure, groaning against the pain lancing through every muscle as the asshole struggled beneath him. Through clenched teeth, Lucas slowly counted to five. By four, the man stopped moving. At five, Lucas hesitated and held him for an extra second before rolling away from him to his feet.

"Fuck," Lucas moaned. He immediately stumbled to his side, slamming his shoulder into the wall. His left knee was fucked to hell and wouldn't hold his entire weight. Blood poured down the left side of his face and at least one eye was swelling shut. The pain became a distant, throbbing thing that he couldn't really focus on. The world swam, blinking intermittently in and out. He couldn't think. Couldn't remember where he'd been going or if anyone had been with him.

Instinct screamed move.

Move or they'll kill you.

Move!

Leaning heavily against the wall for as long as he could, Lucas stumbled out of the alley and to the street. He didn't recognize anything or see anyone so he kept lurching on. At every block he turned, left and then right. No rationale to his movements at all. There had to be somewhere safe. Away from the men who jumped him. Away from others who might be coming.

Lucas didn't know how much time had passed or how far he traveled before he finally crouched down behind a dumpster in the darkness. His head spun and throbbed in time with his racing heart. Pain spider-webbed through his body so that he couldn't tell what was broken. It was all just pulsating agony. Wincing and sucking in a harsh breath, he reached into his breast pocket and pulled out his cell phone. By some slim bit of luck, it hadn't broken in the scuffle. He had difficulty focusing on the screen, everything blurring when he blinked against the bright glare, but he finally managed to call Rowe after three tries.

"Fuck! One of you bastards better be dying!" Rowe snarled into the phone after answering on the third ring.

Lucas wanted to laugh at the irony but he couldn't. "Help," he coughed out. The world shifted around him and the quality of the darkness changed. It was thicker and heavier. He tried to reach out with his left arm to steady himself, but the small movement doubled the pain through his body.

"Lucas? Lucas, where are you?" Rowe barked, instantly becoming serious.

"Don't know." He'd stumbled down so many streets it was all confused now. He couldn't begin to guess where he was hiding. Somewhere blissfully dark and disgustingly smelly. Probably better that it was dark.

"It's okay. I can trace your phone. You just gotta stay on the line with me." Rowe was moving. There was a rustle over the phone followed by a yelping dog. "Talk to me. What happened? Are you safe?"

His friend was trying to keep him awake, but Lucas could feel himself sliding into the darkness and he couldn't stop it. "Hurry," he whispered, or at least he thought he did. He couldn't be sure.

兄弟武士心

Something somewhere was beeping. It wasn't his alarm clock. The pitch and cadence was different. Had he fallen asleep at someone's place? Then why the hell wasn't the guy turning off the alarm? Lucas blindly reached out toward the noise, but something tugged painfully on his arm.

"No, no, Luc. Lay still." Ian's gentle voice drifted across the void. A hand took his and carefully laid it back on his stomach. As Ian drew away, Lucas tightened his own fingers, capturing his friend's hand. "Easy now. You're safe. I've got you," Ian murmured. Fingers ran through Lucas's hair in a caress, moving it from his forehead, easing the panic building in his chest.

Lucas slowly opened his eyes, blinking away the blurriness until he focused on Ian's weary but smiling face. His short, light brown hair was in more disarray than usual like he'd spent the past few hours running his fingers nervously through it. His dress shirt was untucked and rumpled as if he'd slept in it.

"Welcome back," he said, some of the concern slipping from his tired brown eyes.

"Where?" Lucas's voice was rough, his throat feeling like he'd been gargling shards of glass.

"You're in the hospital." Ian's odd little smile left Lucas wondering if he'd answered that question before. His friend typed out a quick text with his free hand, probably alerting the others that he was conscious, before he put the phone in his back pocket again.

Lucas glanced around the small room, taking in the assortment of beeping equipment, medication cart, and nondescript abstract art on the beige walls. His gaze strayed to the window, focusing on the quality of light. It was late afternoon. Something was wrong with that. He wasn't sure what, but he trusted the uneasiness in his stomach. Which was a good thing, because it felt like his thoughts were stuck in first gear when he was ready to get into fourth.

And then it hit him. The restaurant opening.

"What are you doing here?" Lucas demanded when he looked back up at Ian, his voice gaining strength the longer he was conscious.

"What do you mean?"

"You should be at the restaurant. The opening is tonight."

Worry cut deep lines in Ian's face and he pressed his full lips flat as if he was trying to hold back his next words.

"What?" Lucas barked when Ian refused to speak.

"The opening was yesterday," Ian said softly.

"What? Impossible. I—"

"So Sleeping Beauty is finally awake." Rowe strolled into the room followed by Snow in his white doctor's coat. "Well, he ain't so beautiful now. Maybe more like old Rip Van Winkle."

"Shut up," Snow growled, coming to stand at the foot of the bed to glare down at him as if he were already blaming Lucas for his state of distress.

"How long have I been here?" Lucas demanded, ignoring Rowe.

"A day and a half." Snow loomed over him, his frown fierce.

Ian gave his hand another squeeze before releasing it and stepping back. "You've been in and out the whole time." Lucas returned his gaze to Ian, taking in his pale face and the dark circles under his eyes. "This is the clearest you've been since Rowe found you in the alley."

"Did you cancel the opening?"

"No." Ian shook his head, a little smile tugging at the corners of his mouth. "Snow gave me regular updates last night so I'd stay at the restaurant. He said you'd kick my ass if I postponed. The opening was perfect, but I'm sure you expected that."

Lucas closed his eyes, and some of the throbbing that had started in his temples receded. "Of course. Now, go home. Get some rest."

"Damn, Lucas!" Rowe walked closer to the bed. "That's cold even for you."

Lucas's eyes sprang open and he glared at his friend. "He's exhausted and doesn't need to be hovering over me when he's about to drop." He tried to sit up in the bed a little higher, but his body wasn't responding. It felt like his muscles had been reduced to marshmallows.

"No, it's fine," Ian said with a soft chuckle. "He's already sounding more like himself." He patted Lucas on the shoulder one last time. "I'll bring food over once you get settled at home."

Lucas managed to grab Ian's hand and press a kiss to the young man's knuckles. He was proud of him and grateful for his concern, but he just couldn't get the words past the lump in his throat. Lucas knew he was a cold, gruff pain in the ass on the best of days and Ian didn't deserve it. The talented chef had likely put in a full day and night at Rialto then came straight to the hospital. He needed sleep, not a standing vigil at Lucas's bedside.

Ian smiled, squeezing Lucas's fingers before pulling away. Rowe met Ian at the door, and slid an arm around the other man's shoulders before he walked with him out of the room.

Lucas took as deep a breath as he could against the pain in his injured ribs and turned his gaze to the last man in the room, knowing this would be the real confrontation.

"I thought I was going to have to sedate him when Rowe brought you in," Snow said, his tone surprisingly level.

"The stress of the opening—"

"Don't discount his emotions." Snow growled out the words like he had the sore throat.

Lucas's eyes narrowed on his best friend's face. Low-banked rage burned there. The doctor was barely holding his temper in check. Lucas could only guess it was because he was technically at work and didn't want to be caught shouting at a patient. But he wasn't so sure how long that reason would rein Snow in.

"You're the older brother he's always wanted. The one he needs. Seeing you like that—" Snow broke off and swallowed hard. "Don't do this again. You're the center. You hold us together."

"How bad was I hurt?" Lucas asked, shocked to see Snow so shaken.

"You look worse than you are. A couple cracked ribs, some internal bruising, eight stitches above your left eye, and two broken knuckles on your left hand. You're also bruised as hell." Snow slipped into a more clinical tone, probably to help him compartmentalize his emotions. "It's the concussion that's serious. You have to take it easy for a few days. No work. Your memory is going to be fuzzy for a while."

"But nothing too serious," Lucas pressed.

"No. Just don't do this again. Ever."

"Snow—"

"Don't," Snow snarled, cutting him off as his anger surfaced again. "If you're not here, we won't make it. I...I don't know what I'd..."

Lucas wanted to argue, to say something to ease the pain and fear that filled his friend's eyes. But he just didn't have the words. Snow and Lucas had been together since elementary school. They joined the military when Snow needed to escape his family and attended college together afterward. When Snow was offered a residency at University of Cincinnati Medical Center, there had been no question—Lucas packed up and moved with him to Cincinnati. Rowe had been with them in the army and joined them when Snow was in medical school. Ian had been drawn into their intimate crew—the little brother everyone protected—just a few years ago.

But Snow was right. Lucas was at the center that kept them all floating along in the same tight orbit. They all needed each other, but they needed Lucas's calm head and even temper to hold them together, to keep them from drifting apart.

A nurse in blue scrubs padded into the room. "Dr. Frost, this detective wants to speak with Mr. Vallois."

Snow's head shake was short, the hand he waved at the nurse sharply dismissive. "Mr. Vallois is tired. Tell him to come back later."

"But I'm here now." The man who strolled into the room didn't look like any policeman Lucas had ever seen and if he hadn't felt so bad, he would have grinned when Snow lifted one dark brow. On no planet anywhere would this tough guy bend over for Snow and the doctor knew it. Didn't stop him from scoping out that long, rangy body. Wide shoulders filled out the beat-up leather jacket and the white T-shirt underneath did nothing to hide the toned muscles of someone in excellent physical shape. The cop loomed over Lucas as he stopped by the bed. "I'm Detective Banner. I have a few questions for you."

"Who called you?" Lucas asked, voice still raspy. Felt like someone had rubbed sandpaper in his throat.

"Nobody. I'm here on another case and heard the nurses talking. I've been to Shiver and know who you are. It's a nice place." Dark blond hair, just long enough to curl, matched the scruff on the man's jaw. "Kind of chilly."

Lucas didn't say anything.

"You know who did this to you?" Banner asked.

"Bored punks out for cash." Lucas shifted on the bed, winced when it felt like an elephant plunked down onto his chest. "Kids. They had hoods, came at me fast, so I really didn't see anything. It was a simple mugging, detective, so there isn't a reason for you to pursue the details."

"Sometimes we see more than we think. Mind if I come back when you're less groggy to see if your memory gets jogged?"

Something about this guy rubbed Lucas the wrong way. He couldn't pinpoint why either. "My memory is fine."

With one hand on his hip, Banner scratched his jaw, his sharp gaze starting to make Lucas uncomfortable. "Who brought you in? Why didn't you call 911?"

"I was concussed, Detective. Not thinking clearly." Lucas narrowed his eyes. "What's with the interrogation?"

One brown brow went up. "You don't want these guys caught? If you'd called the police to the scene, we could have gathered info, maybe tracked them down." The leather swished as he crossed his arms. "I'm just wondering why a man such as yourself gets rolled and has a friend bring him into the ER on the down low?"

Snow snorted and the cop's gaze shot to him.

"Something funny?"

Lucas's friend leaned against the wall and gave the cop a direct stare as his lips stretched into a rare grin. "Down low? Who talks like that? And why ask who brought him in? You said friend like you already know."

Banner's nostrils flared, his blue eyes turning to chips of ice. "Are you the attending physician? Why didn't you call this in?"

Barked questions would in no way thaw Frost as his body language began to change. His friend's stare sharpened, his relaxed, casual pose flowing into tense muscles as he straightened from the wall. Seemed Snow had the same growing instincts where this cop was concerned. Good. Lucas was worried his judgment was impaired by the meds. And the pain was starting to perk its head up higher, demanding his attention.

If the cop thought he did loom well, he had nothing on Snow, who walked to the end of the bed. "I didn't call it in—*yet*—because I am his friend and wanted to talk to him first. I'm surprised the nurses didn't tell you he just woke up. What's this really about because the last thing my friend needs is some prick barking in his face?"

"That's more your speed, eh? Prick in the face?"

"Depends on the prick," Snow drawled, his chin going up as he observed the cop with hooded eyes.

Lucas certainly didn't mind watching the somewhat hot alpha showdown going on over his bed, but was working to keep his eyes open at this point. "You've got about a minute before I decide sleeping trumps questions, so you better tell me what's going on here, Detective."

Banner pulled his gaze from the doctor and stared down at Lucas for several seconds before he sighed. "You aren't the only rich guy who's been at the wrong end of a fist lately and whoever is doing this, is attacking in groups. It would help if you could tell me anything you remember. Anything at all."

"It's still a blur. Leave your number and I'll call when more comes to me."

Pulling a white business card out of his wallet, Banner dropped it on the rolling table near the foot of the bed. "I'll come back tomorrow." The cop gave Snow once last pointed look before striding for the door. He turned back to Lucas. "Sorry you got beat up, but I hope you can remember more." He paused. "Soon."

Lucas groaned, closing his eyes in relief the second Snow closed the door behind the detective. He was too tired and too sore to deal with this shit. "Guess I should have told him I have no intention of being here another day, huh?"

"Arrogant ass. Let him figure it out on his own." Hands gently smoothed the covers over his chest as Snow snorted and mimicked, *"Hulk is not sorry. Hulk is hulk."*

The chuckle over Snow's Bruce Banner reference made Lucas open his eyes and focus on his friend.

"What?" Snow cracked a grin.

"It was almost like watching you face yourself down in a mirror."

Snow glanced toward the door. "Probably why I didn't like him."

Lucas's thoughts were still slogging through a marsh and he didn't want to worry about saying something he shouldn't to a cop.

But his break was far too short. The door hadn't been shut more than a couple of minutes when Rowe returned followed by a second man he couldn't recall ever seeing. Detective Banner had been good looking in a scruffy, law enforcement sort of way, but he had nothing on this striking man. Nearly as tall as Snow, he had nice, strong shoulders and a broad chest that stretched the black T-shirt he was wearing. His thick shoulder-length hair was so dark it looked black, matching his dark eyes inset under a heavy brow. This man moved with a smooth, hypnotic grace and Lucas suddenly felt better. Good enough to touch.

It took a moment to realize he was ogling the man as he crossed the room. He was never so blatant. Blame it on the drugs being pumped into his body. Lucas looked up to see Snow smirking. It was on the tip of his tongue to deny it when Snow's eyes moved to Lucas's left and then back. Lucas glanced over and nearly groaned. The heart monitor gave him away. The second the man had walked into the room, his heart rate had spiked and Snow saw it.

"I'm not fucking dead," Lucas growled in a low voice, pulling at his blanket as if to settle it more comfortably around him. He was grateful that the drugs and lingering pain were keeping the rest of his body from reacting.

"Thank God!" Rowe, oblivious to what the two men were secretly conversing about, leaned over the bed, his tone a feral snarl. "Because I'm still trying to decide whether to kill you. What the hell happened? And if you say mugging one more time, I swear to Christ I'm gonna crawl into that bed and strangle you."

"Well, at least we finally know what it takes to get him in bed with you." Snow snickered.

Rowe threw the doctor a glare, tensing as if he couldn't decide whether to take a chunk out of Snow or keep his attention on Lucas.

Lucas started to roll his eyes but stopped suddenly when the room swam. "Don't you have rounds or some other doctor things to do?" He didn't need Snow antagonizing Rowe. Judging by the man's flushed face, his blood pressure was already through the roof.

"I'm off the clock now." Snow then dropped into the chair at Lucas's side and set his feet up on the end of the bed as if he were getting ready to watch a show.

"Where the hell is my lawyer?" Lucas muttered. If he was going to get interrogated again, he wanted his lawyer there to protect him from Rowe.

"And that's another thing!" Rowe paced to the door and back. "How the hell did your lawyer get here so fast? You were here twenty minutes and she swoops in like some damn raptor."

"She's listed as his emergency contact," Snow answered before Lucas could open his mouth.

The idea stopped Rowe short. "Are you kidding me?"

Lucas gave a small shrug. "Most days, Snow is here. If I'm brought in, he'll know."

Rowe scrubbed his hand over his face and walked to the far side of the room and then back. "She's a shark, Lucas. You watch her."

"Yeah, she's great," Snow said slowly. "Almost makes me wish I was bi."

Lucas started to smile, but the pain from his split lip stopped him. "She's too much even for you to handle, my friend."

Sarah Carlston was tiny but she was a terror in the court room and the boardroom. Lucas adored her but he was also smart enough to fear her a little. It didn't hurt that he paid her a fat retainer to keep her on his side.

"That wasn't a damned mugging." Rowe's voice dipped low so that it was little more than a rumble of thunder sweeping through the room. "Was this about the Price Hill thing you mentioned a couple weeks ago?"

"It was." There was a lot that was fuzzy about that night, but the three men grabbing him—that was crystal clear. Lucas remembered the anger that filled his veins and then the fear. He hadn't felt fear like that since his tour in Afghanistan when Snow had been pinned down. He did plan to tell the cops the truth, once he figured out a bit more himself first.

"I'm guessing you will decline to follow their advice." Rowe carefully enunciated each word.

"Yes."

Rowe stood at the end of Lucas's bed and leaned forward, planting his fists into the mattress. "One thing: is this about ego?"

Lucas paused, one corner of his mouth quirking. Rowe knew him so damned well. "No, not completely," he admitted. He wasn't going to lie to Rowe or himself. Lucas was not one to cave to pressure when he wanted something. "This is also about that neighborhood getting a second chance."

"And you making a profit," Snow mumbled under his breath.

"Fuck you! You know this project isn't about the money." Lucas's fatigue fled in a rush of anger.

Rowe straightened and crossed his arms over his chest. "All right. I'm in."

"What?" Lucas demanded, trying to sit up straight, but his ribs protested the movement, keeping him lying back on his pillows.

"You're going to need help. Lots of it. I've got eyes and ears on the street." Arrogance threaded Rowe's words—and his smile. "I can help get to the bottom of this."

Lucas shook his head at the ex-Army Ranger, suppressing a shudder. Rowe wasn't the type to worry too much about whether something was entirely legal or even wise when it came to protecting his friends. Hell, even when it came to relieving boredom. The man liked to color outside the lines far too often. Luckily he was good at what he did and knew how to cover his tracks, but that didn't mean Lucas slept easy at night. "For now, we're cautious. Some extra security. We loop in the local cops. By the book, Rowe. This isn't one of your Ranger black ops missions. Contain and control *legally*."

The stocky man took a half step backward and looked like a child who'd had his favorite toy stolen. "Are you sure?"

"Yes." Lucas sighed, closing his eyes. Damn he was tired. He didn't have the energy to rein Rowe's violent impulses in. If he wasn't careful, Rowe would mow down half the city block to take down these assholes.

"Fine. At least you've got Andrei now. When they release you tonight, we'll show you the new security measures. And when you can move, you're coming back in to train with me three times a week. You've gotten sloppy and lazy."

Lucas's eyes snapped open. Most of Rowe's comments slid right by him as his brain locked on one key bit of information. "What? What are you talking about? Andrei who?"

Rowe grinned evilly and even Snow was looking far too pleased. The dark-haired man who'd followed Rowe into the room stepped out of the shadows. How could Lucas have forgotten dark and sexy?

"Andrei Hadeon, your new bodyguard," Rowe announced with a little wave of his hand toward the stranger.

"No," Lucas said vehemently. "Fuck no!"

"Lucas—" Rowe started but Lucas wouldn't let him speak.

"Absolutely not!"

"Yes. You got lucky. They come after you again, they'll kill you!" Rowe's voice climbed to a near yell. "He stays with you. He's with you when you eat. He's there when you sleep and shit."

"And when I'm fucking?" Lucas sneered.

"He's standing at the door with a box of condoms and a bottle of lube!" Rowe shouted back, not missing a beat.

"Fuck you, Rowe—"

"Enough!" Snow said, his icy voice silencing everything but the rapid beeping of the monitors attached to Lucas. "Rowe, out!"

The shorter man looked like he was going to argue but he huffed and stomped out of the room. Snow turned his attention to the silent bodyguard. "Wait outside." Andrei nodded and obediently followed Rowe out.

Snow watched the monitor, while holding Lucas's wrist. "Deep breath."

Lucas did as commanded, closing his eyes. He focused on Snow's larger hand wrapped around his wrist, the steady reassuring presence of his friend eased the pain in his head and the pounding of his heart. He didn't want to think about the panic that had surged through him at the idea of Andrei shadowing his every step.

"He's right and you know it," Snow said, his voice barely over a whisper when he spoke. "Yes, it's an inconvenience but you'll deal with it."

Lucas looked up at the doctor, stretching his fingers to brush against Snow's. He briefly closed his eyes, knowing his friends were right, but still not liking it. "The price I pay for refusing to back down, I guess."

Snow's lips twisted. "At least he's pretty to look at."

"Thanks," Lucas muttered. "Try not to look so amused about all this."

"Sleep. I'll see about getting you released in a few hours."

His eyelids fluttered shut as if following Snow's command. Ian, Rowe, and Snow had left him exhausted. Lucas slipped away, drifting back into sleep, holding his friend's hand.

Chapter 3

Lucas was sick of the piped-in, freezing hospital air and really sick of Rowe's bitching. His hands closed into painful fists to keep from throttling Rowe, who wouldn't stop muttering about Lucas not having any normal people clothes. Still, he helped Lucas pull on a pair of designer jeans and the soft cashmere V-neck sweater he'd brought from the penthouse before settling his left arm back into a sling to help take pressure off his bruised shoulder. But the clothes didn't offer the relief Lucas had hoped for. He still felt dirty and grimy, and he longed for a shower hot enough to remove a couple layers of skin.

Andrei pulled Rowe's monstrous black SUV as close as possible and then climbed into the back while Rowe helped Lucas up into the front passenger seat. So far the bodyguard had yet to utter a syllable and Lucas had begun to hope the man was mute. If he never made a sound, it would be easier to forget he was around. So much better for Lucas's sanity. He preferred it if the men he was attracted to slipped in and out of his life quickly and without fuss. This one offered none of that.

There was no ignoring or forgetting about the dark-eyed temptation who sat directly behind him. While Lucas managed to get out of the car on his own, Andrei stuck close on the elevator ride up to the penthouse and he swore he could feel the other man's body heat seeping into him. A hint of cologne reached him, and Lucas drew in a slow, deep breath, pulling the exotic and spicy scent into his lungs to hold it there. He wanted to pin the man against the cool black wall of the elevator and plunge his tongue deep into his mouth while freeing all that luxurious black hair so he could wrap his hands in it. Hold him in place. Lucas would slowly rock his hips against Andrei's, learn the tenor of the bodyguard's groan, because he couldn't imagine the sound—he'd never heard him speak.

None of this would probably happen because the man screamed straight.

"You know I used to love your place," Rowe murmured after he showed Lucas how to turn off the new alarm system.

"Used to?" Lucas tracked Andrei as the other man preceded them into the condo. Gun out, steps smooth and fluid, it was hard to pull his gaze from him. Between his movements now and that grinding kiss fantasy, Lucas's body had started to perk up—despite the drug store in his system.

"Yeah, now all these huge windows scream sniper's wet dream."

"Sniper?" Lucas blinked, finally jerking his brain from the sight of Andrei's tight, round ass as he passed in front of Lucas to pay attention to the words Rowe was muttering. "I thought your theory was that this was a street gang. You really think they're going to get a sniper?"

"No," Rowe mumbled.

Lucas clapped his right hand on Rowe's shoulder and squeezed. "I have security. I have a bodyguard. I'll be safe. Go home."

Rowe grunted, his eyes scanning the open layout as if checking one last time for some lurking assassin. Beneath Lucas's hand, he could feel taut muscles stretched across his shoulder. His friend's movements remained twitchy and restless, like a squirrel after an espresso, but then Rowe was more accustomed to being in the middle of the fight rather than delegating the dirty work to others. Rowe *liked* doing the dirty work. His marriage and growing business had forced him to slow down, and he was still adjusting.

"Go fuck your sexy wife."

A ghost of a smile passed over Rowe's mouth, easing some of the worry from his eyes. "Stay safe. Be smart." Rowe turned and left.

Fuck. *Finally!* Rowe was gone. Snow was gone. Ian was at work. No more hovering detectives or doctors. A loud sigh rippled through the quiet penthouse and Lucas could feel his body relax despite the pain that was steadily growing throughout his frame. He was home. There wasn't another place in the city where he felt safer.

He shuffled into the living room and sank into the soft fabric of the sofa, closing his eyes against the twinkling lights of the city spread before him. The Ascent was a graceful spire of white stone and blue glass rising up from the riverfront of Northern Kentucky, offering residents an unobstructed view of either downtown Cincinnati or the surrounding Northern Kentucky neighborhoods, complete with rolling green hills in the distance.

Two years ago, Lucas purchased the Pinnacle, the three-story penthouse that looked out on downtown Cincinnati. Not only did it offer security and privacy, removing him from his day-to-day rush of work, but he remained close enough to look down on his domain. The penthouse was mostly an open layout with kitchen, dining room, and a living room he loved. It was a large curving area filled with light honey woods and brushed nickel. But the highlight was the uninterrupted city view across two walls. The second floor held the master bedroom, guest room, and small office. Though, Lucas preferred to work from the dining room so he could watch the lights wink off and on across the city.

A mix of comfortable furniture and eclectic art reflected his personal tastes. And the influences of his friends filled his home. This was no magazine spread of *Architectural Digest* or *Southern Living*. This was a home. And Lucas didn't entertain in his home. If he wanted to throw a party, it was done in a space he rented. Only a select group of people ever set foot into his private domain. People he loved and trusted. That was it.

Exhaustion rode Lucas hard, pushing him down in the sofa until he was sure that he wouldn't be able to gain his feet again. He wanted a shower and his soft Egyptian cotton sheets in his king-sized bed, but he was afraid he couldn't hold himself up in the shower.

He'd just rest there for a moment and then maybe swallow a painkiller before attempting a shower. Whatever they'd given him in the hospital was wearing off and all the aches were seeping back in.

"Mr. Vallois?"

It was the first time he'd heard Andrei speak. Fuck, what a voice. Low and heavy—masculine in a way that made Lucas's body instantly warm. Andrei had an accent—faint, as if he was trying to hide it—but Lucas couldn't place it. Definitely nothing local. The first tendrils of fire curled low in his gut and Lucas wanted to growl. The hunger that had started to make itself known in the elevator was slinking back.

"Is there something I can help you with?"

Lucas's eyes popped open, unable to hide his surprise. Andrei stood directly in front of him, only a battered wooden trunk Lucas used as a coffee table separated them. The man hadn't made a sound.

"I'm sure your employer doesn't want you playing nursemaid," Lucas said, grinding out the flickering spark of attraction. He didn't touch straight men. He also didn't do repeats and there was no pushing Andrei out the damned door after an enjoyable fuck. They were stuck together as long as Lucas was in danger. Acting on this attraction? Too complicated. Too messy. Still, his gaze slid down to those muscled thighs.

"You'll be much easier to protect when you're healthy and mobile," Andrei admitted with a smile that pulled Lucas's gaze back up. Damn. That little twist of his lips drew his eyes, stoking the fire. Andrei's upper lip poked out a bit, a sensual invitation. Lucas wanted to lick it, then work his way slowly down the rest of him.

"So a healthy me is in your best interest?"

The smirk grew into a wide grin. "Both of our best interests."

"Fair enough," Lucas grudgingly said, trying to tap down the crazy attraction he felt. Luckily, he had other aches to distract him. "Where are the painkillers?"

"I put them in the master bath."

Clenching his teeth, Lucas pushed to his feet, instantly grateful the man had enough brains not to help him up. As soon as he took a step, the landline jangled two sharp rings and then paused before repeating. "Could you get that while I find the pills? It's the front security desk."

Andrei nodded, heading for the cordless phone in the kitchen. "You want company?"

"No," Lucas growled. Even a visit from Snow wouldn't have been welcome. He wanted peace and quiet. He wanted to settle back into his routine and forget about what happened in the alley, block out the pain spreading through his body, and work on a plan for how he was going to fix this problem.

Lucas trudged up the stairs to his bedroom, only vaguely aware that Andrei sounded like he was arguing with whoever was on the line. He was just at the bathroom door when Andrei's voice caught him.

"Mr. Vallois?"

Lucas's hand clenched the doorjamb and he closed his eyes for a second. How could Andrei make his voice sound so damned sexy? Lucas couldn't decide if getting him to use his given name would be better or worse. So easily he could imagine Andrei panting his name, a note of pleading catching the last syllable in the back of his throat as Lucas sank deep inside him. Okay, first name would definitely be worse.

He glanced over his shoulder to find confusion bringing together Andrei's dark eyebrows as he covered the phone with his hand.

"There's a woman claiming to be your fiancée. She's demanding to come up. I…I think she's scared the security guard." Surprise threaded Andrei's words.

"Stephanie." Lucas groaned, dropping his head back. Ice water washed over his libido, extinguishing those flickering flames in an instant. "Fuck." The last thing he felt like dealing with was the woman he'd been seeing the last few months. A woman who was certainly *not* his fiancée.

"Mr. Vallois?"

"Let her up. If nothing, it'll be entertaining." Lucas stepped into the bathroom to grab the prescription bottle off the black marble countertop.

He glanced up at the mirror and winced. It was the first time he'd seen his reflection in two days. He looked like shit with one black eye highlighted by stitches and a bruise on his opposite cheek, only partially hidden by two days growth of black stubble. His bottom lip was split and slightly swollen. Shadows hollowed his cheeks, making him look ragged and worn and every bit of his thirty-eight years. He shrugged. It could have been a lot worse. He popped one pill and took a drink of water before shuffling back to the first floor.

Andrei stood in the kitchen, arms crossed, frowning. Walking over to the man, Lucas grabbed his wrist, ignoring the bodyguard's slight flinch and slapped the pill bottle into Andrei's palm with his injured left hand.

"Hold onto these," Lucas muttered. "We both might need one before this is over." Quickly releasing Andrei, he stepped away so the island in the center of the kitchen separated them.

"Wouldn't you rather I went to the guest bedroom?" Andrei offered, still looking confused.

"What kind of bodyguard are you? You're staying out here to protect me." Lucas couldn't stop the grin he knew would look both wicked and tired. "That woman is scary."

Andrei pressed his lips tight together, but there was no hiding the laughter in his dark eyes. Lucas flashed him a wider grin before he could stop himself. Shit. Was he flirting? Fuck, it had to be the drugs. Or, he wanted to be able to blame it on the drugs. But sadly, there was no way the Percocet had kicked in already.

Lucas enjoyed the luxury of slowly examining the other man's face. Closely trimmed dark whiskers accentuated a sharp jaw while a mustache framed full lips that kept drawing his eyes. He had high cheek bones that Lucas wanted to run his fingers along. His thick, black eyebrows accented dark eyes, and were arching like raven's wings right now. Andrei looked young—maybe mid-twenties—but that only piqued Lucas's interest. Rowe was a smart man and hired only those people with the skills to handle this line of work. What was hidden in Andrei's past that had earned him Rowe's trust?

"Ex-military?" Lucas suddenly inquired, but Andrei didn't seem particularly surprised by the question.

He shook his head, his eyes locked on the bottle of pills in his hand. "No. I was a professional mixed martial arts fighter until an injury a few years ago." Andrei lifted his gaze to Lucas, something hardening in those dark depths that threatened to rattle him. "Rowe has seen that I'm thoroughly trained in close-quarter combat, a variety of weapons, and defensive driving."

Lucas smiled slowly, enjoying the flush that dusted Andrei's cheeks. "I don't doubt your skills. Rowe would never have assigned you if you couldn't handle it."

"I'm sorry, Mr. Vallois," Andrei started, breaking into Lucas's wandering thoughts. "I—Rowe—gave me some … confusing information."

Lucas's smile disappeared, but his growing irritation was actually directed at his old friend. "He told you I was gay," he said flatly.

Andrei nodded, looking uncomfortable again.

"Was that just information or a warning?"

"Information, I'm sure." Andrei's dumbfounded expression helped to ease Lucas's ire. It was bad enough he had to allow this stranger into his home, he wasn't going to endure intolerance here as well.

Lucas grunted, staring at the man for another second. "Your boss is an ass. I'm bisexual. I like both genders in my bed."

"At the same time?" Andrei asked and then flushed. It was obvious the man hadn't meant to ask his new employer about his sex life.

Lucas's lazy grin grew, resuming his flirtation with the man. "Only on special occasions."

Andrei's grin returned a little. "And what constitutes a special occasion?"

The sound of keys jingling turned Lucas's head and he answered almost absently. "Just the days of the week that end in 'Y'."

Andrei huffed a laugh but Lucas was listening to the person trying a key in the lock only to fail. There was a muffled curse followed by a familiar hammering on the door.

"Rowe changed the locks?" Lucas inquired, still smiling.

"He changed all your security measures."

"Well, let her in. I'm fixing myself a drink."

Those dark brows came together in concern. "That might not be wise with the Percocet."

"Don't mother me, Mr. Hadeon."

Andrei held Lucas's dark gaze without wavering, making it clear that he would not be a pushover for Lucas. "It's my job to keep you alive, Mr. Vallois."

"Answer the damned door. I'll make a *small* drink."

Andrei gave a soft grunt before turning to the door. Lucas fought to unclench his teeth as he shoved away from the island to walk over to the sideboard. He poured two fingers of whisky into a tumbler and was replacing the crystal top to the decanter when Stephanie Breckenridge's heels clacked across the hardwood floor.

"What's going on?"

"In general or were you after something specific?" Lucas took a sip of the whisky. The Percocet was just starting to kick in, easing the aches and putting a nice protective fog around his thoughts. Andrei might have been right about the alcohol being a mistake, but he just didn't give a damn.

"That security guard wouldn't let me up. Said I'm not on the list." Her tart words were accompanied with a sharp tapping of her foot. "And you changed the lock."

He still wasn't sure why he'd given her a key. Lucas turned toward the kitchen, keeping his back toward Stephanie as he pinned Andrei with a narrowed gaze even though he could feel his grin lurking on his lips. "Shall I ask who Rowe put on the list?" he drawled.

The man flushed, his eyes darting from Lucas to Stephanie and then back. "The three men from the hospital and me," Andrei replied in a low voice. "That's it."

"Lucas?" Confusion and anger colored Stephanie's voice black.

Lucas sighed heavily. Damn Rowe. He loved to cause trouble. He'd once flirted with a BBC reporter in Ankara while using Lucas's name—when they'd been trying to avoid local cops. He'd slowed some since marrying, but Rowe still managed to find ways to cause chaos. It was his *raison d'être*.

"Please add Mrs. Mason to the list," Lucas said evenly. "She cleans on Wednesday and Friday."

"Lucas!" This time, Stephanie stepped around Lucas so he was forced to look at her.

Andrei turned suddenly and coughed, trying to cover his laugh.

Lucas waited for Stephanie to take in his battered appearance. She looked perfect, of course. Every blond hair was in place, her make-up expertly highlighting her large blue eyes and full lips. Her mint green suit hugged her slender form. Outside, she was a beauty, but her insides were as hollow as bird bones. Lucas ignored it for a long time because she'd been a useful accessory on his arm when he needed to make an appearance at some social function. And at one time, she hadn't seemed so…so shallow. But recently, he'd gotten tired of her cruel, dismissive comments and sickened by her overall callousness toward people.

"What happened to you?" she asked. The faint hint of warmth threading her tone felt forced. Faked.

"A small scuffle. Nothing to fret about." He knew his voice dripped sarcasm and he couldn't help it. He settled into the one arm chair, taking another sip of his whisky, enjoying the burn down his chest and into his brain.

"This looks like way more than a small scuffle. Were you in the hospital?"

"Just a couple days."

She genuinely looked confused, but not really upset and that made this easier.

"No one called me," she finally said.

"No need to trouble you from your busy schedule."

"One of your friends should have called me." She wove her way around the furniture in the living room to sit primly on the edge of the sofa closest to him. "I am your girlfriend after all." The last bit was said gently and Lucas nearly laughed out loud.

"That's what I thought." Lucas pointed with the hand holding the tumbler so that the remaining whisky nearly sloshed out of the fine crystal. "But the security guard said you claimed to be my fiancée."

Stephanie gave a little wave of her hand as if brushing off his comment like a stray piece of lint. "Oh that. It's just a matter of time. We've been together almost six months."

Lucas shook his head. "I don't think so." He wanted to feel bad about cutting her loose this way, but couldn't bring himself to frown. Maybe it was the Percocet. Or the whisky. Or sliding helplessly into that thick darkness after a bad beating. "I don't believe this arrangement is working for either of us any longer."

"What? Are you breaking up with me?" Her blue eyes had gone impossibly wide and she gaped at him.

"Yes." He nodded slowly. "I am."

"Now, Lucas, let's just talk about this. You're not thinking clearly. You've been drinking and I'm sure those doctors put you on medication."

"Oh no, I decided this weeks ago. You just haven't been around to tell."

"Well, if you needed more time together, you just have to say. I can always make time for you." She reached to place her hand on his knee but he jerked away. Stephanie frowned, snatching her hand back, curling her slender fingers into a fist.

Lucas reached over to put his glass on the table but missed. Luckily, Andrei was right there to catch it before it could crash to the hardwood floor. He took the glass and placed a cold bottle of water into Lucas's hand. "This might be a good idea, Mr. Vallois."

Lucas blinked. "Can't you make some noise when you move?"

"But then it would be harder to protect you," Andrei said with a half-smile as he straightened.

Lucas smiled back. "Good point."

"Can we have some privacy, please?" Stephanie demanded through clenched white teeth as she glared at Andrei.

"No!" Lucas leaned in his chair so that his body was closer to Andrei than the woman currently turning her glare toward him. "He's my bodyguard. He's protecting me."

Stephanie jumped to her feet. "Lucas Vallois, you're an asshole!"

It was nice to see she was giving up all pretense of caring. He didn't have the energy or even the desire to draw this out anymore. He'd enjoyed his time with her in the beginning, but it had been nothing other than sheer laziness and disinterest that had kept him from pushing her away sooner. "Come now. We both know you can do so much better than me."

"Of course I can." The snarl on her lips didn't flatter. "But you'll never find another woman who is going to put up with you fucking every man to cross your path. You're a cheap, low-class whore and that's all you'll ever be."

"Possibly," Lucas agreed with a solemn nod. "But you knew about my activities from the first day. I told you how it was going to be. And really, Stephanie? Calling me names? When you fucked Tom Chilton, Robert Stapleton, Damien Bryce and … what was that pediatrician's name?" He glanced up at Andrei as if the bodyguard could provide the missing name, but he was now glaring at Lucas's soon-to-be ex-girlfriend.

Stephanie's face turned bright red and her thin body fairly vibrated with rage. "Bastard," she said in a rough whisper. "So it's okay for you, but not me?"

"Of course not. But there's a big difference." Lucas narrowed his eyes. "I never lied."

She glared at him a second longer before spinning on her heel and stomping out of the penthouse. The door slammed loudly behind her and Lucas took a drink of water. He looked up at Andrei with a crooked grin. "I think that went well."

Andrei slowly shook his head. "Normally I'd say breaking up while on painkillers is a bad idea, but that was probably a good call."

"Probably?"

"Well, she is gorgeous," Andrei said with a sheepish grin.

"But that's all she is." He closed his eyes and sighed. Exhaustion slammed into him. He could sleep sitting in the chair.

"Mr. Vallois, I think you'll be more comfortable in bed."

Lucas stared at him, biting his tongue to keep from asking if the man would be joining him. He certainly looked far more appealing company than his frozen ex-girlfriend. But he was too tired to think about enjoying bedroom fun. "Probably."

It took two tries but he finally got to his feet. Andrei hovered close, but didn't touch him as he followed him across the room to the stairs.

"Do me a favor," Lucas murmured.

"Yes."

"The concussion—and probably the painkiller—rattled my brain. Remind me tomorrow about what happened with Ms. Breckenridge. I don't want to do that again."

"Of course." Andrei's words hummed with humor.

Lucas sat heavily on the edge of the bed and started to struggle with the arm sling. Setting the bottle of water on the bedside table, Andrei stepped close and carefully removed the sling. Lucas froze for a breath, trying to soak in the feel the other man's warmth, the strangely reassuring comfort he got from the man's closeness.

"You're a good nursemaid," Lucas said, noticing the slur in his words.

Andrei stepped back and chuckled. "It's easy when your patient is drugged to the gills."

Lucas's head swam for a second. "Are you planning to take advantage of me?"

Andrei laughed again. "No, Mr. Vallois."

Lucas grunted, lowering his eyes to the man's chest. He liked the way his T-shirt stretched over his muscles. "Yeah. Nobody likes rebound sex. All that crying."

"Is there anything else I can help you with?" Andrei asked, sounding like he was fighting more laughter.

Lucas looked down at his heavily bandaged left hand and arm. Getting his sweater off was going to be a bitch. "My shirt," he mumbled. He really did hate asking for help. "But I promise not to take it as you undressing me."

"I appreciate that."

Andrei's low voice sent a shiver through Lucas that he didn't bother trying to hide. The man just shouldn't be allowed to speak. Was it the rough rumble? The hint of an accent that he couldn't quite place? The horrible mix of drugs and alcohol and concussion that was messing with him? Yes to all of the above. Yes.

Andrei took a half step closer, his knee brushing against Lucas's as he plucked up the edge of the sweater. He gathered up the shirt, careful not to brush his fingertips along Lucas's bare skin. With one side pulled up, Lucas slipped his right arm free. Andrei then stepped left, lifting the fabric over his head and then carefully down his left arm.

Lucas rubbed his eyes, trying to push through the fatigue. He couldn't understand this overwhelming need to sleep when he'd been unconscious for the better part of two days. Tomorrow. Tomorrow he'd get back into his normal routine. Or at least close to it.

When he looked up, he found Andrei staring at him, clutching the sweater to his chest with both fists. His knuckles were turning white he was holding the material so tightly. The man's face was an unreadable mask, but his eyes were wide with surprise or maybe panic. His breathing seemed shorter and faster.

"Do I look that bad?" Lucas asked as he glanced down at himself. Had Snow missed a hole in his chest when he'd patched Lucas up? His left shoulder was covered in a reddish purple bruise and more bruises covered his chest and stomach. He also had a nice accumulation of faded, white scars that stretched over various parts of his chest from his years in the Army and earlier, but he didn't think he looked too terribly bad.

"No, Mr. Vallois. Just ... lost in thought calculating your recovery time to full mobility." Andrei dropped his gaze to the shirt in his hands, then turned suddenly and walked to the bureau to lay the shirt down.

"Well, knock a few days off that estimate. I'm not going to sit idle," Lucas grumbled.

"Can I get you anything else?"

"No – wait!" Lucas looked around while patting his pockets with his right hand. "Where's my cell phone?"

"I have it. Your doctor said you can't have it back until tomorrow."

"Fine. Send two texts for me. Tell Candace Parkes to be here at one to work," Lucas instructed as he toed out of his shoes, the only things from that horrible night that apparently hadn't been ruined.

"And the other?"

"Your boss. Tell him he's a fucking asshole."

Lucas flopped down on the bed, pulling the comforter around him with his right arm. He was exhausted and the room was spinning. Sleep and a shower in the morning would make the world a more tolerable, coherent place again. Maybe then he wouldn't feel this unrelenting attraction for Andrei Hadeon.

He never heard Andrei leave the room or flip off the light. He was dead to the world within seconds.

兄弟武士心

Andrei walked out to the kitchen and stood staring out at nothing, trying to get his heart to stop pounding. The blood coursing through his frame felt like it was on fire. His hands shook, forcing him to shove them into his long dark hair just so he wouldn't have to see the evidence that he was obviously cracking.

It was that damned smile. Lucas had looked up at him with that slow lazy grin that lit his soft green-gray eyes with mischief. The combination of painkillers and alcohol had loosened him up, made him so damned appealing. A slow burning fire set loose in Andrei's stomach and all he could think about was leaning down to taste that smile.

Standing at the edge of the bed, it had taken all his control not to grab the man and kiss him until that low growl rumbled back up his throat. He burned with a need to explore every inch of Lucas's mouth and that smile. Find some relief from the tightness of his own skin and the throbbing of his groin.

But that didn't make any fucking sense. Andrei wouldn't have labeled himself as anything more than a little bi-curious. Yeah, he'd messed around with a few guys, but his sexual adventures on that side had always involved copious amounts of alcohol, boredom, and at least one woman to help even things out. There had been no touching beyond what was necessary to get off and there was definitely no kissing.

Lucas threatened to disrupt everything. Yes, Andrei had appreciated handsome men, but he'd never felt an urge to touch, to slowly explore every muscle. *That fucking smile and that low purr in his voice when something amused him.* Andrei had known too few people like Lucas — a man so comfortable in his own skin that nothing seemed to unsettle him. He didn't question himself or doubt himself or who he was. He had an inner strength that was intoxicating to be around, even when the man was drugged out of his mind. Maybe even more so then. That fierce restraint had eased…and made Andrei want to crawl into bed with him. Or just on top of him.

What the hell was he supposed to do? Nothing. Not a damned thing. Company policy strictly forbade any kind of fraternizing with the customer—man or woman. Andrei felt a snicker rise in his throat. Like

Lucas Vallois would give him a second look if his ex-girlfriend was anything to go by. Rich, beautiful, and educated from a good family—that was probably the man's type. He could have whoever he wanted, man or woman.

Of course, it was all the more fitting that Andrei found himself attracted to his boss's best friend. Yes, just perfect. Not only would he lose his job, but Andrei had little doubt that Rowe would beat him senseless if he found out that Andrei took advantage of his injured friend.

That thought was funny in itself. Andrei knew he was not seeing Lucas Vallois at his best, but even concussed, drugged and drinking, no one could get anything past the man. He'd watched the too-smooth Stephanie Breckenridge try to manipulate Lucas and he'd neatly outmaneuvered her.

Fuck, this assignment was going to be rough. Andrei could only hope the unexpected attraction was a fluke. Maybe it would die when he saw Lucas acting more like himself. He was sure he'd seen glimpses of it in the hospital when Lucas locked horns with Rowe. Arrogant and stubborn, Lucas was probably just like every other rich snob he'd protected over the past three years.

Dropping his hands back to his side, he looked up at the time on the microwave and cursed softly under his breath. It was barely nine o'clock. Too early for bed and he was too wired for sleep even if it was late. A few beers would have taken the edge off but Andrei never drank on the job.

He started to reach for Lucas's cell phone in his back pocket when the sound of a key sliding into the lock echoed through the silent penthouse. Andrei pulled his gun from the holster at the small of his back and edged closer to the door. No call from security meant that it should be one of three men, but Andrei was taking no chances.

The door swung open wide but no one stepped in.

"Don't shoot me, Hadeon." Snow's cold monotone voice swept into the room and Andrei breathed a sigh of relief.

"Enter," Andrei replied but he didn't holster his gun again until Snow closed the door behind himself, proving he was truly alone. In one hand, he held a large brown paper bag by the handles.

"Vallois?"

"Just went to bed."

Snow didn't seem surprised, giving only the barest of nods. Stepping forward, he placed the bag on the island with a soft crinkle of paper. "Ian sent food. Save Lucas the Portobello ravioli." He then headed for the second floor without another word.

Andrei waited, straining to hear movement or voices, but there was no sound beyond the beating of his own heart in his ears. With a mental shrug, Andrei dug into the bag, the delicious smell wafting to his nose through the plastic containers. Rowe had mentioned that his friend Ian had opened a new Italian restaurant that was guaranteed to be a four-star joint, and he was eager to try it. The man had sent enough food for an army. There were two fish and pasta dinners, a classic lasagna, two steaks with roasted vegetables, the ravioli, a container of warm bread, and another of salad. At least they had food for a couple days. A peek in Lucas's fridge made him think the man didn't cook much. Andrei wasn't much better, with his skills not extending far beyond steak, eggs, and the occasional grilled cheese.

Grabbing a steak dinner, salad and bread, he packed the rest away in the fridge. He ate standing at the island, letting the silence of the house seep into his tense body. The food and quiet helped to settle his uneasiness. By the time he was cleaning up, he was able to reassure himself that he'd blown everything out of proportion. It was just nerves over watching someone so important to his boss.

Before starting his rounds, he remembered to send both texts from Lucas's phone. The man had missed several calls and texts over two days. Andrei scrolled through, looking only for numbers that didn't have names associated, but none appeared. At least it didn't appear that new threats had been leveled against the man.

Tucking the phone in his back pocket, he double checked the lock on the front door and then swept the first floor before heading to the second. In the small office, Andrei grabbed a recently published thriller from Lucas's collection of books. He found mostly nonfiction on the shelves, but the man indulged in the occasional thriller or crime drama. Andrei figured he'd try to read for an hour before grabbing a few hours of sleep.

Back in the hall, he hesitated in the darkness, unsure of whether he should look in the master bedroom. Snow had left the door partially open as Andrei had placed it so he could hear noises and quickly check on Lucas. Cursing himself and his indecision, Andrei stepped up to the opening and looked in, his heart giving an odd jump. Snow was sitting up in the bed, his back against the headboard. His eyes were closed, but the man was awake. His fingers slowly threaded through Lucas's short dark brown hair again and again in a gentle caress. The only sound in the room was Lucas's deep, even breathing.

As if sensing Andrei's presence, Snow's eyes suddenly flicked open, holding the bodyguard in his steady piercing gaze before he closed his eyes again.

Andrei continued to stare for several seconds, his stomach twisting. Something in his gut said theirs was a strange relationship. He wanted to brush them off as lovers, but it felt too easy an excuse. What he was seeing was something else, something he couldn't begin to define.

The only thing Andrei was sure of was that Snow had not come to comfort or ease Lucas. The injured man was unconscious and utterly oblivious to the fact that he had a bed mate. No, Snow was there for himself. Lucas was a comfort for the doctor, even when he was lost to the waking world.

兄弟武士心

Three a.m. in the hospital. Snow once heard it called the time of gods and monsters. The bitch of it was he wasn't sure which part he played anymore. He looked down at the blood and other body fluids covering his scrubs and grimaced. The hours between his beeper forcing him from Lucas's side to now had been filled with the horrors of a four-car accident.

Two deaths and one person hovering on the edge.

Lives destroyed and all of it had been caused by a teen texting and driving. One who came out with only a broken arm and a few bruises, but would have to live with deaths on his conscience for the rest of his life.

He flashed back to the way Lucas had looked when they'd brought him in. Bleeding, bruised, and unconscious. Just the memory sent fear to pound in his chest. He laid a hand over it as if to stop the muscle from propelling through his ribcage. There were only a few people in Snow's life he loved and of them all, Lucas held the most precious spot in his world. He had for nearly as long as Snow could remember. He wasn't sure he could live through losing him.

Wasn't sure he'd even want to.

The urge to hunt down a stranger he could lose himself in hit Snow hard, then quickly faded. He was too tired to even pretend he wasn't teetering on the monster side of things. When he got like this, his control was for shit.

He cradled his cup of coffee, realizing he'd let it go cold, then set it down. He leaned his head against the wall and groaned when a set of familiar broad shoulders in beat up leather appeared in front of him. He shut his eyes. "Go away, cop."

The leather creaked next to him as the detective sat. "The ER is crazier than usual. Good place to hide. It's quiet here."

"It was." Snow didn't open his eyes. A mix of scents hit him. Leather, smoke and fresh coffee. The last made him open his eyes. He lifted an eyebrow at the cop. "You're not here for me. You came for the coffee."

"Everyone knows the sleep lab makes the best." The cop's tired chuckle was followed by a cough. "Gotta love the irony."

"Damn. I was hoping that secret didn't get out."

Hollis handed him one of the cups he was carrying. "You looked like you could use more."

Snow tilted his head in thanks and narrowed his gaze on the cop. The dirty blond scruff on his head stood out in every direction like he'd been running his hands through it all night and there was a stark, pinched look to his lips. His nose showed signs of too many swipes with cheap tissues. "Bad day?"

"That obvious, huh? Got to crawl around in the remains of a burned house. And here I thought I was ready for the runway."

Snow smirked. He didn't want to like the guy.

"Your friend remember anything more yet?" Hollis coughed again.

That cough sounded nice and wet, so it didn't go along with the smoke odor coming from his clothes. It wasn't from a fire irritant. "You'd have to ask him. Last time I saw him he wasn't talking."

"I plan to see him later today. I didn't actually come here to grill you—just get coffee."

"Spend a lot of time in this hospital, do you?"

"Unfortunately. I'm usually called in here first on most of my cases." He sniffed, pulled out one of those small packs of tissues they sold next to cash registers in drug stores. The cop didn't even flinch when he pinched it over his nostrils.

Snow winced, knowing that had to feel like sandpaper. "Why don't you give yourself a day or two to kick that cold before bothering Vallois?"

"I never get colds."

"Then you should see someone about that drug problem."

The cop snorted.

A soft, rumbling laugh sounded as two paramedics walked through the waiting area. As it did every time the man walked into his sight, Snow's gaze latched onto the one on the right. His black uniform fit his sleek, muscled form in a way that should be illegal. His equally dark eyes landed on Snow, locked with his. They watched each other until the man disappeared around the corner.

It took everything Snow had to keep his breathing even and not give away his body's fiery response to the paramedic who'd been eyeing him from the moment he started the job two weeks ago.

"I haven't seen him here before, so he must be new." Banner leaned forward as if trying to look around the corner. "Damn. You know, with the way he just looked at you, you could take him home right now."

"Not interested."

Hollis gave Snow a disbelieving look. Snow gave in and rubbed his thumb and finger in the corner of his eyes. "Is there anything you else, because I'm leaving?"

"Yeah." Banner handed him a card. "Here's my number. Could you let me know if any more victims come in with the same wounds?"

Snow frowned. "The bruising on his ribs? Or are you talking about the huge bruises on his legs?"

"Legs. Those same marks came up on another rich guy who got rolled. It's not the usual work over from the local gangs."

Thinking about the purple mark that went from Lucas's mid-thigh to his knee, Snow realized he'd seen those same bruises recently. But he kept his mouth shut. He wanted to talk to Lucas before he came to any conclusions.

Banner groaned as he stood up. "Maybe you don't want to drink that coffee. Might by germy. Because of the cold and all." His laughter turned into more watery coughs as he walked away.

Snow had planned to go home, but the pattern of those bruises sent him to the data files instead.

Chapter 4

A low groan rolled out of Lucas's bedroom just after eight in the morning. The man was awake and attempting to move. A ripple of anxiety slipped through Andrei as he got to his feet and slowly walked toward the bedroom. The painkillers would have worn off during the night. Lucas was undoubtedly in pain and groggy. How much would he remember?

Andrei found the injured man sitting on the side of the bed, his hair standing on end as he roughly rubbed his face. At some point in the night he'd shed his jeans so that he now wore only a pair of black boxer briefs. A body like his should be illegal.

Hesitantly, Andrei cleared his throat, causing Lucas's head to jerk around. He stared blankly at Andrei for a couple of seconds before giving a low grunt.

"The bodyguard," Lucas mumbled, his voice warm and sleep-rough.

"Andrei Hadeon."

"I know."

"Sorry, Mr. Vallois. I wasn't sure how much you remembered of last night."

Lucas glanced at him over his shoulder, one eyebrow raised slightly as if he was suddenly uneasy with the question. "Enough. I think."

"Is there anything I can do? A painkiller?"

"Yes," he said with a sigh and then growled almost in the same breath. "No. No painkillers."

"Mr. Vallois, you need—"

"I need a clear head," he interrupted. "I've got work to do today."

"Half a Percocet," Andrei argued. "Too much pain slows your reflexes and movement."

"Fine. After my shower."

Andrei nodded, though Lucas couldn't see it. He remained in the doorway a few more seconds, watching as the other man stiffly rose and walked over to the bureau for clean clothes. Strong muscles rippled and shifted under golden skin that was marred by an assortment of bruises. It was obvious that Lucas Vallois was not a man content to spend his day locked to a desk and a computer screen. He thought Rowe had said he'd been in the Army many years ago, but it didn't look as if he'd paused a day in his physical training.

But the smiling, teasing man he'd spoken with the night before was gone. Andrei could easily blame it on the pain he was obviously feeling from head to toe. Yet, Andrei suspected he was actually seeing the real man. Fuck, he hoped he was. Cold and brusque, he could handle. Anything to kill the low-burning desire he'd wrestled with most of the night. Let Lucas be a pompous, dictatorial ass who treated him like shit. Better to hate him than to crave him.

Andrei silently turned and went back to the kitchen. After throwing out the remains of the coffee he'd brewed earlier, he put on a fresh pot and took the painkillers out of his pocket. He put a half a Percocet on the counter next to a full glass of water. After checking his email for any new updates from Rowe, he completed another round of the penthouse. Everything was quiet and still secure, not that he could really imagine anyone effectively breaking into the place through any entry other than the front door.

Around forty minutes later, Lucas reappeared, his movements smoother than earlier. The hot water must have loosened his stiff muscles. The scruff had been scraped clean from his cheeks, erasing some of the years from his face. Barefoot and shirtless, Lucas wore a pair of dark gray slacks while carrying a white button-down shirt. Setting it on the island, he wordlessly swallowed the pill and drained the water.

"I was not alone in bed last night," he announced, his voice flat. "It was not you."

Andrei blinked twice at the unexpected announcement. The idea of crawling into that large bed among the thick pillows with Lucas momentarily left him flustered and shaken. And then the memory of Snow slammed into his brain. "Dr. Frost stopped by after you fell asleep. He brought food that he said Ian sent."

Lucas stood, his hands flat on the countertop, staring at the empty glass. His shoulders seemed painfully straight. The muscles in his jaw flexed and jumped as if he were clenching his teeth. "Anything else I should know?"

Andrei noticed it then, the overwhelming tension in the man's frame. He'd taken the stillness as him fighting through the pain until the Percocet kicked in, but that wasn't it. He was nervous, on edge as he fought to regain what was missing from his memory.

"I sent the texts that you requested." Andrei pulled Lucas's phone out of his back pocket. He set it down next to Lucas's hand. The man's fingers flinched liked he wanted to reach for it but he stopped himself. "Candace agreed to be here at one pm. And I told Rowe that he's a fucking asshole—as you asked."

Lucas barked out a loud laugh, then cleared his throat. Andrei bit back his own smile. He watched some of the tension ease from Lucas's wide shoulders, relaxing just a bit.

"A Detective Hollis Banner stopped by at seven this morning and left a card. Pretty damned early for a cop visit. He would like you to call him." Reaching into his other pocket, Andrei pulled out the business card and placed it on the counter beside the phone.

"Anything else?"

Andrei cleared his throat, his eyes dropping to the other man's hands. Even with two broken knuckles on the left, they looked strong. Pale white scars stretched across them. They were not the hands of a business man, but the hands of a man who knew how to handle himself, how to handle his problems ... personally.

"Ms. Breckenridge stopped by last night," he said slowly before raising his eyes to Lucas's face. "You ended your relationship with her."

That same lazy grin spread across Lucas's lips while a twinkle jumped into his eyes. Andrei's heart quickened and he struggled to keep from taking a step back.

"I was hoping that I hadn't dreamed that," he said, his voice becoming a rough purr. "At least one good thing came out of last night."

Fuck. Did this man have no idea how insanely sexy he was? Andrei could barely draw a breath. His tongue quickly darted out, licking his lips, as he tried to formulate a thought. The man he'd met last night was back and the world was tilting again. He just wanted to reach out and touch him. So he did the only logical thing. He stuffed his hands into his back pockets and took a step back to lean against the counter.

"You remember?" Andrei asked, praying Lucas didn't notice that his voice had grown rougher.

"Not every blessed word, but most, I think."

"I'm sorry."

"For what? I also recall you laughing. I know I did."

Still grinning, they stared at each other for a second, surprisingly comfortable in the shared silence that stretched between them. But the moment was broken when Lucas's phone vibrated as a new batch of emails was downloaded. Andrei was surprised that the man didn't immediately pick it up.

"I don't know what to do with you, Mr. Hadeon."

Andrei straightened, suddenly wary of the man and his surprising admission. Could he tell that Andrei was attracted to him? Had he stared too long? Laughed when he shouldn't have? "I don't know what you mean."

"I am used to employees whom I give tasks and they leave to do them. They're not just…always…there," Lucas admitted, sounding more than a little uncomfortable. The grin Andrei had enjoyed just seconds earlier was now replaced with a frown.

"Until you are completely healed, I will stick close by. It's easier to keep you safe."

Lucas's smile returned and he took a step closer to the island that separated them. "And exactly how close will you stick?"

Andrei licked his lips again, and there was no missing how Lucas's heated gaze followed that small movement. Heat flushed his cheeks and he battled to keep his breathing even. His brain rushed to figure out an appropriate response to Lucas's question. Sarcasm? Teasing? A serious shut-down that would likely piss off Rowe's best friend or maybe just amuse the fuck out of him because Andrei had stupidly taken serious what Lucas likely didn't mean.

"I will remain close to you in the event that I need to move you out of danger." Andrei decided to ignore the sexual undertones of the question.

"You'd physically move me?" Lucas glanced down at his muscled body.

Andrei nodded, not trusting his voice as Lucas ran his teeth over his bottom lip, his smile growing wider.

"I'm surprised, Mr. Hadeon. I didn't take you for the type who liked it rough."

Andrei's mind was suddenly flooded with the image of Lucas slammed against the refrigerator and pinned there with his own body as he ran his hands across his wide chest, exploring all that warm skin with his mouth. Breathless and shaken, he didn't try to sort through the unexpected desire. Lucas was pure sexual temptation. With those sparkling eyes and sinful lips that seemed to promise so many dirty things without actually saying the words, Lucas was sex.

But he didn't mean it. Flirting was probably like breathing for him. A man like that — rich, successful, talented — he was made to flirt with anyone standing in front of him because he could get away with it.

Andrei opened his mouth and then instantly shut it, catching the comment that nearly slipped out about how he had plenty of experience manhandling stubborn clients. What the fuck was he doing? Flirting back? He'd lost his mind. That's all there was to it. The blood that had left his damned brain was all flowing to his dick.

Clearing his throat, Andrei tried again. "I don't anticipate there being a problem. It's my job to make sure you don't come to harm."

A low, evil chuckle rumbled from Lucas and Andrei had to remove his hands from the back pockets of his jeans as they started to grow tighter. He crossed his arms over his chest, both anticipating and dreading the other man's next words.

"That is not what you were going to say," he taunted.

"No."

"Will you tell me?"

"No."

Lucas shook his head, still grinning. "And I thought you might be more fun than this."

"No."

"Will you remain close after I'm healed?"

"No, I become a shadow. You'll forget I'm even there."

"I doubt that very much," Lucas muttered under his breath, his eyes finally dropping down to his phone as it vibrated again with a new message. "What do you do during the day?" Lucas raised his eyes to him again and the teasing man had been replaced by the cold business man he'd glimpsed before. "Other than hover over me."

"I travel with you at all times. If you are in what would be designated a safe zone, I am more hidden. Inconspicuous."

"Doing what?" Lucas pressed.

Andrei was taken aback by the question. None of the other people he'd guarded had ever asked or cared what he did with this time. "I read, Mr. Vallois," he admitted a tad softly. "I read a great deal."

Lucas shifted, taking a small step back from the island, his eyes widening in surprise. It wasn't the answer that he'd been anticipating, but then the image was a little strange. A fighter with his nose in a book, but then Andrei had loved books since he'd been young. Far easier than trying to make friends.

"What do you read?"

A small grin lifted the corners of Andrei's mouth. "Whatever my client has on hand. I have read the U.S. tax code twice. I've read romance novels about time-traveling Vikings and I've read food labels."

"But what do you like to read?"

Andrei hesitated. He'd seen Lucas's collection of business and finance tomes alongside a few mainstream thrillers. But then Andrei was never one to lie about himself. "Mostly fantasy and science-fiction if I have some personal time."

Lucas gave the barest nod before picking up his cell phone and scrolling through the messages. "I'll have my assistant pick up some books for you. Make a list if you have some in mind."

"That's not necessary."

"It is," Lucas said sharply, still glaring at his phone. "With any luck, this arrangement will last only a couple of days."

Andrei wanted to argue that if Lucas had started a fight with some bastard trying to pressure him out of Price Hill, then this was going to stretch for more than a couple days. But he kept his mouth shut.

"Do you need help with your shirt?" Andrei offered.

Lucas gave a jerky nod. "With the bruised shoulder and ribs, I've lost some flexibility," he grumbled.

Taking up the white button-down shirt, Andrei held it open and allowed Lucas to first slide his injured left hand carefully through the sleeve before he moved behind him. He was stunned that he was only an inch or two taller than the other man. Lucas's personality made him seem bigger, so that he practically filled the room when he entered. Drawing in a slow, silent breath, Andrei tried to ignore the crisp, clean scent that clung to skin fresh from the shower. Down the center of his back between his shoulder blades were tattooed Japanese kanji symbols. Each was barely larger than a silver dollar. It was on the tip of his tongue to ask what each stood for but he swallowed back the question. It wasn't his place to ask such things.

Andrei clenched his teeth as he struggled to touch as little of Lucas as possible while pulling the shirt around to his right side. It wasn't that he thought Lucas would be offended by a stray touch or bump. If his teasing was to be believed, it was quite the opposite. No, it was his own reaction he feared. The man seemed to be one massive temptation. Andrei wanted to run his palms over that smooth expanse of flesh. Badly.

Lucas softly grunted as he reached backward with his right hand, searching for the sleeve. Andrei helped to place his hand in the hole before slowly sliding the soft material up his arms and settling it on his massive shoulders. Silently cursing himself, Andrei stepped back and closed his eyes as soon as the shirt was in place. This was ridiculous. This slow, consuming burn wasn't about Lucas. It was about needing to get laid. He was obviously horny. In a few days, Rowe would come by, give him a few hours off, and he could find a partner willing to give him some relief. He'd been working too much recently and his peace of mind was taking a beating for it.

Repeating in his head that it was nothing, Andrei stepped around to the far side of the island. "We need to set up some ground rules for the house."

"Such as?"

"You don't answer the door." Andrei's voice hardened as he slipped into the comfort of a known situation. "You don't leave the penthouse without me, not even to step into the hall. You don't shut doors. All doors inside the penthouse must be open a little so I can hear noises and quickly enter. I make rounds every hour, checking every room. When we leave, I go with you everywhere. I drive the car. When I say run, you run. When I say hide, you hide."

"Can I just fire you now and save us both the trouble?" Lucas asked, irritation lacing his deep voice.

Andrei smiled broadly, noting how Lucas's jaw had clenched. "No. You're not my employer on this case. Rowe made that very clear. If I must, I am to regard you as my hostage and treat you as such."

Lucas took a step toward Andrei, his eyes narrowed and focused, his expression disturbingly predatory. "I truly doubt you have the fun things in mind I do when you say that," Lucas commented in a voice so low it was nearly a whisper.

Andrei stood his ground, struggling not to react to the other man's taunting. He'd had a few clients flirt with him, but he'd never met someone like Lucas. If the man touched him, Andrei was pretty sure he'd agree to anything Lucas asked just so he could find some relief from the unrelenting ache that had been building in his groin since Lucas had walked into the kitchen shirtless and grumbling.

"Fine," Lucas bit out. "My lawyer, Sarah Carlton, will be here in one hour. Detective Banner will be here in ninety minutes. Do not allow the detective up unless my lawyer is already here. And don't shoot any of them." Stuffing both his phone and the business card in his pocket, Lucas paused to make himself a cup of black coffee before stalking off to his office. Andrei almost felt bad that he couldn't have the cathartic pleasure of slamming the door behind him.

Andrei sighed and put his forearms on the island. Yeah, that was probably closer to who Lucas Vallois truly was.

A year ago while on a job, Andrei had read a glossy write-up on Lucas in *Fortune* magazine. A self-made millionaire, the man had lifted himself up from the worst neighborhood to be this globe-trotting property mogul who still personally managed most of his business interests rather than handing it off to a series of executives. The write-up had also tied him to a series of models and socialites from old money. Each one of them a gorgeous woman.

Lucas was leading a double life and Andrei couldn't deny that he wanted to know more.

兄弟武士心

Cursing, Lucas struggled to button his shirt with his damned broken knuckles, but there was no way in hell he was going to ask for Andrei's help. Hell, he'd gotten hard just when the man had helped him into the shirt. What the hell was wrong with him? He couldn't use the excuse of the drugs. He was on half a dose now and the pain was still biting at him.

And then last night … Did he remember? He remembered every smile and laugh and comment. Lucas had flirted with the man like some half-wit twentysomething in a nightclub. Fuck. He'd flirted with him again this morning. He couldn't control himself. His first instinct every time he opened his mouth was to say something provocative to see the flush rise in Andrei's cheeks. When Andrei had leaned against the counter, his hands in his back pockets, Lucas's wanted to drop to his knees and suck the man off until he came apart, shouting Lucas's name.

Flopping into the cushioned leather chair behind his desk, Lucas dropped his head into his hands. What was wrong with him? He had rules about this shit. No emotions. No sleeping over. No repeats. And at the top of the list in big bold letters: No fucking straight men. They just weren't worth the trouble. Lucas was happy to leave that kind of emotional wreckage and chaos to Snow when the doctor was feeling particularly twisted.

Everything about Andrei screamed straight.

Except…there had been a moment last night when Andrei had helped him with his clothes. It could have been the drugs, but Lucas had seen a glimpse of interest. Or maybe he was just desperately grasping at straws.

With a shake of his head, Lucas turned his attention to the two days of neglected emails and piles of reports that needed his attention. He spent a minute on the phone with his lawyer and another two minutes with Detective Banner, setting up a meeting. Lucas lost himself in his work, forgetting for a time about Andrei and the attack. His world settled back into known figures and expectations, feeling safe and predictable again.

Lucas wandered to the kitchen an hour later for a second cup of coffee when he was greeted with a sight he had been dreading.

"Damn." Hollis Banner walked right by Lucas, past the dining room table, to one of the walls of windows. "I always wondered how Odin saw the world from so high up in his tree."

"Who let him in?" Lucas lifted an eyebrow at Andrei, who was standing near the island in the kitchen.

"I brought him up with me," Sarah announced as she clicked into the room on her high heels. Heels that still didn't bring her up to the detective's shoulders. "I've met him before. He's a real detective even if he seems like an amalgam of every bad boy cop movie actor you've ever seen."

"Hey now. My feelings could get hurt." Banner turned back to the window and waved as he leaned closer. "Hello, peons!"

"Don't grease up the glass with your face! It'll make Lucas grumpy." Sarah scowled at the cop, then walked to Lucas. She didn't stop until he was forced to look down into her eyes. She tilted her head up, her sharp black suit impeccably spotless, her even sharper gaze going over his face. "You look better." She nodded. "Good."

"So glad I have your approval." He gave her a smile to take out some of the sting in his voice. That damned cop rubbed him the wrong way. He looked at him just as the man sneezed and fumbled for a tissue out of a pack he'd had in his pocket.

"Sorry," Banner said, his voice considerably more nasally.

"You weren't sick when we saw you yesterday." Lucas tilted his head, took in the rumpled clothes. "And you're wearing the same clothes. Rough night?"

"Yeah, but I wanted to see if you remembered anything before I headed home and collapsed."

The cop did look beat—like *to the bones* beat. Lucas would bet that only sheer determination and bull-headed stubbornness held him up. Lucas motioned for them to sit on the sofa while he settled in the one chair. He started to cross his ankle over his knee, but his bruised thigh complained with the first movement. "Three men grabbed me outside the Laundry Room, and no, it wasn't a random mugging." Lucas caught the slight lift of Sarah's eyebrows, questioning the wisdom of his words. He hadn't discussed anything with her yet about what had happened. She was willing and able to swoop in if he said the wrong thing, but that was only after the words were out of his mouth.

"The Laundry Room has a particular reputation..." Hollis drawled, pinning Lucas with his piercing gaze.

"It's a gay bar," Lucas said. There was no beating around the bush or hedging on this. He had nothing to hide. "As my companions likely told you already, I was there with Dr. Frost and Rowan Ward. And before you stumble forward with any more inane questions, no this wasn't a hate crime either."

"Seen them around before?"

"I didn't get the impression that was their kind of place."

"What can you tell me about them?" Banner stuffed his tissue in his pocket.

"Not much." Lucas lifted a hand and started to run it through his hair but stopped suddenly with a wince of pain. He had five stitches on the back of his head from where it had busted open on the concrete. "It was dark. After two in the morning. They were careful to keep their faces covered. Hoods, remember? Two of them were big, muscular. The third was only about five seven or so, but he was fast, strong and fought with a shitload of anger. Liked to kick." Lucas touched the slacks on his bruised leg. "We could probably get his shoe size off the bruise on my thigh. He also had a thick southern accent, like he was straight out of the tobacco fields."

"You heard his voice then. What did he say?"

Lucas frowned, fighting to get the words out. The idea of pulling the cops into his business rankled him to no end, but he'd just told Rowe the night before that they were sticking to the goddamned straight and narrow on this and that meant cluing in the cops. "He told me I should have stayed out of Price Hill. That I might not get the chance to sell it now."

Banner jerked upright, his mouth hanging open for a second. "Wait. They were telling you to get out of Price Hill? What the hell is that about?"

"No idea. The property I recently purchased there has been vacant a long time so I'm not sure what their interest is in it."

"And you didn't think this was a little strange?"

Lucas forced himself to sit back, resting his hands on the arms of the chair rather than clenching them into fists. "Less strange the second time around. It was the same thing someone else said to me two weeks ago as I was leaving Rialto."

Hollis flopped back on the couch, his long limbs going loose as he stared incredulously at Lucas. "And you didn't think this threat was important enough to report to the police?"

"Mr. Vallois does not have to answer that question," Sarah interjected sharply. Lucas held up his hand, keeping her from continuing. She was practically growling from where she sat next to Hollis, ready to pounce on the unsuspecting detective.

"It was a brief, random encounter. I didn't think anything of it."

The detective didn't look convinced. His glare was impressive, or at least it would have been if he wasn't sniffling and looking utterly miserable. "Anything else?" he bit out after several seconds of silence.

Lucas paused. Something had struck him about the fight…beyond the bastards' fists and knees. Detective Banner caught the hesitation and slid forward to the edge of the sofa, leaning in closer. "What? You hear a name? See a tattoo?"

"They weren't your typical thugs."

"And how would you know that?"

"Lucas doesn't have to answer that," Sarah inserted and Lucas smiled at the detective. He was definitely going to let her have that one.

"Fine. Not your typical thugs. Could you explain?"

"One used Muay Thai."

"Muay what?"

"Muay Thai. It's an eastern fighting style."

"You mean that MMA shit?"

"Yes."

"How can you be sure that you recognize Muay Thai? There are lots of fighting styles out there."

"Lucas—"

He held up his hand, halting Sarah's words. "I know Muay Thai and would be happy to give you a demonstration."

Hollis grinned. "I'm sure you would. How common is Muay Thai?"

"More than it used to be, but it's not what I'd call common. Takes years of training and dedication. The guy was good, experienced. Not great, but good."

"What about the other two?"

"One was a boxer, or at least had a more traditional, all-fists approach. Nothing unique. The other was a wrestler or maybe someone who specialized in small circle jujitsu. I didn't let him kick my ass long enough to verify his style of fighting."

"So you got rolled by three pros over some property in Price Hill?"

Lucas shrugged and winced at the pain that shot through his shoulder. "I don't know if they were pros. They just weren't your average street thugs."

"Something about all of this sounds familiar and if I wasn't fighting a little man with a sledgehammer in my skull, I could remember from where." He covered his mouth when a loud cough sent him bending in half. When he straightened, he apologized again. Lucas got the feeling that wasn't normal for him. Neither the coughing nor the apologizing.

"Do you remember anything else?" Banner asked, his voice closer to normal.

Lucas shook his head, his eye snagging on Andrei as he quickly crossed to the front door. Banner's coughing had covered up the sound of a key unlocking the door. His heart thudded as the bodyguard put his hand on the butt of his gun hidden under his jacket, ready to place himself between Lucas and danger.

The door opened and Andrei instantly relaxed, his hand falling limp at his side. Banner and his annoying questions were instantly forgotten at the sight of Ian carrying bags that had actual steam coming out of them. The room filled with the scents of chicken, shrimp, sausage and more. Lucas knew that smell. Lucas *loved* that smell. "Paella? You brought paella? I love you so hard right now."

"You always love me hard because you know that's how I like my loving." Ian's cheeks turned bright red as he noticed the others in the room. His brown eyes moved over Sarah and locked onto the detective. "I meant…I mean…I didn't mean that the way it sounded."

"You totally did, and you know it," replied a teasing female voice.

Lucas smiled at the cheerful woman who followed Ian inside, a black garment bag slung over her shoulder. It faded fast when he saw the expression on the cop's face. Looked like someone had hit the big guy in the solar plexus and put him on stun mode. The hair on the back of Lucas's neck stood up. Oh no. *Fuck no.* Not only had Lucas's gaydar completely missed the cop—which was unusual and had to be due to painkillers or concussion—but from the look on his face, Ian was just his type.

His gaze swept to Andrei, who leaned down to allow Melissa to place a sweet kiss on his cheek before he accepted the bag from her. A small twinge of something…uncomfortable ran through Lucas at the gesture. It was not surprising that Melissa knew one of her husband's employees, but he wasn't overly thrilled that she'd apparently gone to the man's place and packed a bag for him. Touched his personal belongings. That kiss was a too-painful reminder that Melissa was more his type than Lucas.

He pressed the heel of his hand into his forehead and rubbed hard. What the fuck? This was Melissa. She adored Rowe. And Andrei… Andrei wasn't his. Never would be his. These damned painkillers and this stupid concussion were making him crazy.

He looked back to Hollis. How could the cop have not looked over Andrei if he were gay? The bodyguard stood quietly watching from the kitchen, his elegant features composed, his silky hair back in a short tail on his neck. Hollis had barely nodded at Andrei. How could anyone look at the bodyguard and not stare?

He had to pull his gaze from Andrei as he slipped away to the guest room to deposit his bag and locked his eyes on Banner, who looked only slightly more composed. Fucker was still staring at Ian like he was picturing him naked.

Ian, who was impeccably dressed as usual in a soft beige mock turtleneck and formfitting brown slacks, set the bags on the table and cleared his throat. "I brought several things."

"We still have food you sent with Snow from last night. You're spoiling me."

The smile that Ian gave him was his favorite. Exactly the first one he'd seen years ago when they'd met. Shy and so endearing it still made Lucas want to wrap him up and keep him safe from the world. That smile had even melted Snow.

The doc would hate the way Banner was looking at their friend.

"Melissa mentioned that she was dropping some things off for Andrei, so I thought I'd tag along." Ian walked toward the detective, his hand out. "Hi. I'm Ian Pierce."

"I wouldn't shake his hand," Lucas said, butting in. "Germs." Lucas walked over and wrapped a protective arm around Ian's slender shoulders, gathering him close.

Banner's nod was interrupted by another cough. He covered his mouth and rose from the sofa so he could step back from Ian as if he didn't want his germs anywhere near the pretty man.

This nudged Banner up a notch in Lucas's eyes. Just a nudge. The way those blue eyes ran over Ian still bothered him and the cop wasn't being that blatant about it. But if Lucas recognized anything, it was lust. Even when that lust was tempered with the misery of a cold.

Ian's expression softened as soon as he realized the detective was ill and he hurried back to the bags. "I have just the thing for that cold." He pulled out a container. "There's enough paella for everyone else, but I brought a container of avgolemono soup in case the paella was too much for Lucas. It's warm and comforting, has chicken, rice, lemon, egg and some fresh spices. Oh, and it's creamy but has no other dairy products in it so it won't make your cold worse." He walked to Banner and handed him the container along with that smile.

And it did what it had done to the rest of them. Banner took the container in his big hands, his gaze not leaving Ian's mouth. He still didn't say anything. Lucas hoped the sun streaming in from the windows was baking the cop in that leather coat and that's why sweat had popped up on his forehead.

Sarah snorted, breaking the tension in the room. "That soup is one of the reasons I live and you want to waste it on the cop?"

Ian shot her a frown and her mouth snapped shut.

Lucas had to work to keep from laughing when Sarah didn't respond. Ian had that effect on most everyone and even his shark-like lawyer seemed to have a hard time mouthing off to him. There was only one man Lucas knew who hadn't felt protective and loving toward the slight, young man. And just the thought of that evil monster reminded him why a scruffy big, street-hardened guy like Hollis Banner had no business looking at Ian like he'd rather eat him than the soup. And that soup made his mouth water.

Lucas did love Ian's avgolemono.

Banner cleared his throat. "Thank you." He cradled the container to his chest.

Before Lucas could bark at the detective, Melissa stepped in front of him, her gentle hands cupping his face, turning it left and then right to look him over. "Oh, honey," she said in her smooth southern accent that wrapped around him like a warm blanket. "You look horrible. Who's going to fuck you now?"

"Thanks." His lips twitched against a laugh. Much like her husband, there was no filter between her brain and her mouth, resulting in the most disturbing things crossing her bow-like lips. And he absolutely adored her for it.

"I guess you could always aim for a pity fuck but I really didn't think men went in for that rough and tumble look."

"Melissa, darling, how does your husband put up with that sharp tongue of yours?"

She flashed him a wicked grin, dropping her hands down to his waist. "My husband has learned to keep my sharp tongue busy."

Lucas bit his bottom lip. There was no reason to pursue that line of thought. "What did you pack for my new best friend?"

She gave a little shrug. "Oh, you know, the usual. Playboys, lots of lube and an assortment of nipple clamps and butt plugs."

"Jesus fucking Christ," Andrei said with a groan. Lucas turned to find the bodyguard's face bright red and his eyes wide in horror. A loud laugh erupted from Lucas, filling the room. He ignored the pain in his ribs as he clasped Melissa to him, hugging her tightly.

"You have always been my favorite," he said in her ear.

She snorted, hugging him back. "Please, everyone knows Snow is your favorite."

"You're my favorite female."

Lifting her head, she gave him another devilish smile. "I'll buy that."

"I do have one important question for you." He jerked his head over, motioning toward Andrei standing just across the room. "Boxers or briefs?" There was no missing the glare Andrei was directing at both of them, but it certainly wasn't going to stop her.

"Actually, brightly colored banana hammocks."

"Melissa!" Andrei closed his eyes.

Lucas turned, putting his back to the rest of the room, so that he could direct his heated gaze toward Andrei. "That puts a lovely image in my head," he said in a low voice.

"She's not serious." Fire lit up Andrei's cheeks. Lucas couldn't tell if it was from embarrassment or anger or maybe both.

"That's a shame." Though personally, he hoped that wasn't true. He'd never liked the look of those. Give him a nice tight pair of boxer briefs any day.

Melissa leaned up on her toes and brushed a quick kiss to his cheek. "Actually, I didn't pack any for him so I would imagine that he's going to be going commando very soon. You have fun with that." She patted his chest twice.

兄弟武士心

It was nearly one when everyone finally left. The detective had tried to put a protective detail on him, but Lucas turned it down. It was bad enough that he had Andrei on his heels every hour of the day, tempting him. He didn't need a second set of babysitters watching his every move.

Sarah, unfortunately, wasn't pleased with his decision, confident that one bodyguard wasn't enough to keep him safe. Lucas felt no need to inform her that Rowe would be cooking up more defensive measures to keep him safe. For now, Lucas had needed Sarah only as a witness to prove that he was fully cooperating with the law.

When the front door was shut and locked, the silence in the penthouse was almost unsettling. Melissa's laughter mixed with Ian's pleasant chitchat with the nearly mute detective had made a somewhat boisterous atmosphere while Lucas tried to evade Sarah's attempt to prod him for more information. Of course, dodging his lawyer made keeping Ian and Hollis separated difficult. He didn't want that damned detective too close to Ian.

And then there was Andrei. More than once during that long hour, Lucas had looked up, his eyes searching for his guardian to find him standing almost hidden near the back wall, watching everything. Alone and detached. He could feel the man's shadowed gaze on him. He'd been torn between wanting to pull Andrei into the conversation that flowed so easily about him, to see that elusive smile spread across his lips at some ridiculous, teasing comment, and wanting everyone else to get the fuck out so he could be alone with him.

Now when he looked up, Andrei was nowhere to be found. Disappeared back to the guest bedroom or making his rounds. Lucas ignored the feeling of disappointment, clutching tight to the physical ache that wracked his body. The half pill he'd taken wore off more than an hour earlier and now he didn't want to contemplate the long walk back up to his office to answer more emails before Candace arrived.

Pushing away from the door, he took two steps when he noticed a bottle of water on the kitchen island with a note taped to it. He changed direction and entered the kitchen to find a half Percocet next to the bottle. In neat, tight handwriting, Andrei had printed:

Take the Percocet. Eat lunch. Portobello ravioli is on the top shelf. Your assistant doesn't deserve your bitchy attitude.

Lucas bit his lower lip, unsuccessfully fighting a smile. The man was right. He was cranky and Candace would silently tolerate it, but she didn't need to. Popping the pill and draining half the bottle, Lucas grabbed the ravioli out of the fridge. He banged around the kitchen, making far more noise than necessary, expecting Andrei to come investigate, but he never did. Lucas finished eating alone and he was disturbed by the disappointment that continued to nag him. Andrei had said he would become little more than a shadow in his life when he was present and he was proving true to his word.

The phone rang, not letting Lucas think on it long. The security desk called up wanting to know if they should allow Candace Parkes up to his penthouse. Lucas agreed and hung up. He started for his office, planning to warn Andrei that his assistant was on her way up but he nearly ran into the man as he descended the stairs.

"Candace is on her way up." Lucas paused on the stairs and sighed. He was pissed at himself and his lack of control, not at Andrei. "Mr. Hadeon, thank you for the note. You were right."

"You're welcome, Mr. Vallois."

Lucas shook his head at the man's surprised tone but continued up the stairs without another word. Damn, he must come off as a real dick if Andrei was surprised that he'd appreciate the man's thoughtfulness. Or Andrei was just convinced he was insane. He spent half his time flirting with him and the other half barking at him. Lucas was simply grateful to get back to his office and lose himself in work. The woman said nothing about his appearance or his injuries. She pulled out a pile of files, contracts, and other reports for them to work through as if she were in the office with him rather than his home. His assistant was all business, and while he might occasionally tease her about it, he found solace in her demeanor. It gave him normal and he needed normal.

"Oh!" Candace exclaimed in an uncharacteristic moment of surprise. "I almost forgot." She seemed to be talking to herself as she searched through her purse. She had been in the middle of packing everything up at the end of the day, but she was now pulling it all apart again as she dug for something.

It was well after six. He'd conducted four conference calls while Candace set up other meetings for later in the week. Contracts were reviewed and approved while plans were lined up for him to tour some property on the east side on the outskirts of Hyde Park the following week.

She softly sighed as she pulled a white business card out of her wallet and handed it to Lucas. "That gentleman that you pointed out last Friday at Shiver. His name is Chris Green."

Lucas chuckled, looking at the woman rather than the business card in his hand. "You asked him for his business card? I really thought you'd be more circumspect and subtle than that."

Candace threw him a dark look as she shoved items back into her purse. "I didn't. I stopped by Shiver on Saturday to talk to Gerald about the delay in the shipment from Carrington Spirits. Mr. Green stopped me. He'd seen us talking on Friday and asked if you'd be back in. Then he gave me his business card."

"Thank you. I never doubted you."

Candace shouldered her purse and her leather messenger bag, the epitome of efficiency and class in her neat, expensive suit and short hair. "Will I be meeting you here tomorrow?"

"Yes."

Candace nodded and then left without another word. Lucas glanced down at the card in his hand. The name on it was Christopher J. Green, Marketing Director, Cincinnati Financial Group. The man had been attractive and definitely interested from their one brief interaction…and yet… Lucas felt nothing. Not even the slightest hint of interest. No desire to call him for drinks and then a quick fuck to blow off some of this frustration. No, Andrei was on his mind now and there was no escaping that as long as the other man was close. Lucas started to toss the business card in the trash and caught himself. Soon, Andrei would be gone and he would need to find someone to amuse him. Lucas dropped the card into a drawer and closed it.

Pushing away from his desk, Lucas stretched, testing out muscles. His ribs were tender, but not as sore as they had been. He flexed his fingers on his left hand before he unraveled the tape on the two knuckles. They were still swollen, but he could move his fingers and lightly grip things. He had to remember not to slug anyone with his left. His shoulder was still another matter altogether. He didn't have full mobility and couldn't put any of his weight on his left arm, but it would come back. He needed more time.

"Feeling better?"

Lucas's head jerked up to find Andrei standing in the open doorway, his hands shoved into the pockets of his dark slacks, looking somewhat unsure of whether he should be standing there.

"Getting there," Lucas replied, a wry grin lifting his lips. "Melissa pack you a tie?"

Andrei nodded. "Hot date tonight and need a driver?"

Lucas snorted and shook his head. "I think not. I wouldn't put it past you to follow Rowe's orders to the letter."

"I may be willing to slide the condoms and lube under the door and pretend not to listen." Andrei grinned, clearly remembering the argument from the hospital.

"Go get dressed," Lucas ordered, fighting not to laugh. "We're heading out."

"Destination?"

"Rialto. If I'm out in public, Ian might stop checking on me."

Lucas didn't miss the skeptical look on Andrei's face as he turned away and headed down the hall to the guest bedroom. Yeah, it was probably unlikely Ian would stop checking on him—Ian liked to take care of his close friends. And in truth, Lucas looked forward to the young man's visits, even though he already had a week's worth of food packed in his fridge.

As he walked back to his bedroom, Lucas paused and looked down at the door to the guest bedroom. Was this a bad idea? Yes, it was likely to be an absolutely horrible idea, but he had to get out of the penthouse. Staying in all night with Andrei close at hand had to be worse.

Chapter 5

The early theater diners were clearing out when Lucas and Andrei arrived at Rialto. The restaurant was less than a block from the Aronoff Center, which was currently running *Wicked*, the Cincinnati Arts Center, and Fountain Square. The Taft Theater was less than two blocks away. The restaurant couldn't have been better placed to capture the vibrant Cincinnati nightlife. It was already paying off. Rialto was packed, making Lucas grateful he'd had the presence of mind to text both Ian and the general manager, James Dunkle, ahead of time. Otherwise, it was likely they would have been dining in the manager's office.

When they were seated at a secluded table that gave Lucas a good view of the dining room while still affording him some privacy, Lucas caught Andrei's amused look and his heart skipped. In the soft lighting, the man was stunning. His dark eyes were nearly black and Lucas longed to reach across and touch the hair brushing against the collar of his navy suit jacket.

"I'm a good friend?" Andrei murmured in a low voice as soon as the hostess left them alone. When the general manager had rushed out to glad hand Lucas on his arrival, he'd introduced Andrei as his "good friend," surprising Andrei when he'd expected to be overlooked and brushed aside.

Lucas gave a little smirk. "Yes, well, bodyguard just sounds so damn pretentious."

Andrei chuckled, looking down at his menu. "Never you."

Lucas stared at the man for a moment, surprised by the unexpected teasing and the fluttering it caused in his stomach. But it also felt familiar, right in a strange way. Had Andrei teased him that first night? Maybe. He knew there were things he wasn't remembering correctly. Had he seen the beautiful smile before and couldn't remember it?

He started to comment when a tall, lanky man dressed all in black appeared at their table and filled their water goblets with sparkling water. He began to rattle off the specials of the night, but Lucas waved him off, just requesting that Ian come to their table. The man visibly paled and hurried away without another word.

"You were going to say something," Andrei prompted, his eyes still lowered to the menu.

"How would you know?"

Andrei looked up and his grin grew so that amusement lit his eyes. "Because there's no way you could let a comment like that go without offering a rebuttal."

Lucas struggled to hold back his own answering smile, keeping his frosty exterior in place. "And to what do I owe this new outspoken attitude?"

"Maybe it's because I'm a 'good friend' tonight."

Lucas sat back in his chair, letting his gaze slide over the other man in open appreciation. His smile slipped free and his eyes became hooded. "And what would I get if I'd introduced you as a lover?" he asked, his voice barely more than a rough purr.

Andrei held his gaze. His only reaction was a slight widening of his eyes and a faint flush to his cheeks that left Lucas wondering. Lucas's heart pounded as he waited to hear how Andrei would either answer or evade his question. The seconds stretched and the world around them faded away so that the clink of silverware and crystal over the soft murmur of conversation went unnoticed.

Finally, Andrei lifted one eyebrow. "Lover?" He paused, still smiling.

"Lucas!" Ian exclaimed, appeared at their table, startling both men and shattering the moment.

Ian bent and wrapped his arms around Lucas, hugging him tightly. Lucas bit back a groan as Ian put pressure on his left shoulder. He pulled away and looked Lucas up and down with a critical eye before giving a little nod. "You look good," he said softly. "Much better."

"It's only been a few hours since I last saw you," Lucas muttered.

Ian shrugged. "You looked tired and stressed."

"He needed a painkiller."

Lucas threw him a dirty look, but Andrei just grinned.

The chef turned to Andrei, his smile becoming a little hesitant and Lucas realized he hadn't had a chance to introduce the two men at his place. Not with Ian's attention pretty much locked on Hollis and his cold.

Andrei smoothly pushed to his feet and extended his hand to Ian. "Andrei Hadeon, good friend of Mr. Vallois. Congratulations on the opening of the restaurant."

Ian took his hand and shook it. "Thank you," he said slowly, still looking a little confused.

Lucas gave a soft snort. "Rowe was kind enough to introduce us last night after my little mishap."

"Oh!" Ian gasped, shaking Andrei's hand with new vigor when it dawned on him that Andrei worked for Rowe and was protecting Lucas. "It's very nice to meet you."

"Thank you," Andrei said, returning to his seat when Ian released his hand.

Lucas watched as some of the amusement drained from Andrei's eyes and the smile lingering on his lips grew more forced. It bothered Lucas and he wished Ian would leave so that he could ask him about it. But it could wait.

Ian turned and pulled over a chair so that he was between Andrei and Lucas. "So? What do you think?"

"It's perfect," Lucas said with a broad smile, swept up in Ian's enthusiasm. The restaurant was amazing, a cut above everything else in the city. And Lucas had had very little hand in it all. Ian had hired the decorator, designed the menu, hired every member of the staff, and more. "Are you happy?"

Ian gave a little laugh and slumped in his seat. "It's exhausting. There's always so much happening and so many things that could go wrong. I'm always worrying about something, but then I walk in here and…and I'm just astounded every time." He laughed again, sounding surprised. "Yeah, I'm happy."

Leaning forward, Lucas cupped the side of Ian's face with his right hand so that the young man was forced to meet his gaze. "I am proud of you. No matter what happens from here, succeed or fail, I am proud of you. You have created something brilliant and people love it."

A crooked smile twisted Ian's mouth and he blinked rapidly. "Yeah, I created it with your money."

Lucas made a scoffing noise in the back of his throat. "No! You would have done this one day. I have no doubt. I just sped it along because I'm an impatient bastard and I couldn't wait to share your genius with the world."

"Thank you," Ian whispered in a rough voice.

"One more thing. If you decide you're done, say the word. You walk away. No questions asked."

"Lucas!" Ian gasped, jerked backward out of the other man's grasp. "I couldn't. I mean, the money—"

"It's just money. I can make more. Your happiness," Lucas paused, fighting the need to clear his throat. "I pushed you into this, Ian. I know that. I need you to be happy."

Ian leaned forward again and embraced Lucas tightly. "I am happy."

Ignoring the protests of his shoulder and ribs, Lucas returned the hug as relief coursed through him. Lucas hadn't realized how much he'd been worrying about the younger man until he'd walked into the restaurant. It was a lot to put on the shoulders of a twenty-five-year-old. Even if Lucas was offering a safety net, he knew Ian was worried about pleasing him.

When Ian released Lucas, he sat back and gave another nervous laugh. "Dinner?"

"Sounds excellent," Lucas said with a nod.

Jumping to his feet, Ian put the chair back away and snatched up their menus when he returned. "In the mood for anything in particular?"

Lucas motioned for Andrei to proceed and the other man just looked up at Ian a little surprised. It wasn't every day that the chef of a four-star restaurant waited on your every desire.

"No, not in particular. I've enjoyed what you sent to Lucas already." Andrei's smile looked a little more genuine now.

"Oh, you did?" Ian said, glowing with the praise as if he were somehow surprised that anyone liked his cooking. Then his brow immediately furrowed. "If you've been stuck with him," Ian began, pointing his thumb over his shoulder at Lucas, "Then all you've had is Italian. And paella. Lucas doesn't even know how to turn on his oven."

"Hey!" Lucas snapped.

Andrei shrugged, his grin growing. "I'm not much better. I don't venture far beyond steaks and grilled cheese."

"Barbarians," Ian muttered under his breath, glancing over at Lucas. Ian quickly peppered Andrei with questions, uncovering any hidden allergies and preferences before giving a final nod. "I've got something." Ian started to leave when Lucas reached forward and grabbed his elbow.

"What about me?"

Ian smiled and patted Lucas on the cheek. "You'll eat what I make you."

Lucas flashed him a dazzling smile and released the young man. "Yes. Yes I will."

When Lucas sat back in his chair again, relaxing, he found Andrei watching him with a somewhat mysterious smile. He couldn't begin to guess what the man was thinking, but he was eager to find out.

"He's very nice," Andrei ventured after a lengthy stretch of silence. "And an excellent chef."

"He's brilliant."

"You're close."

"We're not lovers," Lucas said, still smiling at Andrei, who blushed. "Never have been. Never will be."

Andrei shifted in his chair, sitting up a little straighter. "I-I didn't mean to imply."

"I know, but you were wondering. Particularly since you know about my preferences."

Their conversation paused when their server quietly swept in and poured red wine into both of their glasses. He didn't offer the bottle or say a word, and Lucas wasn't surprised. Ian loved surprises. He knew Lucas's taste and the young man would have undoubtedly picked something that perfectly matched whatever he was cooking up for him and Andrei.

"It's not my place to inquire about your love life," Andrei said a bit stiffly when they were alone again.

"But it is the place of a 'good friend,'" Lucas teased, but was disappointed when the smile didn't returned to Andrei's lips. "I said something earlier that bothered you. What was it?"

"No, you didn't." Andrei's response came fast as he picked up his glass to sip his wine.

"Don't lie."

Andrei's eyes snapped to Lucas's face and narrowed over the rim of the glass. Setting the glass carefully on the table, Andrei sat back in his chair. He looked as if he were trying to appear relaxed and at ease, but there was no missing the tension in his frame. "If we'd met under normal circumstances, do you think we could have been friends?"

"No," Lucas said without hesitation.

Andrei gave a jerky nod, his jaw clenching at that emphatic declaration.

"My answer has nothing to do with you," Lucas continued. "I don't have friends. At least, not what you have in mind."

Andrei frowned. "What about Dr. Frost and Rowe and Ian?"

"They are my family." Lucas paused and picked up his glass, swirling the wine for a moment. He watched the color wash over the fine crystal, catching the light. "For me, there is my family and then there's the rest of the world. There's nothing in between." Lucas took a sip, savoring the wine as he set his glass on the table. He looked at Andrei for several seconds before venturing a tentative smile. "But talking to you has me thinking that I may need to reconsider adding a new layer to my life."

"Forgive me if I don't hold my breath. A controlling bastard like you would probably need a few years to examine the pros and cons of such a decision."

"Without a doubt," Lucas said, his grin returning.

"So it's got nothing to do with the fact that I come from a poor family and that I work for your family and I'm still trying to get my bachelor's degree from an online college and not some ivy league college and—"

Lucas's loud bark of laughter halted Andrei's list as he slumped in his chair. Swallowing the last of his chuckles, Lucas leaned forward, both his hands sliding across the crisp white tablecloth as if he were struggling to keep from reaching for Andrei. He pinned the other man with his eyes and Andrei dragged in a deep breath. "The only one at this table who cares about where you came from is you."

Lucas saw it then. The last of the tension fell off of Andrei and his smile became more open. He hadn't even realized that the man was holding some last protective barrier around him, but when it finally fell away, Lucas was…shocked. As they talked and enjoyed their food, Andrei's face became more animated when he spoke and his laughter tumbled from his lips a little easier and fuller. The light he had been guarding inside of him had been set free and Lucas was simply in awe that he'd shielded it that effectively.

"Are you straight?"

Andrei's entire body froze except for his gaze, which jumped to Lucas's face. Their plates had just been cleared away and they'd been easily chatting all evening. Lucas almost regretted the wariness that crept into Andrei's eyes, but he simply couldn't hold back the question any longer.

What surprised Lucas was that Andrei didn't immediately answer. Seconds stretched on and the other man stared at him like a deer in the headlights. That was almost more telling than any answer he could utter now.

"Why?" Andrei finally replied.

Lucas smiled slowly and they both knew Andrei had evaded the question. "I'm curious. You asked about my preferences. It's a fair question."

"I don't know."

Lucas's frowned. "You don't know if it's a fair question?"

"I don't know…if…I'm…straight," Andrei admitted haltingly.

Lucas carefully smoothed his face of expression while his heart lurched in his chest. That was certainly not the answer he'd been expecting. He'd fully anticipated a lusty and maybe even a laughing YES that would finally stomp out the last of his attraction for Andrei. But that…was thrilling and frightening… and even hopeful.

Andrei looked torn. Panic edged his gaze. If Lucas said the wrong thing here, Andrei would forcefully shut him down and there would be no broaching this topic again. Lucas needed Andrei to feel safe and comfortable with him, but that wasn't exactly his specialty. That was more Ian's domain. He was going to fuck this up.

"That's a surprisingly honest answer," Lucas said carefully. "Have you been with a man?"

Andrei glared at him, clenching his jaw.

Lucas inwardly winced. That was wrong. "I'm sorry. Is this too personal for two good friends? Should we talk about something else? What chance do you think the Bengals have of making it to the Super Bowl this year?"

A surprised laugh jumped from Andrei, the sound echoing through the restaurant. Out of the corner of his eye, Lucas saw a few diners look up and stare for a second, but he didn't care. They only wished they were at the same table. Andrei's laugh reminded him of Snow's—when the doctor loosened up enough. Loud and open and truly joyous.

"Two good friends, huh?" Andrei teased, his body relaxed again.

"I'm considering it." Lucas tried to sound serious as he fought back a grin. He was on firmer ground now.

"That's a much faster time table than I thought you capable of—considering what you told me about family earlier."

Lucas shrugged his right shoulder. "I can be an impatient man."

Andrei chuckled, stirring his largely untouched coffee, allowing them to fall into a comfortable silence again.

"You never answered my question," Lucas pressed after a minute.

Andrei kept his eyes on the coffee. "I'd hoped you hadn't noticed."

"No."

The younger man looked up, meeting Lucas's gaze. His expression was unsure, as if he were stepping out on a too-thin branch, knowing if he said the wrong word, the branch would snap beneath him. Lucas almost felt the need to warn him that he was confessing to the devil, not an angel, but he couldn't bring himself to do it.

"Yes," Andrei finally admitted. "A few times. I told myself that it was about boredom and being adventurous and having too much alcohol."

"You're probably right."

"But..." Andrei's sexy lips tightened, his unease obvious in the draw of his brows as his dark eyes locked on his coffee.

"Things have changed," Lucas finished when Andrei's voice drifted off.

Andrei gave one sharp nod and Lucas shrugged again. "Happens." He dropped his hands to his lap and curled them into fists on his legs to keep from reaching across the table to touch.

Tension eased from Andrei's expression, though he was looking at Lucas a bit incredulously.

"Does it scare you?"

"Not knowing?" Andrei cocked his head to the side, truly considering Lucas's question. "No."

"Anger you?"

"No."

"Confuse you?"

"Yes."

Lucas nodded, tossing his linen napkin on the table. "Then you'll be fine."

"Just like that, huh?"

Lucas leaned forward, smiling at Andrei. "You'll figure it out. Rowe wouldn't have hired you if you were a complete idiot. Now let's get out of here. I want to show you something."

It took everything Lucas had not to let his grin turn wicked with those words. As it was, the flush on Andrei's cheeks let him know that the bodyguard's mind had gone the same direction.

兄弟武士心

Andrei followed in Lucas's wake through the restaurant, flummoxed by the man. He was like the planet Jupiter—a massive force within the solar system, drawing others into his orbit like small moons by the sheer weight of his presence. Andrei had been surprised by his warm affection for Ian. And even more flabbergasted when he'd asked about Andrei's sexuality so bluntly. Was Lucas attracted to him? Yeah, Andrei was pretty sure Lucas was. The endless flirting seemed to grow more heated each time. Would he do anything about it? No, not a chance in hell. Lucas was undoubtedly a man bound by rules and screwing around with an employee had to break a rule or two of his.

"Were you serious?" Andrei inquired when they stepped outside.

Lucas looked over and gave Andrei a dark look that he was beginning to recognize as Lucas's favorite expression. "I'm always serious." He buttoned his jacket against the cool night air, gaze locked with Andrei's. "But you might need to be specific about my previous seriousness."

Andrei snorted as he waited for the valet to bring around Lucas's car. "About being friends."

"Ah, yes. You may ask me again after you complete the written exam."

"Bastard," Andrei muttered, trying not to laugh.

"True, but I've been known to keep life interesting."

"Let's just focus on keeping you alive for now," Andrei said in a low voice as the valet hopped out of the car. Andrei stepped forward to open the back but Lucas slipped around him and opened the front passenger door. Andrei quickly moved out of the way, as Lucas slid into the car, throwing one last smirk over his shoulder at his bodyguard.

Grumbling to himself, Andrei hopped into the driver's seat and pulled the car out into traffic, heading south toward the Ohio River.

"Where are we going? Somewhere to get you some action?" Andrei asked when they stopped at the next traffic light.

"Why the hell would I want to show you that?"

Andrei groaned dramatically but he was enjoying their banter. "Sometimes talking to you is like trying to nail gelatin to the wall."

"I wouldn't know. I've never tried to fuck gelatin," Lucas replied.

Andrei couldn't stop his laughter. When he looked at Lucas, he was watching Andrei with a decidedly heated gaze that caused Andrei's throat to become desperately dry. He licked his lips and locked his eyes on the road in front of him.

"Come to think of it, the men I've nailed to the wall never complained."

"Are you done?" Andrei was proud that he managed to sound bored by Lucas's attempts to rattle him. Because the image of Lucas nailing *him* to the wall took a prominent spot in his mind and made him feel like he should pull over.

Lucas nodded. "For now."

"Where are we going?"

"Price Hill."

Yes, the fun was definitely over. It was time to get to work.

Chapter 6

Both men fell silent on the drive west out of downtown and across the tracks to Price Hill. Tension thickened in the car, but it was not due to any discomfort between them. Andrei knew he should say something as his hands flexed on the steering wheel. The sexy banter was now forgotten, pushed off to the side. This was a bad idea and he needed to make that clear.

Andrei parked the car under a dingy street light, but didn't turn off the engine. Nothing felt good about this. The shadows in the area were heavy, crowding close to old homes fallen into disrepair and vacant buildings where business owners had given up. Trash and dead leaves clogged the gutters, while sidewalks were cracked and crumbling. Hope had abandoned this part of town years ago, leaving its occupants to trudge along like vacant-eyed zombies, beaten down by life and despair. It was all too familiar.

A muffled click jerked Andrei from his grim thoughts, drawing his gaze to Lucas to see him removing his seat belt and reaching for the door. Andrei moved faster, hitting the lock button so that a loud thunk echoed through the car.

"Where the hell are you going?" Andrei demanded before he could stop himself. The area had him too on edge to censor his words.

"Getting out. I want to show you something."

"No."

Lucas stared at him, his brow furrowed in confusion and what looked like shock. Hadn't anyone ever said that word to him? Well, he was going to have to get used to it. There was no way in hell Andrei was letting the man out of the car when someone was desperate to do him harm.

"What?"

"I said no. We're not getting out. In fact, I shouldn't have even driven you here. We're leaving. It's not safe." Andrei started to reach for the gear shift in the console between them and Lucas lurched forward, grabbing the key and pulling it free. The car fell silent with a shudder, leaving them wrapped in a deepening silence.

"We're staying. Just for a few minutes."

"Give me the key."

Lucas smiled as he shoved the key in his right pocket. "Come get it."

Andrei swore violently under his breath, gripping the steering wheel with both hands, before glaring over at his companion. Lucas was lounging back in his seat, the shadows caressing his features, making him look all the more enticing with that lazy grin on his lips. "Damn it! This isn't some fucking game. Give me the key now."

"Just slip your hand in my pocket and take it. Then we can leave." The tip of Lucas's tongue slid across his upper lip and Andrei couldn't stop his gaze from following the motion before he finally closed his eyes and shook his head. This man was going to drive him insane.

"Be serious. You've been attacked once," Andrei said evenly, forcing his voice to remain calm. He could appeal to the man's common sense. "We're in the area they've warned you away from. You think they're not watching this place? We step foot out there and they're going to try to kill you. I'm one person against an unknown number."

"And I'm telling you that there's no reason for them to protect this place. It's nothing. There's nothing to watch." Lucas's growing anger made him clearly enunciate each word. "Besides I'm not about to be run off from *my property* by a bunch a fucking hoods." He flicked the latch, unlocking his door, but Andrei immediately hit the button again. "Andrei…" The growl rumbled through the car in warning. Lucas hit the latch again and Andrei punched the button.

Lucas started to move but Andrei was faster. Twisting his body, he slammed his left hand against Lucas's door, holding his lean body mere inches above the other man's, as he blocked his escape. "I fucking said no. You may be used to getting your way, Your Highness, but it's my job to keep you alive. You're not getting out of the car. So give me the damned key."

Tension ratcheted up between them until Andrei could feel his skin tingling. Lucas's lips parted and a harsh breath escaped him. Andrei made the mistake of looking at them and he nearly groaned. They were inches apart. Lucas tilted his chin up, closing the distance by a tiny amount. His mouth looked soft, so fucking soft. Andrei had never kissed a man before and now that he was so damned close to Lucas, it was all he could think about. He tried to imagine the feel, the taste, the sound he might make as their mouths met and he simply couldn't.

Lucas ran his teeth over his bottom lip, tugging at it. He'd watched the man do that several times in the past when he was amused or thoughtful and now it was like he was fighting something and losing. Andrei didn't care. He longed to pull that lip into his own mouth and suck on it.

Catching the moan that rose up his throat, Andrei lurched away from Lucas, falling back into his own seat. His knuckles were turning white, he held the steering wheel so tightly. His harsh, rapid breathing was the only sound in the car. He was becoming obsessed with the man's perfect mouth.

"Andrei, it's okay," Lucas said softly after a couple seconds. Out of the corner of his eye, he saw Lucas reach for him and he flinched. Lucas stopped and pulled his hand back, dropping it into his lap.

"It's not fucking okay," Andrei gritted out.

"We'll be in and out in five minutes," Lucas coaxed. "No one will even know we were here."

Andrei's eyes jerked to Lucas in confusion, his mind stumbling out of its lust-filled haze to realize that he wasn't talking about the fact that he'd nearly kissed the man within an inch of his life. No, Lucas was still talking about getting out of the car. Hell, that seemed less dangerous now compared to the edge he'd been balanced on just seconds earlier.

He barely reacted to the soft thunk of Lucas's car door unlocking yet again. "Come on," Lucas pressed. "Let me show you this. I need you to help me figure out why I'm being targeted." Andrei reluctantly dragged his gaze over to Lucas's face to find him tentatively smiling. "Sooner we figure it out, the sooner you never have to see me again."

That didn't make him feel better. Andrei just shook his head, closing his eyes for a second. "You're the most stubborn man I've ever met."

"It's one of my more endearing qualities."

Andrei snorted, some of the tension starting to flow out of his shoulders. "I still don't like this."

"Five minutes and then we're gone." Lucas pulled the door handle, popping open the door, but he stopped it from swinging wide.

"Stay. You follow my lead," Andrei said firmly, waiting for Lucas to nod in agreement.

Andrei exited the car and stood holding the top of the door as his eyes slowly scanned the area. Everything was ragged and worn. The darkness didn't help much to hide the sagging homes and broken sidewalks. He knew the vacant store fronts, broken windows, and weed-choked lots. He couldn't understand what Lucas saw in the area. They'd parked just down from an old two-story warehouse.

Removing his jacket, Andrei tossed it onto the driver's seat, revealing the shoulder holster he was wearing. With any luck, the gun tucked under his left arm would be effective in deterring anyone from bothering them. The street was quiet. It was after ten, but no one was in sight. The sound of cars rushing from one place to another echoed through the city, but on the little block where Andrei stood, it was empty.

"Okay," he said in a low voice before stepping away from the car and shutting the door. He continued to scan the area as Lucas stepped out and led the way across the street to the dilapidated warehouse. They paused only long enough to unlock the single door and then Andrei entered the building, using the flashlight on his phone to beat back the darkness.

The small, thin light panned over the crude tables built using saw horses and the other random building supplies. Orange water coolers dotted the area along with coils of thick extension cords. The entire place was dusty and in various levels of disrepair.

"What do you think?" Lucas asked after more than minute of silence had passed.

"I think you may have lost your mind," Andrei said, continuing to sweep the flashlight over the building. There were signs of rust on some of the metal I-beams and chunks of the concrete floor had deep divots. "Is this really worth risking your life over? This building?"

"Yes."

Andrei turned back to face Lucas, his interest piqued by that single word. Lucas had infused it with passion and determination. He turned off the flashlight, letting his eyes adjust to the moonlight and street light pouring in through the skylights and windows high on the second floor.

"This building, it's the beginning. It's ground zero for where I plan to change this entire neighborhood," Lucas explained.

"How? I thought you were building another nightclub."

"I am, but like I said, it's just the beginning. I've bought six other buildings in this area under another holding company that hasn't been directly linked to me. I don't want people to know I'm moving into the area beyond this building or the fuckers will jack up the property values."

Andrei lifted his eyebrows at the man's back, surprised he'd admit to such a sneaky tactic. "Is that legal?"

"Yes," Lucas hissed, sounding more than a little irritated.

"So what are the other buildings for?" Andrei asked, fighting a smile that he hoped Lucas wouldn't notice in the darkness.

"Shops. I'm opening a green grocer and funding a bakery. I'm going to have one refurbished for a bookstore. After that, I'm starting on some of the homes in the area, rebuilding them. The nightclub and the restaurant that's going next door will be my cash cows. They'll bring people in with their money, but the stores and the homes, that's to rebuild the area."

"That sounds...amazing." Andrei was surprised by the feeling of awe that swept through him when he looked at the other man. "But what about the people that live here already?"

Lucas waved one finger at him, a broad grin on his face. "See, I thought about that too. Cincinnati already pulled this trick with Over the Rhine. The police came in, swept out the gangs and the violence, and poured money into cleaning everything up. All that was great. But as soon as all the shops opened up and OTR became the cool place in the city, none of the people already in OTR could fucking afford to live there. The goddamned hipsters priced them out!"

"And you're not going to let it happen?"

"Fuck no!" He threw his arms wide, as he turned back to look at Andrei, his light eyes narrowed in his vehemence. "I was strategic in my purchases so that no one can come in and buy huge swaths of land because I won't sell. I'm not building high-priced condos or freaking coffee shops that charge $20 for a latté. I'm bringing money to an underserved neighborhood and letting it remain working class, but with a better standard of living."

Andrei couldn't look away from him. Lucas had stepped forward in a beam of light shining down from the ceiling and his expression was filled with a sort of fierce pride and hope. He gazed around the crumbling building, apparently seeing opportunity, beginnings, and new life.

"Why?" Andrei couldn't stop the near whisper.

Lucas's gaze snapped back to Andrei and he frowned. "What?"

Andrei pressed on. "Why? Why do it? I mean, it sounds like you're going to be lucky to break even on this deal."

One corner of Lucas's mouth lifted in a mocking smile. "I like a challenge."

"Ehhh," Andrei said, making a buzzer sound. "I'm sorry, that was the wrong answer. Please try again."

The mocking smile morphed into a wide grin. Amusement made his eyes glitter. "I want to give back to a community that has given me so much."

"Ehhh," Andrei said again with a snicker. "Strike two. Do you think you can recognize the truth under all that manure?"

Lucas spread his legs and tucked his hands into the pockets of his slacks, staring at Andrei through narrowed eyes. "I know what it's like to grow up in a neighborhood where you feel like you have no hope of ever getting out alive and no hope of things getting better. I want to create better *now*."

Andrei smiled. "Good answer." Fuck, he wanted to kiss Lucas all over again, but for an entirely different reason.

Lucas's grin turned decidedly wicked and he lifted one eyebrow. "And what have I won?"

"My grudging respect and admiration."

Lucas shook his head. "We need to discuss these prizes. Not at all what I was hoping for."

"Yeah, well, what you're hoping for probably wouldn't get past the censors," Andrei muttered under his breath.

"God, I hope not." Lucas turned his back on Andrei to wander around the warehouse.

"So what is this place going to be like? Another Shiver?"

Lucas stopped and looked over his shoulder at Andrei, his gaze suddenly assessing, as if he were weighing some secret information. "You've been to Shiver?"

"Everyone's been to Shiver," Andrei replied with a shrug.

"And?"

He laughed deeply, tipping his head back. "Great place for a one-night stand."

"Isn't that every nightclub?" Lucas drawled.

"Nah, some places I have to work at it. Not Shiver. I'm big and warm and chilly women like to snuggle." Lucas looked like he was going to say something, but Andrei interrupted, trying to direct them away from the more sexual banter. "What are your plans for this place?"

"I'm going retro. Industrial goth." Walking over to Andrei, Lucas started pointing out his plans for where the bar was going to be and the stage for performances or a DJ. The lighting would be low and subtle while the tables and art would be modern. Waving for Andrei to follow, Lucas led him up the wide staircase to the second floor that overlooked the first floor.

"Look here," Lucas said excitedly, snatching up a rag draped over the railing. He wiped some of the dirt caked on the window and pointed out. "That's the biggest reason I bought this place."

Andrei leaned forward, peering through the smudged window to see the beautiful view of the glowing downtown skyline. It was a prime location worth millions because of the view. The city of Cincinnati was settled down in a river valley and was surrounded on almost all sides by hills. Some of the most exclusive clubs, restaurants, and homes were those with views of downtown and now Lucas had claimed one for his own.

"Brilliant," Andrei whispered.

"Most people don't know about this. They forget this plot is on a rise with an unobstructed view. I'm going to knock out the back wall and put a patio on the first floor and a deck on the second floor for private parties."

"Not bad for the summer months."

"With heaters and some well-placed curtains, it will be available in all but the coldest months."

Andrei stepped back, a smile playing on his lips as he looked at Lucas. This man was not what he'd expected and was leaving him feeling extremely unsteady. He'd witnessed the commanding figure, in control from a hospital bed, and he'd watched the tenderness directed toward Ian. And then of course, there was the ex-girlfriend who he could only guess was part of the image he portrayed to the world. Andrei was an intruder, given a rare glimpse of the inside of this man's life, something only an elite few ever saw.

Lucas cocked his head to the side slightly, his brow furrowing. "What?"

"What?" Andrei took another step back.

"You've got this look on your face. What are you thinking?"

Andrei gave a shrug, fighting the urge to break the man's direct gaze. He stepped back so that his shoulders were now leaning against the cold stone wall. "Just trying to figure you out. You're not what I'd expected."

Lucas's expression tightened and he slowly prowled toward Andrei, his movements sleek and smooth. "Don't try to whitewash me." Lucas took a step forward, closing the distance between them so that mere inches separated their chests. He lifted his right hand and slowly touched a strand of Andrei's hair, rubbing it between his index finger and thumb as if he simply couldn't help himself. There was something in his beautiful eyes, something anxious and uneasy he seemed to be trying to tamp down. Andrei could hear it in each uneven breath Lucas dragged over his parted lips.

Andrei remained perfectly still, afraid that if he flinched or shifted, this strange moment would shatter and Lucas would jerk away from him. He'd pulled himself back from the edge in the car. He simply couldn't do it again. The pounding of his heart was so loud that it nearly drowned out Lucas's whispered words.

"I'm a bastard, Mr. Hadeon. Never forget that. I use people. Manipulate them to get what I want."

"And you don't want me in your bed?" Andrei demanded, grinning at the other man. He needed to chase away the anxiety clouding those green-gray eyes.

Lucas's fingers clenched in Andrei's hair and for a heartbeat Andrei thought Lucas was going to finally drag him across the tiny distance to seal his lips across Andrei's. His hand relaxed and pressed against the wall next to his head. "I never said that."

"Then why are you working so hard to scare me away?"

Leaning forward, pressing their chests together, Lucas brushed his cheek against Andrei's, his nose digging against the man's jaw near his ear so that Andrei could hear his deep inhale. Andrei wanted to wrap his hands around the other man's waist, but he settled for fisting them at his side. He tilted his head away to expose his neck. Lucas's every movement was absolutely predatory and Andrei could feel his body responding, longing for this man to tear into him. Sexual tension zinged through him. Every instinct screamed that Lucas could destroy him, but damn he still wanted it.

"You smell like a horrible mistake," Lucas said, slowly pulling back.

Andrei huffed a laugh. "I'm sure you've never made one of those."

A genuine smile parted Lucas's lips at last, making him appear more relaxed. The dark protective layer he'd wrapped around himself slipped away. "Never."

"So we do nothing?"

"Nothing."

"We ignore this."

Lucas's gaze dropped from Andrei's eyes to his lips. He lifted his left hand and ran his thumb along the man's lower lip, seemingly mesmerized by the soft bit of flesh. "There is no this," Lucas whispered. "Nothing to ignore. You don't do this kind of thing unless you're bored. Are you bored, Mr. Hadeon?"

"No, definitely not bored." Andrei slowly opened his mouth and lightly bit Lucas's thumb. Holding Lucas's surprised gaze, he ran the tip of his tongue along the warm flesh. There was no missing the hard shiver that ran through Lucas. Andrei was playing with fire and he couldn't stop himself. This man was temptation incarnate and he was tired of fighting these crazy new feelings. He wanted more.

"Fuck." The soft word jumped from Lucas, more an expulsion of air than sound.

Lucas withdrew his thumb from Andrei's lips and hovered for a second, seeming to fight the urge to close those last couple of inches, indecision filling his light eyes. Andrei lowered his chin the tiniest bit, his breathing ragged as he tried to keep from swooping in, praying the other man would kiss him to put them both out of their misery. He just needed a taste and then he would be able to walk away from Lucas Vallois, never give the man another thought.

Lucas's warm breath danced across Andrei's lips as he sighed, a sound of capitulation, giving into the swamping need that was drawing them closer.

A loud scraping echoed through the warehouse as the door was forced open. Both men jumped, startled by the intrusion. Andrei recovered first, using his left arm to shove Lucas behind him, deeper into the shadows while he pulled his gun with his right.

"Is there an exit on this level?" Andrei whispered, his eyes trained on the entrance as two men entered carrying heavy, awkward objects.

"No.

Andre wanted to groan. Of course there wasn't an easy way out of there. They'd have to get past the two intruders in order to escape. Sadly, Andrei couldn't decide if he was pissed or relieved they'd interrupted what would have been his first kiss with a man. But now was not the time to think about it. He needed to get Lucas out of there safely and then call the cops.

"How many exits?"

"Three. One in the front, back, and on the far side. All on the first floor."

Andrei nodded, keeping his eyes on the two men as they moved toward the center of the room. If they kept moving toward the back, Andrei planned to grab Lucas and hurry him down the stairs. He could lay down some cover fire so Lucas could make a run for the door. Of course, Andrei was hoping that the two didn't have any companions waiting outside the building.

Texting and calling for help was also out of the question. The light from their phones would instantly give them away in the darkness of the place. They were trapped.

"So? How are we goin' do this?" The taller man stopped in the middle of the room with his heavy container. "We could just put a rag in one and light it."

"This ain't no Molotov cocktail, you fucking moron!" his companion shouted. "We splash it on everything and leave a puddle on the floor in the middle. I've got a wick that'll stretch to the door. That way we can get out of here before the whole fucking place goes up."

"What the hell?" Lucas whispered. He took a step, moving as if he planned to march down the stairs to confront the two thugs.

Andrei soundlessly spun around and pressed Lucas against the wall, leaning in so that his face was close to the other man's. "We're going to sneak out before they set it on fire."

"But—"

"No. We're out. I never should have brought you here. We need to figure out where the others are." Andrei turned away from Lucas to look past the temporary wooden railing down to the first floor where the two men were opening the containers. He prayed they were smart enough to start at the back of the building and work their way toward the front door.

"Others?"

Andrei frowned and then bent to yank of up his pant leg. He pulled out a snub nose revolver and handed it to Lucas. "There should be one more at most—a driver of the getaway car. Keep your head down and just run for your car. I'll be behind you."

The two men continued to talk as the first splash on the concrete floor echoed through the empty warehouse. Noxious fumes from the gasoline filled the air, threatening to gag Andrei. Reaching back, he grabbed a fistful of Lucas's jacket and pulled him toward the stairs as the men moved steadily deeper into the building. The patter of dripping gasoline hitting the various surfaces while the men loudly talked helped to cover their movement down the grime-covered stairs.

Andrei's heart pounded and he was cursing himself over and over again for allowing Lucas to even get out of the car. It was just his bad luck that they'd timed their trip with a pair of arsonists.

Lucas had reached the bottom step when their luck took an even bigger turn for the worse. They were less than a hundred feet from the door when one of the intruders looked back and caught sight of them. His shock briefly showed in the dingy moonlight, but he didn't hesitate long. Dropping his plastic container of gasoline, he drew his weapon and pointed it at Lucas.

Andrei shoved Lucas down and fired at the man. Both he and the other guy dove to the floor, but the thug holding the gun returned fire. Pain ripped across Andrei's bicep, but he ignored it and kept firing while he focused on getting Lucas to his feet again so he could scramble toward the door while Andrei kept them busy.

But Lucas got no farther than a step when a great whoosh engulfed the back of the building. Andrei had only enough time to react. He launched himself at Lucas, tackling the man to the floor once again as he covered him with as much of his body as he could, tucking his face in the other man's neck. The ball of fire rushed forward, seeking oxygen to feed the ravenous flames. Heat scorched across Andrei's back, drawing a pain-filled cry from his lips but he didn't move as he continued to tightly clutch Lucas beneath him.

The fireball dissipated after a second, retreated to the back of the building where the bulk of the gasoline had been spread. Wincing, Andrei jerked at Lucas, getting the man moving again toward the door. Adrenaline pumped through Andrei, pushing aside the pain for the short term. As soon as he hit the night air, he raised his gun, expecting to find yet another attacker waiting for his companions but there was no one in the beat-up old Chevy parked in front of the warehouse.

They turned, looking up at the building that was now glowing brightly in the darkness as black smoke billowed out of every hole, crevice and broken window. Even as Andrei dialed 9-1-1, he knew there was no saving the building or the men inside.

Chapter 7

Lucas sat naked from the waist up on the edge of a bed in a private room in the hospital. He smelled of sweat, dirt, and smoke. A chill crept into his bones, gnawing at him. The hospital was cold, but then they were always cold, right? Helped to distract the patients from their pain. It wasn't helping. His mind kept going around and around about how everything had turned to shit in a matter of seconds and only he was to blame.

The EMTs that arrived with the fire trucks and the cops had taken one look at them and immediately shoved them both into the ambulance, shuffling them off to University Hospital. He'd been separated from Andrei, who was looking worse for wear and had not spoken a single word beyond the occasional grunt since stepping outside the burning building.

A doctor appeared a moment after Lucas had been shown to the room and flashed him a small smile. "Mr. Vallois, I was not expecting to see you again so soon."

"I've never seen you before," Lucas grumbled, giving the man only a cursory glance. He needed to get out of that room and find Andrei, needed to know that he was okay and that the staff who were so quick to take care of him were actually helping his bodyguard. Guilt and frustration burned through him like acid, eating through his soul. Andrei was hurt and it was his fault.

"No, you wouldn't remember me. I was the doctor who attended you when you were brought in a few nights ago with a concussion." He pulled on a fresh pair of rubber gloves with a soft snap and positioned his stethoscope in his ears. "Don't worry. I believe a nurse was notifying Dr. Frost of your arrival as he came out of surgery."

"Fuck." Lucas sighed. Why couldn't this shit have happened on a night that Snow had off? The man was going to lose it. "Can you send someone to tell him that I'm not hurt?"

"Why don't we just check to make sure that's true first and then we'll update Dr. Frost on your status?" The doctor pressed the cold metal disc to Lucas's chest.

Clenching his jaw, Lucas closed his eyes and fought the urge to punch the man. His condescending words didn't merit a response. His entire body ached, but that had more to do with his original set of injuries than anything new he'd sustained. He should have taken another painkiller more than an hour ago, but he wasn't going to bring it up or the fact that his head was swimming. Sleep and a Percocet would have done wonders, but he was hours away from that relief. He endured the exam with his patience scraped thin as tissue paper, not speaking unless he absolutely had to and then he said as little as possible. By the end of his exam, the doctor was flushed and his hands trembled as he flinched under Lucas's piercing gaze. The doctor scrambled to leave, mumbling something about updating their records, as he struggled to jerk the door open and slide out of the room.

And then Snow blew in, looking like the wrath of God. He wasn't wearing his white coat, so he must have just gotten off duty. His blue button-down shirt made his eyes look like chips of frozen sky. He had on loose faded jeans, the ones that rode low on his hips. Snow's laze-at-home clothes. *Terrific.*

Lucas lowered his head and cursed under his breath, unable to meet the other man's gaze. When he did finally look, his friend's expression made him peer closer. Anyone looking at the man would see the anger, but it would take a close friend to see the fear. "Hey," he said softly. "I'm okay. Come see for yourself."

Snow didn't move closer. His nostrils flared, his lips tightened, and Lucas half expected real ice bolts to shoot from those eyes any second. Lucas lifted an eyebrow.

"What were you thinking?" Snow's voice, low and threatening, sounded gritty like he'd swallowed glass. "Or were you even thinking at all? Has the hot bodyguard forced all your blood too far south?"

"You think he's hot?"

"That's what you hear?" Snow shut his eyes and a small shudder ran through him as if he were straining to hold back an explosion. "Not the point here, Vallois." He spoke through clenched teeth as his eyes snapped back open. "I don't give a shit if you're boning the bodyguard. I care that you got attacked—again. You know, *fucking know*, that they specifically targeted you and you go to the one place that instigated the attack? And with a concussion?"

When put like that, it did seem stupid. "Snow, I honestly didn't expect such a blatant attack. Not there. It doesn't make any sense."

"The criminals are dumb shits. And so is your bodyguard!"

"No." The quietly spoken word came with a rush of anger that tightened Lucas's chest. "Don't talk about him like that. He tried to talk me out of it." He flexed his hand, wincing at the stretch of not-healed scrapes and busted knuckles from the fight. "The criminals were dumb shits. Or not worried about being caught."

Snow came closer and leaned down until Lucas could see the tiny dark flecks in his eyes. "Which makes them reckless and deadly."

His friend had a point. The men who'd beaten him had been cocky, skilled, and carried a careless arrogance—almost like they knew they wouldn't get caught. Or knew they'd get free if they were. Even their hoodies had been the bare minimum effort of disguise.

"I noticed you didn't deny boning the bodyguard," Snow said, gaze sharp.

"I'm actually not."

"You want to."

With Snow, Lucas could be honest. Always. "Of course I want to. Anyone would want to. Did you really look at the man?"

Snow sighed and walked to the sink where he wet paper towels. He came back and started swiping the soot and dirt from Lucas's chest and shoulders. "Best to wait until he isn't working for you."

"He's not working for me—he works for Rowe."

Lucas let Snow take care of him, knowing it made the doctor feel better. Truth to tell, the attention worked for him, too. He needed his friend as much as Snow needed him. Hell, he should probably tell him that more often.

A loud clatter in the hall outside the room caught their attention. It was followed by a familiar sound and Lucas cocked his head to the side, listened.

"Hear that cough? I think we're about to see the detective again." Lucas groaned when he reached for his shirt.

"What are you doing? You can't get dressed. We need to run a scan over that new bruise on your back."

Lucas scoffed. "You and I both know I can have my clothes on for that."

"Maybe I was enjoying the make-shift sponge bath."

"Perv."

Snow grinned and surprised him with a quick hug. "Always."

"How did you know there is a bruise on my back? You haven't seen that side of me."

Snow tossed the blackened paper towels onto the tray by the bed. "The attending ordered the scan."

Lucas rolled his eyes. "Half a dozen hospitals in this city and they keep bringing me to this one."

"How about you just stay out of them altogether?"

The loud sniff by the door made them both look. Banner leaned on the door jamb, his face flushed, his nose so red, Lucas winced in sympathy. "You two argue like you're married." He pointed from Snow to Lucas, his head cocked slightly to the side. "So, you together? Because I could have sworn I saw sparks between you and the dark statue at your place."

Lucas didn't bother to answer the question. "Damn. You look worse than I do. You should be in bed, Detective."

"We haven't even had a date yet. I like to be wooed, receive a good meal before I go ass up." Banner grinned and while that sexy smile probably got him what he wanted usually—in another healthy galaxy—

right now, he just looked pathetic. Lucas kind of felt sorry for him. Kind of.

Snow snorted.

The cop screamed top so Lucas doubted he ever gave that up. He sighed as the aches and pains from the explosion started making themselves heard now that Snow appeared calmer. "Why are you here?"

"Heard you went to Price Hill. I can see I need to reevaluate my gift of first impressions because you didn't seem like a complete dumb ass to me then."

Lucas caught Snow's smirk out of the corner of his eye and turned to glare at him.

"What?" the doctor said, raising his hands. "I don't have to like the guy to agree with him. And going there right after getting your ass beat *was* a dumb ass move."

"You don't like me?" Banner tried to pout but a cough ruined it. He grimaced, glanced around the room and walked to the paper towel dispenser by the bed. "I'm a likeable guy. Give me a chance." He started to wipe his nose, but Snow made a sound of disgust and walked into the bathroom.

He came back with tissues and handed them to the cop. "I don't appreciate you sharing your germs with someone who's been in a hospital twice in less than a week. Let's save the questions for when you don't have a fever."

"I don't have a—" he broke off. "Okay, yeah, sorry." He walked back to the door, but didn't leave. "Don't suppose you got a good enough look to identify the crispers in what's left of your building?"

Lucas shook his head. "No, but I recognized one of the voices from the other night. Not the guy with the accent, but one of the bigger ones. He cursed a few times—his voice was distinctive. Deep and nasally."

"Hear anything that could let us know why they torched the place?"

"Only that they had no idea what they were doing. Arson wasn't something they normally did, so I'm guessing someone ordered or paid them to do it."

"Okay, good enough for now." Banner wiped his upper lip with the tissue. "Keep your phone handy tomorrow in case I have more questions."

"Will do." Lucas watched him straighten up but stopped him before he was out of sight. "Hey Banner? The avgolemono? That better not be considered a good meal."

Banner chuckled. "That meal was not merely good. It was the best. So... is GQ seeing anyone?"

Snow clued in fast and Lucas didn't have to ask why. Ian had been cooking that Greek soup for them long before he opened his own restaurant. His friend growled, actually growled, as he stalked to the cop and clapped his hand on his shoulder. "So Holly," Snow drew the name out. "We're gonna have us a little chat about GQ as I walk you and your fucking germs out of my hospital."

Lucas chuckled, winced, then frowned when he realized he had to wait for the scan and he just wanted to go home. Or better yet, find Andrei then go home.

He had barely enjoyed a moment of peace when Rowe stepped into the room, a scowl deeply etched into the man's face. Shutting the door carefully behind him, Rowe leaned against the wall with his hands shoved into the pockets of his worn jeans, glaring at Lucas as he continued to sit on the edge of the bed.

"Just save it," Lucas muttered with a tired wave of his right hand. "I've already been ripped up by both Snow and Banner. I don't need the same speech from you."

"I'm still tempted," Rowe grumbled. "A little repetition might finally drive the notion of safety into that thick skull of yours." Rowe looked down at the floor, shaking his head. "What the hell is wrong with you? Have you gotten so damned cocky that you think your money is going to keep you safe?"

"No."

"Then what? My God, you used to be smarter than this. You watched all our fucking backs in Afghanistan. Nothing got by you." Rowe pushed away from the wall, clapping his hand on Lucas's shoulder. "And now this? A bunch of stupid thugs have sent you to the hospital twice now."

"I got sloppy. Underestimated them." Lucas knew the self-disgust was obvious in his tone. He *was* better than this, but ducking for cover and watching his back, that was more than ten years ago. A lifetime. For too long the only knife aimed at his back was a metaphorical one wielded by a rival investor. Physical attacks were almost a forgotten thing in his world.

Lucas shook his head before lifting his eyes to meet Rowe's worried gaze. "It won't happen again, I swear. I know what I'm doing now. Hadeon and I can handle it."

"No, not anymore."

"What?" Lucas's heart seemed to stop in his chest as Rowe's calm demeanor started to sink in. It was suddenly hard to draw a deep breath and the world seemed to swim away from him on a wave.

"Andrei's done. I fired him."

"No!"

"He let you get hurt. He's supposed to be fucking protecting you! But you're in his care for twenty-four hours —*twenty-four fucking hours* — and you're back in the hospital."

"It's not his fault!"

"Of course it's his fault!" Rowe paced away to the far side of the room, skirting a chair and some equipment, and then back to Lucas. "He should never have let you near Price Hill, and certainly not at night. What the hell, man! He's lucky I don't file charges for reckless endangerment."

"I told him to take me there."

"And he should have said no!"

Lucas shoved both of his hands through his hair, ignoring the pain that lanced through his shoulder at the movement. "He did. You can't do this to him. It's my fault."

"To him? What about to you? He put you in danger! His job was to keep you safe." He turned to the door, stopped and glared back at Lucas. "He was my best. The BEST I had and you managed to get in his head or something. I don't know, but it's obvious his common sense is now fucked. He's gone. Done. I'll get someone else to watch your back even if I have to do it myself."

Lucas launched off the table, slamming Rowe against the wall beside the door so the entire room rattled. He pressed his right forearm across the man's throat, pushing into his windpipe but not yet cutting off his air. Rowe grabbed both of Lucas's upper arms, trying to throw him off, but there was no moving Lucas. He had both height and muscle mass on the smaller man, not to mention he was pissed beyond rational thought.

A feral grin spread across his lips and he leaned close to Rowe so that their noses nearly touched. He had forgotten what this felt like, what it was like to physically take control of a situation. Too long he'd settled arguments across a boardroom with a squad of high-priced lawyers or with a checkbook. But this…this was intoxicating. Adrenaline thrummed through his body, shoving aside the lingering aches.

"I guess I haven't forgotten how to watch my back." The whispered words slithered between them, causing Rowe's eyes to flare.

"Let me go."

"Rehire him."

Rowe's brows beetled together over his nose, throwing his eyes in shadow as the muscles in his jaw flexed. He knew that stubborn look too well. "He's useless to me."

"You fucking rehire him," he snarled, his body vibrating with rage. There was nothing useless or worthless about Andrei Hadeon. He'd very nearly given his life to protect Lucas and he would not allow

Rowe to throw that away. "If you want me to have a bodyguard so bad, then you give me Andrei. That's it. No one else."

"Luc!"

"No one else!"

The door burst open next to Rowe and Snow tried to pull Lucas off Rowe, but Lucas planted his free hand in the middle of Snow's chest and shoved hard, causing the man to backpedal several feet to keep his balance.

"Fix this," Lucas ordered in a harsh voice, while watching Snow out of the corner of his eye.

"What the hell is going on?" Snow demanded.

"No, he's done," Rowe interjected before Lucas could answer.

Lucas's smile returned and he applied pressure to Rowe's throat, slowly cutting off the airflow. "You think he can't take care of me? That maybe you're the only one who can watch my back?" He gave his head a little shake. "Look at you now. Pinned by an injured man. How hard would it be for me to slide that hidden knife off your belt right now?"

"Stop it, Lucas," Snow ordered. "This isn't a game."

"I won't let him hurt Andrei." The urge to press down on Rowe's throat was becoming overwhelming. Thoughts scattered, fragmented and painful through his brain, until the only thing that was clear was the unrelenting need to protect Andrei. He was somewhere in this hospital, in pain, injured because of a choice Lucas had made. Lucas had to protect him, keep him safe. The only thing that was clear through the fog was that Rowe was a threat to Andrei.

The doctor cursed under his breath before he ran over the locked medical dispensary and punched in a code. When he turned back, Lucas was aware the man had something in his hand and it wasn't going to be good.

Twisting his fist in Rowe's shirt, Lucas growled as he threw Rowe across the room into Snow where they slammed into the opposite wall. With his legs spread and knees bent, Lucas fell easily into a defensive stance, ready to protect himself from anything the two men might attempt. For a moment, everything slowed and the sounds of the busy hospital just beyond the closed door faded away. He was operating purely on an instinctive drive to protect himself. To protect Andrei.

"Whoa, man. Easy." Rowe used a low, controlled voice as if trying to talk down a jumper balanced on the ledge of a twenty-story building. "There's no need for this."

"Really? You attack Andrei and now he's trying to fucking drug me?" Lucas's voice jumped slightly higher than normal as his gaze darted between the two men. "Tell me I don't need to watch my own back."

"You saying you can't trust me?" Snow said in a low voice.

"I don't know, Dr. Frost. Are you still holding the syringe?"

Snow lifted the syringe for Lucas to see before extending his hand out to the side and dropping it. The little plastic container clattered and bounced once on the floor before it rolled away. "It looked like you were trying to strangle Rowe. I just wanted to calm you down."

"Bad idea, wasn't it?" Lucas snarled.

"Yeah, obviously," Rowe muttered, rubbing his throat with his left hand.

Lucas narrowed his gaze on the smaller man, not missing that his right hand was hovering close to where he kept a knife hidden on his person. "You will go to Andrei now. Fix this. He leaves with me or I do this shit alone. You got me?"

"Why the hell is Andrei so important to you?"

"Don't talk. Just do."

"Go," Snow ordered before Rowe could open his mouth again. He stepped away from Rowe so he had a clear path to the door. "Just fucking fix this."

Lucas stepped back, his fists tightening as he shifted his gaze back and forth between the two men. He was on edge, tension radiating from his body. Everything in his brain had become a shattered mess. Heart racing and temples throbbing, he was having trouble remembering why he even attacked Rowe, but panic screamed through every nerve ending. *Rowe had threatened Andrei. That was it. And Andrei was hurt because of him. Hurt and in pain somewhere in that hospital and there was no one to protect him.*

Snow took one step forward. "Talk to me, Lucas."

"No. It's nothing." The words were fired from his lips, sharp and sure, to stave off the doubts before they could overwhelm him.

"You look like you're willing to beat me to death."

The horror of Snow's words plowed through Lucas and he finally looked down at his bruised fists. "Ash," Lucas whispered, Snow's little-used real name slipping out past trembling lips.

Snow immediately stepped forward, his hands covering both of Lucas's, threading his fingers through, loosening them before he pulled the man into his arms. He held Lucas gently, comforting him without making him feel trapped. "What happened?"

"I-I don't know. Is… Is this from the concussion?"

"Was that a flashback?"

Lucas jerked his head up so that he could look his friend in the eye. "Flashback?" The word sent a chill through him.

"From Afghanistan."

He quickly shook his head, shoving the past back into the deepest corners of his brain. There was no reason to call up such dark memories. Both he and Snow had discovered uncomfortable truths about themselves during those four years, and Lucas never wanted to think about them again. But they were still there. He'd felt hints of it, a darkness in himself that had tried to surface, when he'd pinned Rowe.

"Everything. I'm just so uneven. Out of control." Lucas reached with trembling hands and tightly gripped his friend's waist. His forehead dropped to the man's shoulders and he squeezed his eyes shut.

"What's this about Andrei?"

"Rowe fired him," he mumbled, not lifting his head. He took a deep breath, pulling Snow's scent into his lungs, holding it there as it calmed his frazzled nerves. Even when Snow was irate and on the edge of losing control, his simple presence gave balance to Lucas's world. Yet it wasn't working like it should have. Snow couldn't fix what Andrei was upsetting. "It wasn't his fault. I-I lost it."

"Why? You've known the guy for a couple of days."

"It's not what you're thinking. Andrei risked his life for me. He would have died to protect me tonight. And...and Rowe was just going to toss that aside. Called him *useless*."

"It's okay."

"No, it's not! How many people would die for you? For me? How many people have?"

Snow gripped both of Lucas's shoulders tightly, meeting his wide gaze. "Hey! Stay with me here. You're safe. Andrei is safe. Rowe, I'm going to kill for putting your mind here." Carefully, Snow pushed Lucas back to sit on the edge of the bed. Pulling a little flashlight from his pocket, he checked Lucas's eyes before taking his wrist for his pulse. The familiar procedure helped Lucas step back from the mental ledge and begin to put some order to his thoughts.

Satisfied that Lucas wasn't going to jump out the nearest window or take a nurse hostage, Snow stepped back toward the door.

"Relax. I'll check on Rowe and get you out of here."

A sigh escaped him when he was finally alone in the room. His body ached from a mix of old injuries and new bruises. He was overdue for another painkiller, but he didn't want to take another. His head was fucked up enough as it was without the Percocet fog. But the aches were nothing against the dull throbbing pain in his chest. Reaching up, he rubbed the heel of his hand over his heart.

He should have said something to Snow, let the man talk some sense into him. That was the problem, though. He didn't want to listen to the logic that Snow or even Rowe would pound into his head. It was the same reason he wouldn't let Rowe remove Andrei from his life. He wasn't ready to let go yet.

Lucas clenched his teeth. He couldn't bring himself to admit that he wanted to pitch it all out the fucking window. Break all his rules.

Andrei lit a fire in him that he simply couldn't extinguish. The man made him laugh and feel. He made him reckless and alive for the first time…in so fucking long.

Chapter 8

It was after two in the morning when Lucas and Andrei finally shuffled through the front door of the penthouse. The silence weighed thick and heavy, like a living presence stood between them, pushing them apart. Lucas had thought of and tossed out half a dozen comments to kick start a conversation. There were too many things scattered in his brain and nameless emotions he didn't understand.

"Stay," Andrei commanded when they walked inside.

Lucas grunted, locking the door behind him and resetting the alarm. He turned to watch the other man move through the rooms, a gun in his right hand. His dress shirt was gone, replaced by a dark blue scrub shirt. Andrei's movements were stiff now and he occasionally winced as if in pain, but Lucas didn't know the extent of his injuries. Lucas had escaped the building with nothing more than a few scrapes and some smoke inhalation, even if he did have to suffer through another CT scan.

When Andrei returned from his check of the second floor, he gave Lucas a nod and then paused in the kitchen. His brow furrowed and his eyes narrowed as if he were thinking hard about something, but couldn't find the words to explain what was bothering him. Lucas wished he could read the man's mind. Was it the fire? The fact that they could have been easily killed? That he'd been canned and rehired in the span of an hour? Or that they nearly kissed? Lucas mentally snorted at his own thoughts. Their "almost kiss" was probably long forgotten in the face of their bigger problems.

"Why burn down the building?" Andrei asked after several empty seconds.

Lucas walked over to the fridge and pulled out two bottles of water. He offered one to Andrei and then leaned back against the sink, holding his with both hands. Standing in the dim light cast by the work lamp over the stove, Andrei's eyes were hard obsidian gems. Lucas couldn't take his gaze off him. "I don't know. The building itself was worthless. I'd been tempted to level it and start over."

"So…what? A scare tactic?"

Lucas allowed himself a little smile. "Pretty shitty scare tactic. A fire isn't going to get me to walk away, even if I was in the building at the time."

"Then what are we left with? Beyond a name, that is."

Lucas stopped in the process of lifting the bottle of water to his lips. "What name?"

"Rowe said in between bouts of shouting at me that Thomas Lynton also suffered an attack recently. I think Dr. Frost might have pulled some info and Rowe's been digging. Lynton's been very reluctant to talk to the police about it. He's told everyone else that he was in a car accident."

"I know Thomas," he said as his mind raced off, trying desperately to connect dots between his situation and what he knew of the other man. "He owns a local investment firm with Patrick Laughlin and has a couple luxury condo developments on the East Side."

"Business associate?"

Lucas shook his head. "No, we just have mutual acquaintances."

"Ah, fellow old rich guy."

He glared at his companion. "I'm going to ignore the age comment, but yes, we travel in some similar circles."

"Why did you ask Rowe to rehire me?" Andrei asked suddenly. The words escaped him in a rush, as if he'd finally worked up the nerve to ask.

Lucas frowned, biting back his initial response. He didn't ask Rowe to rehire Andrei. He had very nearly strangled his best friend while ordering him to rehire the man. But Lucas was still working out all the logic, or rather the lack of logic, behind his actions. For the most part, he'd been operating purely on instinct, fueled by an unhealthy dose of frustration, rage, and guilt. He certainly didn't want to share that with Andrei.

"Because it wasn't your fault. It was mine."

"Why go at all?"

"Something you said in the restaurant," Lucas started slowly. He dropped his gaze down to the bottle of water in his hands. "About your working class background. It's not so far off from my own. You're the only one I've shown Price Hill. The only person I've told about all my plans. I feel like this is something you would understand. Someone who could understand what I'm fighting for. More than the others."

"What about Dr. Frost? Rowe said you grew up together."

Lucas lifted his eyes back to Andrei and grinned. "If you asked Snow, he would tell you he was hatched fully grown from an egg. He doesn't claim a childhood and I don't blame him."

"Thank you."

"Thank *you* for saving my life."

Andrei jerkily nodded, his eyes on his unopened bottle of water clenched in one fist. The awkward silence stretched between them and Lucas spent it mentally kicking himself. Was his rationale true? Had he said too much? Fuck if he knew. It sounded true, but his brain was so scattered he would have claimed belief in the tooth fairy at that moment. He just didn't want Andrei to leave, which made his next words all the more painful.

"If you want to leave, I would understand and wouldn't blame you."

A slow smile lifted the corners of his mouth, but Andrei didn't meet his gaze. "I've never walked away from a client because he was a stubborn bastard. Good night, Mr. Vallois."

Lucas continued to lean against the sink, sipping his water while cursing himself and his choices recently. Rowe was right in that he'd completely underestimated his opponents. It had been years since he'd last been physically threatened by another. There had been a few times that Snow had unsettled him, but even then, he'd been more afraid for his friend than himself. Through it all during the past several days, even weeks ago when the threat first surfaced, he'd never truly taken it seriously.

But he had a new thread to tug at, thanks to his friends' snooping. Lucas even had a good idea of how best to start with Thomas Lynton, and it would certainly be safer than trekking into Price Hill late at night.

Shoving away from the sink, Lucas climbed the stairs, his ribs protesting the continued movement. His body was demanding that he fall into bed despite the fact that he smelled of sweat and smoke. He paused at Andrei's partially open door on the way to his room, noting that the light was still on. He knocked on the door, pushing it open a little farther.

"Do you want to split a Percocet?" he asked, figuring the man could use something to take the edge off whatever pain he must be feeling.

"Fuck that sounds good," Andrei groaned, dropping his hands back down to his side. He stood in the middle of the Spartan guest room near the foot of the bed. His shoes had been kicked off and he was now struggling with his shirt.

"What happened?"

"Someone set fire to the building I was in," Andrei said sarcastically. He started to reach over his head to grab the back of the shirt as if trying to pull it over his head, but stopped suddenly with a hiss of pain.

Lucas leaned against the doorjamb and glared at him. "I meant how were you injured?"

"A bullet grazed my arm and my back got scorched a bit. Kind of like a bad sunburn."

Entering the room, Lucas paused to put his water on the nearby bureau and stepped up to Andrei. He picked up the edge of his shirt, trying to ignore the feel of Andrei's warm, smooth skin under his fingertips. "Lift your arms."

"That's the problem. It hurts like hell when I lift my arms over my head."

"How'd they get you in the shirt in the first place?"

"With a lot of swearing and shouting."

Lucas smiled at Andrei, leaning a little closer. "Suck it up, buttercup. Looks like that's how it's coming off."

Not giving Andrei a chance to argue, Lucas started pulling the shirt up, revealing hard abs and a sculpted chest that sent desire through him. Andrei swore under his breath as he lifted his arms and stepped back, bending down as he pulled free of the shirt. His breathing was heavy and ragged when Lucas dropped the offending garment on the floor and stepped around to look at the man's back.

It was bright red as if he'd lain out in the summer sun for too long. There was a pair of tan stripes cutting diagonally across his shoulder where the leather bands of his holster had given some added protection to his skin. The worst was at his shoulders, but there was a patch along his left side that stretched down to the waist of his pants.

"Sit," Lucas said, pointing at the end of the bed. "I've got a couple things that will help."

"I'm not taking your Percocet," Andrei called after him as Lucas disappeared down the hall. He made a quick run down to the kitchen before hitting his own bathroom. He snapped a pill in half and popped one half in his mouth before returning to Andrei's room.

The younger man was seated on the edge of the bed, his elbows balanced on his knees and his head hanging down. Exhaustion had put dark circles under his eyes and that lush upper lip was pinched. The enjoyment they'd found at Rialto appeared to have been forgotten and maybe that was for the best. The easy flirtation would have created nothing but trouble, Lucas told himself. He just wasn't sure he believed it.

"Here," Lucas said, standing in front of him with his palm outstretched.

Andrei looked up and grimaced. "I can't take it. I need to be sharp."

"You think the pain is making you sharp?" Lucas mocked. "I need you mobile and not lost in pain. Take the damned pill. I already took my half."

Andrei grumbled, but took the pill, then accepted the bottle of water from Lucas a second later. "What the hell is that?" he demanded when he put the water on the floor, his gaze catching on the bottle in Lucas's other hand.

"To help with the burn."

Moving around Andrei, Lucas put his knee in the center of the bed and sat behind him. He kept one leg extended off the edge, running along Andrei's without actually touching him while his other was bent behind the man's lower back. A little tremor ran through Lucas and he finally stopped to wonder how this could possibly be a good idea. Heat poured off of Andrei and it wasn't all due to the burn. The man before him was all lean, sinewy muscle wrapped around a tall frame. Only the occasional scar marred his perfect skin, which was this rich, swarthy tone. Lucas couldn't begin to guess his family's heritage. Something Mediterranean maybe.

Pouring the gel into his right hand, Lucas barely touched Andrei's shoulder when the man completely came off the edge of the bed, cursing. Andrei lurched around, glaring at Lucas. "What the hell! It's fucking cold!"

"Of course. It's kept in the fridge."

"And you weren't going to tell me? What the fuck is that shit?"

Lucas gave a dramatic sigh and held up the bottle. "It's sunburn treatment. It's got aloe, moisturizers, and other *shit* that helps leach out the heat. Now sit your pansy ass back down. Or would you rather not sleep tonight?"

Andrei hesitated, frowning at Lucas before he returned to the edge of the bed with a huff.

Lucas had to bite his lip to keep from laughing. He really should have warned Andrei that the gel was cold, but the man's reaction had been worth it. He continued applying the gel to the burned area in a slow circular motion. Andrei's curses and twitches eased after a minute and a low sigh slipped past his lips as his head dipped forward.

"Better?" Lucas asked.

A grudging grunt was his only reply and Lucas did chuckle then.

As the other man calmed, Lucas allowed himself to enjoy the feel of Andrei's warm, soft skin beneath his fingers. Muscles rippled and moved in reaction to his touch. He longed to lean close and kiss down his spine, but he contented himself with just the slow caress.

With his left hand, he at last gave into temptation and sank his fingers into Andrei's thick, black hair. The loose curls wove around his finger as he lifted them up off the back of the man's neck so he could cover the top of his shoulders with the gel. His hair was incredibly soft, but there were some surprising rough ends that brought a frown to Lucas's lips.

"Your hair was singed," he murmured.

"A little." Andrei's voice was low and relaxed. The gel was doing its job, pulling the painful heat out of his back. "It's long overdue to be chopped."

Lucas's hand involuntarily tightened around Andrei's curls as if to protect them from some invisible barber's shears. "I've got someone who can repair it."

"It's just hair."

"Beautiful hair," Lucas whispered, slowly pulling his fingers free. Andrei turned his head to look over his shoulder at Lucas, but Lucas avoided his eyes, looking down at the bottle by his knee. He shouldn't have said it. *Fuck, he shouldn't have said that.* Should have bitten down, held those two stupid words back. He'd teased and flirted shamelessly with Andrei for two days, but now it seemed wrong. Beneath his hand was an injury that Andrei had suffered because of his stubbornness. Something he didn't want to think about had driven him to Price Hill, to use that place to bridge this gap between them, and it only succeeded in hurting Andrei.

"Can you lift your arms?" he asked, the question coming out a little harder than he'd meant.

Andrei slowly lifted both of his arms, wincing. "It's better. Can you put a little more on my shoulders?"

"Not such a bad idea, was it?" Lucas muttered, some of the apprehension flowing out of him again.

A low groan slipped from Andrei as Lucas resumed putting the green gel across Andrei's shoulders and back. "You're a horrible nurse."

"I gave you half a Percocet. What more do you want?" Joking was easier. The laughter helped him forget this miserable, sick feeling in the pit of his stomach.

"A little compassion. A sweet disposition. A pleasant bedside manner."

"Fuck," Lucas moaned. "Next you're going to complain that I don't have a nice set of tits to fill out my white uniform."

Andrei laughed. "I said you were a horrible nurse. I didn't say you weren't a sexy nurse."

Lucas froze, letting Andrei's joking words sink in. His heart sped up and he fought to keep his voice light when he could order his brain to function again. "I have a feeling you didn't mean that like it sounded."

"Maybe I did." All laughter and joking left his voice, becoming a soft caress that had Lucas clenching his teeth against a real moan.

His body had hardened the moment he sat down behind the man and all he longed to do was pull him firmly against his chest so he could run his hands over every inch of Andrei while kissing along his neck. But he couldn't and Andrei was now pushing the flirting too far. Lucas was strung out from too much stress and uncertainty in his life. He couldn't trust himself to make the right decisions, certainly not where Andrei was concerned.

Lucas shoved off the bed to stand back on his feet, intending to put the sunburn gel on the bureau on his way out of the room, but Andrei stood at the same time. The space between them shrank instead of grew and Lucas's tight control wavered.

"Wait," Andrei started but any other words seemed trapped in his throat when Lucas was just suddenly there. Their bodies brushed from knee to chest so that the growing bulge in his pants pressed briefly against Andrei's thigh. The man needed to know exactly far he'd pushed Lucas.

Leaning close, Lucas pressed his nose into Andrei's cheek while his sticky fingers twisted in the silken strands of his hair, trapping his head so that he had nowhere to go. No more hiding. No more teasing dance of words. He closed his eyes, becoming lost in the scent and heat of the man. With each harsh, ragged breath, their chests rubbed, igniting a fire in Lucas's blood.

"Say it," Lucas growled. "Tell me you're straight and I will stop." His lips barely grazed the rough stubble on his cheek.

"Is that one of your rules?"

"Yes," Lucas hissed. "I look at you and I know that you're going to break every one of my damned rules. Now say it or I'm going to kiss you and I won't stop until we've both lost our minds."

"No."

"Please, Andrei…" Lucas's voice trembled on his last plea, trying one last time to save them both.

"Kiss me."

Those two whispered words snapped the very last of Lucas's control. But he didn't pounce. He dragged his mouth along Andrei's jaw, savoring the prickles of his whiskers. He kissed him slowly, a tantalizing caress of his lips moving along Andrei's, learning the contours of his mouth, the softness, the gut-wrenching fullness of his lower lip. Lucas pulled away and Andrei chased after him, opening his mouth on a soft moan.

Lucas deepened the kiss, plunging his tongue into Andrei, tasting him at long last. Strong hands clamped down on his waist, pulling him flush against Andrei's long body, making it impossible to hide that both men were aroused. One kiss would never be enough. Not even a dozen kisses stretching straight on until dawn.

Reluctantly, Lucas drew away so he could look at Andrei's flushed face and dark hooded eyes. The man was a fucking wet dream. Was one night even going to be enough?

"What do you want?" Lucas demanded in a voice that sounded harsh and raw to his own ears. He was trying desperately to get his brain working again, but Andrei was determined to wipe every thought from his head.

"More," Andrei immediately replied. He leaned the last distance to claim Lucas in a demanding kiss that had both men groaning. Andrei clasped the back of his neck, pulling him close so that he could crush their mouths together. His tongue plunged into Lucas's mouth, tangling with his own so that another groan was trapped between the two men. Lucas rocked his hips, sliding their hard cocks against each other. It was perfect. The sharp desperation biting at them, pushing them between languid exploration to aggressive thrusting.

"Lucas," Andrei said on a gasp for air, a shudder running through his body. It was the first time his given name had slipped past Andrei's lips and it sounded like heaven.

"I'm serious," Lucas ground out through clenched teeth. "I need to know how far you want to take this."

Andrei blinked a couple times, some of the haze of desire clearing. They stared at each other for several seconds, the silence shattered by their heavy breathing. "I want whatever you're willing to give me."

"Have you bottomed?"

"No."

A slow smile spread across Lucas's lips and he pressed a kiss to the corner of his mouth. "You're not ready for what I want."

"I'll try." Andrei's words were thick and heavy, a tremor going through the hands clasping Lucas's waist.

Lucas closed his eyes, enjoying the shiver that ran through him at those two words. Dear fucking God, this man was going to break him and he was going to love every damned second of it. He leaned forward and pressed his face into Andrei's neck, breathing in the musky scent of the man under the lingering hint of smoke and sweat.

"Not yet. We'll get there." He kissed him again, rough and messy, driving the heat back up between them so that Andrei's hips jerked against his. He moaned as he sought more friction. His body ached to enter the man in his arms, but he was going to behave. He would go slow. Andrei was worth taking this slow.

"Damn, Lucas," he groaned. "Forget the other shit. I'm going to come in my pants if we keep this up."

Sucking in a loud, deep breath, Lucas released Andrei and took a shaky step backward. He held his hand out, warding the man off when he attempted to close the distance between them. Andrei's face had an attractive flush to it and his full lips were swollen from their kisses. Only his sparkling dark eyes were confused, detracting from the all-too-fuckable picture he presented.

"I've got to leave now while I can still stop myself." Lucas swiped his hand roughly through his hair. For now, all body aches and pains were forgotten. Well, except for the throbbing ache at his crotch, but that couldn't be helped.

"Maybe I don't want you to stop."

"Let me do one smart thing tonight. I don't sleep with straight men."

Andrei snorted and adjusted himself, allowing his fingers to linger over his hard cock as it strained against his pants. "Considering that I'm hard as steel and desperate to attack your mouth again, I'd have to argue that I'm not really all that straight."

"Yeah, I'm learning that."

With a sexy grin, Andrei crooked one finger and beckoned Lucas back to his side. "Then let's keep going."

A shaky laugh jumped from Lucas and he managed to take one more step backward. He couldn't remember the last time he'd wanted anyone so badly. But he wouldn't give in tonight. He was already too jacked up and there was no way he could go slowly. And Andrei needed slow. Lucas wanted to make sure it was good for him and he didn't have the control for that. Not tonight. Not after risking the man's life. Not after nearly losing him. He needed time to get his head on straight again, to figure out what he was doing and what he wanted.

Licking his lips, Lucas smiled. "Not tonight but soon," he said in a voice that was nearly a growl. "Strip down. And when you jerk off tonight, think about all the things I'm going to do to you. I want you to imagine me sucking your cock until your eyes roll back into your head. And just before you come, I'm going to flip you over and fuck you until you scream my name."

"Is that what you're going to think about when you jerk off?" Andrei demanded, the words low and hoarse and he pressed his hand into his cock as if trying to relieve some of the ache.

"Definitely." Lucas left the room, walking briskly down to his own bedroom before he could give in to the temptation to follow through with that lovely image. For once, he was going to do the right thing, even if it killed him.

兄弟武士心

Andrei awoke in pain. He started to roll onto his side but stopped suddenly as his back screamed, drawing a hiss out of him. His shoulders and side were on fire. Apparently, both the soothing gel and the Percocet had worn off. The fog around his brain lifted. He done exactly as Lucas had instructed. After stripping down, he sprawled across the bed and stroked himself to thoughts of Lucas's mouth and strong hands as they ran over his body. He hadn't even gotten to thoughts of sex, he'd already been so fucking excited from their abbreviated make-out session. Lucas looked so damned hungry and desperate, otherwise Andrei would worry that he'd never get another shot at that man's mouth. No, this wasn't over. Andrei might not understand why Lucas had stopped, but his control wasn't going to hold out for much longer, that he was sure of.

But that kiss. He'd never kissed a man before. Guys had sucked his cock and he'd even fucked one once, but he'd never sought that kind of intimacy. And that's exactly what that kiss had been with Lucas. A searing, blindingly intimate moment that reached down into his gut and threatened to turn him inside out. And now hours later, with his passion cooled and pain lancing through his body, he found that he wanted more. He wanted to continue kissing Lucas until his growls and groans filled his ears. He wanted to see that slow, lazy grin directed just at him. Was he in danger of getting in too deep with someone who probably didn't care about him at all? Yes, but he was enjoying himself too much to put a halt to it now. Did this mean he was gay? No idea, but it was far too early in the morning to contemplate such things.

Pale light washed across the floor, creeping up from the first level. Wincing with each movement, Andrei quickly pulled on his boxers before grabbing his gun and the gel. If Lucas was in trouble, he'd need the gun. If he wasn't, he was begging for another coating of the gel so he could get back to sleep.

He hesitated on his way to Lucas's bedroom and instead silently slipped downstairs to find Lucas sitting on the sofa staring out the window at the city skyline and the gradually lightening sky. Dawn was less than an hour away. He had no way of knowing how long Lucas had been sitting there, seemingly lost in thought.

His stomach twisted uncomfortably. Was it what they'd done that was keeping him awake? Comments from his ex-girlfriend, their own easy banter, and even things Rowe had said left Andrei feeling as if one-night stands with men were a common occurrence for Lucas. But then, the complication was that Andrei was still there and would continue to be in his life as long as there was a threat. Was that what had stopped Lucas from allowing their kissing to progress any further? Lucas might already be eager to have Andrei anywhere but in his penthouse and yet he was stuck.

Of course, Andrei hadn't yet given in to the temptation to contemplate his own tangle of emotions when it came to Lucas. He'd almost begged the man to fuck his ass! Never in his life had he thought such words would cross his lips. Not only had he said those words, but Andrei had a feeling that he'd say them more than once for Lucas. The grim man staring at the skyline was just different. He couldn't peg it. But Lucas made Andrei want things he couldn't explain or even want to understand. The one thing he was clinging to was that none of it felt wrong.

"Regrets keeping you up?" Andrei asked as he crossed to the living room to stand beside the sofa.

"That depends on what kind of regrets you're referring to," Lucas said softly, still staring out of the windows in front of him. Bare chested, Lucas wore only a pair of soft sleep pants, as if he'd attempted to go to bed after leaving Andrei but had given up when it proved impossible. His skin was pale and mottled with an assortment of bruises from his beating just a few days earlier. Even with that, he was still incredibly sexy with large, powerful muscles filling his frame.

"Regrets about what happened upstairs?"

A smile broke across Lucas's face briefly when he looked up at Andrei. "Nope."

Lucas pushed to his feet. He stood before Andrei and placed his palm on Andrei's stomach, then slowly moved up to caress his chest. He stopped over Andrei's pounding heart. "I don't regret a simple kiss. I don't regret wanting to do it again. I refuse to regret wanting to do a hell of a lot more."

"Good."

"Why are you up?"

"Back is killing me."

Lucas glanced down at the gun and gel in Andrei's hands and chuckled. "So, what? You were going to hold me at gunpoint until I applied more of the gel."

Andrei grinned. "Something like that."

"Gotta love a plan." Lucas snickered as he took the gel and motioned for Andrei to sit on the footstool in front of the chair that Lucas dropped into.

Andrei remained quiet through the first coat of the gel. It wasn't as cool as when Lucas had applied it the first time since they hadn't bothered to put it in the fridge, but it still worked to kill the heat. Lucas's hand felt good on his back, massaging away the tension and loosening up muscles. It was on the second coat that Andrei finally raised the courage to speak again.

"What regrets were keeping you up?"

Lucas paused for several seconds before he released a soft sigh. His hand swept down along Andrei's left side, slipping just under the waist band of his boxers to get one little patch of burned skin. "I needlessly risked your life tonight and I'm sorry. You were right. We should never have gone to the warehouse at night. It was stupid. I was showing off and we got lucky that you weren't hurt worse."

"This is my job. I know the risks," Andrei argued, wishing he were facing the man.

"Yes, but I can make better, smarter decisions to reduce the risks to both of us. Rowe and Snow are right, though I'll deny it later if you tell them I said that." Lucas gave a little growl of frustration and snapped the cap of the bottle closed. "I've got more common sense than this. I'll be more careful going forward."

Andrei rose and turned to face Lucas who stood at the same time. "Thank you."

Lucas lifted his clean hand and ran it through Andrei's hair. Andrei had to fight the urge to close his eyes and lean into his palm. He was quickly learning that Lucas loved his hair and now that they crossed certain boundaries, the man was frequently giving in to the temptation to touch it as if it soothed him.

"I'm sorry you were hurt," Lucas said. His voice was rough and he was no longer meeting Andrei's gaze.

"Thank you. But it's not so bad. If it means you've got to put that green goop on my back for a few days, I think I can suck it up."

"You're too kind," Lucas muttered, giving Andrei's hair a little tug before releasing it. "Let's go back to bed. I told Candace not to stop by the penthouse until after ten so we can catch a few more hours of sleep."

Andrei nodded, following Lucas back toward the kitchen where the other man placed the gel in the fridge. His eyes caught once again on the Japanese kanji tattooed down Lucas's spine between his shoulder blades. The black ink was just so damn sexy and unexpected against his perfect skin.

"What do the symbols mean?" Andrei asked.

Lucas's right hand reached over his shoulder as if to touch the tattoo, a slight look of surprise filling his gaze. "The first two mean brother. The second two mean warrior and the third is heart."

"Snow, Rowe, and Ian."

Lucas didn't reply, but one corner of his mouth kicked up in a half smile before he motioned with a jerk of his head for Andrei to follow him back to the second floor.

Andrei stopped at the door to the guest room when they reached the second floor and watched Lucas continue down to the master bedroom. The other man turned, his eyes almost glowing in the dim morning light, as they stared at each other in silence for several seconds. Andrei's body heated from head to toe. Just a few steps and he'd be back at Lucas's side, his lips against his, his tongue thrust deep into his mouth until they both moaned. Something in him knew if he went down there Lucas wouldn't turn him away. Not again.

But he didn't move. Maybe Lucas was right. Maybe it was too fast. They needed to think about this. Lucas was still his client. Could they work together if they let their arrangement become physical? Was it the danger of the fire that was driving them together? Andrei didn't think so, but he could wait one night. Get his head on straight and then he'd try again. Good night," he murmured.

Lucas's gaze raked over him. "Good night," he whispered back and then disappeared into his own room.

Yeah, they weren't done yet.

Chapter 9

Andrei wasn't really surprised when Rowe showed up while Lucas was ensconced in his office with his assistant. He didn't bother to get up from the barstool in the kitchen where he'd settled with coffee and a book. He hadn't been reading, just holding the book and staring at the gathering of clouds in the overcast sky.

And thinking a lot about what was happening between him and Lucas.

He had nothing to compare them to—these feelings Lucas raised in him. Nothing even remotely close to the fire that had burned him alive the night before. Rowe stalking into the kitchen forced him to shove all that aside.

His boss didn't look any less pissed than he had when he'd stormed into the hospital room for the second time last night to put Andrei back on the job. Truth was, Andrei loved this job and felt like a part of the family when it came to Rowe's business. He'd been to dinner at Rowe and Melissa's more times than he could remember, so even though he'd felt he deserved the firing for not putting his foot down, it had still hurt at the time. If he'd learned anything the last few days, it was that Lucas meant everything to the men in his circle. Everything.

And Andrei understood more and more why with each hour he spent with the man. He rubbed his chest, wondering about the tightness he felt there, the inability to take a full breath when he thought about how he'd felt with the man's hands and mouth on him the night before.

Rowe stood in the kitchen, thumbs tucked into the pockets of his jeans as he stared at Andrei. It looked like maybe he'd stayed up most of the night, too. Dark circles shadowed his green eyes and lines bled out from lips pinched tight. His auburn hair stood in spikes over his head.

"Coffee?" Andrei pointed at the carafe on the island.

Sighing and shaking his head, Rowe walked with casual familiarity to the cabinet that held the mugs and grabbed one of the large black ones in the back. "Is there still food from Ian in the fridge?"

"A lot." Andrei marked his place in his book and laid it down. "I had some of the leftover paella for breakfast. I thought about asking for a raise so I could afford to eat at Rialto every night but figured now wasn't the best time." Might as well jump in and get the tongue-lashing over with.

Some of the tension eased from Rowe's spine and he turned to stare at Andrei while leaning against the refrigerator. "No, it's not. What the hell were you thinking?" He held up a hand. "Wait. I bet I can guess. Lucas just barreled all over anything you said, didn't he?"

"Pretty much, but I still shouldn't have given in. I knew it was a risk—though, not the kind of risk it turned out to be."

Rowe pointed at him. "I thought you, more than any of the others in my employ, would have the backbone to stand up to Lucas."

"I do."

With a small shake of his head, Rowe finally broke eye contact and sipped his coffee, his mind seeming to turn away from Andrei's failure to other problems. "Can you remember anything more than you told me last night about the men who set the fire?"

"Other than the fact they were completely clueless, no. I got the distinct feeling they were only there on orders. Someone a lot higher up has designs on Price Hill. If you want to watch Lucas an hour or so, I'll run home and get my laptop—do some research on people who bid on the property."

Rowe rolled his eyes. "You really think I don't already have Gidget on it?"

Andrei grinned. "I figured you did."

"You need to run home for any other reasons?"

Andrei thought about his small, one room apartment. He had no pets, no plants, nothing that required his attention. And nothing really worth stealing, so he didn't need to check on things. He shook his head. "Melissa brought more than I needed."

Rowe continued to stare at him until Andrei had to fight the urge to fidget. Or touch his mouth. Were his lips still swollen from the kissing? It was better to change the subject, not that he wanted to talk about what was on his mind.

"There another reason you put me on this job?" Andrei asked in a low voice, struggling to hold Rowe's gaze.

Rowe's eyes narrowed. "What are you talking about?"

"I heard Lucas's description of his attackers yesterday when he talked to the detective. Thugs with some fight training."

A little smirk tugged at the corner of Rowe's mouth and he relaxed. "Well, it doesn't hurt that you've got some experience in that field. You can handle a more skilled physical attack." His smile disappeared before it fully formed and he folded his arms over his chest. "Any insight?"

Andrei stared down at the book laying on the countertop, wishing there was something he could offer while at the same time wishing he didn't have to think about his former life. "No. I'm three years out of that world and the kind of people who would do this…not the type I talked to if you get me."

"Yeah, I get it."

"You want me to let Lucas know you're here?" he asked, feeling a little better that Rowe had had some kind of confidence in his skills. Maybe not so much now, but he could work hard, earn his trust again.

"I can let him know myself if that's what I wanted." Rowe shook his head again and turned to dig containers out of the refrigerator. He peeked in a few, then pulled down a plate and filled it with a little from each.

Andrei couldn't help but laugh.

"I love the kid's food." Rowe stuck the overflowing plate into the microwave. "I danced for joy when he finally caved in to Lucas and set up Rialto."

"Lucas took me there last night. It's great." Andrei inwardly winced at his word choice, instantly wishing he could pull them back but it was way too late for that.

Green eyes narrowed on him. "Is there another reason I should be pulling you off this job, Hadeon?"

Again, Andrei fought the urge to squirm. It wasn't usual for him—he'd faced down bigger men than Rowe. But he wasn't stupid. The man might not be that tall, but he was strong and mean and wouldn't hesitate to work Andrei over if he felt the need. Even if they were friends to a certain degree. Not the kind of friends he was with Lucas. No, what the four men had was something a lot deeper.

He honestly felt envious of the bond they shared. Andrei had nothing like that in his life.

"Andrei, are you fucking my friend?"

"No." He didn't elaborate, didn't share anything more. He wasn't fucking Lucas. But he probably would be sooner or later. At least once when this job was over.

He had to know what it felt like to be with him. Had to.

The microwave dinged and Rowe opened a drawer and pulled out a potholder so he could get his plate. He set it on the bar a couple of seats down from Andrei and began shoveling food into his mouth. He groaned as he chewed, then swallowed.

Andrei grinned. Melissa didn't cook much. She worked just as many hours at her job as her husband and from what he'd witnessed, they argued over whose turn it was to cook most nights. Hell, Andrei had cooked once at their house. Steak, of course. And bagged salad. He constantly sent out thanks to whoever came up with that idea. Though, eating Rialto food was going to spoil him. He bet Ian never touched a bagged salad, could even imagine the horrified dismay on the pretty guy's face when confronted with it. He grinned.

"What's funny?" Rowe sliced into a wedge of steak.

"The thought of Ian eating bagged salad."

Rowe snorted. "Never gonna happen. Never."

Andrei relaxed. It seemed the subject of his stupidity last night was over. It was a good thing because he still wasn't sure he was comfortable with why he'd let Lucas talk him into going inside that warehouse.

Rowe never bothered Lucas, and Andrei figured out he'd only come to check on him and the situation. Probably to steal some of the food, too. The rest of the afternoon passed with only the occasional glimpse of Lucas or Candace. The two worked long hours. When Lucas finally emerged in the early evening, it was only to announce that he had to check on another of his clubs that night.

兄弟武士心

"You been here before?" Lucas asked Andrei as they walked inside Gaile. Andrei scoped the crowd and never removed his hand from Lucas's arm, the heat from his skin burning through Lucas's jacket.

"No. It's nice." Andrei's gaze roamed the crowd.

"Have you even noticed the décor?" He waved toward the massive mirrored wall behind the bar with the glass shelves of collectable vodka bottles, the buttery gold and red round couches that circled low, walnut tables. He'd created a mix of modern and old world comfort, sort of meshing two bars he had good memories in. One in Vegas and one a small pub in Ireland. He grinned. Such fond, fond memories of that pub.

"The décor isn't where the danger lies." Andrei did sort of glance around then. "Comfy. What does the name mean?"

"It's Gaelic for steam. Snow and I had a pretty hot time on vacation in Ireland once." Lucas winked. "I modeled some of this place after a sweet little pub we frequented."

Andrei's gaze locked onto Lucas's. "Hot time? Together?" The hand on Lucas's arm tightened, almost possessively, but Lucas wasn't sure that Andrei was aware he'd done it. He wanted to just lean in and run his tongue along Andrei's lips, teasing them from the tight line he'd pressed them into, urging them to part for him again.

Everyone who spent any time around them asked that question sooner or later, so Lucas wasn't at all surprised. "Snow and I are friends. Just close friends." He didn't bother to explain their friendship further. It wouldn't even be possible.

"Shiver, Steam—are all your clubs named like that?"

"Not all, but I do like my...sensations." Smirking, Lucas tugged on Andrei's shirt. "Come on. I called ahead and made sure the best table was clear."

"You mean there isn't a table that stays permanently clear for you?"

Lucas shook his head. "I usually stay behind that wall of glass." He pointed to a dark wall. "I can see everything from in there."

"Looks safer. Let's go there."

Andrei gave him a look Lucas wasn't sure he knew how to interpret. Did the man want to get him alone behind that wall? The thought of fucking up against that one-way mirror sent heat spiraling through Lucas's body. Andrei, that black silk shirt unbuttoned and hanging open, his pants shoved down to his knees. Lucas would press him to the glass, make him watch the people barely a foot away from them as he tangled his hands in all that black hair and pushed slowly into his body.

Seeing Snow sprawled on one of the red couches surrounding the table he'd reserved sent that fantasy to the back of his mind. He could do nothing about the hard-on barely contained in his slacks. The blond twink currently trying to crawl into Snow's lap would hopefully keep his friend from noticing Lucas's predicament. He shook his head, smirking as Snow grinned at the kid, picked him up and set him on the couch next to him.

Lucas narrowed his eyes. *Kid was right.* Was he even legal? He picked up the pace, wove through a tight crowd and stopped at the table as the obviously drunk young man tried to crawl into Snow's lap again. "Problem?" It took effort to hold back a laugh as Snow winced and grabbed the kid's hips.

"I think you need to card this one," the doctor said through gritted teeth. "Hey." He clutched the blond's arms, pulled the wandering mouth off his neck and pushed him away. "Do you have someone you can call to come get you?"

"God, you smellsogood. Don't wanna go home. Seen you before here a lot. AnatShiver. Been hopin' to find you."

The slurred words came with the flirtiest smile Lucas had ever seen. The kid really was a beauty—if you went for young, adorable, and pretty. Nearly platinum curls framed a pixie-like face with big blue eyes. And holy shit, the kid's plump, pouty lips were made for blowjobs. *For someone his own age.* Lucas had to hold his breath to keep from laughing when the boy started rolling his hips in a sinuous move that sent his ass right over the doctor's crotch.

Snow winced, cursed, and picked him up, this time setting him on his feet. "No." He used the kind of voice one would with a toddler.

The muffled chuckle behind him let him know Andrei was having just as hard a time not cracking up.

"Come on," the kid whined. "I promise we'll have a good time. I'm Goh...Geoffrey."

"Of course you are." Snow's mutter came with a frantic look at Lucas, followed by a grunt when Geoffrey jumped back into his lap.

"Okay, come on now." Andrei moved around Lucas and helped pull Geoffrey off Snow. "Let's see an ID."

"Why does everyone askforit? Showed it to three bartenders here already." He frowned, stared down at Snow as he dug his license out of pants that had been painted on.

Andrei took the card, lifted a dark eyebrow. "He's twenty-six. It's real." Shock widened his dark eyes as he looked back at the kid.

Lucas didn't blame him. The kid, no, man stood all of five foot five and with those delicate young features wasn't going to look like an adult until his late thirties probably. That could either hinder him horribly or work in his favor with the right boyfriend.

"See?" Geoffrey waggled his white brows at Snow. "Wanna come play now?"

Snow's grin surprised the hell out of Lucas because instead of cutting the kid down like he usually would, this smile was actually friendly. "It's still no. Maybe you can find me again when you're sober."

Geoffrey's hands tightened into fists and his cheeks turned pink. The humiliation that swamped him hit Lucas like a wave and he felt bad for the young man as he turned and lurched away. Lucas waved one of the bouncers over to make sure the guy was safely seen into a cab. In both his state of mind and inebriation, someone with way less scruples would take advantage. He watched the bouncer follow Geoffrey before settling onto the couch across from Snow. "Would you really get with him? Never seen you go for anyone like that."

Snow's look of incredulous disdain should have burned a hole through Lucas. But all he did was laugh and give the doctor's crotch a pointed look. There was definitely wood pushing against his jeans. Lucas felt the rush of surprise again. Wasn't like Snow to hit a nightclub like this in jeans. But he looked good in them and the blue of his shirt made his eyes even sharper than usual.

That disdain turned into a scowl. "You have a tight, little bottom like that one rub all over you and see if you don't react." His ice-blue gaze flicked up to Andrei who stood behind the couch. "Are you going to hover like that all night?"

Lucas looked over his shoulder to see the bodyguard's attention wasn't even on Snow. He had his gaze zoomed onto something across the room if the narrowed eyes were an indication. Turning his head, Lucas scanned the crowd, but he didn't see anything other than people dancing and a very decent amount of people crammed around the bar.

This club had been open the longest and had stayed surprisingly steady. People seemed to like the mix of cozy and sleek. Snow sure as hell did.

Andrei must have decided whatever threat he'd seen wasn't one after all because he came around and sat on the couch with his back to the wall. He could see everything from that spot and because the rounded couches were set back from the table in the center, he wouldn't be pinned in there. Andrei's dark red tie with the fine black striping was drawing Lucas's attention, causing him all kinds of internal problems. He changed the earlier fantasy image to Andrei with his back to that mirrored wall, his shirt still open, that tie bouncing on his abs as Lucas pushed one of his legs high—

Low chuckles pulled him from the image and that was a good thing. He'd been about to embarrass the hell out of himself. He glared at Snow, who only stared back, still laughing. His friend knew him well, probably had a pretty good idea what he'd been thinking about. He looked at Andrei only to find those black eyes locked on him.

Fuck. Andrei had a pretty good idea himself.

Not one to apologize, Lucas just shrugged and gave the man his sexiest smile, then watched as Andrei's breathing picked up. Lucas wasn't even sure Andrei knew he had reached up and loosened the tie around his neck.

Snow threw his head back and laughed like he usually did with Rowe. "Oh, to be a fly on the wall in your penthouse right now. It's probably the best show in town. If not already, then it will be soon. Rowe aware you two are here on a date?"

"It's not a date," Lucas assured him. "He's still here in an official capacity and I'm working."

"Makes the role-playing that much more fun, doesn't it?" Snow's attention was snagged by something over Lucas's shoulder.

He glanced behind him to see someone a lot more Snow's type giving him a look from the next table over. Nobody could ever call that wide-shouldered man a twink. Lucas looked again at Snow to see the lurid plans already forming in his friend's head. He barely held back from rolling his eyes. Instead, he waved the hovering waitress over and had her get him a whiskey and Snow a refill. He looked at Andrei.

"Soda water with lime."

He hadn't expected the man to order alcohol while on duty, but sometime he hoped to see Andrei drunk. He couldn't help but wonder what it would be like to watch that tight control disappear.

"So," Snow said slowly as if dragging his mind from the temptation he'd spotted. "That detective—Hollis—returned to the hospital and asked that I let him know if more people come in with the same bruises on their thighs. I went through the files because I generally don't get called to handle beatings. Besides you, there has been only one other — Thomas Lynton."

Lucas nodded, glaring down at the table. "That what Rowe told us." He'd been hoping for a little more information, something that might shed some light on who was behind this and why.

"But I did make a couple of calls."

Lucas's head snapped up and for once Snow looked a little uncomfortable. "Do I want to know how many laws you've broken?"

"None yet," Snow growled. "But if I dig any deeper I could definitely lose my job."

"Snow—"

"Two others suffered similar attacks. Obvious beatings but the bruising was similar to yours."

"Who?"

"That's what I'm not allowed to know. HIPAA fucking privacy rules."

"Rowe's got someone who can find out that information," Andrei volunteered. He scooted to the edge of the sofa, resting his forearms on his knees.

Lucas forced his mind away from the enticing fact that Andrei's knee was just a few inches from his own. So close it wouldn't take much to reach out and run his hand along that strong thigh. But his mind jumped back to the idea of Rowe sending his hacker through protected hospital files. There went the straight and narrow.

"No," Lucas sighed.

"But—"

"Not necessary," Snow interrupted Andrei. "One was taken to St. E. South in Kentucky and the other was taken to Good Sam. I don't have names but my contacts confirmed that both likely had more than seven figures in their bank accounts."

Lucas swore, shaking his head. "Someone has hired these bastards out to put pressure on Cincinnati's rich. Why? I'm the only one buying in Price Hill. I've checked."

"Then what?"

Without warning, Geoffrey was back, followed by a red-face, angry bouncer. The little guy wrapped his arms around Snow's neck from the backside of the couch and whispered something in the doctor's ear. Snow's mouth dropped open.

Lucas gave his employee a withering stare.

"He's little, fast, and slippery," the guy said, holding up his big hands. "He was in the cab and on his way off, I swear. I didn't even see him slip back in until he was nearly here." He put his hands on Geoffrey's hips and tugged him.

Lucas could tell the bouncer was trying not to hurt the guy and he got it. He was pretty sure he'd never seen anyone that delicate looking in his life.

"Come on, little dude. It's time to go all the way home this time."

A loud shot sounded and a hole appeared in the couch right next to Geoffrey. He pulled away from Snow, frowned, stared at it. "Whatzthat?"

There wasn't time for a response as Lucas found himself on the floor with over two hundred pounds of muscled bodyguard on top of him as loud gunfire drowned out the music. Glass shattered and Lucas twisted to see shelves of vodka bottles exploding along with the mirrored wall behind them.

Screams and stampeding feet overpowered the music and everything became a blur of noise. He saw Snow's shoes as the doctor jumped to his feet.

"Idiot! Get down." Andrei reached out and snagged Snow's hand and tugged him hard enough to make the man lose his balance. He hit the floor with a grunt. "I know your first instinct is to help, but you have to wait. Lucas's bouncers had one down already and were close to the second man."

It was hard to hear him over the screams. It took everything Lucas had not to flip them, so he protected Andrei. He worked his head around so he could see under the couch and found Geoffrey flat on his back. Alarm filled him and at first, he was sure the little guy had been shot. But he started wiggling and it was obvious the bouncer was holding him down.

The shooting stopped, the screams dwindled to mostly cries as the DJ finally turned off the damned music. "I think they got them," Lucas said. "You can let me up."

Andrei rolled off him, but kept one hand on the nape of his neck as he looked around. "Okay, it's safe." He let go and stood.

Lucas scrambled to his feet and got his first look. Two of his bouncers held one of the gunmen on the ground while the other two were busy helping people out. The fifth—the one who'd been on top of Geoffrey—had placed himself between Lucas and the rest of the crowd. Right next to Andrei. Lucas moved around them, feeling the heat of Andrei keeping close, as he stepped around overturned tables. Broken glass crunched under his feet. Liquor dripped down what was left of the shattered mirror behind the bar. Several couches had been flipped to use as barricades. Blood soaked into one and Lucas stopped to stare, his heart pounding. Snow already knelt on the other side of that couch, barking out orders to the people gawking around them.

Lucas touched the bouncer's arm. "We should keep the rest of the people here. The police will want to question every eye witness."

The guy nodded and hurried ahead.

There was a piercing ring in Lucas's ears as he tried to take everything in. He walked to where the bouncers held the gunman on the floor and arrived just as the police did. He squatted next to the guy, took in the blank stare. The man knew he'd been beaten. There was no getting out of this one. "Who sent you?" Lucas grabbed his face just as a cop placed his hand on Lucas's shoulder.

The gunman only stared straight ahead, he didn't acknowledge anyone around him.

A cop touched Lucas's shoulder. "We'll get it out of him."

"There was another shooter," one of the bouncers said. "He got away."

Lucas blinked, bringing the man into focus, noticing that he had blood on his right shoulder. "There's a doctor helping others back there." He pointed to where he'd left Snow. "Go see him and let the cops handle this guy." He made sure to look at both the men who worked for him. "You did well. Went above and beyond. I won't forget that."

The injured one nodded and they stood as the police took the gunman into custody.

As the horror of the moment threatened to overwhelm him, Lucas crushed his fist around his emotions and jumped into the fray. With a sharp voice, he directed his employees in caring for the customers while others helped organize areas where the police could start taking statements in an orderly manner so that people could leave as soon as possible. By sheer force of will, he bent the chaos under his control.

But there was no getting around one fact. He'd have to close the club until an investigation was finished, but it wouldn't matter. Gaile had seen its last night. The kind of crowd that would brave the nightclub after a shootout wasn't the type he was interested in serving. The thought of Gaile not being around cut deep. He'd designed the place for Snow. But then, after tonight, he knew his friend would never want to set foot in it again.

Lucas turned and his gaze locked with Andrei's. The concern in those dark eyes seeped in to help negate the numb horror freezing his heart. He stepped closer to the bodyguard and wondered if Andrei realized he'd been rubbing his palm up and down Lucas's back the entire time they'd stood there as Lucas surveyed the damage.

Three hours passed before Lucas and Andrei were able to leave the remains of Gaile. He'd answered questions, but there hadn't been much information that he could provide. The men hadn't made any demands, hadn't said anything, before they opened fire. Lucas had overhead from one cop that most of the shots had been fired at the ceiling rather than into the crowd, but it was cold comfort for the woman who Snow had desperately worked on until the ambulance finally arrived. He didn't get a chance to talk to Snow, but he knew it hadn't been good considering the drawn expression on the doctor's face.

A block over from the nightclub, Lucas and Andrei walked into the parking garage where Andrei had parked. As they drew near the gleaming black Mercedes, Lucas swore loudly, his pace quickening. Andrei tried to grab his arm to slow him, but he threw off the bodyguard's hand. Something was sticking out of the front hood of the car.

"Fuck!" Lucas snarled, barely noticing when Andrei finally grabbed him, forcing him behind Andrei's larger body. Someone had stabbed a large knife into the hood of the car to hold a fluttering piece of paper in place. Moving close, he could easily read the big block letters written with a magic marker:

This is your last warning. Get out of Price Hill. The next bullets won't miss.

Lucas looked up in time to see Andrei dialing 9-1-1 on his phone. With a strong hand, he clasped Andrei's wrist before he could connect the call. "Don't."

"You don't want to tell the cops?"

Grinding his teeth, Lucas forced himself to take a deep breath and release Andrei's wrist. They'd destroyed Snow's club, threatened his customers, and now they'd fucked with his car. He was done letting the Cincy PD dick around in his life. Rowe was getting carte blanche.

"Take a picture. Then pull the knife out of the hood. Get the knife, the note, and the picture to Rowe tomorrow. Tell your boss to do his fucking job."

Chapter 10

A long, heavy sigh slipped from Andrei. He slumped against the side of the elevator when the doors slid shut and dropped his head back to watch Lucas with hooded eyes. Lucas had been quiet since they'd left the nightclub, but then he was undoubtedly preoccupied. His business had been shot up and his customers threatened. They'd had to tolerate nearly two hours of questions from the police and they still were no closer to knowing the culprit. At least Lucas hadn't gone to the hospital again. That would have been fun to explain to Rowe.

Lucas leaned against the opposite wall, staring back at Andrei, his face an unreadable mask. "Well," Andrei drawled with a smirk playing on his lips. "I've had better dates."

"Let's make it better," Lucas said. Andrei barely had enough time to turn his words over in his mind before Lucas pushed off the wall and lunged at Andrei, covering him with his larger body. A grunt shot from Andrei and then any discomfort was lost to Lucas's lips. Andrei's slump made them the same height, allowing Lucas to kiss him deeply without needing to tip his head up. There was no tentative exploration or slow seduction. The kiss was scorching heat, burning away thought and doubts. His tongue plunged into Andrei's mouth, dominating him as a low moan rose up from his throat. Andrei lost himself in that kiss as Lucas threaded his fingers through Andrei's hair, clutching the strands so he could hold his head captive.

Lucas pulled back slightly, sucking Andrei's lower lip, tugging at him. With a growl, Andrei chased him. Fingers tightening in the smooth material of Lucas's jacket, he jerked the man back, tongue darting into Lucas's mouth to glide over his tongue. They ground their bodies together so that there was no hiding their arousal. After dragging his hand across Lucas's chest, Andrei started unbuttoning his shirt, fingers skimming from the soft material to warm, naked skin. Lucas made a hungry noise in the back of his throat and Andrei briefly wondered if he was about to get fucked in an elevator. They had been dancing around this edge since their first meeting. Last night's kiss had only made it worse, leaving Andrei constantly thinking about the softness of his lips, the hardened muscles wrapped in smooth skin, and his hands. Those goddamned hands were so strong and so sure. Those hands made him shudder.

A soft ping broke Lucas and Andrei apart. They both looked up to stare vacantly at the elevator doors as they opened. Their heavy breathing filled the small car and they looked out into the hall that led to the penthouse, but neither moved as if they couldn't comprehend where they were or why they were there. It was only when the doors started to shut that Lucas cursed softly, the spell broken so that he could lurch forward to hit the button to open the doors again.

Shaking his head, Andrei watched the other man step out of the elevator before he followed behind him. "Damn, Vallois. You're going to kill me," Andrei muttered, searching for his key to Lucas's door while putting his other hand on the butt of the gun tucked under his arm.

"Never before sex," Lucas promised in a low voice, smiling at Andrei with enough heat to send a throb of longing through him.

"I think we need to concentrate on finding the bastard who's causing all this bullshit." Andrei unlocked the door, hoping to put both their minds on the problem at hand rather than the smoldering desire that was quickly turning all of Andrei's common sense to ash.

Pausing just inside the entrance, Andrei tapped in the code, turning off the alarm before flipping on the overhead lights. For the moment, the gnawing hunger for Lucas was pushed aside as his eyes searched what he could see of the first floor. No one was there and nothing had moved. Stepping the rest of the way into the penthouse, he moved aside so Lucas could enter before locking the door behind him and setting the alarm. Sinking comfortably into protector mode, Andrei could forget about personal worries and needs so that his entire being was focused on the job at hand—protecting Lucas.

"I'll check the penthouse," he announced, pulling his gun from his holster. Its familiar weight in his hand soothed him as he easily swept through the kitchen, living room, and first floor bathroom. He was aware of Lucas following him, but the other man said nothing. Andrei led the way up to the second floor, checking the guest room, the bathroom and then the office before finally venturing into the master bedroom.

Unlike the other rooms, Andrei didn't bother to flick on the light. It was still dark, but the light from the wall of windows beat the thick shadows back enough that his eyes easily adjusted. He made a quick pass at the massive walk-in closet and the master bath before returning to find that Lucas had turned on one of the small bedside lamps.

The penthouse was empty except for them. Everything was still secure. They were safe.

Nerves flooded Andrei so that he stood, almost paralyzed, staring out the floor-to-ceiling windows toward downtown Cincinnati. Roebling Bridge glowed, bathed in warm yellow lights along its pale blue suspension cables as they stretched across the Ohio River, leading the way into downtown. The skyscrapers were shining bright, white diamonds surrounded in a velvet blanket of night. The Queen City had never looked so serene and elegant.

"Stunning view," he murmured, trying to tear his eyes away while at the same time decide how to move forward. Did he just shrug off what happened in the elevator and return to his room? It was after three in the morning. He was wired now, but if he remained still long enough, sleep would finally claim him.

Lucas stepped up behind Andrei and slid his sports coat off his shoulders and down his arms. He dropped the jacket to the floor with a heavy thud before he started on the shoulder holster that soon joined the jacket. Andrei tried to turn and face him, but Lucas stopped him.

"Don't," Lucas commanded, his voice nearly a growl.

"What?"

"Stay."

Andrei froze, some of the same tension he'd felt in the elevator returning to his frame as he stood with his hands loose at his sides. Moving closer, Lucas slipped his hands around Andrei's waist and up his chest, pulling him so that his back was molded to Lucas's front. On a soft moan, Andrei dropped his head to rest on Lucas's shoulder. Pressing slow open-mouthed kisses along his exposed neck, Lucas ran his hands up and down Andrei's chest, exploring hard muscles.

This felt different from the frantic kiss in the elevator or even from the night before. The searing hunger was still there, but Lucas's movements had become more controlled and measured. Every touch and lingering caress was designed to burn Andrei up. And even though Andrei could clearly see Lucas's seductive plan, it didn't stop it from working. His taller frame trembled with need. It was taking all of his control not to turn and pin Lucas to the nearest surface so they could both go up in flames.

Any remaining questions about whether he was gay and if this was wrong were drowned out. They had no place when Lucas touched him. Something that felt so perfect, so all consuming, could not be wrong.

Fingers danced down his chest, unbuttoning his shirt, shaking slightly in their haste to strip it from his body. "I need to touch you," Lucas murmured against his neck. As he finally tugged the shirt free of Andrei's pants, Lucas bit down hard on Andrei's shoulder while his hands glided up the taut muscles of his stomach to his chest. Andrei hissed, reaching back to grasp Lucas's hips to pull him flush against his ass.

As Lucas's hands swept across his stomach, he moved one down over Andrei's hardened cock. Andrei's hands tightened on Lucas's hips to the point of bruising.

"Fuck, Lucas," he groaned.

Lucas drew his hand back to Andrei's hip while the other snaked up across his chest, holding him captive. "Should I stop?"

"No," he said, his voice full of gravel.

"What do you want me to do?"

Andrei paused, nerves starting to surface through the throbbing haze of pleasure and hunger. "I don't know. Don't care. More than the last time."

A soft chuckle rumbled from Lucas and his hot breath brushed across Andrei's ear. "Oh, I think we're both way past a little kiss."

"Fuck me?"

Andrei could feel every muscle in Lucas's frame tense against his for a split second before the other man dragged in a long, deep breath and then released it. Pressing his face into Andrei's neck, he kissed him slowly as his hands started moving over his body again.

"I've got another idea."

"I hope it gets at least one of us off," Andrei moaned.

Lucas laughed, a low, wicked sound as he lifted his head. "Let's play a game." He released Andrei and walked around in front of him. Andrei watched him warily. This was not what he'd expected. He'd anticipated finding himself face down in the mattress while Lucas fucked him into oblivion. A game actually sounded more uncomfortable.

"Oh, don't worry. You'll like this game," Lucas teased as he set about removing Andrei's clothes as he pressed a series of slow kisses along his chest. As soon as his arms were free, Andrei resumed his earlier work on Lucas's shirt, pulling it off his strong arms, finally forcing his mouth back up to Andrei's. Their tongues dueled, leaving both men panting and desperate again. It was only when Lucas slid his hand inside of Andrei's boxer's, wrapping his long fingers around his straining cock that Andrei even realized that the man had managed to get his pants down around his knees.

Andrei cursed on a gasp, trying to suck air into his lungs. He blinked, meeting Lucas's heated gaze. In the dim light, his eyes had become darker, more green than gray. Like wet leaves or spring grass, sharp and bright. Haunting.

Lucas licked his lips and withdrew his hand as he took a step backward toward the windows. Glancing over his shoulder briefly, he motioned for Andrei to approach him. He didn't question it. He was too fucking far gone. He needed Lucas. His touch, his kisses, everything this man had to give. Andrei tried to press against Lucas again, but Lucas stopped him with a hand in the middle of his chest.

"What?" Andrei demanded.

Lucas grinned. "Put both hands on the glass in front of you."

Andrei frowned at him for a second, questioning, but he followed his directions, placing both hands, palms flat against the window just above Lucas's shoulders. The glass was cool and he could feel the wind buffeting the building. Lucas leaned in, kissing along his jaw. Andrei moved his head, trying to capture his mouth, but Lucas evaded.

"Keep your hands on the glass."

"This is the game?"

"Yes."

"I just keep my hands on the glass?"

"Yes."

"If I don't?"

Lucas leaned back to look Andrei in the eye and smile. "I stop and you go to your room."

Andrei's heart picked up and he licked his lips. "I'll keep my hands on the glass."

"We'll see," Lucas whispered as he suddenly dropped to his knees in front of Andrei. His large hands swept up the back of Andrei thighs to cup his ass and squeeze before moving slowly up over his stomach and across his chest in a thorough caress.

Andrei stared out through the window, the lights of the city shining brightly right in front of him while one of the most powerful men in Cincinnati was on his knees, stroking his body as if he were worshipping it. Every touch was intoxicating. Then Lucas leaned forward, his lips brushing against Andrei's hard cock through his silk boxers, and Andrei knew he was in trouble. A shiver of pleasure ran through the length of his body and there was no hiding it.

"Fuck," Andrei growled and Lucas chuckled. There was no way he was going to be able to keep his hands on the glass and if Lucas stopped, he was going to die. That's all there was to it. He was going to die.

Before Andrei could organize his thoughts enough to either stop Lucas or prepare himself, Lucas pulled Andrei's boxers down to his knees. He looked down in time to see Lucas lick him from root to tip. He sucked in a hard breath through clenched teeth but couldn't drag his eyes away as Lucas swallowed him down.

A string of incoherent curses rained from Andrei as he watched his cock slide in and out of Lucas's hot mouth, his full lips tight around him while his tongue worked along the skin to the engorged tip. The whole time Lucas looked up at him, holding his gaze with dark, glittering eyes as if Andrei were the only thing in all the world. In that moment, he knew he'd never seen anything so sexy in his life.

Andrei fought to remain still when everything in him was dying to thrust his hips, to force his cock ever farther down Lucas's throat. Skilled hands moved over him, continuing to caress him, squeezing and massaging tense muscles so that his entire body was on fire.

Slowly pulling away, Lucas let Andrei's cock pop free from his mouth. He licked the tip before starting to stroke him with one hand. "Hands on the glass?" Lucas asked in a teasing voice.

"Fuck yes."

"Shall I continue?"

"I'll die if you don't," he ground out, spreading his fingers along the glass as if to ready himself. He was already hovering close to the edge and nothing was going to stop him from finally finding a release with Lucas.

With a smile, Lucas stuck two fingers in his mouth while continuing to stroke Andrei. He lifted on eyebrow in question. There was no doubt what he was planning to do, but he was waiting for Andrei to agree. Andrei grunted, ignoring the frantic beat of his heart as he spread his legs just a little farther for the man.

Removing his fingers from his mouth, he slid that hand behind Andrei, pressing one wet fingertip against his hole. Before Andrei could even react to the pressure, Lucas ran his tongue along his sack, gently sucking one ball into his mouth. Andrei jerked forward, crying out in a mix of pain and pleasure so intense he could see stars. Lucas moved back and took his cock in his mouth again, sucking him hard while pressing against the tight muscles of his ass until his finger entered him.

Andrei gasped. The orgasm was building fast now, his focus shattered from the new sensations accompanied by blinding pleasure. "More," he groaned. There was pain, but it was perfectly matched with the pleasure from Lucas's mouth on his cock. Lucas pressed his finger deeper, stroking his ass, opening him up a little more.

The lights of the city blurred in front of Andrei's eyes. He couldn't watch Lucas any more. He was on edge, struggling to push back the orgasm racing down his spine, but it was a losing battle. Dropping his head down, he met Lucas's hot stare and gasped.

"Gotta stop," he bit out. "I –I can't… almost," he hissed. But Lucas didn't pull away. He sucked him harder, his free hand clamping down on his hip as if to hold him should he attempt to escape. Fingers bit into him, threatening to leave bruises, mark him. A shout ripped from his throat in the form of Lucas's name as he came hard, shooting himself down Lucas's throat. And Lucas took everything he had, prolonging the orgasm as long as possible as he stroked Andrei's cock with his lips and tongue. Andrei's head jerked up and he saw the city stretched before him, the lights shining so damned bright. The world tilted and in that second he felt like a god, floating above it all.

It was only when Andrei shivered hard, his body swaying slightly as his knees threatened to give out that Lucas pulled completely free, possibly fearful that Andrei might collapse on top of him. He wiped his mouth with the back of his hand as he stared up at Andrei, his eyes still hungry but also very happy.

"Hands still on the glass," Andrei murmured, trying to get the blood to return to his brain.

"Impressive," Lucas murmured as he carefully pulled Andrei's boxers back into place. Before pushing to his feet, he kissed along the man's stomach, working his way up to Andrei's chest. Andrei couldn't stop watching him. How the fuck had he ever thought that he was in a position of power by being on his feet? Lucas might have been on his knees, but from the first moment that he'd touched him, Lucas had been in control the whole damned time. Andrei would have done *anything* he'd asked.

Lucas tried to kiss Andrei's throat, but Andrei ducked his head, capturing his mouth in a drugging kiss. His tongue swept through his mouth, taking in the mixed taste of himself and Lucas. It was something he'd never thought he'd find appealing, but then he couldn't think of anything about Lucas that he wouldn't find a fucking turn on. Every kiss, every touch, everything just left him craving more of this man and he just didn't give a damn anymore.

Breaking off the kiss, Andrei slid one hand between them. Before he could reach Lucas's cock, Lucas clamped a hand down on Andrei's wrist stopping him.

"Don't," Lucas choked out before giving Andrei a crooked grin. "You don't have to. I don't expect…"

Andrei stared at the man for a moment, his eyes glazed with an aching need and no small amount of pain. He was giving Andrei an out. Lucas would let him walk out of the room and not think less of him. But Andrei didn't want out. He wanted more. He craved it.

Dropping his head, he pressed his nose into Lucas's cheek, dragging down to his neck so that Lucas tilted his head up, offering up more skin. "Don't think I'm ready to suck you off…yet," he admitted in a low, warm voice before biting his neck. He twisted his wrist just a little and Lucas released his hand, allowing him to run his hand along the hard ridge in his pants. Lucas's hips jerked and he hissed softly but didn't move otherwise. "But I'm dying to see you come."

Pushing Lucas back, he roughly maneuvered him so that the other man was now pressed against the window, the city spread behind him, but Andrei could see only Lucas. He stepped back long enough to kick out of his pants, shoes and socks, leaving him in only his boxers before he returned to a bare-chested Lucas watching him through hooded eyes. He could help but smile.

"Should I put my hands on the glass?" Lucas mocked.

Andrei shook his head, closing the distance between them so that he was now standing between Lucas's thighs. "You can put your hands wherever the fuck you want. I'm not leaving this room until you're shouting my name."

Grasping Andrei's shoulders, Lucas could only groan, his eyes closing as Andrei quickly undid his belt and opened his pants. He shoved both his pants and his boxer briefs low on his hips, freeing Lucas's cock. He couldn't draw his eyes away from Lucas's face as his wrapped his hand around his hard cock, earning another low moan, Lucas's hips thrusting forward. He stroked his hand up and over the head, catching on this soft, damp skin. A slow smile pulled at his lips as he caressed the slick tip.

Andrei leaned in, nibbling at Lucas's lips, then pulling away before Lucas could deepen the kiss. "Did you come a little when you sucked me off?"

"Fuck yes," he hissed. Lucas's eyes flicked open, drilling through Andrei with such heat. "You are so damned hot. Taste so damned good. And the noises you make." His body tensed, his hands tightening on Andrei's shoulders until Andrei was sure the man was going to have more bruises in the form of fingerprints. His breathing picked up.

Threading the fingers of his free hand through Lucas's hair, he pulled his head back, trapping him for a hard, punishing kiss as he stroked him faster. Their bodies nearly pressed together so that Andrei's knuckles swept across both their stomachs as he moved his fist. Andrei could feel himself growing hard all over again, need beating at him, but he shoved it down. He needed this more.

"Andrei...." Lucas drew out his name, gasped.

"That's it. Come for me," Andrei growled, picking up his pace. "I want to watch you fucking come all over me."

Lucas's breath hitched in the back of his throat and then he cried out, shouting Andrei's name as his entire body jerked under the force of the orgasm that ripped through him. Andrei continued to pump his cock, spreading his come across both their stomachs. As soon as Lucas started to drift back down, he grasped Andrei, kissing him deeply.

When Andrei pulled away, he kept his forehead pressed against Lucas's as he grinned. His hand was still wrapped around Lucas's slowly softening cock, trapped between their bodies. Never in his life had he jerked another man off, never even considered doing it. But that realization didn't compare to the expression of the man in his arms. Lucas looked utterly sated and relaxed. Lines of worry had disappeared and new laugh lines around his mouth had appeared that Andrei hadn't noticed before. His eyes almost seemed to glow in the semi-darkness, still the deep green of earlier.

He was beautiful.

Andrei's heart stuttered.

Lucas slipped his fingers through Andrei's shoulder-length hair in a slow, gentle caress. "I'm a mess."

"Yeah," Andrei said with a note of pride and amusement. "But look." He jerked his chin toward the window, getting Lucas to glance over his shoulder. "Still a stunning view to fuck to."

Lucas's deep laugh filled the room before he kissed Andrei. He was still laughing when he broke off the kiss and Andrei stepped away. Andrei turned and grabbed up his slacks, wiping off his hands and stomach. Out of the corner of his eyes, he saw Lucas kick off the last of his clothes before strolling into the bathroom to clean up. A shower would be nice. But even as the thought hit Andrei, exhaustion from the long day crept up on him. He could always shower in the morning.

"How's your back?" Lucas called from the bathroom.

"Stings," he admitted as he bent and picked up his clothes scattered around the room. He'd completely forgotten about his back since they'd entered the penthouse. But now that he thought about it, there was a lingering pain as if from a slowly healing sunburn. In another day or two, the pain would be completely gone.

Lucas stepped into the open doorway with a white towel in his hands. "Need more of the green goop?"

"You gonna put it on?"

"No, I thought I'd watch you struggle with it," he replied sarcastically. As he walked to Andrei, he pulled the clothes out of his hands and thrust the towel into them. "Lay on your stomach. I'll be right back."

Andrei watched as Lucas unselfconsciously sauntered naked through the room on his way back to the kitchen. He seemed to be moving better than he had been just a couple days ago. Even with the faint bruises, he was a stunning man.

Shaking his head, Andrei let out a little sigh as he used the towel on himself before dropping it on the counter in the bathroom. Lucas had taken all his clothes, leaving behind only his gun and holster. Was he supposed to crash in Lucas's bed? Let him put the goop on and then crawl back into his own bed? Hell, he had a feeling that it was the latter. Lucas didn't seem the type to let his sexual partners linger after he was done with them. Even so, the cool aloe gel sounded nice.

He was moving pillows around on the king-sized bed when Lucas returned. The bed was comfortable, covered in the softest duvet and sheets Andrei had ever felt. Maybe he would angle to sleep in here. This had to be like sleeping on a cloud.

"What's with all the pillows?" Andrei demanded as Lucas approached.

"What do you mean? It's a king-sized bed. It needs lots of pillows."

Andrei flopped down on the side closest to the door, tucking one pillow against his chest, while two more propped under his head. "I thought only chicks needed this many pillows in the bed." He glanced over his shoulder at Lucas to find the man glaring at him. "I think you have this many pillows so you don't have to share your bed." As he spoke, Andrei grabbed two pillows and threw them off the end of the bed, making more room.

"Let's see if I can make you scream again," Lucas said in a low voice, holding up the chilled gel, ready to have his revenge.

Somehow Andrei managed not to jump from the bed like the first time, but he couldn't hold back the curses as the ice cold gel hit his heated skin. But the worst of it passed and he was able to just enjoy the feeling of Lucas's hands working the gel into scorched flesh, letting his mind travel back to the reason why Lucas was suddenly in his life.

"I've been thinking," Andrei announced after several minutes of silence. Lucas flinched and stilled. Even though he was touching Andrei with only his hands, Andrei felt the sudden tension in the man. "About your case," he clarified. Lucas instantly relaxed and resumed his ministrations. "I really don't like asking this question."

"Then don't."

He paused, glaring at the man over his shoulder. That wasn't going to stop him. "What happens to everything if you die?"

"Making plans?"

"Fuck you. I'm being serious. You're not married. No kids. Everything go to your family?"

"God no," Lucas gasped, his lip curling in disgust. He pushed back to his feet and walked to the bathroom to get a towel.

Andrei sat up in the middle of the bed, his legs folded in front of him. "Then what?" Andrei threw out his hands wide, prompting Lucas when he returned. "You can't tell me that you've amassed this empire and haven't planned out every detail of it."

"My shares in Rowe's company go to him and my shares in Rialto go to Ian." He grabbed a clean pair of black boxer briefs and pulled them on before coming back to the bed. "I've got something set aside for Snow, but other than that, the majority of my holdings will be sold off and the money will be split across several charities that support the city."

"Have you told anyone about your plans?"

Sitting with his back against the headboard, Lucas frowned, no longer looking Andrei in the eyes.

"What?" Andrei demanded in a low voice, his body tensing as he waited for the answer.

"In an interview with *Forbes* last year, I admitted that I was part of the Giving Pledge."

Andrei's brow furrowed and he shook his head. "What's that?"

"It's a pledge started by Bill Gates and Warren Buffett where the person agrees to give away at least half of their wealth to charity either during their lifetime or after death."

"Oh. That's nice."

Lucas shrugged, looking embarrassed. "Yeah, well, as you said, not married and no kids. I admitted in the article that the majority of my wealth will go to charities in the city that adopted me."

"And when they sell it all off, that would include your newly acquired land in Price Hill." Andrei groaned, dropping his face into his hands.

"Do you think this bastard will go so far as to kill me?"

Andrei dropped his hands and slowly lifted his eyes to Lucas. "No idea. He's been content to try to scare you so far." He still refused to think about how close that first bullet had come to where Lucas had been sitting on the couch.

"And piss me off."

It was hard not to smile at him. Only Lucas would see a guy stalking him and threatening his life and business as an irritation. "But you've admitted to being pretty damned stubborn…"

"Whatever," he growled, getting out of the bed to jerk down the blankets and sheets. "It's late. We'll solve this bullshit tomorrow."

"Right. Thanks for the goop. Night," Andrei said, still grinning. He started to climb off the bed but Lucas grabbed his wrist in a tight, hard grip, halting him.

"You either sleep in here or you put my fucking pillows back on the bed."

Andrei froze. For a moment, he simply didn't know what the right answer was. He hadn't expected this. Hoped, maybe, if he let himself think about it. Lucas tugged his arm, pulling him off balance so that he leaned close, allowing Lucas to easily brush his lips across Andrei's. It was a light kiss that sent his heart skipping for a reason other than the burning heat they'd felt earlier. This was…something else.

"I'll get this stuff on your sheets," Andrei said because he couldn't think of anything else.

Lucas snorted. "I've got more sheets. Lay down. I'm fucking tired."

Without further argument, Andrei slid under the sheets and lay on his stomach while Lucas flipped off the lamp on the nightstand by his side of the bed. As soon as Lucas was settled under the covers, he pulled Andrei close, wrapping their bodies together so their limbs were tangled under the cool sheets.

"Better than a pillow," Andrei murmured, his lips grazing Lucas's neck.

"Fuck you. I'm using your ass as a shield in case someone breaks in here." Andrei huffed a laugh, not missing that his glib words were undermined by the fact that Lucas was slowly running his fingers through Andrei's hair in a soothing caress.

Chapter 11

A noise woke Andrei. He blinked, fighting the urge to jump immediately to his feet. The bedroom was bright with sunlight, but it wasn't his bedroom. It was Lucas's. Somehow he'd forgotten that he'd fallen asleep wrapped around the larger man. Now he lay on his still tender back with Lucas pressed against him, his arm across Andrei's chest. They couldn't have been asleep for more than four hours, but it had been a deep, peaceful sleep that left Andrei feeling more rested than he'd been in a long time.

Very carefully, he slid out from underneath Lucas and stood by the side of the bed. Relaxed at last, Lucas was even more handsome. The lines around his mouth and eyes had disappeared, taking years off his face, softening some of the man's sharp edges.

Another noise echoed up from the first floor and Andrei bit back a growl of frustration. He'd rather climb back into the nice, warm bed and wrap around Lucas's pliant body for another hour, see if he'd be willing to wake to more of what they'd enjoyed last night, but someone was in the penthouse. Considering that the alarms hadn't gone off, Andrei was willing to bet that it was one of Lucas's trio of friends, but he wasn't going to take a chance with Lucas's life.

Grabbing the gun off the nightstand, Andrei paused, looking around the bedroom. His clothes were missing. Fuck, Lucas had walked off with them, likely throwing them back in the guest room. With a frown, he snatched up a pair of sleep pants draped over the arm of a chair and pulled them on. They would be fine until he got rid of the intruder. Then he could either get his own clothes or climb back into bed in his boxers.

Andrei descended to the first floor on silent footfalls. He'd tried gazing over the railing on the second floor to get a glimpse of the person, but he couldn't see that part of the kitchen from where he stood. As he turned the last corner, Andrei raised his gun in both hands, ready to put a slug in the bastard's chest.

Ian rose from where he'd bent over to pick up a bag and shouted, dropping the eggs in his hand on the hardwood floor. "What the hell!"

Andrei breathed a sigh of relief and immediately lowered the gun. "What are you doing here? Mr. Vallois didn't warn me that you'd be coming over."

"Lucas probably doesn't even know what day it is," Ian grumbled as he grabbed the paper towels off the counter to start cleaning up the eggs. "I stop by on Wednesdays and Fridays to have breakfast with him."

Andrei put the gun on the island counter and bent to help him pick up the egg shells. "I'm sorry I startled you."

As the last of the mess was cleaned up, Ian stepped back and he started to say something when his eyes snagged on the sleep pants. Andrei's heart gave a little jump as he prayed that the other man didn't recognize them. But all hope was lost when a slow smile spread across Ian's face and his eyes narrowed when he met Andrei's gaze.

"Nice pants," Ian drawled. Andrei waited. There was going to be more. "I gave those to Lucas for Christmas. I recognize the little skulls."

Andrei couldn't stop himself from looking down. The design had looked innocent, but Ian was right. What he'd thought were little white dots were actually skulls.

"I forgot to pack something to sleep in and Lucas loaned them to me," Andrei said. It wasn't a complete lie. They were on loan from Lucas even if the other man didn't know about it. The rest of his comment was complete garbage and they both knew it.

"Mmmhmm," Ian hummed with a smile.

Andre almost growled. "It's not what you think."

Ian turned back to the counter and started pulling food out of his canvas bags. "And what am I thinking?"

Andrei didn't know what to say that wouldn't make it worse, but Ian didn't need to think that something was happening between them. It was only a matter of time before word got back to Rowe. Then he'd be out of a job fast ... again. Or maybe something worse.

Before he could come up with a way to deflect Ian's question, Lucas's heavy footsteps echoed across the first floor. Both men looked up to find a barefoot and bare-chested Lucas crossing to the kitchen, one hand rubbing his eye as if he were still trying to wake up.

As soon as he reached Andrei, Lucas grabbed a handful of his long hair and twisted, holding him captive as he roughly kissed him. His tongue plunged into his mouth in the most possessive, draining kiss Andrei had ever received. A low moan rose up his throat and he lost himself in the heat and passion. He had just enough time to clasp Lucas's hips before the man broke off the kiss.

Lucas pressed his forehead to Andrei's, loosening his grip on his hair. "Next time, wake me," he said, his voice hoarse from both sleep and the low-burning hunger that was still eating at them both.

When they parted, Andrei looked up to find Ian staring at them with his mouth hanging open. Well, there went that secret.

"Ha! I knew it!" Ian exclaimed, pointing at both of them.

"Let it go, E," Lucas grumbled, stepping around the island to pour himself a cup of the coffee that Ian had already started. "It's not what you think."

"You know, that's exactly what Andrei said."

"That's because he's not an idiot." Lucas picked up the folded newspaper that Ian had brought in with him and moved to the small dining room table, while Ian continued cooking breakfast, occasionally throwing Lucas a dirty look.

Out of place and off-kilter, Andrei struggled to find his footing as if he were trapped between two worlds. After a couple seconds of indecision, he retreated to the one he knew. Grabbing the gun off the counter, Andrei turned to head back upstairs. He could shower and get dressed while Lucas spent some time with his friend. Maybe he could read a chapter of the book he'd been working on the other day.

"Where are you going?" Ian demanded when Andrei hadn't taken more than two steps. Andrei turned back to find Ian looking utterly confused and maybe even a little hurt that Andrei was leaving.

"Shower and get dressed." Andrei turned a little to look at Lucas. "I'll be ready when you want to leave for the office, Mr. Vallois."

"Sit," Lucas growled, not even looking up from the paper.

Ian smiled at him. "I'd do it. He's a bear until he's had a couple cups of coffee. I'm making crêpes today."

"With bacon," Lucas added.

"No."

"Sausage."

"No. Fruit."

That brought the newspaper down so that Lucas could glare at Ian. "Damn it! You've got to stop this healthy shit, E. I need meat in the morning. Sausage, bacon, steak, ham. Something with substance."

Andrei bit back a smile as he fixed himself a cup of coffee and took the seat next to Lucas, content to watch the byplay between the two friends. They really were like brothers. Ian was incredibly easy-going and quick to smile, while Lucas was definitely bear-like regardless of whether he had his coffee. He was prone to giving orders and simply expecting everyone to fall into line.

"That healthy shit is going to keep you from having a heart attack in a year. Besides, last week was the omelet with the four different meats. You can't have that every time."

"Watch me. Crêpes with fruit? Come on, E—"

Ian slammed a knife down on the counter and glared at Lucas. "Are you seriously criticizing my cooking?" he demanded in a soft voice that sent a chill down Andrei's spine. The guy wasn't very big, but damn.

"Fuck," Lucas grumbled under his breath. To Andrei's amazement, Lucas's shoulders slumped and it looked as if he were slightly cringing. "Of course not. I'm just saying—"

"If I were you, I'd stop now or I might choose to stop pretending that I didn't get a fucking call from Rowe two nights this week and that I don't know you spent last night being shot at."

Andrei jerked, frowning. He'd hoped that their recent escapades had escaped Ian's knowledge. They'd had an enjoyable time at Rialto just two nights ago and he'd wanted the man to think the night had ended with that. Lucas's hand dropped to his wrist, his thumb lightly rubbing against the top of his hand. He looked at the other man to find him trying to reassure him. Andrei blamed himself for that mess in Price Hill and that wasn't going to change. They'd both made mistakes in judgment and other people had gotten hurt because of it.

Pushing to his feet, Andrei walked over to the island to stand next to Ian, wary of the knife still clenched in his fist. "Is there something I can do to help?"

Ian froze at his words, his head lifting so he could look at Andrei in shock.

"I'm a horrible cook, but I can chop and wash."

"Yeah, sure," Ian said slowly as if still trying to shake free of his surprise. "Cut up these strawberries. Small but not fine, please."

Andrei set to work, doing each task Ian set before him, checking with the young man every so often to make sure that he was doing it to his exact specifications. Occasionally, Ian would give him a tip or a trick. But within a couple minutes, Ian was smiling again, his carefree nature back in place. They chatted companionably, with Ian talking about learning how to cook and some of the disasters he'd created, while Andrei added his own tales.

As they finished, Andrei looked up to find that Lucas had set his newspaper aside and was just watching them work, a smile haunting his lips. Andrei quickly looked away, trying not to think about the strange swirl of emotions in his chest that look created. This was just breakfast. And Lucas was just a job. They'd enjoy some physical distractions, but when the job was over, Andrei would go back to his life and Lucas would go back to his. There was no overlap. No chance of their paths crossing again. Andrei was simply trying to make sure that Lucas could go back to his life with as few problems as possible when it was all over.

With that firm reminder in place, Andrei sat down with Lucas and Ian to enjoy a delicious breakfast where the conversation was no more serious than grumbling about the new streetcar construction going slower than expected and that traffic would continue to be bad into the new year. When they were done, Lucas excused himself to make a phone call, giving Ian a quick hug before disappearing up the stairs.

Ian chuckled to himself as he picked up his plate and Lucas's and walked it over to the sink. "Always doing ten things at once. I learned a few years ago that if I didn't bring him food, he wouldn't eat unless it was part of a meeting. I had to threaten his new assistant to schedule more lunch meetings just for that reason."

"Don't tell Rowe," Andrei blurted out as he handed over his plate.

Ian lifted his brows in surprise, a smiling growing on his face. "I thought there was nothing going on."

"There's not."

"But..."

"I don't want to lose my job over nothing."

"I find it hard to believe this is nothing when Lucas has already threatened Snow and Rowe over you."

Andrei lurched back a step, feeling as if the air had been knocked out of his lungs. "What?"

Ian winced. "Oh, you didn't hear that, huh?"

"What are you talking about?"

"Rowe told Lucas he'd fired you and Lucas...kind of lost it. Snow talked him down." Ian smoothed over the news. It wasn't helping much since Andrei was tightly clutching the edge of the island with one hand. "Lucas can get protective at times."

Andrei nodded, trying to organize his thoughts. "It was a stressful night."

Ian continued to clean up the area, wiping a damp cloth over the counters even though they didn't need it. "I feel like I should warn you about Lucas," he started a bit awkwardly. He glanced over his shoulder at Andrei and gave him a weak smile. "He can be…difficult."

"I've learned that firsthand."

"And closed."

Andrei leaned back against the island, crossing his arms over his chest, trying to appear relaxed when he was feeling anything but. "Seen that too."

"Lucas doesn't date men. Ever. He's got these rules."

"He seems the type to have lots of rules," Andrei said when Ian paused.

"Actually, no, but when it comes to his sexual exploits with men, he's got very specific rules. The only reason I bring it up is that it looks like he's breaking his rules for you and I worry."

Andrei smiled at Ian. "You're worried that he's going to get hurt."

Ian didn't return his smile when he turned to face Andrei. In fact, his eyes looked incredibly sad. "No." Dropping the rag in the sink, Ian leaned against the sink, folding his arms over his stomach. "I think you could be good for him. You're a hell of a lot better than that Breckenridge bitch. But I think Lucas will fall back into his old ways as soon as this is over and…"

"I'll be kicked to the curb."

"Even if he does have feelings for you."

"Can I ask you a question?"

Ian hesitated, his frown growing deeper. "Yes, but I might not answer. I don't like betraying Lucas's privacy, but I also don't like the idea of you going into this blind."

"Is Lucas in denial about being gay?"

Peels of Ian's laughter rang off the high ceiling, lightening the mood. "No," Ian said, still chuckling. "Lucas knows he's gay and accepts it in his own way. His problem is that he's got this perfect idea of who he wants to be in the professional world, this ideal of the rich, successful man, but he's convinced himself that that image can't include being gay. I don't know. Maybe he reads too much of *Forbes* or *Fortune*."

Andrei gazed off toward the stairs, weighing Ian's words. "He seems pretty perfect already to me," he murmured, more thinking aloud than actually talking to Ian.

"When he's happy, he is."

Andrei looked back at Ian. "And when he's not?"

"Get a hose, because the world will burn."

A smirk lifted half of Andrei's mouth. "Thanks for the warning."

Andrei watched Ian moving easily around Lucas's kitchen, wiping off counters and drying the few pans and utensils he'd used while cooking. There was an easygoing air about him, as if he were completely content with life and the world flowing around him. Andrei had met too few people in life that exuded that kind of peace.

"Have you always been gay?" Andrei asked, the words tripping past his lips before he'd even realized they'd escaped. Andrei's mouth dropped open in horror as the other man looked at him strangely. "Holy fuck," Andrei groaned. "I can't believe I just said that. I'm so sorry, man. I didn't—"

Ian's laughter rang through the open room. "I don't think I've ever been asked that."

"I'm sorry."

"I don't know about always, but I've known for a long time."

Andrei nodded, dropping his gaze down to the countertop. He didn't know why he'd asked Ian that question. Or maybe he did but he certainly didn't know how to keep going. Everything that he was feeling, everything in his life that surrounded Lucas Vallois, was now this tangled knot. Every time he tugged on one strand to untangle it, the whole ball tightened up, making the knot worse.

"But everything is new and confusing for you." Ian leaned against the island opposite him, a dishtowel twisted in his hands. He shook his head. "You scream straight. I'm surprised Lucas has let anything happen."

"He was...reluctant," Andrei admitted and then gave a little shrug. "But I've been with men."

Ian lifted one disbelieving brow. "We're not talking about a quick fuck and then gone here. No, Lucas was your first kiss. Your first touch. He's the first one to reach you in here." Ian tapped his chest over his heart, smiling gently.

Andrei gave a jerky nod. He didn't question why Ian could read him so well, he was just grateful that he could. "I just...It changes things. I had this idea of who I was and now I don't know if that's changed."

"Because you're attracted to a man?"

He shook his head. "No." He stopped and clenched his teeth. It was almost painful to say the words, the embarrassment burning through him, but he needed to talk and damn it, he felt that Ian could understand a little. "It's that I'm attracted to Lucas. He's..."

"Beautiful," Ian supplied and Andrei glared at him. That word went without saying. "But I think you mean that Lucas is one hundred percent pure alpha. He's controlling and dictatorial. He's dominant and there's no way around that. It's his comfort zone and I have a feeling it's the only way he knows how to be."

"Yes."

"And you think there can be only one dominant in the bedroom."

"Yes."

"And you were sure that that was your role."

Andrei lifted his eyes back to Ian's face and nodded. He was holding the edge of the island so hard that his knuckles were turning white. Andrei had spent the majority of his childhood and too damned many of his teen years being bullied. He was nearly twenty before he finally gained real muscle bulk and dedicated his existence to fight training. Everything had driven him to being a professional fighter. It was his way of taking charge of his life, of stomping out the bullies.

But the injury that took that future from him had left him floating the past three years. Had he lost everything that he'd been fighting for? Had he given up that power? That control?

Ian smiled at him. It wasn't a look of pity but understanding. "I have two things to say to that." He held up one finger, "First, submissive does not equal weak. You've got to get that stupid thought out of your head right now." Reaching across the island, Ian tapped Andrei's forehead twice hard. "If you choose to be submissive to Lucas's dominant, do not think for one second that he will believe you to be weak. He trusts you with his life and he wouldn't do that if he didn't think you were a strong, capable person. Besides, Lucas Vallois doesn't tolerate weak people in his life."

"And second?" Andrei prompted, nearly giddy with the relief that was unwinding tense muscles through his body.

Ian's smile became something sly and almost wicked, giving Andrei a glimpse of a totally different side of the man that seemed to be perpetually hidden beneath his sweet exterior. "With the right person, a submissive has just as much power in the bedroom as the dominant. In fact, I'd wager with the right person, a submissive can get a dominant to do whatever he wants."

Andrei straightened, feeling the blush creep back into his cheeks at Ian's words, but there was no mistaking his meaning. He'd already seen hints of it with Lucas. The right touch, a slight brush or caress to manipulate Lucas one way or another. Yes, Lucas was dominating, but he turned himself practically inside-out trying to give Andrei as much pleasure as possible. It was a subtle power, but it was intoxicating all the same.

"But the key is finding the right person," Ian stressed, his smile disappearing completely. "Lucas is a great guy and I love him. I'd do anything for Lucas, but for you, is he the right person?" He shrugged.

"I think…I'd like the chance to find out."

This time Ian's smile was sad and a little pitying. "I hope he gives you the chance." Ian turned and folded the dishtowel in his hand before placing it next to the sink. "Oh and being gay doesn't change who you are. At the end of the day, you're still Andrei Hadeon, badass bodyguard."

Andrei gave a little snort. "And you're Ian Pierce, kickass chef who is on the fast track to making me fat."

"And don't worry. I won't say anything to Rowe. It may seem like we tell each other everything, but…well…there's nothing to tell."

After Andrei locked the door behind Ian, he did a quick sweep of the first floor before heading up to the second. He glanced in the guest bedroom, placing his gun on the bureau, before peeking into Lucas's bedroom to find it empty. He continued on to the office where Lucas was pacing behind the desk with his cell phone to his ear. When he caught sight of Andrei, he held up one finger, keeping him from backing out of the room again. Lucas issued a couple of sharp orders and then ended the call.

Coming around the desk, Lucas wrapped his arms around Andrei, being careful not to touch his back while pulling him flush against him. The kiss was rough and hungry. Andrei pulled back, nipping at Lucas's lips, teasing him before Lucas finally captured his head again with one hand twisted in his hair so that they could resume the passionate kiss that had started between them. Andrei couldn't believe how much he loved the way Lucas took control, setting a fire between them that was burning away all of Andrei's doubts and lingering hang-ups. Ian's warning words, while well meaning, were forgotten under the onslaught of strong hands exploring his body and intoxicating kisses.

Lucas pulled away, moving to rub his nose along Andrei's cheek. "Thank you," he said roughly.

"For the kiss?"

"For Ian. You made him happy. I'm…I'm not good at it sometimes."

"He doesn't need to suffer because we're a pair of jackasses."

Lucas huffed a laugh before turning his face back for another kiss. It was like they couldn't get enough of each other.

Andrei groaned when Lucas's hands slipped inside of his boxers and cupped his ass, pulling his groin more tightly against Lucas's. "Should we continue this in the shower? I'm curious as to what you look like pinned against the wall, coming on my chest."

Lucas jerked away from him suddenly. He held out one hand toward Andrei as if to keep the man at arm's length. "No."

"Really?"

"I have to be in the office in an hour."

Andrei licked his lips and a shudder went through Lucas. "I'm pretty sure I can get you to come in less than an hour."

"No doubt, but then I'll want to get you off. And we'd be useless after that."

"Later?"

"Fuck yes," Lucas moaned as he turned toward the door.

Andrei caught him before he could reach the hall, wrapping one strong arm around the other man's chest while pulling Lucas's back against his chest. Andrei buried his face in Lucas's neck, his hot breath dancing along his ear. "Are you going to think about me when you jerk off in the shower?"

"Yes," Lucas hissed, tilting his head to the side as Andrei ran the tip of his tongue along his earlobe.

Andrei slid his hand along Lucas's stomach and down into his loose pants. A loud moan slipped from Lucas as Andrei wrapped his fingers around his hard cock and slowly stroked him. His thumb swept lightly over the engorged tip, sliding over the pre-come that was leaking from him. His own cock swelled painfully and he moaned, thrusting his hips against Lucas's ass. They were both on edge, needing relief, but the desperate rush was also part of the fun. Andrei kept up with the motion only until Lucas jerked his hips higher, seeking even more friction before he released him and stepped back.

"Just to get you started," Andrei taunted. When Lucas looked back over his shoulder, Andrei lifted the finger he'd run over the head of

Lucas's dick to his mouth and licked it, his hot gaze never wavering from Lucas's face.

It almost sounded like a growl escaped Lucas, but he shook his head and continued down the hall to his bedroom. "Longest fucking day ever," he muttered under his breath.

Yeah, but Andrei was pretty sure that Lucas was going to be a hell of a lot of fun when they got home that night.

Chapter 12

Lucas's office was enormous. Andrei tried not to gape when his gaze skimmed over the two walls of windows that looked out on the Ohio River, the long board room table, and the scattering of modern furniture that contrasted strangely with the old-fashioned dark mahogany desk. The office was bigger than his entire apartment. Andrei ruefully shook his head, trying to ignore the butterflies in his stomach. This was a different world entirely.

Candace attempted to follow Lucas into his office as soon as he and Andrei arrived, but Lucas cut her off, telling her to come back in twenty minutes, giving them a short time alone. Andrei watched Lucas as he stood in front of his desk, his hands opening and closing at his sides as if he were suddenly uneasy. So reminiscent of their first day together when Lucas simply didn't know what to do with him. Was that truly just three days ago? It felt like so much more time had passed. He knew this man. Didn't he? As Lucas's expression hardened, settling into the cold businessman that he presented to the world, Andrei began to doubt that he did.

"I don't expect to need to leave my office today," Lucas announced. "I'll have my meetings in here."

"That'll make things easier. I'll stay out of the way." Andrei pointed toward a chair in the corner of the office with a little reading lamp beside it. "No one will notice I'm there."

"I will."

Andrei frowned. "I can sit outside your office. In the reception area. Screen people before they walk in."

"No," Lucas said sharply. "You're in here. Can't give Rowe an excuse to fire you."

Andrei stared at the man, unable to tell if he was joking or if he was completely serious until Lucas smirked slightly. It was on the tip of his tongue to mention the threat he'd apparently delivered in the hospital, but he swallowed the words. Now was not the time to get into that.

"Candace will bring lunch at one. Sushi, I think." He motioned off to a door half hidden behind a large palm. "That's my private bathroom and there's a mini fridge under the bar there with juice, water, and tea if you need something to drink."

Andrei frowned as he looked around the office. "I forgot the book I was reading," he mumbled and then looked over at Lucas. "I was cruelly distracted this morning." Lucas fought back his own grin as he stepped behind his desk. They'd run into each other in the hall as they finished dressing. Several heated kisses later, Lucas had been forced to turn back for a new shirt because the one he had been wearing was suddenly missing most of its buttons.

Lucas picked up a bag with the name of a local bookseller on the front and handed it over to Andrei. "Candace picked these up yesterday for you. Hopefully there is something in there that you will enjoy."

Andrei's jaw dropped to see close to twenty paperbacks in the bag. He glimpsed over some of the covers. All appeared to be science-fiction or fantasy, the hottest titles on the market and most he'd not found a moment to pick up himself. Not one client had ever thought of his comfort or entertainment while he passed a long day in relative boredom. He'd suffered long days and nights, cold, starving, and sleepless to keep his clients safe. Lucas was the first person to treat him as a human being and not as a piece of furniture or lifeless weapon.

"Thank you," Andrei said, unable to lift his voice above a rough whisper. His hands tightly clutched the plastic bag so that it loudly crinkled. "I'll pay you back for these. I—"

"Stop."

Andrei jerked at the unexpectedly harsh tone. He blinked, surprised to find Lucas glaring at him. "What?"

"If this desk wasn't separating us right now, I'd be kissing you so stop."

"Sorry?" Andrei grinned.

Lucas sighed and continued in a low voice as if he were afraid someone would overhear him. "No kissing in the office. No...anything here. Just go sit."

Andrei nodded and turned away, heading to the chair in the corner. "Yes, Mr. Vallois."

"And that's another thing," Lucas said, halting Andrei. "Never call me that again."

"What? Mr. Vallois?"

"Yes," Lucas hissed. "It sounds wrong now. Don't say that."

Andrei nearly laughed out loud. Lucas looked so frustrated and twisted up that Andrei wanted to have pity on the man, but he just couldn't. He walked over to the desk, standing close enough that his thighs were pressed against the front. "And what am I supposed to call you? Sir?"

"Andrei," Lucas nearly growled.

"Lucas," he replied in a matching growl. The other man closed his eyes as if in pain. "Lucas," he repeated on a gasp.

Eyes flicked open and Lucas started to reach for Andrei when a knock on the double doors echoed through the office. Lucas jerked back, his cheeks flushed like a teenage boy getting caught with his hand down his pants. Andrei's head dropped back on a deep laugh that he could no longer contain. The other man glared at him and pointed toward the chair, sending the bodyguard to his corner with his books. Lucas would probably get even later when they were alone at the penthouse, but it was worth it to see the man flustered.

Candace marched into the office with a pile of files, a tablet and a laptop in her arms. She never glanced at Andrei as she crossed the office and took a seat in front of Lucas. Andrei sat and watched them work for several minutes as she plowed through one item after another with precision and efficiency. At the same time, Lucas maintained an impressive speed, never hesitating as he snapped one order after another.

Smiling to himself, Andrei turned his back on them and conducted a quick inspection of the office to make sure there were no other ways in or out before settling in his selected chair. It certainly wasn't a bad place to spend the day and he had plenty of books to read. But getting lost in a book was the last thing Lucas was planning to let him do.

Candace scurried away less than thirty minutes later only to have the receptionist usher in a tall, black man dressed all in black carrying two large bags. Andrei immediately came to his feet, moving to stand between the stranger and Lucas.

"Luc, dear, you do not even want to know how many appointments I cancelled for you today," the man announced, dramatically dropping both bags on the floor with a heavy thud. "Carol Sanderson spent twenty minutes screaming her bottle-blond head off at Julie this morning. But then I just grabbed the phone and said, 'Lucas Vallois needs me.'" He snapped his fingers sharply. "And that shut her up."

Placing a hand on Andrei's shoulder, Lucas gently squeezed, reassuring him without a word before he attempted to step around his bodyguard. He gave the newcomer a reserved smile that didn't quite reach his eyes. "You're the only one I trust, B."

B immediately started to flutter around Lucas, touching his short brown locks, moving them here and there like a bird settling the feathers of its chick. "Everything looks fine here. You're finally using that conditioner I gave you."

"It's not me."

The black man's eyes immediately jumped to Andrei and widened. "Well, hello beautiful," the man purred, his grin widening. He started forward and Andrei lurched back two steps, turning his wide, confused gaze on Lucas. "Oh sweetheart, I don't bite on the first date."

B moved a little slower this time as he stepped around Andrei to pull out the band holding his hair back. B ran his fingers through the strands. His touch was gentle yet firm. "Oh sweetheart, what have you done to your beautiful hair? What is this? Burned?"

"Something like that," Andrei replied, but his eyes were locked on Lucas who was grinning at him.

"Can you fix it, B?" Lucas inquired. "We have a business appointment this evening and he needs to be perfect."

"Of course I can fix it! What a ridiculous question!"

"Get to it then. Set up in here." Lucas gave an absent wave of his hand, indicating anywhere in the office. He started to walk back to his desk, but Andrei roughly grabbed his elbow, stopping him.

"Can I speak to you a moment, Mr. Vallois?" Andrei demanded through clenched teeth. Lucas's eyes narrowed on him and he gave a curt nod before allowing Andrei to escort him to the farthest point of the room.

Out of the corner of his eyes, Andrei saw B setting out a drop cloth, and getting all his equipment organized so he could work. All the while he was humming to himself.

"What the hell are you doing?" Andrei demanded, fighting to keep his voice low.

"What are you talking about?"

"The books and now this haircut. I'm not comfortable with this."

Lucas stared at him, his brow wrinkled in confusion. "Why?"

Andrei's mouth fell open for a second and then shut as he struggled for the right words. "You can't spend money on me like this. It's...weird," he finished a bit lamely, his gaze skipping away from the other man to dart out the window and then back.

"Your hair was damaged because of my stubbornness. It's my responsibility to fix that."

"But—"

"And you wouldn't have left me alone in the middle of the day to take care of that, right?"

"No, but—"

"So I brought B here to fix my mistake."

"And the books—"

"To keep you from getting bored during the day and prowling the office, distracting me from work," Lucas bit out as if it were perfectly obvious.

Andrei glared at him for several seconds and Lucas returned it, making him feel as if *he* was the one being utterly obtuse. "Is this how you've succeeded in business? You drive everyone else insane?"

Lucas's glare dissolved into a smug grin. "I'm very good at getting what I want."

"Not everything, Mr. Vallois."

"We talked about that." There was a bite to his voice as he took a step closer to Andrei. Andrei saw something uneasy flit through Lucas's eyes. It had been brief, but Andrei had a feeling Lucas had thought he'd back down.

Andrei licked his lips, his heart picking up its pace when Lucas's eyes followed the movement. He had better ways to get even with the domineering Lucas Vallois that didn't include physical violence. "So…no kissing in the office?"

"No."

"Ever?"

"Not. Ever."

"Does that ban include other fun activities?"

"Yes."

Smiling, Andrei stepped around Lucas to the end of the boardroom table, running his fingers over the slick, glossy surface. He lifted hungry eyes to the other man, wringing a hiss out of him. "That's a shame because I think this table was made for fucking."

"Andrei…" he said in a near groan, closing his eyes. The muscles in his jaw flexed and jumped as he ground his teeth together.

Andrei took the opportunity to step close, brushing his arm against Lucas's. The man flinched, sucking in a harsh breath, but he didn't open his eyes. "Shame you also don't date men, because I can think of a half a dozen places in this room alone that I'd like to fuck you and then I want to take you home and christen every room in that damned penthouse. Hell, everywhere you look in this office and everywhere you look at home, I want you to remember how we fucked there. I want those memories burned into your brain. And that…takes time."

Lucas's eyes jumped open and Andrei basked in the scorching heat pouring from the man. Andrei couldn't remember ever being on the receiving end of such a desperate, hungry, stunned look. It took all his self-control to not grab the back of Lucas's neck and drag him closer to a kiss. With a smug smile of his own, Andrei turned and walked over to where B had finished his set up. He felt Lucas's eyes burning into his back as he moved across the expansive office before the other man returned to his desk to work.

Unfortunately, Andrei's triumph was short-lived as B dragged him to the bathroom to wash his hair in the sink. Shucking his jacket, shirt, and holster, he shoved his handgun in his pants and quickly washed his hair himself, straining to hear anyone who might enter the office. B complained the entire time, but Andrei brushed the man off, finishing the shampoo in record time so he could return.

As he settled in the chair B indicated, Andrei's eyes drifted to Lucas. The handsome man's brow was furrowed as he read through a sheaf of papers, a pen tapping against his jaw. He was lost in his work again. But Andrei was curious at how well Lucas could completely block him out.

"So, my angel, what are we going to do with your hair?" B inquired as he brushed it out. "Luc wants me to clean it up, but shall we change the style?"

"Chop it off. Make it short. Really short," Andrei said firmly.

"No!" Lucas thundered, proving that he was paying attention to them. B and Andrei both looked up. "Preserve the length, B. Don't take off a single centimeter you don't have to."

Andrei's laugh filled the office and Lucas blushed before dropping his eyes to the papers in his hand. *Busted!*

"Yes, sir," B said softly and quickly set to work without another word.

Smiling to himself, he started asking B questions, trying to set the man at ease again. Within a couple of minutes, the stylist happily explained that B was short for Ben—not even Bernard or Benjamin or Benedict, but plain old, boring Ben—which was just far too mundane for a man of his obvious personality and style.

Work continued around them. Each time someone needed to come into the office, Lucas would tell Andrei and Andrei would force B to stop his work so he could stand, his hand on his gun until Andrei could judge that Lucas was safe. Everyone took this strange arrangement in stride, never questioning it. They either didn't find it bizarre or they knew better than to question Lucas about it. Andrei had a feeling that it was the latter.

The trio was alone when B finished his work on Andrei's hair with a flourish. He stepped back, arms extended, waiting for Lucas's judgment on his work.

"Nice job," Lucas said, barely looking up from the report he was reading.

Andrei nearly choked a laugh. Poor B was crushed by the man's lack of reaction after his adamant stance on how little was to be cut off. Andrei ran his fingers through his hair, appreciating the softness. It was off his shoulders but long enough to easily grab a fistful, which should please Lucas. Andrei didn't want to stop and really think about why that was important to him.

"It's perfect, B," Andrei said, smiling up at the other man, as he handed back the mirror he had been holding.

"Thank you." B sniffed, giving Andrei an unexpected hug before starting to clean up his area.

Lucas walked over when B was packed up again. He handed the man a white envelope and smiled. "I appreciate the rush and your skill."

B paused in the act of taking the envelope, his dark eyes sliding over to Andrei. "I'll cut my price in half if you let me keep him."

Lucas's smile widened. "No."

"My entire fee?"

"No."

B looked over his shoulder at Andrei and gave a wistful smile, batting his large brown eyes. "You know where to find me, sweetheart. I'm all yours."

"Flirt," Andrei said, smiling as he slipped into his suit jacket.

B winked at him and then waltzed out of the office with his bags on his shoulders as if he didn't have a care in the world.

Andrei turned his attention to Lucas who was watching him with an unreadable expression. "Look okay?"

Lucas merely nodded, his jaw shifting as if he were clenching his teeth.

Andrei's grin widened. "You want to touch it?"

"More than I've wanted anything in a long time," Lucas admitted with a low voice that sent a tremor through Andrei.

He blinked and there was suddenly a wealth of open longing in Lucas's vibrant green-gray eyes. It took his breath away.

Andrei took a step toward him and Lucas immediately shuffled backward, a pained looked crossing his face as he shoved his hands in his pockets. Lucas was telling the truth. He did want to run his fingers through his hair. He was obviously determined to keep that private life separated from his professional life, even if they were alone in his office. A sharp pain ached in Andrei's chest, but he hid it behind a little smirk.

"Care to tell me about this business appointment I have this evening?" he asked, dispelling the tension that had thickened in the air. He'd teased the man enough already and they had bigger concerns to occupy their time.

Lucas smiled back, no longer clenching his teeth. "*We* have an appointment." He walked over to the windows looking out on the river and Great American Ballpark, home field for the Cincinnati Reds baseball team. "I thought we would conduct a little research tonight."

"I'm afraid to ask how much this is going to piss off your friends." Andrei came to stand beside Lucas.

"Assuming nothing goes wrong, not at all."

"Yeah, but when has 'nothing gone wrong' happened so far?"

Lucas's shoulders slumped and he glared out the window. "It's a black tie gala for charity at the Cincinnati Art Museum. The kind of money strolling around that place means there will be plenty of security. Nothing is going to happen. We'll be there and back within a couple hours, safe and sound. No problems."

"Ugh," Andrei said, pressing his hand to his stomach. "You saying 'no problems' actually made me sick. I think you just jinxed us."

"Shut up," Lucas grumbled.

"What kind of research are we doing at the Art Museum?"

"Thomas Lynton will be there."

Andrei's eyebrows jumped in surprise. He hadn't expected Lucas to want to track down Lynton, but then he probably should have. Lucas definitely wasn't the type to sit back and let others take care of things. "You sure?"

"He's a major sponsor for the gala. He is every year. He'll be there. I want to ask him a few questions."

Folding his arms over his chest, he leaned one shoulder against the glass. "Are you sure he's going to talk to you? You said you were only acquaintances."

"I think he might be more willing to talk to me after I confess that I wasn't in a car accident as Candace has been telling everyone."

"If you were in a car accident, what has your assistant been telling people about me?"

Lucas turned, leaning his shoulder against the window facing Andrei, his hands shoved in his pockets. "You? You're my nurse."

Andrei snorted. He couldn't pass for a nurse in any way, but it was a fun lie. "Am I a sexy nurse?"

His smile grew wider as his eyes slowly swept down from the top of Andrei's head to his feet and back up again. "Definitely. And I'm not sharing you with B or anyone else so long as I have you."

It was a struggle for Andrei to remain perfectly still when everything within him demanded that he close the few feet between them so he could touch Lucas, kiss him, something. A thousand comments crossed his mind, demands to know if he would have to share Lucas and how long Lucas saw this arrangement lasting. He thought about making a similar proclamation and even making a joke, but in the end, he settled for silence and a smile. Ian's words of warning were ringing in his head and he was afraid anything he said would push Lucas away. In truth, Andrei didn't know what he wanted from Lucas. He just knew he didn't want it to end before he figured that out.

"If this is a black tie event, I might have a problem," Andrei finally said. "As I don't have a black tie."

Lucas grinned and pushed away from the window as another knock echoed from the door. At his call, a pair of men in suits carrying a variety of garment bags bustled into the office.

"Fuck, Lucas. We've got to talk about this," Andrei growled, his good humor dissolving.

"Oh, I'm charging Rowe for this," Lucas quickly countered, his grin turning evil. "He really should supply his people with the proper attire to keep up with their client's schedule."

Scrubbing his hand over his face, Andrei tried to settle the unease building in his stomach. Lucas spending money on him constantly didn't sit well with him. Maybe the idea of trying to develop something more with Lucas beside a few hot fucks was stupid. How much did they actually have in common? They traveled in different circles and likely enjoyed completely different things.

A hand clamped down on his shoulder and Andrei looked up to stare directly into Lucas's worried gaze. "This is bothering you."

"Yes, it's fucking bothering me," Andrei snapped. "You can't keep making decisions that impact me without telling *me*. I'm not some brainless Ken doll that you can dress up and move around. I'm an adult and can take care of myself."

"I know. I thought it would be easier if I handled it."

"It's not." Andrei struggled to keep his voice low.

Lucas's brow furrowed and he looked out the window. "I'm sorry. I didn't intend to piss you off."

"You can't keep spending money on me. It's wrong."

Lucas's gaze returned to his face. It was obvious by the furrow in his brow that he still didn't understand, but he finally shrugged, releasing Andrei's shoulder. "Fine. You've got dinner after the gala. Pizza. Pepperoni, Italian sausage, and black olives. I trust you know a place."

Andrei could only shake his head as he walked over to the newcomers. He gave himself over to a series of measurements and fittings as the two tailors made adjustments to an existing tuxedo so that he could wear it that evening. After making a few initial comments, Lucas slipped over to his desk to resume his work. Again, people came and went, but no one seemed to react to the odd things going on in the office.

At lunch, Lucas and Andrei attempted to brainstorm why Lucas's investment in Price Hill had made him a target, but neither of the two men felt as if any progress was made or even could be made until more information was gathered from Thomas Lynton.

Andrei fell into a book after lunch while Lucas worked for the rest of the day. Time slipped away and it was after six when Lucas announced that they needed to return to the penthouse so that they could dress for the evening. The tailors had said Andrei's tux would be delivered to The Ascent by four p.m.

As they rode the elevator down to the parking garage, Andrei looked at Lucas's reflection in the silver doors. "Is this a normal day for you?"

"You mean the fittings, haircuts, and meetings?"

Andrei nodded.

"No. It's usually just meetings."

"Thank you. You didn't have to. We could have worked something out. Rowe could have gone in my place," Andrei offered up a little haltingly.

Lucas turned his head so he could meet Andrei's gaze. "I trust you with my back. I want you there." Lucas sighed as he tacked on, "But I also want you comfortable. It's…it's a different world. They're…"

"Judgmental. Critical. Elitist," Andrei supplied with a smile when Lucas's voice trailed off.

"Yes."

"Do you like it? That world."

Lucas frowned and looked up at the digital readout of the floors as they steadily ticked lower. "No," he whispered. "I have little time that's my own and I can think of several other things and other people I'd rather be with than these people. But…"

Andrei grunted in understanding. This was the life that Lucas was fighting so hard to build for himself. He wanted so badly to be considered a part of this rich elite that he was willing to suck up a crappy evening with a bunch of people he didn't like and probably didn't respect.

The elevator pinged and the doors slid open with a soft rumble. Andrei moved first, stopping in the doorway. He held both doors open, blocking the way so Lucas couldn't pass. "Do we have time for a little fun when we get to the penthouse before we put on your fancy duds?"

Lucas laughed, deep and loud, and Andrei relaxed. It was the first true laugh he'd heard out of the man all day.

"I wish."

"No?"

Lucas shook his head. "The gala starts at 7:30 and I want to get there as close to the start as possible."

Andrei's shoulder slumped and he groaned. That didn't sound enticing at all. Not when he had other things in mind to pass the evening.

Lucas closed the distance between them and threaded his fingers through Andrei's hair, so that the other man sighed happily. "Get there early. Leave early. And the rest of the night is ours." Lucas's hot breath danced across Andrei's ear.

"Thank fucking God," Andrei growled, grabbing Lucas's arm to pull him out of the elevator and toward the car. Lucas's laughter echoed through the parking garage, bouncing off the concrete structure so that it wrapped around them. It lifted Andrei's spirit. The cold, distant man he'd spent the day with was fading, giving way to the man that sent chills through him and made him long for something more.

Chapter 13

The Art Museum glowed with twinkling white lights and candles in delicate hurricane glasses reflecting off shining marble. Cincinnati's elite had turned out in their finest to flaunt their wealth and, if anyone happened to remember it, raise money for the Fine Arts Fund. Lucas had attended only once several years ago at the request of a woman he'd been dating at the time. The relationship had ended the next day and Lucas had been content to cut a check each year rather than make another appearance. In fact, he had a rule that he only attended these functions if he could accomplish other business while making the required social appearance.

Tonight held to that rule if he could get in a few words with Thomas Lynton while making his usual donation. But instead of a high-heeled beauty wrapped in a designer gown on his arm, Lucas walked next to a man who simply took his breath away. When Lucas had first seen Andrei in his tailored tuxedo, he was sure he'd never seen anyone look more handsome. His raven-black hair shone as it fell free and framed his clean-shaven face. It cast his dark eyes in shadow, making him look even more mysterious and exotic. Lucas was torn between wanting to show Andrei off to the glittering elite and locking the door of the penthouse so that he would never have to share the man.

"Any last words of advice?" Andrei said in a low voice after Lucas handed over his tickets and they stepped inside the museum.

"Smile. Keep it simple. And if anyone asks you a question, spout a bunch of useless gibberish. No one will question it."

A snort escaped Andrei and he grinned, causing Lucas's heart to quicken. "Got it."

"And don't leave the main room without me."

Andrei lifted both eyebrows in surprise.

Lucas smirked. "Both the men and women at these things are wolves. They get you off alone and they'll eat you alive."

Andrei coughed, covering up his laugh as Lucas smiled and strolled over to the nearest bar. He bypassed the champagne and various wines for a tumbler of bourbon while Andrei stuck with water and a slice of lime. They paused for a moment, surveying the scene.

"With all this security, it doesn't look like you needed me tonight," Andrei said as he lifted his glass to his mouth.

Lucas frowned, his eyes skimming over the guards in obvious blue uniforms mixed with the grim-faced men with ear pieces and bulges under the jackets marking them as part of the private security force. Would any of them risk their lives to protect Lucas? No. But that wasn't why Lucas had brought Andrei along. If he was honest with himself, security hadn't even crossed his mind, but he wasn't ready to face those thoughts just yet.

From there, Lucas launched into the fray with Andrei at his side. It had been months since Lucas had made a social appearance and everyone was eager to hear about his supposed car accident and the unfortunately break between him and Stephanie Breckenridge. Lucas deftly dodged and maneuvered through the pointed questions like a championship boxer, while introducing Andrei as an old friend who was in the security business.

To his surprise, Andrei took to the party and the people as if he'd been born to it. More than once, Lucas found himself staring as Andrei easily chatted about one thing or another with a voice of authority and then switched to politics or the Bengals season with a natural ease. Andrei was a chameleon and briefly, Lucas was jealous. He'd had to work so hard to become comfortable around these people, to give himself the right polished shine so that he wouldn't betray his own humble beginnings. But Andrei just made it look…easy, almost enjoyable.

While the sponsors made their speeches, Lucas and Andrei slipped away to a nearby gallery, pretending to look over the items for the silent auction.

"I'm impressed," Lucas said, keeping his voice low so they couldn't be overheard by the few people who were lingering nearby.

"Thought I'd embarrass you?" Andrei murmured.

"No, I just never thought you'd be so at ease considering your comments about your past."

Andrei grinned. "It's easy for me."

Lucas stopped in front of a large painting of the skyline done in a brilliant watercolor, but barely paid it attention. There was only Andrei. "Why?"

"I just tell myself that after tonight, I'll never see these people again. I can pretend to be whoever I want."

Lucas jerked his head back to stare at the painting, fighting to keep his face expressionless. Why did that statement hurt? His chest tightened and it was suddenly hard to draw in a breath. Andrei was right. In a few days, they would likely discover who was behind the threat and Andrei would walk away, returning to his life and moving on to his next assignment. There would be no reason for them to see each other again. He had his friends. His interests. His life. And Lucas had his small family.

It was such a sharp contrast to the hint that Andrei had dropped earlier in the day about dating. That tease had sucked the air right out of Lucas's lungs. Never for a second had he thought that Andrei would want to linger in his life. But once the seed had been planted, it had been the only thing he could think about, making it nearly impossible for him to get any work done. To keep Andrei in his life for more than a night. To touch his smooth skin each night, to hear his laugh, to watch his eyes burn with hunger or anger again and again—he was becoming obsessed with the idea.

"Shall we go see Mr. Lynton?" Andrei inquired after Lucas had remained silent for several minutes. "Or would you rather put a bid on this item?"

Lucas shook his head hard, freeing his mind from the quagmire of thoughts and emotions that were threatening to bog him down. He couldn't worry about his future with Andrei...as if they had a future.

"Let's go," he said a little sharper than he'd meant to. He closed his eyes for a second, centering himself and shoving his tangled emotions down. When he was sure he could speak evenly, he continued, "I spotted him at a table in the corner with his wife."

Leading the way into the main room, Lucas deftly wove through the crowd, shaking hands and smiling, promising to chat with others as he worked his way to Thomas Lynton's table. He slowed as they drew close, taking in the man's gaunt appearance. A cane leaned against his hip and there were more lines in his face. This was a man under stress and it was taking its toll on his health. His wife didn't appear to be much better with shadows under her eyes and one hand resting constantly on his arm, as if she were afraid that he would suddenly disappear. They would need to be delicate.

"Thomas, it's good to see you again," Lucas proclaimed with a broad smile when he reached their table.

The older man looked up, appearing slightly surprised Lucas was addressing him. "Lucas. It's been a while." He extended his hand.

"Thomas, Marilyn, may I introduce an old friend of mine, Andrei Hadeon?"

"A pleasure to meet you, Mr. Hadeon." The silver-haired woman held her hand out to Andrei and he smoothly captured her fingers and bent over them as if he'd done the motion a million times in his life.

"Andrei, please, Mrs. Lynton. And the pleasure is all mine."

"May we join you?" Lucas inquired, putting a hand on the back of a chair next to Thomas. The older man nodded, looking hesitant.

"If you don't mind my asking, how are you doing, Lucas?" Marilyn inquired, leaning forward a bit so that she could be heard over the string quartet playing on the other side of the room. "I'd heard that you were involved in a horrible car accident and then you and Miss Breckenridge parted ways."

Lucas gave her a winsome smile and a shrug. "My accident was more damaging than the end of my relationship."

Thomas chuckled softly. "And you look to have recovered from the accident quickly enough."

"Thank goodness. I never liked that idea of you with Stephanie Breckenridge," Marilyn admitted with a surprising burst of passion.

"Really?" Lucas sat back in his chair, unable to mask his surprise.

"That whole Breckenridge clan is nothing but a group of backstabbing, scheming trash." Thomas's gaze following some people passing nearby.

Marilyn reached across and patted Lucas's hand with her soft, wrinkled one. "Yes, you need to find someone nice. Someone who can take care of you and make you happy. Settle down at last."

Lucas narrowed his eyes on the older woman with the enigmatic smile. He thought it odd that she'd said someone rather than some girl, but he brushed it aside. Of course, it was likely just paranoia on his part because Andrei's presence felt more like a date than a friend, especially considering what he had planned for the man when they returned to his penthouse.

"Thank you, but I fear Thomas has snatched up the only angel at this party."

Marilyn giggled softly, blushing as she shook her head at him. "Silly boy," she murmured and then directed her attention at Andrei. "And what about you, Andrei? Are you married?"

"No, Mrs. Lynton. I've not been lucky enough to find the one I'm looking for."

She clucked her tongue at him, smiling. "Marilyn, please."

"I understand that you were in an accident not too long ago as well," Lucas said, directing the conversation around to why they'd attended the party in the first place. He noticed the way Marilyn's hand tightened on Thomas's sleeve and her smile dimmed while Thomas stiffened, his expression growing grim. "I hope you've recovered."

Thomas grunted, thumping his cane on the marble floor once. "This is a permanent addition, my doctors say, but I'm good otherwise. I appreciate your concern."

"Marilyn, do you dance?" Andrei suddenly asked, surprising everyone at the table.

"Ah...yes, sometimes."

Andrei smoothly rose to his feet and extended his hand to her. "Would you do me the honor?"

"Oh, I don't know if I should."

"Please. I enjoy dancing, but Lucas has warned me against most of the women here. I feel that I would be safe in your hands," Andrei pressed, earning a laugh from Marilyn.

"My, you are very smooth," she said even as she placed her hand into his.

Andrei grinned, slipping her hand on his arm as he led her away from the table. "My mother taught me to be a gentleman always."

Thomas and Lucas watched as the couple walked onto the dance floor. Andrei held the older woman as if she were a piece of priceless crystal, leading her slowly about the floor in a waltz. The two moved as if they had been dancing together their whole lives. Andrei was a source of endless surprises for Lucas. He couldn't wait to ask the man where he'd learned to dance and when.

"If I didn't know better, I'd say that friend of yours was determined to seduce my wife," Thomas announced gruffly, drawing Lucas's gaze from the dance floor.

Lucas smiled at the older man. "She's in safe hands."

Thomas nodded, giving him a grudging smile.

"I was hoping to discuss your accident," Lucas said and the man's smile dissolved.

"There's nothing—"

"It's my understanding that we were involved in similar car accidents," Lucas interrupted. Thomas's eyebrows rose slightly, but he said nothing. "May I ask if you recently acquired some land in Price Hill that might have caught someone's attentions?"

"No. Corryville."

Lucas slumped his chair and frowned. This was not what he had expected to hear. He looked over at the dance floor, watching Marilyn laughing at something that Andrei had said as he continued to twirl her about the floor.

"I was told to get out. To sell," Thomas continued. "You?"

"The same."

"Do you know who is behind this?"

Lucas shook his head. "Have you sold?"

"Not yet. I'm arranging the paperwork." Thomas sighed and pounded his fist on the table, rattling their glasses. "I'm too old to fight this, Lucas. The strain is too much for Marilyn."

"Have you informed the police?"

Thomas shook his head, the lines in his face digging deeper as his eyes searched out Marilyn. "They threatened my wife. My kids. They got to me so easily…" His low, rough voice faded and he cleared his throat. "I can't risk their lives."

"Have you had any more problems?"

"No, we added some security, but no one else has approached me."

Lucas leaned across the table, holding Thomas's gaze. "Slow up the papers. Give me a few days."

"You're fighting this? You know who's behind it?"

"No, but I will. I'm not going to be fucking run off." Lucas pushed to his feet and extended his hand to Thomas.

The older man shook it, clasping it in both of his. "You be careful."

Lucas graced him with a cocky smirk. "Of course. That's why I have Andrei."

He deeply laughed, drawing a few gazes to them before people went back to their conversations. "You've got the devil's luck, Lucas Vallois." He paused and looked at Andrei, a smirk tugging up one corner of his mouth. "And that man has his charm."

"Keep your head down, Thomas." On impulse, Lucas reached into the interior pocket of his jacket and pulled out a business card and a pen. Bending down, he quickly wrote his cell phone number across the back. He slid it across the table to Thomas. "You hear anything, call me. And if you or Marilyn need anything, call me."

Thomas caught his wrist as he started to lift his fingers from the card. "I admire what you're doing, but you've got to remember that it's just a chunk of land."

"I won't be bullied," Lucas replied, nearly growling.

He nodded, but he didn't look pleased by Lucas's words. He turned in time to see Andrei escorting Marilyn back into her seat, which he held out for her. She was flushed and her eyes were once again vibrant. For a time, Andrei had helped her forget about the worries plaguing her and her husband. They might not have accomplished what Lucas had hoped, but he couldn't call the night a waste after seeing the smiles on both their faces.

Lucas's own happiness was cut short when he gazed around the room to see a newcomer enter the museum. Biting back a curse, he stepped over to Andrei and laid a heavy hand on the man's shoulder. "Thank you for the wonderful chat. I hope we can get together sometime soon."

"Yes, I was telling Andrei we should do brunch this Sunday," Marilyn quickly chimed in.

Lucas's surprised gaze jerked to Andrei who only smiled at him. The man was too charming by half. "Thomas has my number. Call me and we'll arrange it." He took a step backward.

Keeping his hand on Andrei's shoulder, Lucas gently guided him toward one of the galleries off the main entrance, slipping through the crowd. Tension tightened the muscles in the man's shoulder, indicating that he was at least aware that there was a problem, but his face showed nothing.

"Problem?" Andrei inquired when they were through the crowd of people.

"Detective Banner just arrived. After last night's adventure, I'd prefer it if he didn't see us."

As Andrei stepped around a couple, he glanced over his shoulder, scanning the crowd before they disappeared down one exhibit hall. "I wouldn't get your hopes up about that. He was frowning and moving through the crowd toward us."

"Shit." Lucas picked up his pace, cutting through one exhibit hall after another. It had been a while since he'd spent an idle Sunday afternoon wandering the halls of the museum but he was pretty sure that he still remembered the layout. With so many people milling around, he was counting on all the doors being unlocked with security guards stationed at strategic locations to keep an eye on the guests. Two more turns and Lucas finally spotted the double doors he had been looking for.

With a wide grin, Lucas grasped Andrei's sleeve and carefully shoved open the door, trying to make as little noise as possible when he hit the push bar. Cold air slapped them in the face as they stepped into the shadowy garden courtyard. Lucas pulled Andrei along, his heart rate speeding up at the thrill of evading the detective. At the far end of the garden, Lucas found a spot behind a tree where the small yellow lights failed to reach.

With a shove, Lucas pinned Andrei against the stone wall of the museum and pressed close, using the deep shadows to hide them from view. The night air was cool enough to keep the gala guests inside the warmth of the building rather than seeking a late-evening stroll in the fall garden. Standing pressed against Andrei, Lucas suddenly recalled the smooth movements of his companion on the dance floor, the way his tux hugged his muscled form through each sinuous movement.

"You're having fun, aren't you?" Andrei demanded in a whisper, his breath gusting across Lucas's cheek.

"Some." Lucas lifted a hand to cup the side of Andrei's face, his thumb moving over the man's chin to his cheek bone in a slow caress.

It was dark enough that he couldn't clearly make out his features, but he was more than willing to explore him with his hands and lips.

Andrei turned his face into Lucas's hand, running his parted lips over the palm of his hand. "And what if someone comes out and sees us?"

Sliding his hand to grasp the back of Andrei's head, Lucas pulled him down to his lips. "Fuck 'em," he growled. The kiss was rough as Lucas let go of the hunger that had been building since that morning. He'd fought it down all day while Andrei had been in the office with him and he'd battled it while watching him dance with Marilyn. He clenched his teeth and smiled as every woman flirted with Andrei. Lucas was tired of holding the façade in place and pretending that he didn't want this man with every fiber of his being.

Andrei growled, returning the kiss with the same fire. His hands slipped between them and unbuttoned Lucas's jacket so he could slide them inside and up his back. Lucas shoved a knee between Andrei's legs, forcing them apart so he could stand between his thighs. Groans rose up from both men as they pressed closer, their bodies touching from shoulder to knee. And it still wasn't close enough.

"I need you," Lucas whispered between kisses, biting Andrei's lower lip before plunging his tongue into his mouth yet again.

"I—"

The scrape of the door opening halted Andrei's reply. Both men froze but didn't pull apart, relying on the deep shadows to keep them hidden. Lucas looked over his shoulder to see Banner outlined by the light from the museum, standing in the open doorway. He held his breath, his heart pounding in his chest as he waited for the detective to enter the garden. There was another exit, but Lucas and Andrei would have to cross through the light, giving themselves away.

Seconds ticked by before they heard Banner mutter "Shit" in a low, harsh voice before turning back into the museum.

It was only when the door banged closed behind Banner that Lucas chuckled. They had escaped the persistent detective for now. He had no delusions that Banner wouldn't track him down tomorrow, but it looked like they were in the clear.

"You need to do anything else here tonight?" Andrei asked, his fingers tightening where they dug into the muscles of Lucas's back, pulling him tight against him again.

"No."

"Then let's get the fuck out of here."

Tipping his chin up, Lucas brushed his lips against Andrei's in a teasing kiss. "Good idea."

Sadly, they didn't get as far as Lucas would have liked. Andrei had handed over the ticket to the valet and they were waiting for Lucas's car to be brought around. They hadn't bothered to go back inside, but used a side exit from the garden to cut to the front, hoping to escape not only the notice of the detective but also anyone else who might have tried to stop Lucas for gossip.

"Vallois!"

Lucas jerked around and nearly groaned to see the detective hurrying down the stairs toward them. He didn't look happy. "Fuck," Lucas muttered, looking over at Andrei to find him frowning at the detective.

"Well, I guess our good luck has run out for the night."

Lucas suddenly smiled, his eyes on the main drive leading toward the museum. "Maybe not. That's my car."

Andrei wagged his eyebrows at him. "You want to try to make a run for it?"

It was a tough choice. They could deal with the detective here and risk him killing their good mood, or run and risk him following them to the penthouse, where he would definitely kill their mood. He opened his mouth to answer as the valet jumped out of the sleek black car and rushed around to open passenger side door for Lucas, but something else caught his attention. A dark car zoomed up the drive on squealing tires and was turning through the drive, but didn't appear to be slowing enough to let out passengers. Instead, the window on the passenger side rolled down.

"Down!" Andrei shouted, launching his body at Lucas so that he tackled him hard to the ground a second before gun fire filled the silent night air followed by the sharp screams of innocent bystanders. Lucas cringed, burrowing under Andrei against the harsh sound. He clenched his teeth, willing the noise to finally stop. It couldn't have lasted more than a couple seconds but it felt like an eternity that he was trapped helpless. He had no gun and he was all too aware of Andrei's body vulnerable above him.

The end of the gun fire was punctuated by more squealing tires as their attackers fled the scene. Andrei immediately rolled off him and to his feet, staring after the car. Lucas didn't hesitate, but ran for his vehicle. These bastards were not getting away that easily. To his relief, Andrei was right behind him, sliding over the hood to jump into the driver's seat.

"Oh hell no, you aren't leaving me behind!"

Lucas twisted around in his seat as the rear passenger door jerked open. Hollis dove inside right as Andrei hit the gas and the cop cursed as he slammed into the back of the seat then hit the floor. Lucas had to face front again, using his hand as a brace on the dashboard to keep from hitting the window as Andrei took the first curve fast. The car thumped hard as they went over a curb.

"Oops," Andrei muttered.

"Where's the goddamned seatbelt?" Hollis grumbled from the back. His face must have smashed into the seat on the next curve because all Lucas heard then were muffled words. Something about backseats and evil sentient vacuums.

Lucas reached for his own belt, then hesitated. Andrei was using both hands as he navigated the winding road and couldn't do his own. "I'm going to reach across you and grab your belt, okay?" He figured warning him was a good idea considering his focus on the road. Navigating with the other cars had to be tricky.

Andrei nodded. "I can see their taillights. We're not far behind." He lifted his elbow to give Lucas access, then cursed and swerved.

There was a loud thump from the back seat. "Ow. Fuck!" the detective yelled.

Andrei shot Lucas a glance, amusement twisting the corner of his mouth, before his attention zipped back to the road.

Something in Lucas's chest went tight and he rested his palm briefly on Andrei's side before he grabbed the seatbelt and pulled it around him. He then quickly fastened his own. He didn't miss the bodyguard's second fiery glance and he certainly didn't know how to explain what that had been about. One shared glance and Lucas felt like he'd been burned from the inside.

"This is so not right."

Lucas ignored Banner, watching the taillights ahead of them. He had to admire Andrei's competence in keeping up…and in keeping them from going over the drop off on their right.

"I shouldn't be in the back. I'm the cop."

"Shut up, Banner. You wanna stop and switch seats now so we'll lose them?" They hit the next curve so hard, Lucas's head would have slammed into the window if he hadn't been belted in. Yellow light shimmered between the trees from Mirror Lake's fountain to his right as another thump sounded from the backseat. It was followed by a muffled cry. If Lucas hadn't been so pissed about being shot at, he would have relished the detective flying all over the back seat. "Whoever this is, took it to a new level fast. I can't believe this! Did anyone get hit back there?"

"Yeah," Hollis said. "The valet. Saw blood on his shoulder. He'll live."

"They're getting braver. The attack at Gaile was to scare Lucas, I'm sure. But this—this was a hit." Andrei swerved. "What the hell? How did they pass—" He broke off.

Lucas saw that another car was now between them and the bad guys. "They must have passed to the left."

"Into the oncoming traffic?"

With the stream of lights they passed, Lucas couldn't see how they'd accomplished it either. Tires squealed again as Andrei made a hard left, pulling onto the four-lane Eden Park Drive. The dense black trees of the park pulled back from the road, giving glimpses of the towering skyscrapers and office buildings of downtown. Back to the nerve-tingling edge of civilization. Traffic was relatively light for that time of night, but as they barreled down the first hill toward the intersection, Lucas's entire body tensed as he prayed the light held green because Andrei was showing no signs of slowing up in his pursuit of the black Dodge Charger.

Banner's hand grabbed the seat next to Lucas's head. "Why were you two avoiding me back there? Or did you just go outside to make out?"

"You saw that?" Lucas frowned, wondering if he'd been the only one. Not that he really cared. The thought gave him pause. Surprised him. And maybe even delighted him.

"Shadows weren't as dark as you probably thought. It was hot. Thought about sneaking around to get a more private viewing."

"That's just wrong." Lucas turned to glare at him, caught the wicked grin and knew the cop was messing with him. "What were you doing there anyway? And dressed like that?" He raked his gaze down the wrinkled, white T-shirt and gray sweats. The cop had obviously thrown his leather jacket on after rolling out of bed. Even his hair stuck up all over his head and his jaw had a thicker layer of brown scruff.

"Black tie isn't really my thing. Too confining." He shuddered, turned away and covered his mouth as a stream of coughs erupted from his throat.

"Looks like you crawled out of bed to chase us down at the museum. Why?"

Hollis groaned. "I did. Crawl out of bed, that is. Where I was enjoying the last of that fantastic soup, by the way. I would give the world to be able to eat like that more often. Job keeps me existing on burgers and Chinese takeout most of the time. But your doctor friend called me and he was upset."

"Snow?"

Hollis cleared his throat, the sound wet and rumbly. "Yeah. Another beating vic came in. High profile one. Patrick Laughlin. He didn't make it."

"Fuck," Lucas cursed softly, his eyes drifting over to his window as the cityscape blurred past him. Patrick had been Thomas Lynton's business partner for years. This was going to hit Thomas hard, pressuring him to act now to protect his family.

The detective leaned closer and ended up grasping the back of the seat when Andrei hit the brakes, then sped up again. "Your doctor friend was about to storm the museum and drag you home. He talked about protective custody and some other stuff about handcuffs or chains. I didn't realize you two had that sort of relationship. He doesn't mind you boinking the smoking bodyguard?"

"Hey, the smoking bodyguard is right here," Andrei muttered. "And there isn't any boinking going on."

Banner snorted. "Not yet maybe," he murmured, then cursed, his attention shifting back to their attackers. "They're getting onto the highway. You gotta keep them in the left lanes if you can. If they cross the bridge, this could get tricky." He started coughing again. "Don't know what kind of hell bug crawled into my system but I'm pretty sure I caught it at the hospital. Should go into that place in a Hazmat suit."

Andrei snarled curses under his breath as he whipped the car into another left against the light, dodging a silver SUV to grab the Interstate 71 south on-ramp. He gunned the car, deftly maneuvering through the traffic as if the other cars were standing still, positioning the larger Mercedes on the right side of their attackers. But they were quickly running out of room as they approached the tunnel that would pour them out onto Fort Washington Way.

"Hold on to something," Andrei said under his breath as he pressed on the gas.

Lucas's heart slammed as the car sped up and they got close enough to better see the back of the car. He leaned forward, hands once again on the dash as he tried to peer inside. "Can't make anyone out through the tinted windows. And the fucking license plate is missing."

"Let me try to get a little closer," Andrei murmured as the car picked up even more speed. They drew even with the other car as they hit the tunnel.

Lucas held his breath, looking for something, anything, to tell them who they were chasing. But his breath came out in a panicked whoosh when the back window came down and a gun appeared. "Shit, Andrei!"

"I see it," he bit out as he abruptly slowed.

The other car weaved, the tail end swerving and hitting the front of Lucas's Mercedes. The shot missed them completely. Lucas looked over his shoulder to find Banner pulling out his gun. "You shoot that in here and we all go deaf."

"We'll have to get closer before I can fire at them anyway. Can't risk hitting all the civilians."

"They don't seem to have that worry." Andrei released a growl as another shot went wide over the top of their car. "We have to stop them before they hit someone else."

The lights from the city came back into play as they exited the tunnel. Downtown rose up on their right while glimpses of Great American Ballpark and Paul Brown Stadium zipped by on the left in a blur of golden light and gray concrete. "They're grabbing the ramp to 75 north," Lucas said with almost a relieved sigh. He definitely didn't want to play chicken with these assholes speeding across the Ohio River along Brent Spence Bridge. "They've already fucked up my car." He glanced at Andrei. "Think you can clip them? Send them into a ditch?"

"Hell yeah." The intense focus that came over Andrei's face sent Lucas's already fast heart into overdrive. With his hair shoved back from their earlier scuffle, his sharp features were perfectly clear. Even with his lips tightened, that slightly pouty upper lip was sexy as hell.

Damn, the man was sexy.

Lucas shut his eyes briefly. They were in a life or death car chase with men shooting at them and he was thinking of peeling his bodyguard out of his tux. Snow would be laughing his ass off at him…after he was done being pissed about the whole car chase, whizzing bullets issue.

"Hang on to something." Andrei floored it, clipped the back of the Charger and instead of sending them into the ditch like Lucas expected, their car swerved, then flipped. Over and over.

Andrei veered to the side, spinning the car and coming to a stop with them facing the opposite direction on the shoulder of the interstate.

All three of them sat there, breathing hard for what felt like forever before Banner whooped so loud from the back seat, Lucas flinched.

"That. Was. Fucking. Awesome! You ever think about joining the police force?" The detective leaned over the seat to thump Andrei loudly on the shoulder. "Or maybe racing? You got skills, man."

Lucas watched for movement from the car, which had ended upside down. "Think we killed them?"

"I'll go check." Banner got out of the car and knocked on the passenger window. "Stay here. Call 9-1-1." He held out his gun as he approached the car.

"Shouldn't he be calling for back up or something?" Andrei asked, unbuckling his seatbelt. He reached inside his jacket and pulled out his own gun, checking it with a kind of practiced skill that should have set Lucas at ease, but instead left an unsettled feeling in the pit of his stomach. "Cop knows they have guns."

Lucas frowned. If their attackers were alive and conscious, Hollis was outgunned. He might not like the guy, but he didn't want to see him dead. "I think he's high on adrenaline. And Nyquil. The man's not right."

He stared at Andrei, his gaze running over features he was starting to think were the finest he'd ever looked at. In the next instant, he grabbed Andrei by the lapels and hauled him closer. "He was right about one thing. You drive like a professional and it was hot as hell." He slammed his mouth over the other man's, groaning when Andrei immediately opened his mouth and sucked his tongue inside. The kiss grew hot and dirty fast, but Andrei shoved him back against the passenger door before it could blaze out of control.

"Call 9-1-1 and stay in the damned car," Andrei ordered in a rough voice before throwing his own door open and sliding out into the cold air. Lucas started to argue but he swallowed the words as the door slammed shut in his face. His every instinct screamed to follow Andrei out to back up Hollis, but he knew he couldn't. Without a gun, he was only a target, endangering Andrei and possibly even Hollis.

Swearing loudly to himself in the empty car, Lucas pulled out his cell phone and dialed 9-1-1 as instructed, giving their details to the operator. It was likely cops were already racing to their location considering the way they'd already torn through the city, but he was sure at least one of the men in the overturned car was going to need an ambulance.

Chapter 14

Lucas followed Andrei through the penthouse as he made his rounds, checking to make sure that no one had intruded while they were out. The younger man movements were tense and hurried, as if he were struggling to keep his mind on the task at hand. And all too soon, he reached the last room—Lucas's bedroom. All the locks were still set. Nothing was out of place. They were safe but Andrei didn't looked relaxed. He looked...haunted.

After dropping down on the small sofa in the sitting area of the bedroom, Lucas untied his dress shoes, removing them and his socks. The night was gone. The black skies just past his wide windows were giving way to a deep slate gray of the coming dawn. They spent two hours at the crash site, answering questions and watching three bleeding men get pulled from the car and loaded in a pair of ambulances. Then Lucas, Andrei, Hollis were shuffled off to the police station where they were met by Sarah for another three hours of questions. Lucas didn't want to think about the legal tap dancing/bullshitting that had been done by both Sarah and Hollis, but they were released at last. Lucas would be stunned if Hollis still had a job this morning.

But through it all, he couldn't pull his mind from Andrei. Something was tearing him apart. Before the EMTs had arrived, Hollis had flashed the IDs of the three men who'd shot at Lucas. He'd not recognized them, but he'd seen a subtle shift in Andrei's jaw, the tiniest flicker in his eyes before Andrei denied recognizing them.

"You lied to Banner," he stated as Andrei moved to leave the master bedroom. The man stopped but didn't turn around to face Lucas so he continued talking. "You recognized those men. Why?"

Andrei lowered his head and turned slightly. "I wanted to talk to Rowe first. I don't want you pulled into this. Or the cops."

"Were you involved in something illegal?"

Andrei grunted. "Briefly."

"Rowe know?"

"Yes."

"Drugs?"

"No," Andrei growled, his hand clenching at his side.

"Prostitutes?"

Andrei swung around to glare at Lucas as the man reclined on the sofa, staring at him. "Is that really what you think of me?"

"No, but you're not volunteering information so I'm left to guess worst-case scenarios until you finally tell me. Were you an enforcer for a loan shark?"

"No! Fuck! Maybe it's none of your business."

Lucas lifted one eyebrow at Andrei's outburst, patiently waiting for the man to speak. Andrei was right that his past wasn't his business but he didn't care. He wanted to know. He wanted to know everything about Andrei, and that included his past.

Andrei tried to shove both hands through his hair, but the tux jacket restricted his movement so he roughly stripped it off and tossed it over the back of a chair. He forced himself to take a deep breath that he released noisily through his nose. "Illegal fights," he snapped as if he couldn't hold back the words any longer. "I fought on the amateur circuit, trying to get my professional break into MMA, but it's fucking expensive. I used to pad my income by participating in illegal underground fights in the city. A few months before my injury, John—the driver of the car—started appearing at the fights. The other guy, Matt, I heard about from some people I'm still in contact with. He was in the backseat."

"Organizers?"

"Fighters." Andrei frowned and shook his head. "I didn't recognize the third, but looking at the build and scarring, I'd easily wager he's a fighter too."

Lucas nodded. It made sense now. The men he'd encountered in that damned alley the previous week had been too skilled to be just a handful of street thugs. They'd blocked blows and used moves that most people wouldn't have been able to. Lucas had thought that maybe this asshole had recruited a few guys from the local dojos as muscle, but if he had access to the underground fights in Cincinnati, then this was fucking bigger than he'd thought.

With his hands shoved in his pockets, Andrei wandered over to the wall of windows and stared at the city skyline glowing before him. His shoulders were stiff and tense while his face was pulled into a grimace. Old memories and new fears mixing together.

"How is this bastard getting all these fighters working for him? Money?"

"Isn't that how you buy anyone?" Andrei asked. Bitterness twisted in his words, leaving Lucas aching to go to him, but he remained where he was sitting on the sofa, letting the words pour out of Andrei as if he were purging an old poison. "A lot of money changes hands at these things. Bets are placed. The winning fighter gets a cut, but then you can also bet. Even on your own fight. Some fight for the rush, but most…most are desperate for cash. And if you're not careful, you can wrack up some sizable losses with the house." Andrei turned his head slightly, but Lucas got the impression the man was looking at Lucas's reflection in the window. "The bastard after you likely holds markers on these guys. They kill you and he forgets their debts."

Sighing, Andrei turned around and leaned his shoulders against the window to look at Lucas. "I've seen guys crippled in these fights. Some even killed. And the fighters keep coming back. They get in deep and they say just one more fight to get on top again, but their bodies can't do it."

For the first time since Lucas had met Andrei, the younger man looked lost and vulnerable, struggling with memories of a life that he'd escaped and Lucas couldn't feel anything but relief.

"Were you ever that desperate?"

"No." He paused and sighed, his dark eyes rolling up to stare at the ceiling. "Yes. I never got in with the house. Never bet. But there were times when I knew if I didn't win, I wouldn't have money for food for a week or I wouldn't have rent for the month and I'd be homeless." He closed his eyes and took another deep breath. "But you knew when you were standing opposite a guy that he was just as desperate as you. He had a baby to feed or a debt hanging over his head that could mean his life. And...and you just couldn't let yourself think about it as you're beating the shit out of him because if you didn't win, you didn't eat."

Lucas pushed to his feet and walked over to stand in front of Andrei, the only sound in the room the soft rustle of his slacks. Andrei opened his eyes as Lucas placed a hand on his neck, his thumb stroking his jaw. "I'm glad you were injured."

A wry smile lifted one side of Andrei's mouth, though sadness still filled his lovely dark eyes. "Really?"

Lucas leaned in and placed a small, open-mouthed kiss on Andrei's chin, letting the tip of his tongue slide along the prickle of whiskers. "That injury means that you're right here with me in this moment."

"Is this a good moment?" he asked, his voice becoming husky. There was a thread of something else in his tone, wariness and maybe a vulnerability that tugged at something deep within Lucas, prodding him on.

Lucas continued to kiss along Andrei's jaw until his lips brushed against his ear. "It's the start of a very good moment."

"Is this a mistake?"

Every muscle in Lucas's body froze for a second and then another as he considered Andrei's question. It was the same question that had hammered against his brain since Andrei first strode into his hospital room. Fear of the unknown claimed that his every move toward Andrei was a mistake, but instinct said it wasn't. It couldn't be a mistake, not when he needed him so damned bad.

"Does it feel like a mistake?" Lucas replied, hating that he'd answered his question with an evasion.

"No."

"Should I stop?"

"No." The denial escaped Andrei as a harsh exhalation as he wrapped his arms around Lucas. "No regrets."

Lucas wasn't sure if the man was talking to him or himself, but the concern was immediately shoved aside when Andrei roughly kissed him. Everything—the people threatening Lucas's life, Andrei's past, Cincinnati's moneyed elite, their friends, the expectations of the world—was forgotten in the growing heat of their kiss.

Long fingers pulled at Andrei's bow tie, sliding it from around his neck before moving down to unbutton his shirt. An approving hum rumbled up his throat as Lucas parted the material, fingertips brushing against bits of skin.

"Are you seducing me?" Andrei asked.

"Yes." Lucas gathered up fistfuls of Andrei's shirt and jerked it free of his pants so he could run his hands up his bare stomach and across the hard muscles of his chest.

"How could anyone say no to you?" Andrei chuckled, leaning a little to press his chest into his hands. He was a cat stretching in the afternoon sun, soaking in the attention.

Lucas placed an open-mouthed kiss on his neck, his tongue skimming along warm skin until Andrei shivered. "I've never seduced anyone like this," he confessed. "Never wanted anyone as badly as I want you." His hot breath brushed across the damp skin, sending another shiver through him.

Stepping back, Lucas shrugged out of his jacket, letting it fall to the floor, followed quickly by his tie, shirt, and T-shirt. Andrei's dark eyes followed his hands, his gaze growing hungrier with each motion.

"Why seduce me?" Andrei's voice was low and rough, as if he'd dragged it up from the bottom of his soul.

"Because I want you as desperate as I am. I want you moaning and begging beneath me." Lucas slowly unbuckled his pants and Andrei's hands clenched at his sides as if he were fighting to keep from grabbing him. "I want to make you come so hard you shout my name loud enough for the neighbors to be jealous."

Unbuttoning his pants, he shoved them down to his ankles, leaving on his boxer briefs. They did nothing to hide his straining erection pushing against the soft material. Andrei licked his lips, his eyes skimming over the other's man body, wringing a groan out of Lucas. He took one step forward and Andrei finally snapped free, meeting him in a clash of rough hands, running over as much exposed skin as they could find and it wasn't enough. Lucas jerked at garments while his tongue tangled with Andrei's. The room was filled with low grunts and the occasional tearing of seams.

When Andrei was finally naked, he shuddered against Lucas. Each movement built the heat between them. The soft tug of skin as flesh pulled along flesh. Lucas threaded both hands through Andrei's hair and twisted, holding his head captive, as he thrust his hips against Andrei's.

"Do you want me to fuck you?" Lucas growled, trying to control the trembling need burning through him. Damn, how was he going to do this and do it slowly? His body was heavy with need and aching. Everything screamed to bend Andrei over and plunge inside, just find the relief he'd craved for too many days. But he wanted to go slow for both of them. He was desperate to have Andrei enjoy this just as much.

Andrei's hands sank into both his ass cheeks, kneading the muscles as he pulled him flush against his body. "Fuck yes. Don't tell me no. Not tonight."

Lucas actually managed a choked laugh. "I think saying no would actually kill me tonight."

When Lucas relaxed his hold, Andrei dipped his head, grabbing Lucas's lips in a brief, hot kiss. "Can't have that."

Lucas stepped away from Andrei and pushed him toward the bed. "Get in my bed."

Andrei didn't hesitate but stretched out on his back across the king-sized bed. With his legs spread and feet flat on the mattress, Andrei put one arm behind his head while his other hand snaked down to wrap around his cock, stroking it slowly as he watched Lucas. This might have been new territory for Andrei, but there was certainly nothing shy about him.

Lucas stole a moment to admire the man's long, lean form. Covered in tanned skin with dark hairs on muscular legs, Andrei was beautiful. Every fucking inch of him. His rich coloring was perfectly set off against the deep red duvet, as if Lucas had chosen it just for Andrei to lie against. But even with acres of perfect male form in front of him, Lucas's gaze kept drifting back to his eyes. Those dark, sinful eyes haunted him like nothing else in his life. Andrei's every mood was reflected in his eyes no matter how he tried to hide it. Pain, joy, fear, and mischief flashed through them. But now, Lucas saw only stark, raw hunger. And maybe a hint of trepidation.

From the nightstand on his left, Lucas pulled out a bottle of lube and a condom, tossing them on the bed. He pulled off his boxers and crawled onto the bed, kneeling between Andrei's knees. He ran his hand up over the man's legs, squeezing the powerful muscles in his thighs, pulling a low moan from other man, as his eyes drifted closed and his legs widened. Capturing the hand Andrei was using to stroke himself, Lucas pulled it up, trapping it next to Andrei's head as he leaned over the man with his wider body. Andrei's eyes opened, questioning him, and then Lucas moved his hips, rubbing his hard cock against Andrei's.

"Oh fuuccckkk," Andrei groaned, his head tipping back. Muscles tightened and strained, pulling Andrei's body taut. "That's…weird."

Lucas hummed, lowering his head to bite his neck. "As in, that's weird, Lucas, please stop?"

"As in, fucking do it again."

Lucas swallowed his laugh and did as commanded, shifting his hips and pressing down so that their cocks slid against each other, pulling another groan out of Andrei as he lifted his hips as well. "Kiss me," Andrei demanded in a rough voice, tilting his head up. Lucas couldn't pass up the sweet offering of his full, parted lips. He devoured the man's mouth, tasting him, their tongues tangling together as he continued to thrust against him. Fuck. A demanding Andrei was pushing Lucas closer to losing his mind. He was the one who was usually in control, but there was something addictive about having a strong partner to match him. He wanted to fulfill Andrei's every request and be rewarded with pleasure-filled moans and gasps.

Lucas pulled his lips away to kiss down along Andrei's jaw and run the tip of his tongue over his soft ear lobe. A tremor ran through Andrei's frame. "Lucas," he moaned.

"What would you like me to do now?"

Andrei turned his head, a slow smile spreading across swollen lips while a mischievous light filled his eyes. Lucas didn't think it was possible for him to get any harder, but that look alone did it. His mouth went dry and he nearly begged Andrei to fuck him.

"Get your lube."

"And?"

"I want you to slide your fingers in my ass while you suck my cock," Andrei's voice had become thick and warm like syrup, sliding through Lucas's brain so that he could barely think.

"How many fingers?"

Andrei grinned. "Let's start with one and add more until you can fit your fat cock in there."

Lucas sucked in a harsh breath, gathering his control. "You're going to fucking kill me tonight."

"I've got to at least make you work for my virgin ass," he joked, but Lucas didn't miss the hint of uneasiness that passed through Andrei's eyes.

"When I'm done, you're going to wonder why you waited so damned long," Lucas muttered, sitting back on his heels. And he was going to deliver on that promise.

He grabbed the lube and poured some on his fingers before tossing it aside. With a wicked grin, he ran his tongue along the length of Andrei's swollen cock while at the same time running his slick finger along his pucker. Andrei lifted his hips and gasped at the two sensations. A series of curses rolled off his tongue and not all of them sounded like they were in English. Lucas lapped up the pre-cum oozing along the slit while carefully pressing against the ring of tight muscles until the tip of his finger was inside of Andrei.

Andrei's hand clamped down on Lucas's head, fingers threading tight into his hair as his breath exploded from him in harsh gasps. "Oh Jesus fuck yes," Andrei exhaled. "More."

Unsure of which Andrei meant, Lucas pushed his finger up to the second knuckle while swallowing his cock down. Andrei cursed again, his head thrown back and the thick, corded muscles in his neck were straining. He was beautiful. Lucas continued to work him, sucking his cock while adding a second finger, stretching his asshole until Andrei finally pulled his hair, lifting him away from his weeping cock.

"Stop," he growled.

Lucas froze, his fingers still deep inside the man. "What?"

"Get inside me. I'm close. I don't want to come until you're inside me."

He didn't question it. Nodding, he pulled his fingers free and Andrei released his hair. "Flip onto your stomach."

Snagging up the condom, Lucas make quick work of the packaging and rolled it down onto his throbbing cock. He quickly slathered it with lube, trying to ignore the shaking of his own hands. He'd never been so desperate to get inside of someone. It was more than each sigh and groan that slipped from Andrei's lips that night. It was days of smiles, touches, laughs, and kisses that had worked to this moment.

Andrei might have had an inch on him in height, but Lucas was wider, allowing him to almost completely cover Andrei with his body. He kissed his back, pressing him down into the mattress. Old pains tried to creep over him from the beating he'd taken days ago, but the incident and injuries seemed too distant. Not worth paying attention to when pleasure vibrated from Andrei. He rubbed his hard cock against his ass until Andrei moaned and thrust his hips backward.

Lucas broke off the kiss, shifting his weight so he slid his hands down Andrei's smooth back to rest on his narrow hips. "I'm not going to hurt you. I stop when you tell me to stop."

"Even if it kills you?" Andrei's voice was muffled from where his face was buried against the red duvet.

"Even if it kills me," Lucas repeated. And he was pretty sure it would.

Lining the head of his cock up with Andrei, he carefully pushed past those tight muscles to slip inside him. Andrei tensed beneath him, his fists twisting up the duvet while Lucas cursed. He stopped as he got the head inside and drew a shuddering breath.

"Good?" he gritted out.

"Don't stop." Andrei's voice sounded pained and Lucas hesitated. He slid his hand from his shoulder, running it down the rigid muscles of his back. Andrei was sinuous, long and lean. The need to touch Andrei, *to constantly touch him*, was overwhelming. He would never get enough, but for now, he had to focus his energy on making it good for Andrei. He grasped Andrei's cock and ran his thumb over the head before he began a gentle rocking motion that slowly pushed him deeper inside of Andrei. Muscles tightened around Lucas, squeezing and massaging until he swore he was going to lose it.

"Fuck," Lucas moaned. He gasped, trying to control his entrance. His thoughts fragmented, becoming nothing more than leaves caught up in the wind. "You feel so good."

Andrei pushed back, taking more of Lucas and they both swore softly. "That's it," Andrei growled. "I want all of you. Fuck me, Lucas."

Lucas's control snapped and he pushed completely in, burying himself. The breath was sucked out of his lungs as he froze, fighting to give Andrei time to adjust to being so completely filled. Lucas closed his eyes, trying to count backward in his head from twenty, focusing on anything besides the perfect heat from Andrei's body. As control returned, Lucas moved again, pulling part of the way out before sliding easily back in, wringing groans of pleasure from them both.

He struggled to keep his pace slow, but Andrei's moaning and pleading for more were sapping all of his good intentions. Nothing had ever felt so amazing in his life. This was pure heaven and he was already falling over the edge.

"Lucas! Fuck me harder. I need it. Harder." Andrei groaned, his words caught somewhere between commanding and begging.

With a growl, he pulled completely out of Andrei, ripping a gasp out of him. Moving to the edge of the bed, Lucas flipped Andrei onto his back before climbing into position. He smiled down at the man as he wrapped Andrei's legs around his waist and plunged inside of him. Pleasure soared through him as Andrei arched deliciously off the bed and a long moan filled the room.

"That's it," Lucas growled as he once again clasped Andrei's cock while his hips picked up an almost frantic pace. The slapping of their bodies was nearly drowned out by Andrei's swearing and pleading. "This is what you needed, isn't it?"

"Fuck, yes," Andrei whimpered. "Don't stop. Don't ever stop." His hands clawed at the sheets as he tried to lift his body into Lucas's pounding thrusts.

"Look at me. I want you looking at me when you come."

Andrei's eyes snapped open, his dark gaze holding Lucas's. He could see every emotion pouring through Andrei, captured in his hooded eyes. More desperate words tumbled from Andrei's lips, but they were no longer English. His entire body tensed, the muscles of his ass tightly clenching Lucas's cock so that he could barely move, but he kept plunging inside even as his rhythm broke. Clasping the bed just above his head with both hands, Andrei's body bowed, every muscle rigid and trembling. Andrei shouted his name as he came, covering Lucas's hand and his stomach.

A broken cry escaped Lucas's lips as he could no longer hold back his own orgasm. He came hard inside of Andrei, his entire body jerking and shaking as he shattered. Darkness crowded his vision and Lucas was tempted to let it swallow him. Nothing had ever felt so good, so complete. He dropped to his forearms. Pressing his forehead against Andrei's, he laughed. They were both panting so hard they couldn't kiss.

"So...." Andrei said, struggling to catch his breath.

"Yeah…"

As his breathing slowed, Andrei smiled crookedly as if he couldn't get all the muscles in his face to work properly. "We're doing that again, right?"

"Fuck yeah," Lucas said before finally grabbing the kiss he'd wanted the moment clear thought had started to return to his blood-starved brain. Andrei kissed him back slowly, savoring it.

It was with a great deal of reluctance that Lucas pulled out of Andrei and shuffled to the bathroom on shaky legs to dispose of the condom. He came back with a towel and tossed it to Andrei, who quickly wiped his stomach clean and threw the towel on the floor.

Sliding into the bed, Lucas heaved a contented sigh. Andrei rolled to his side, throwing one arm around Lucas's waist to keep their bodies pressed together as he kissed him again and again. Lucas marveled at how he still craved this man's touch. The sex had been mind blowing, draining everything from him, and yet something deep within his soul needed more of Andrei.

"Sorry," Andrei murmured, his lips still brushing against Lucas's. "This is probably wrong, isn't it?"

Lucas wanted to laugh at the slight surprise and confusion in his voice, but he couldn't. This was new for both of them. After every other sexual escapade, Lucas had rolled to his feet upon completion and immediately dealt with the condom so he could begin dressing again. There were no lingering kisses or touches. But now he needed them.

"Don't stop," Lucas whispered when Andrei started to pull away. He ran his fingers through Andrei's dark hair, pushing it away from his face simply because he couldn't stop touching the man.

Andrei laughed. "We should or you'll have to fuck me again."

Laying his head on the corner of a pillow, Lucas smiled at Andrei as a lazy contentment stole over him. "I can't imagine when I won't."

"Won't what?"

"Need to fuck you."

Andrei closed his eyes and hummed his approval. "Sounds good to me. I didn't expect it to be like that."

"Like what?"

"So…intense."

Lucas stared at the other man's face, memorizing each line and the curve of his lips. Heavy eyelashes lay fan-like on his cheeks and there was a small bump on the bridge of his nose as if it had been broken once. He was starting to know this face better than his own. Lucas could close his eyes and see this face burned in his mind.

"Are you good?" he asked firmly.

"You mean other than the fact that my ass is tender?" Andrei said with a slight mocking sneer.

"Yes."

Andrei's eyes flicked open and he licked his lips. "Yeah, I'm good," he replied in a low voice that nearly sent a tremor through Lucas. This was more than a physical good. This stretched down to Andrei's being and it warmed Lucas, setting lingering worries at ease.

"Couldn't have been too bad if you were speaking in tongues," Lucas teased, trying to lighten the mood again when all he wanted to do was pull Andrei close and settle his face into his neck, breathing in his scent.

Andrei's eyes dropped to Lucas's chest and his body stiffened to Lucas's surprise. "Did not. You just weren't getting blood to your brain anymore."

Lucas pushed against Andrei, putting the man on his back again so Lucas could hover over him. "No. You were shouting in another language when you came. What was it?"

A frown played on Andrei's lips and he looked anywhere but Lucas's eyes. "Romanian," he mumbled.

Lucas couldn't hide his shock. "You speak Romanian?" It wasn't a language that Andrei would have learned in school and he had to imagine that he must be fluent if he slipped unconsciously into it.

Andrei's eyes darted up to Lucas, looking completely uncomfortable with the conversation. "My family is Romanian. My grandparents moved to the U.S. when my mom was a teenager. My father is Romanian too. I grew up learning both English and Romanian."

"I don't understand. Why does that bother you?"

Andrei shrugged. "Grew up hearing a lot of Roma and gypsy bullshit. Gets old fast when people automatically assume you're a thief or a con man because you're Romanian."

Leaning forward, Lucas pressed his lips against Andrei's temple, soothing some of the tension. "But it's incredibly sexy," he whispered, earning a small laugh from Andrei. "Hearing you lose control like that made me come."

"You're ridiculous," Andrei said, but his voice was warm and smooth like honey again.

"Say something else."

"Lucas…"

"Do it," he pressed. "Please."

Andrei rattled something off, the foreign words wrapped in his deep voice, so they sounded incredibly sexy and inviting. Lucas pulled back to look Andrei in the eye. "What did you say?"

"Your monkey has stolen my bicycle."

Lucas fell against the bed, his laughter filling the room. He leaned forward, grabbing Andrei's mouth in a rough, brief kiss. "And you call me ridiculous."

"Well, you are the man who just fucked his bodyguard. You can't get more ridiculous than that," Andrei said with a derisive snort. "I mean, they've made sappy chick movies about that shit."

"I don't think we're what Hollywood has in mind."

Andrei stretched beside him, still grinning. "Damned shame, because you are one sexy motherfucker when you're coming, shouting my name at the top of your lungs."

Lucas couldn't tear his eyes away from Andrei. His happiness was infectious. Dark eyes danced with laughter and the world just felt lighter. Did he share that lightness with the world or was it just his as they lay alone in his bedroom looking down on Cincinnati? Something incredibly possessive raised its head. He'd been Andrei's first, and he already wanted to do it again. Lucas tamped the feeling down, enjoying instead the shiver that swept through Andrei as Lucas ran his hand over Andrei's chest. He was amazingly responsive and that was a high all on its own. Lucas wanted to fuck Andrei all over again, but he held back. Andrei had already made a comment about being tender. He didn't want to hurt him.

This was nothing like the casual fucks he'd enjoyed in the past. Walk away from Andrei? Hell no! Walking away meant allowing someone else to touch him and kiss him and fuck him. And while Lucas wasn't willing to think about whether he could have a tomorrow with Andrei, he knew without a doubt that he couldn't let him go to someone else.

"What's wrong?" Andrei demanded, jerking Lucas from his dark thoughts. "You're scowling."

"Thinking about tomorrow," Lucas mumbled as he pushed to his feet. He grabbed his pants and pulled out his cell phone.

"Everything okay?" Andrei demanded, leaning up on his forearms to watch Lucas.

"Just telling Candace to cancel my meetings tomorrow." He typed out a quick text to his assistant.

"Playing hooky?"

"We've got other things to take care of tomorrow."

Andrei grunted, his smile sliding away. Reality was crashing back in around them, destroying the remains of the moment. Lucas instantly wanted to take the words back, but it was too late. It was time they both remembered they had problems that needed to be dealt with.

"Should I go back to my room? Would it make you more comfortable?"

Lucas shook his head as he reached for the bedside lamp and turned the light off. More comfortable? Yeah, it probably would. Lucas had never slept with someone after sex. He'd always been happy to send them on their way. But not this time.

"It's going to be a hassle to come get you when I wake up needing to fuck you in a few hours." Lucas pulled the blankets down to slide into the bed.

Andrei rolled to his feet and quickly joined Lucas under the covers. "I would hate to inconvenience you."

A smile played on Lucas's lips as he relaxed in the bed with Andrei beside him. He managed to fight the urge for all of five seconds before he growled and grabbed Andrei, manhandling him until he was wrapped around Lucas. It was the same position they'd fallen asleep in the previous night and it settled a lingering ache in Lucas's chest.

Andrei gave a little snort as he settled his head on Lucas's shoulder. "I'm not the only cuddler."

"Shut up," Lucas muttered as he slid his fingers through Andrei's hair.

Closing his eyes, Lucas welcomed sleep. He didn't want to think about how his world just felt…better with this man stretched out beside him. More complete. He didn't want to think about how he longed to ask him about his childhood and if his nose had truly been broken. He didn't want to think about how he needed more nights like this. Such ideas didn't fit with his plans. But letting go of Andrei wasn't an option either.

Chapter 15

Andrei felt sick. This was going to be ugly. There was no avoiding it. He'd known his course of action since he'd heard the names from Hollis last night. Common sense would have naturally argued that sex was a mistake, knowing what he planned to do, but he'd caved with the first touch of Lucas's lips.

Hell, Lucas's smile was burned into his brain. It cut through everything, pushing him to say ridiculous, teasing things so it would keep reappearing. He was addicted to that slow, lazy grin and the unspoken promise behind it.

Fuck, he was going to destroy that smile. If he'd learned anything during his short time with Lucas it was that the man was incredibly protective and possessive. Something had changed between them, even before Andrei had begged Lucas to fuck him. And Andrei's plan was going to make it impossible for Lucas to protect him.

Rowe would need little convincing. His priority was keeping Lucas safe and this plan would end the threat to his friend. No, the problem was going to be Lucas.

Leaning against the wall in Rowe's office just behind his boss, he could stare at Lucas all he wanted without Rowe being aware of it. Lucas was doing an excellent job of ignoring him as they talked about the few things they'd discovered. It was only when Rowe went digging in his desk for something that Lucas dared to flick his eyes up to Andrei, a small smile tugging at the corners of his mouth. Andrei couldn't even fake a smile.

"Are you sure you never heard who was masterminding the fights?" Rowe demanded, swinging suddenly around in his chair to look at Andrei

"Never," Andrei shook his head. "There were plenty of middle men running around, lining up fights and handling the money. No one cared so long as they got paid."

Rowe frowned, staring at Andrei as a grim look entered his gaze. Andrei had a feeling his boss was starting to have the same thought, formulating the same plan.

The door opened suddenly, stopping either man from speaking, and Hollis strolled in wearing his usual leather jacket, rumpled shirt and jeans. The circles under his eyes weren't any darker so maybe the man had managed to catch a few hours of sleep since they'd last seen him. His dirty blond hair was a disheveled mess from him running his hands through it one too many times.

"Do you have any idea how sick I am of seeing you two?" he announced, pointing from Andrei to Lucas.

"Trust me, Detective, the feeling is more than mutual." Lucas frowned as the other man dropped into a chair beside him in front of Rowe's desk. Lucas had opted for slacks and soft V-neck charcoal gray sweater that made him look as if he was ready for a fashion magazine photo shoot. Two men couldn't have been more different.

"Look, Vallois, I'm not in the mood to play today. I'm tempted to run your adorable boy toy in after he lied to me last night."

Andrei curled his lip—not liking the boy toy tag at all.

Lucas shifted in his seat, sitting a little straighter. Muscles jumped in his jaw as he clenched his teeth. Fucking Hollis was playing with fire and there was no missing the fact that Lucas was more than willing to tear into the man. Andrei wasn't liking the cop too much either, but this was not going to help him at all.

"How about I tell you everything I know after you tell us what you got out of the men you interrogated last night?" Andrei interjected wearily. It was better to head this off now before it escalated. They had bigger issues coming.

Hollis made a face, seeming to think about Andrei's proposal. Of course, the cop was telling them the truth. He could haul Andrei in on obstruction charges and make him spill what he knew, but it was always so much easier when everyone was playing nice.

"Fine," Hollis said in a huff. "None of the men could give me a name for the person gunning for Vallois. They claim to have no idea why they were shooting at him. The orders arrive by courier. All three are in deep at the Locker."

"The Locker?" Lucas asked, looking over at Andrei.

"Local name for the underground fights," Andrei replied, crossing his arms over his chest as he grew more uncomfortable under Hollis's cold gaze. "Anything else?"

"Altura Unlimited LLC."

"What's that?"

"The company that owns the abandoned warehouse where the fights were held last month. Also, the same company that put a bid on the land that Lucas owns in Price Hill."

Lucas's frown deepened and he turned his gaze to Rowe. "I bet that's not the only thing this company has been involved in. We need to do some digging."

Rowe grunted, pushing to his feet. "Find the owner." He walked around to the door and jerked it open, half hanging out. The office was up on the second floor of an old warehouse that had been remodeled. The first floor was more of a training center so that Rowe could be sure that his people were being trained in the latest fighting and defensive techniques. "Hey! Where the hell is Gidget?" Someone shouted back, but Andrei couldn't make out the words. "Send her up here now!"

Turning back, Rowe flopped down in his chair behind the desk, his worried eyes flashing back over to Andrei. "If we find the owner of Altura, can we actually tie the attempts on Lucas to him?"

"You're going to need more," Hollis chimed in. "A lot more. But it would be a solid start considering we've got nothing more than a bunch of fighters with a hard on for Vallois."

"And Thomas Lynton," Lucas added.

Hollis's lips twisted into a wicked grin. "So you know about him too?"

"I've got connections."

"What else have you discovered that you haven't thought to share with the CPD?"

"Nothing."

"I find that hard to believe," Hollis snarled. "We're at risk, trying to protect your sorry ass—"

"Actually, the only one risking anything is Andrei," Lucas corrected sharply. "From what I've seen, you're just following along on our heels like a mongrel begging for scraps."

Hollis lurched to his feet, shoving his chair away so that the legs scraped loudly along the hardwood floor. Lucas was up just as quickly, his fists balled at his side. Andrei rolled his eyes to see Rowe lean back in his chair, the hint of a smile already on his face, his hands folded over his stomach as if he was content to sit back and watch the fight. His boss was no help. Andrei jumped between Lucas and Hollis, pushing them apart.

"This isn't helping," Andrei growled.

"I'm sick of doing all the work for him," Lucas snapped.

"I—" Hollis started, but he was interrupted by a new voice.

"Andrei!"

All four men turned instantly toward the door to find a small blonde in a flower-patterned ankle-length skirt and a modest white blouse. Her gamine face was alight with joy as she stared at Andrei.

"Hey Jen," Andrei replied, dropping his hands from Lucas and Hollis to turn completely to face her.

She immediately launched herself at him, wrapping her arms around his waist while the top of her head barely reached his shoulder. "It's so good to see you again. Between this new job and the last, I haven't seen you in weeks. Are you finally back?"

"Not quite." Andrei looked over the woman's head at Lucas. The man was a storm cloud ready to rain destruction down on all of them, and the focus of his ire was the tiny woman in his arms. Andrei couldn't have stopped the smirk that pulled at his lips if his life had depended on it. Lucas was jealous. He was so jealous that he was about to rip into a woman who was completely oblivious to his claim. Jen could never be more than a little sister to him and that suited both of them just fine.

"Oh, I'm sorry, Mr. Ward." She looked around Andrei at Rowe. "I didn't mean to interrupt. Daniel said that Andrei was back and I had to pop in for a visit before he disappeared again."

"I was looking for you anyway, Gidget," Rowe said with a dismissive wave of his hand. "I've got a job."

"Oh!" She lit up even more. "How can I help?"

"This is your hacker?" Hollis demanded incredulously. "She looks like a fucking kindergarten teacher."

Andrei fought to pick between the urges to gather Jennifer close or break Hollis's nose. But there was no need. She could more than handle herself.

"And who are you?" she asked crisply, slipping into what Andrei thought of as her mom voice.

"Detective Banner. Hollis." Andrei said, grinning.

"Your attitude is very unkind, Detective." She narrowed her eyes. "I'm sure that you were raised to treat strangers and ladies far better than that. I'm also sure you have no wish to dishonor your family in such a disgraceful manner."

Hollis blushed and actually took a step backward. "No, ma'am. My apologies."

Lucas snickered and Jen's eyes snapped to him. Lucas narrowed his own gaze on the woman and his grin became positively evil. Andrei could almost hear Lucas begging for the woman to give him shit because he was aching to snap at her. She still had her arm around Andrei's waist. A shiver ran through Andrei. Lucas's jealousy burned hot enough to singe.

"Here, Jen. Sit and Rowe will give you the details." Andrei pushed her down into Hollis's open chair. He sent a warning look at Lucas who just smiled at him before Andrei returned to his place against the wall behind Rowe. The space helped, but it did nothing to get rid of the feeling that they were on a runaway train racing toward someone doing something incredibly stupid.

Rowe gave Jen a quick rundown of the situation and what little they had managed to learn. Taking a piece of paper and pen from Rowe, she scratched out a few notes in her own unique shorthand. She chewed on her bottom lip, taking in the information and turning it over at lightning speed to look for new angles. If anyone could uncover the identity of the business owner, it would be Jen. She'd told Andrei that she'd acquired her first computer when she was ten and there was very little that she couldn't accomplish with one. She was an activist, determined to fight for and defend the weak and the helpless. Andrei was just glad Rowe had snatched her up and pulled her into his company. He helped to set boundaries for her, giving her a good cause to fight for that wouldn't land her in jail or worse. Sure, her techniques weren't *entirely* legal and Hollis had been correct when he called her a hacker, but she didn't care for that term. She preferred researcher. She just didn't let things like passwords and firewalls stop her.

"Need anything beside the owner?"

"Complete list of employees if you can find it," Lucas said. Any hostility he might have felt toward the woman seemed to have disappeared as they directed their attention to the problem at hand. "Also, see if the company or any subsidiaries have been purchasing any other land. Lynton and I might not be the only ones who've encountered resistance."

"Areas I should focus on?"

"Anywhere in the loop," Rowe directed, referring to the I-275 highway that encircled the tri-state area with Cincinnati at its center.

Jen nodded, making a couple of last notes. "Got it."

"How long will this take?"

"If this guy's careless or reckless, a day or two."

"And if he's not?"

Jen's eyes darted over to Hollis and then held Rowe's for several long seconds. "If we're talking a Nevis LLC buried inside of a Cook

Islands trust, I'll have to be creative. Could take weeks, maybe months. Those darn lawyers have gotten sneaky."

Rowe nodded. "Get started. Do what you have to."

Jen jumped up from her seat and swept around the desk to give Andrei one last hug before hurrying out of the room again.

Hollis pinched the bridge of his nose with his thumb and forefinger before rubbing his eyes. "So I'm going to pretend that I never met that woman and didn't hear that conversation at all."

"It's just a little research on the Internet," Andrei said with a smirk. "She would never do anything illegal."

"Yeah and I'm the fucking tooth fairy. Don't give me grief right now, boy toy. I can feel the ulcer forming in my stomach each second I spend with you three." He glared at all three men and shook his head. "You got anything else for me? Anything useful?"

"No," Andrei sharply said before anyone could speak up. He had a plan, but he knew that he couldn't include the cop in it. The man might not always stick to the straight and narrow of things, but Andrei didn't want to risk him stopping them.

Hollis eyed him for several long seconds before cursing them all and stomping out of the room. Yeah, he knew there was something in the wind, but he also couldn't do anything to make them admit to it. Worst-case scenario, Lucas just had to call Sarah in to growl at the detective, forcing him to back away. Hollis was trapped.

Andrei waited several seconds before he looked down at the back of Rowe's head. "You know we can't wait a week or longer for Jen. She's good, but this guy is escalating. The first few were little more than scare tactics, but the drive-by was aimed to kill. Patrick Laughlin's death has made this asshole desperate. He's either afraid we know something or he's running out of time to get to Lucas."

"I know," Rowe said in a low voice, staring down at the top of his desk. He sighed and turned in his chair to look at Andrei. "You got a plan?"

"Fire me."

"What?" Lucas shouted, coming out of his chair. "How the hell does that fix shit?"

Andrei refused to look up at Lucas, couldn't meet his eyes. No, he kept his stare on Rowe, whose expression had become hard and unreadable.

"You sure about this?"

"We need someone on the inside," Andrei said firmly. "Not only have I been there, but they'll come to me if they think I'm pissed at Vallois."

"No, Rowe!" Lucas thundered. "No! You're not doing this! You're not even considering this bullshit."

"Lucas, calm down. He's right. We need someone on the inside."

"Then let the fucking cops do it. It's their job!" Lucas pointed at the door Hollis had just exited through.

"I doubt they have anyone on the inside. I'm your best bet." Andrei finally looked up at Lucas who was watching him with glittering pale eyes. Every muscle in his body was tensed as if he were fighting to hold his anger and desperation inside his body. "I've been there. It's only been three years since I fought last. If they believe I'm unemployed and desperate for cash, they'll not question it."

"Will you have to fight?" Lucas asked in a deceptively low voice. Andrei hesitated, pressing his lips together in a tight, thin line. "Will you?" Lucas snapped, his voice cracking through the tense air like a whip.

"Yeah, a few times. I have to make it believable."

"No!" Lucas glared down at Rowe, who had been watching his old friend very closely. "He's been injured. He can't fight. That's why he gave it up in the first place."

"I know."

"Then you can't allow this. He's going to get himself killed!"

"He's still a strong fighter. Just needs to get a little sparring practice in, knock the ring rust off, and he'll be fine."

"No! I forbid it!"

Andrei waited until Lucas met his gaze. "I can handle this."

Lucas drew in a slow breath as if trying to pull himself together when it was obvious that he'd rather tear the office apart in a fit of rage. "Get out, Rowe," he said in a low, calm voice. "I want to talk to Andrei alone."

"Luc," Rowe started, but his next words were caught in his throat by the dark glare Lucas turned on him.

"It's okay," Andrei said.

Rowe gave a sharp nod and pushed to his feet. Andrei clenched his teeth, swallowing the groan that rose up when he met Rowe's eyes one last time. His boss knew or at the very least had some serious suspicions. Fuck. There was a good chance that Rowe wasn't going to have to fake fire him. By the end of the day, Andrei was going to be fired for real (again) and very likely have the shit beaten out of him for breaking company policy with his boss's best friend.

Lucas waited until the door closed behind Rowe before he moved. Kicking Hollis's chair out of the way, he rounded Rowe's desk and stepped up to Andrei, putting his hands against the wall on either side of Andrei's head. Pain and anger radiated from him in waves until he vibrated where he stood. Andrei watched as he took in a deep breath as if trying to control himself.

"And here I thought being jealous of some tiny woman was going to be the worst part of my day," Lucas started in a low voice.

"No need. She's like a little sister," Andrei replied, trying to smile. "But I am flattered. I thought you were just interested in my ass."

"No," Lucas gritted out through clenched teeth. "You don't get to make jokes."

"Lucas." Andrei sighed. He reached up to lightly touch his cheek, but Lucas jerked away. "It's my job to protect *you*. It's what I do."

"If that's the case, then I'll tell Rowe that we've been fucking. Tell me that's not grounds for termination right now. No job. No reason to go through with this stupid scheme you've cooked up."

"That won't stop me."

"No! You are mine and no one touches you."

Andrei smiled. He'd expected that reaction, but that didn't stop the flutter in his chest to hear the words cross Lucas's lips. They'd been constant companions for just over four days and he already knew this man so well. Lucas was the born protector of his small group of friends. He rallied them, pushed them, supported them, and when the time came, protected them with everything he had. And somehow, Andrei had found his way into that small group…at least where Lucas was concerned.

"Doesn't that mean you're mine? That I have a right to protect you? That I can snarl at every fucking woman who looks at you, calculating the best way into your bed? And I sure as hell have the right to take a baseball bat to any man who smiles at you."

Lucas looked lost, the anger draining from his face, as if he were truly stunned that anyone would feel that same level of possessiveness. He obviously didn't know how to handle it. The ground was slipping away under his feet.

"I know you," Andrei whispered, smiling to try to ease the sting of his words. "I know this isn't going to last. You don't date men. When you're safe again, I'm gone. I get that. But while I've got you, I can't accept you being in danger. I can end this by going back to the fights."

Lucas squeezed his eyes shut. "I am so royally bad at relationships. I mean epically. Worse than Snow even." He cleared his throat, but his voice still sounded hoarse. "But you'd rather risk your life than stick around to see how monumentally I could fuck us up." When Lucas opened his eyes, Andrei was drowning in a sea of moss green.

"I would still love to see how you can fuck this up, but I need you safe first."

"Andrei…"

"Listen to your analytical side. You know this is the best way to get at the bastard. It saves you and Thomas and anyone else he might be threatening."

"I can't. You've fucked everything up. I can't think any more."

A ripple of warmth swept through Andrei and he had to fight the urge to kiss Lucas right there. But he didn't. Lucas was at the edge, nearly ready to give in. He had to keep pressing. It was what was best. What was right.

"I get in. Get the info. Get out. Nothing more."

"And if they discover the truth?"

"They won't."

"How long?"

Andrei hesitated, so very tempted to lie, but he couldn't. "A few weeks at least."

"How many fights?"

"I don't know. As few as possible. Just enough to make it look like I'm genuinely desperate and pissed."

"And when you get back…"

"You can fuck me until I can't walk," Andrei promised with a half grin.

Lucas nodded, one hand sliding through his hair. He gently stroked the soft curls, his eyes moving over Andrei's face. "Say it again," he commanded, his voice low and rough. "About the monkey and the bicycle."

Andrei smiled and repeated the same bit of nonsense Romanian he'd said the night before, but his tone was low and soft like a caress or a promise. Lucas didn't smile as he'd hoped. Tipping his chin down, he kissed Lucas slowly, tasting him. This time it wasn't about building the fire that seemed ready to flare between them at all times. It was reassurance. It was a promise that this wouldn't be their last kiss.

When Lucas pulled away, he cupped Andrei's cheek. The look in Lucas's eyes stole his breath. Something had hardened in the man in those last seconds, stopping Andrei's heart in his chest.

"Be safe. Come back to me."

Because if you don't, the world will burn.

The words hung unspoken in the air. The man who was willing to negotiate, threaten, and even plead to get what he wanted was gone.

Lucas would step away and let Andrei take this risk. But if he failed, if he was hurt or killed, Lucas Vallois would rain fire on this city and no one would be safe.

Chapter 16

With his arm against the window, Lucas leaned his forehead on his wrist. The glass was cool to the touch as the brisk wind buffeted the building. The local weathermen were speculating that the city could see its first dusting of snow by Halloween. It was a sad thought considering the trees were still green on the hills surrounding Cincinnati.

But Lucas didn't feel the cold or see the shivering trees thick with leaves. The world was little more than a garish blur of noise and faded colors. Life had been squeezed down to work, sparring with Rowe until his body was aching and trembling from exhaustion, and the occasional update on Andrei's status. So far, Rowe's hacker had turned up nothing and Lucas's own discreet inquiries into who was buying up land around Cincinnati had not resulted in any new players or even useful information.

Two weeks. It had been two fucking weeks since that afternoon in Rowe's office. Nothing happened for the first week. Andrei contacted his associates in the fights and Lucas returned to his normal routine with a new bodyguard hounding his steps. Lucas never spoke to him. Never looked at him.

One week ago, Andrei had his first fight and Lucas lost himself in a bottle of bourbon to get through the night. When he closed his eyes, all he saw was the long scar along Andrei's knee from where he'd had ACL surgery. The injury would slow him down, make him just a little less mobile, make that knee just a little weaker. All Lucas could wonder was if that knee injury would be what made Andrei lose.

It was dawn when Rowe appeared to tell him Andrei had suffered only some minor injuries and had come through his first three fights victorious. But there would be more. The fights would keep coming until Andrei's body finally gave out or the bastard hunting Lucas offered Andrei a job.

Heavy footsteps thudded down the hall, approaching his study. Lucas turned back to the desk and picked up the 9mm sitting on a stack of papers. His finger rested on the safety and he drew in a slow breath, waiting. He started to lift the gun until Rowe stepped into the open doorway. Flipping the safety back on, Lucas wordlessly returned the gun to the papers and stayed behind the desk.

Rowe frowned at the weapon before he looked up at his friend. It wasn't the gun that Rowe had given him. No, this one came with a silencer and Lucas knew his friend was unnerved.

"I was getting ready to come see you," Lucas said, sitting down in the big leather chair behind his desk. He shuffled some papers, placing them in tidy stacks. Maybe he'd be able to work with a clear head later. He needed to hit the heavy bag for a while, burn off some of this excess energy.

"With that?" Rowe jerked his chin toward the gun still sitting out in the open.

Lucas didn't bother looking up as he shoved a file in his briefcase at his feet. "I thought you'd prefer it if I had some protection."

"Yeah, that's why I gave you George. The bodyguard is the one to handle the weapons, I thought."

"Speaking of which, where's that knife you promised me?" Lucas demanded, looking up at Rowe.

The other man made a face and then sighed heavily as he reached inside of his jacket and pulled out the black-handled folding knife. Leaning forward, he slammed it down on the top of Lucas's desk, but kept his hand over it, forcing his friend to meet his gaze. "We need to talk."

"Later. When we're sparring," Lucas said gruffly, clenching his teeth.

"Now. Something's up with you." Rowe pushed back to stand in front of Lucas's desk with his arms folded over his barrel chest.

Lucas reached forward and picked up the blade, his fingers moving over the patterned matte black grip. "There's someone trying to kill me." With a flick of his wrist, the four-inch blade jumped from the handle. It was also a dull black except for the shine along its incredibly sharp edge. Lucas continued to inspect the blade, testing its weight. He wasn't as good with knives as Snow. No, he preferred a gun or even his fists, but a blade could work in tight quarters. "You track down that fixed blade I asked you about?"

"It's on backorder," Rowe replied without thinking and growled. "You know, I should find this fun. I like it when you stop by once a month and visit the gun range. I like sparring with you. But this," Rowe paused, motioning toward the knife and gun. "This is too much even for you. Where the hell did you even get that gun?"

Lucas lifted one eyebrow at him and smirked. "Did you really think you were my only supplier?"

"YES!"

A dark chuckle slipped from Lucas as he closed the knife and slipped into his pocket. "Weren't you the one who said I needed to take this more seriously? That I should be more cautious? This is me being cautious."

"No, it's fucking not and you know it!" Rowe shouted, pointing at Lucas. "This is you preparing for war. I've seen it before. That time you found out that we were gonna be sent on recon near that Khost training camp. You started going dark and loading up on weapons, things that weren't standard issue."

Lucas stared at his old friend, but for once there were no flashes of his time in the Army while stationed in Afghanistan. He saw nothing. There was just his need to prepare. A feeling of anger and dread were building in him and the only thing that could combat that feeling was the knowledge that he could take control again…or at the very least, take revenge. And for both those scenarios he needed to be prepared.

"Snow stopped by today," Rowe announced in the silence that had stretched between them. "He said that he hasn't seen you in two weeks and that you haven't actually seen Ian in over a week."

"It's safer if I don't see them. It's dangerous to be around me," Lucas said, his voice empty of all emotion.

"He said you fired Candace."

Lucas flinched. That he regretted. "She was belligerent."

"For calling you on being a maniacal douche bag? She should have been given a medal for putting up with your shit!"

Lucas blinked, his eyes focusing on Rowe who was staring at him as if he had lost his mind. "Are you done?"

Rowe threw his arms up in the air and paced a short distance away as if trying to get his temper back under control. "Man! I haven't seen you in two weeks."

"You've seen me every day."

"No! I haven't seen *my friend*, the man I love and respect as a brother, in two fucking weeks. You've just become this cold, soulless bastard who acts likes he preparing to unleash Armageddon on the world." Rowe paced to the desk, standing over his friend. "It's like you've abandoned us to hide in your tower and plot your revenge."

Lucas jumped back to his feet, his fists twisting in the collar of the soft navy Henley Rowe was wearing, holding the man so close that their noses nearly bumped. "I have never abandoned you when you needed me. Never," he snarled. "I have been there for you every time you've needed me through everything."

Rowe clenched the back of Lucas's neck, lowering his head so that his forehead hit Lucas's. "Then why are you pushing us all away?" Rowe's words came out as little more than a rough whisper. "Snow, Ian, me, you know we'd all die for you."

Lucas shuddered and he could feel cracks forming in the wall he had built around his emotions to keep them at bay so he could simply function each day. He longed to step back and let the wall fall, but he couldn't. He had to keep holding the wall up, to hold himself together should something go wrong. He had to be the strong one. He had to be the one to hold the line and protect his friends…his family.

"Maybe I don't want anyone dying for me." Lucas pulled away.

Rowe released him and straightened, frowning at his friend. "Is this about Andrei?"

"The guy is risking his life for me. He's risking getting beaten to a bloody pulp in those damned fights. Even without that, if this asshole discovers that he's a fucking spy, he's dead." Lucas could feel the tension ramping back up in his frame with each word he spoke. He suddenly felt trapped in his own office. He needed to be out, doing something, taking some action that would get him closer to having this whole thing finished so no one else would end up hurt or dead.

Rowe shrugged. "It's his job."

"It's not his fucking job to do this!" Lucas roared before he caved to the need to move and walked over to the windows, massaging the muscles in the back of his neck. His entire body was one tense muscle and he could only find relief when he was fighting with Rowe or deep in a bottle of alcohol. But the next morning he always woke hating himself, knowing that if he'd been needed, he would have been unable to help anyone.

"Luc?" He turned back to find Rowe rubbing his right hand nervously through his hair, looking incredibly uncomfortable. "Is there more going on with you and Andrei?"

"You mean, am I fucking him?"

Rowe gave him a dirty look, dropping his hand to his side. "That's not what I mean. It's obvious to even me that you're fucking him. Which I totally blame you for since I was pretty damn sure that he was straight when I assigned him to you." Lucas opened his mouth to defend himself but Rowe threw up both hands, halting the words in his throat. "Don't want to hear it. Really. I don't."

"Then what are you talking about?"

"Is it…is it more than fucking?"

"No."

"Are you sure?"

Lucas glared at Rowe, but the man didn't flinch and didn't yield. "He—" Lucas started and suddenly found that he simply couldn't continue the sentence. What the fuck was Andrei? No, the man wasn't just some random fuck that he'd never speak to again and be happy to forget. But he couldn't be more because there wasn't room in Lucas's life for more. There was his family and then there was the rest of the world.

But he wouldn't be feeling like this if that were the case.

"I just don't want him dead because of me," Lucas finished lamely, inwardly cringing at his own words. He sounded so fucking weak. And it felt like a damned lie. Shaking his head, Lucas let his shoulders slump, copping to the one truth he could deal with. "This whole situation…Andrei in the fights…it's out of my control. I'm just sitting here, twiddling my thumbs, waiting for other people to cover my ass. I can't take this helpless bullshit."

Rowe slipped his hands into the pockets of his worn jeans, shifting from one foot to the other. "Trust me, I know. I'd rather be in those underground fights with him, but if this guy knows you, then he fucking knows who I am. There was no way in for me."

Lucas watched Rowe for several seconds, fighting another frown. Yeah, the ex-Army Ranger would understand. Rowe loved being in the middle of the action. He lived for the hunt, that middle of the night sneak into enemy territory with only your brothers. The man would still be a Ranger if it hadn't been for the injury to his heart. He'd been forced out far sooner than he'd planned and now he was stuck as a civilian, constantly on the lookout for the next adventure to get his blood pumping.

With a sigh, Lucas looked over at one of his oldest friends, wondering not for the first time why the man put up with his shit over the years. "Do you think Candace will come back?"

Rowe grinned. "Sure. But you're going to need to offer her a seriously fat bonus for coming back. And lots of vacation time. Maybe you should send her to that island with all the hot, half-naked guys serving drinks with those little paper umbrellas."

Lucas grinned. "What island is that?"

"I don't know," Rowe said rolling his eyes. "When was the last time I took a vacation?" He paused, his brow furrowing in thought. "She is straight, right?"

"Yeah." Lucas snickered.

"I don't know. All those women in business suits come off hungry and angry. My best friends are all gay. Obviously I can't tell anymore who's straight or bi or gay or a purple fucking people eater."

Rowe's exaggeration forced a loud bark of laughter out of Lucas. He grinned back. Lucas knew that he was the serious one of the group, but he'd taken brooding down to Snow's level and their little family couldn't handle two Snows.

"Come on. Walk me out," Rowe said, waving for Lucas to accompany him.

"Hot date?"

Rowe groaned. "Mel bought new curtain rods. I promised I'd be home early to help hang curtains." He made it sound like he was being dragged off to a Siberian gulag for ten years of hard labor.

Lucas chuckled as he followed Rowe down the hall. "Married life is rough."

"Fuck you."

They'd reached the living room when Lucas's new bodyguard stepped in the front door. He was an older man with a scarred face and bulky frame. Rowe had said that the man was an ex-cop and could be trusted. Lucas had barely looked at him and was only vaguely aware that his name was George. Sadly now that Rowe had talked a little sense into him, Lucas was starting to feel a smidge bad about dismissing the man so completely. Since Lucas was staying at home, he had requested that the man take up his post outside the front door rather than in the penthouse. He also wasn't staying over at night, which hadn't pleased Rowe at all.

"Mr. Vallois? There's a Chris Green here to see you," he said, his voice rough and scratchy.

"How did he get up here?" Lucas demanded, walking into the kitchen.

The bodyguard shook his head. "Do you want me to send him away?"

"Who is he?" Rowe's entire body tensed as he went on alert.

"That guy you shoulder checked at my club a few weeks ago. Before the incident. I thought..." Lucas's voice drifted off as he ran out of words. He thought there might have been something, a one-night stand to blow off a little steam, but then Andrei stepped into his life and Lucas lost all interest.

"Let him in," Rowe said firmly as the bodyguard waited for an answer.

Lucas frowned at his friend, but bit his tongue. This was a good test. With Andrei out of sight, could he also be out of mind? Lucas had his doubts, but he was willing to test it.

Chris Green was a handsome man in his early thirties with brown hair and fair skin. His brown eyes skimmed over the penthouse, taking in the wall of windows that looked out over the city before settling on Lucas and Rowe standing near the island in the kitchen. He seemed taken by surprise to be faced with someone other than Lucas, but he quickly slipped his smile back in place, seeming a little unsure and nervous.

"Hi, I know we haven't been formally introduced. I'm Chris Green. We...um...ran into each other at Shiver a couple weeks ago." He extended his hand to Lucas.

Lucas stepped forward and quickly shook his hand, but still kept the island between them, not wanting to close the space more than necessary. "I remember you, Mr. Green. This is my friend, Rowan Ward."

Chris started to reach for Rowe, but Rowe actually took a step backward and leaned against the counter, watching the man through narrowed eyes. Lucas wanted to chuckle. There was nothing welcoming about Rowe. He was quite talented at making people uncomfortable when he was feeling overly protective.

"Can I ask how you got up here?" Rowe demanded.

He flushed. "My boss lives a few floors down. I was delivering some contracts to him to look over. He mentioned that you lived here," he said, his eyes shifting to Lucas. "I thought I would drop by. I haven't seen you at Shiver since that night and I'd heard that you were in an accident." He gave a shrug and nervously clutched the edge of the counter. "I thought I'd just drop by. Check on you."

Lucas forced a small smile. "Thank you for your concern, Mr. Green."

"Chris, please."

"Thank you, but as you can see, I'm just fine."

"Then would you have dinner with me?"

Lucas paused, staring critically at the man. Dinner was definitely out. But he could so easily usher Rowe out the door and guide Chris up the stairs to his bedroom. That would release the last of the tension humming through his body. But even as he thought it, Lucas knew it wasn't going to happen. There was nothing. No spark. No stirring. No hint of interest. Whatever had captured his attention at the nightclub just weeks ago was gone. The man seemed pale and thin and flat compared to Andrei. There was nothing in his eyes that burned with life and passion. There was just…nothing and for a moment, Lucas couldn't decide if he was relieved or disappointed.

"I don't think so, but I appreciate your invitation, Mr. Green," Lucas said, trying to sound friendly.

Chris's smile slipped a notch, but he nodded as he backed toward the door. "Well, I'm glad you're better." He then slipped out without looking back again.

"That was disappointing," Rowe muttered, straightening.

"How's that?"

"Figured you'd just say let's skip dinner and let me fuck you against the fridge," Rowe drawled with a grin. "You know, work some of your sex magic."

"Not my type."

Rowe snorted and shook his head. "No, you're craving someone else now."

Lucas glared at his friend, his good humor slipping away. "I just want him safe."

"He'll be fine."

"Really?" Lucas snapped.

Rowe paused, taking in his friend's new sharp tone. "What?"

"Do you truly think he can handle this? Will he be fine?"

"Of course."

Lucas shook his head, clenching his fists where they rested on the top of the marble counter. "I know you, Rowe. I know you better than anyone else. You wouldn't hesitate to sacrifice someone else if it meant protecting me, Snow, Ian, or Melissa. Can he truly handle this?"

Rowe dropped his eyes, his body tense. Stepping closer to Lucas, he pulled him into a quick hug, holding him tightly for a few seconds before thumping him on the back. "It'll be over soon."

It wasn't the answer that Lucas had been looking for, and for a second Lucas couldn't breathe. He wanted to strangle Rowe, but he never doubted where Rowe's priorities were. He protected his wife and his family above all else. Lucas just prayed that Andrei didn't pay the price for Rowe's blind love and devotion.

Chapter 17

Andrei clenched his teeth, struggling to regulate his breathing. This fight had already gone longer than he'd expected. He just reminded himself that this opponent was the last one in the series. He'd taken out the previous two easily, giving this asshole the chance to watch his moves. The fucker was being cautious, staying out of Andrei's reach for the most part. But they were both winded. The fight needed to end soon.

The asshole with the bleach-blond hair came in with a one-two punch. Andrei was a second too slow and the first landed, grazing the side of his jaw, while the second missed wide when Andrei ducked low. His opponent took advantage of the move, landing a knee to Andrei's solar plexus, sending Andrei stumbling back a few steps, gasping for air. Blondie followed as Andrei expected, keeping the pressure on with a flurry of punches that Andrei deftly blocked, using the moment to gather his wits about him while catching his breath.

As much as he hated to admit it, Blondie had a few skills. He was certainly faster than most of the bastards Andrei had been fighting for the past two weeks and had a few more tricks up his sleeve. He still wasn't worried that he wouldn't come out on top of this fight, but he was beginning to become concerned as to whether he'd escape injury.

Blondie threw a lead hook, aimed for Andrei's jaw right near his ear. Andrei stepped in, blocking the punch with his arm before turning it into a hook that crashed into the man's jaw. Andrei immediately followed with another one-two punch before lowering his body to take the man out at the knees. But he was too slow. His body was tired and his own knees were fighting him. Blondie saw it coming and grabbed him by the back of the head. Andrei caught sight of the knee rushing toward his face and blocked with both hands, pushing them apart.

For a moment, the roar of the spectators watching them on two sides of the squared-off ring permeated Andrei's mind. They were losing their mind. But then, they sensed it too. This fight was fucking over. Taking advantage of this new distance, Andrei delivered a stomp kick to the center of the man's chest, hitting directly on the man's sternum to lower ribs. Blondie was sent sprawling backward into the crowd, his larger mass and momentum knocking two people down before he finally stopped. Hands grabbed the man's arms and shoulders before shoving him back into the open ring. Andrei was waiting. Taking one step, Andrei launched himself into a flying Superman punch that crashed into the man's mouth and chin.

Blondie fell backward, limp, his head bouncing off the hard concrete twice, but it didn't matter. He was unconscious before he hit the ground.

Andrei forced himself to look away as they dragged his unconscious opponent off to the side while a couple of fight workers splashed bleach across the blood-splattered concrete. They weren't trying to clean up the mess as much as they were trying to destroy the DNA evidence. The fights moved regularly, springing between abandoned warehouses and even the occasional fields out in the middle of nowhere just to keep the local cops off their scent. It was only when a mangled body popped up in the ER or the morgue that things went quiet for more than a week as the fight organizers waited for the heat to be off them.

Lifting his wrist to his mouth, he tore the tape with his teeth and started to unravel the black hand wrap he'd used to protect his knuckles. The cotton material was soaked with blood and sweat. He'd have to burn it later. He wanted to burn it all. The illegal fights made him sick to his stomach. And it wasn't the brutality that could be found in both the amateur and professional circuits. No, this was an utter disregard for human life. There were no doctors tending wounds or refs to make sure that the fights didn't go too far. In these illegal fights, there were no submissions. The fight wasn't over until at least one man was unconscious on the ground.

He was ready to be done with his undercover work and return to his life working security for Rowe. His job might not always be entirely legal, but he at least felt like Rowe gave a shit about whether he was safe and healthy. The ex-Ranger was constantly training him, improving his skills, making sure that Andrei had the very best equipment. Of course, it was a little hard not to feel utterly disposable as he wandered through hell, but Lucas needed him here even if the man wouldn't admit it.

But to get home, Andrei had to keep his eye on the prize. For now, that was Paul Roethke. He was the man who set up the fights, set the odds, and handled the payout. He was typically the most powerful man on the fight floor on any given night.

Tonight, he was talking to a newcomer in a suit and both men were closely watching Andrei as he approached them.

"There's my champ!" Paul crowed when Andrei was only a few feet away. "Another win for the gladiator!"

"What's my payout?" Andrei bit out, having no problem playing up the disgruntled asshole. Being back in the underground fights, his body aching while the bitterness of broken dreams threaten to swallow him whole — it all put him in a bad place.

Paul handed over a stack of bills. "Fifteen hundred."

Andrei quickly counted it, struggling a little with his right hand still wrapped. "Fuck, Paul. Why are you holding out on me? These have got to get bigger. I'm busting my balls out there for you."

"And you've won every fight since coming back," Paul said with a shake of his head. "It's getting hard to find another idiot to face you."

"If I lose to make you money, I get nothing but broken bones." Andrei shoved the money in the front pocket of his dirty, blood-stained jeans. "Fucking Vallois," he muttered under his breath before pulling at the tape on his right wrist.

"You work for that security company, correct?" the stranger inquired, his eyes narrowed on Andrei as if he were inspecting him like a prize horse up for auction.

"Worked," Andrei corrected. With an angry jerk, he pulled the wrap off his hand and balled it in his fist. "Fucking snotty ass-bag client pulled some stupid shit and I got canned. No warning. No severance. Just shoved out the damned door."

"Bastard," the man muttered but Andrei didn't miss the glitter to his pale blue eyes or the hint of a smile on his thin lips. "But this could work out for you."

Andrei glared at the man in the expensive gray suit. His thinning hair was slicked back, making his narrow face look even more pinched. He was smooth and tried to give off the aura of money but after spending days with Lucas, this guy was nothing but a cheap knock off.

"How?"

The man jerked his chin, motioning toward an empty section of the old warehouse. "Walk with me."

Andrei fought to keep his features schooled into a scowl as his heart took off. His aching ribs and throbbing knees were forgotten. He was close. They were close to having this done. Of course, now it got dangerous.

"I've been watching your fights, kid," the stranger began. "You've got a lot of skill. Too much to be wasting your time here with Paul's sideshow freaks."

Andrei snorted. "I've spent most of my life in training. I know how to handle myself."

"That would explain why Ward recruited you two years ago to join his little company."

The man's words sent a chill straight to Andrei's bones. This fucker knew a lot more than Andrei would have expected. Had Rowe loosened the security, allowing them to rummage around in the company's files so they could research Andrei? He prayed that was the case.

"Ward knows talent," the man continued.

"He also threw away his best man because his friend is a fucking idiot," Andrei snarled, letting his growing discomfort come out as irritation.

"We heard you were protecting Lucas Vallois," the man murmured when they were alone in the shadows.

"We?"

"Me and my employer."

"And who the hell are you?"

He flashed a grin full of yellow, crooked teeth. "Jake Heath."

Andrei nodded. Either he was lying or he didn't expect Andrei to live long enough to use the name against him.

"Yeah, I protected Vallois. Risked my life for the bastard only to get shafted."

Jake snorted. "Considering the prick's preferences, I'm surprised he didn't try."

Andrei kept his face blank, trying to look as if he didn't understand when all he wanted to do was slam his fist into the man's nose. It was bad enough that he had to lie about Lucas. He didn't want to listen to any derogatory words about him as well.

Jake cleared his throat and continued. "Did you recognize any of the men chasing Vallois?"

"Yeah, a couple," Andrei mumbled, looking away from Jake to gaze around the warehouse, as if the other man wasn't able to actually hold his attention.

"But you didn't tell the cops."

"Nope. My job was to keep him alive, not solve his problems. He's not earned any loyalty from me."

"Besides, you solve his problem and you're out a job."

Andrei smirked. "Exactly." He shrugged and then winced at the pain in his shoulder. "Glad I didn't. Fucker deserves what he gets."

"Would you like to help my employer in that respect?"

"What do you mean?"

"Vallois has hurt some people. Taken advantage of them and we just want to make things square." Jake spread his hands as if trying to make his argument seem like he and his employer were the good guys. Robin Hood stealing back what was theirs from the evil Sheriff. "You give us a little inside information on Lucas's habits and we can make it worth your while. Better than risking your life in those fights."

Andrei rubbed his jaw, making a show of thinking things over. "What kind of information?"

Jake smiled slowly. "Nothing too detailed. If you were with him a while, you've got to know his schedule. Any habits? Places he goes on a regular basis where we can meet him and…talk to him."

A harsh bark of laughter escaped Andrei. "You can kill him for all I care." He dropped his hand back at his side and glanced up at the other man. "I don't know about his usual schedule. I was with him for less than a week, but I know that tomorrow night he's supposed to go to the jazz bar across the street from Fortune off of Main Street with that doctor."

Jake nodded and stepped closer. He was shorter than Andrei by several inches so it was odd when the man tried to intimidate him, but then the two larger men who stepped up next two Andrei from behind certainly helped. "Now, you understand…that since you were working for Vallois and you've suddenly shown up here with information, it does look questionable. How do we know you're not a spy or just bait?"

Andrei met his narrowed gaze and smiled. "You don't."

"Then you won't mind if you stay with me for a couple days. Just until after we pay Mr. Vallois a visit. We'd hate for you to have second thoughts and warn him."

"Not fucking likely, but yeah, I get it. You gonna feed me?"

Jake laughed deeply, throwing his head back before clapping his hand on Andrei's shoulder. "Yeah, we'll feed you. You're probably gonna break the fucking bank when it comes to food."

Andrei shrugged, trying to push down his nerves as Jake started to walk him toward the exit accompanied by the other two thugs. "I'm not asking for steak. Just pizza with more than one topping might be nice."

"You get me Vallois and I'll make sure you're eating steak every night for a fucking year." Jake laughed.

Andrei's cheeks hurt from the fake grin and he was fighting a wave of nausea. He and Rowe had discussed this. Even though they hadn't told Lucas ahead of time, they knew Andrei would have to prove that he was on the level. They'd set up a series of potential times when Lucas would make an appearance somewhere. When Andrei failed to send his check-in text tonight, Rowe would assume that he was in custody and that Lucas would have to make his appearance with Snow. He just prayed Rowe had a solid plan for keeping Lucas safe when these bastards hit the bar, because he had just sold out the one person who was starting to mean way too much to him.

Chapter 18

Snow took in Lucas's deceptively lazy sprawl and smirked. His friend was fooling no one with those tense muscles and scowl. They'd been at this ridiculous bar for two hours now. Whoever designed the place had no imagination. Everything was so red, Snow's eyes felt as if they were bleeding. Even the whiskey choices made Snow wish they could leave. He glanced around the shadowy room. Rowe had parked himself near the main entrance and in addition to the new bodyguard covering Lucas, two more of Rowe's staff were strategically standing near doors. Still, Snow couldn't help but stay tense. He'd been jumpy since the shootout in Gaile. One of the people who'd been shot hadn't made it. He knew there'd been nothing he could do by the time he got to the woman—she'd bled out fast—but it still cut into him.

He hated losing anyone. It was the one part of his job he never could get past.

The way she'd stared at him, as the life drained from her eyes, had been keeping him up nights. He gulped more of the crappy whiskey, hating that it burned wrong, but still trying to shove the image away. The last person anyone should see as they lay dying in this world was him.

Running his gaze over Lucas, he took in the black jeans and black cashmere sweater that made his friend look like some kind of dark pirate and managed to grin. Lucas leaned against the wall in their small booth and he'd spent most of the two hours frowning at the live band. Snow snickered. "Tell me again how we came here to check out the band for one of your places. I dare you."

Lucas's scowl grew darker. "Fuck you. You know why we're here."

"You didn't want another of your own places getting shot up?"

One black eyebrow went up. "You think I'd have brought you along if I thought they'd have guns again?"

"Like you could stop me."

In truth, Snow was just happy to see Lucas again after his two-week absence. Even if Lucas did look like hell and his patience had become absolutely microscopic. The dark shadows under his eyes and constant, angry tic of muscles in his jaw spoke of a man pushed to his limits. In all their years together, Snow couldn't remember ever seeing Lucas so frayed…and all over some guy he'd known for barely a week. Something fluttered in Snow's chest that he didn't want to examine too closely. Was he jealous? Threatened that someone commanded Lucas's attention so completely? Or just pissed that Andrei could hurt his friend?

Fuck. He felt like he should do or say something. Lucas was hurting, though he would never admit to that, and Snow felt so utterly useless. Lucas was the one who handled these things. He smoothed the waves and soothed the pain. The man instinctively knew the right touch, the right amount of force and murmured words to pull Snow out of his dark places. Snow should be able to give back. To not fail his friend.

Snow sneered at himself and picked up his whiskey again, watching the ice swirl in his glass and wishing he could hear the clink against the sides. Grimacing, he set it back down. He was spoiled and he didn't care. This slop wasn't worth the pain it would give his stomach later. He glanced up at the back of Lucas's current bodyguard's head. The man had squeezed into the booth behind theirs and Snow was pretty sure he wouldn't be able to get out fast enough to save anyone. "Maybe you should have greased the new guy up before forcing him into one of these booths."

"Trust me, I have no interest in oiling that man for any reason." Lucas traded the scowl for a faint smile. "He looks tough enough to take you on." He leaned closer. "Come to think of it, you seem good—you get all that anger worked out?"

"Been too busy to worry about it." Snow shrugged, unwilling to talk about his own problems. Those eyes. Staring at him. Desperately wanting him to stop what she knew was happening…"I think we need to be focusing on you right now. I'm fine. You're not." He slowly smiled, telling himself to just fucking man up and wade in. "You got it bad, my friend."

Lucas opened his mouth, but Snow cut him off.

"Don't even bother to deny it. The worry is coming off you like some kind of noxious gas."

Lucas's lip curled. "Pleasant. I'll leave the hooking up to you tonight then."

"Like it was even a possibility. For you. " He wiped all amusement off his face and leaned over the table. "You slept with the hot bodyguard."

Lucas just shrugged.

Snow nodded. "I thought so. And you didn't just sleep with him. What—did you fucking bond or something?"

"Shut up, Frost."

"I'll give you that he's cute and got a great mouth on him," Snow teased, giving a little shrug as he continued, "But is he really worth—"

Lucas's hand slammed down on the table, rattling their glasses with enough force to nearly topple them. "Ash! Drop it. This is not open for discussion."

The proverbial wall slammed down between them, fifty feet high and made of solid stone. There would be no reaching Lucas, not here at least. That was the worst part of their relationship. Lucas could dig at all of them, get them to pour out their pain and fear, as if he were the pope taking confessions on Sunday, but when it came to his own pain and fear, they remained locked away and untouchable. Hell, if Andrei could touch that side of Lucas maybe he wasn't so bad after all.

"He'll be fine," Snow offered up, his voice pitched so low that it barely carried over the music.

Lucas dropped his head back against the wall and closed his eyes, his façade cracking with a heavy sigh. He took another breath and Snow started to reach for the arm resting on the table when Lucas lifted his head, blinking as the controlled mask fell back into place.

"You're right." Without looking at him, Lucas grabbed Snow's hand and squeezed. They were still good.

Before Snow could come up with a response, a sexy grin and blatant invitation caught his eye. The man stood next to the hall that held the restrooms and as soon as Snow snagged his stare, that grin grew wider. He had dark, curly hair and a long elegant body and smile that reminded Snow of that damned paramedic at the hospital. Heat curled in his gut. Here was a way he could kill the film reel of that woman and her terror, something to temporarily drown out his worry about Lucas and his friend's obsession with his bodyguard. "Seems there's something somewhat decent here after all. I'll be right back. This shouldn't take long."

Lucas turned to look in the direction Snow had and shook his head. "Thought you'd gotten bathroom hookups out of your system years ago."

"Good blowjobs are never out of the system and that is a good one just waiting to happen." Snow stood and made sure to keep eye contact with the guy as he walked up to him, then past him. He didn't bother to look back—he'd be followed.

Empty stalls greeted him and as soon as the guy walked into the restroom behind him, Snow had his shirt in his fists and was backing him into one of them. He kicked the door shut and turned his face when the man tried to kiss him. He wasn't here for that. Instead, he opened the fly of his slacks, ran his hand down a taut, muscled chest and lifted an eyebrow. The guy dropped to his knees. Snow could read this sort of thing right every single time. Some men loved to give head. Some men, like him, loved to receive. Though, he did have his times he liked giving just as much. Writing on the wall above the man's head read, "For a good time, call Jehovah." Snow smirked, tilted his head back and closed his eyes, more than ready for something good to come out of this night.

The slam of the outer bathroom door didn't faze him as the man opened his slacks further with eager fingers and dove in.

"He's here. Has a new bodyguard, but tell the boss the fighter came through."

Even the strong suction on Snow's dick couldn't keep him from paying attention then. He put his hand on the head below him to stop him and angled his own to try and look between the door and the stall wall.

The hooded figure on his phone reminded him of Lucas's description of the men who'd attacked him. Fury filled him and he had to work to rein it in as he tapped the guy in front of him on the head. He shook his head no, gave him what possibly resembled a polite "never mind" smile then shoved open the stall door. He didn't bother to refasten his pants.

Before the new man could shut down his call, Snow had him against the wall with both hands on his throat. "Tell *who* the fighter came through?"

"Hey! What the hell, man? Get off me!"

He squirmed but Snow merely tightened his fingers. "I'm a doctor and I know exactly where I can hurt you…" He tightened his fingers again. "Or worse. It's just your bad luck I happened to be in this bathroom and heard you."

"Dude, I'm not a fag!"

Snow chuckled, loving the way the man's face bled white with the noise. "I have no interest in putting my dick anywhere in you. I just want to know who you work for."

"None of your damned business!" The words came out strangled because of the pressure Snow was putting on the man's throat.

"I've seen you at the hospital before. You're a fighter. Tell me who sent you to check on my friend."

"Hey," another voice interjected.

Snow had forgotten all about the man he'd left in the stall. "You don't want to be a part of this. Catch you someplace else sometime."

"Sure. Whatever." The bathroom door slammed behind the guy as he left.

"Look, man. I don't know who is calling the shots. I was paid to come here and see if the rich guy showed. That's it." He shuddered. "Could you at least put your junk away?"

"I've got my hands wrapped around your throat and you're worried about a dick?"

"I told you, I'm not a fag!"

"You're not too bright either, are you? Just why do you think my cock is out when I wasn't alone in that stall? Think we were having a fucking pee party? Maybe you should think about your choice of words."

"You're a sick piece of shit. Let go of me."

"You think it's a good idea to throw around words like fag when I'm twice your size and had obviously been getting my dick sucked when you came in here and interrupted?"

The bathroom door opened and the low laughter that spilled into the room made Snow see red. Again. "Not now, Rowe."

"I saw you come in here with another guy who left really fast and looked pretty damned pissed. So, I thought I'd see what was going on. This one looks nothing like your usual type."

Snow grinned and hoped Rowe would play along. "This one likes it rough. Wanna join in?"

Rowe came up behind Snow and pressed in close. Snow had to fight not to lift his eyebrows in surprise. Rowe had some fantastic muscles in that taut body of his. "Want me to lock the door so we can really go to town on this guy?" Rowe breathed over his shoulder, while wrapping one arm around Snow's waist. "Do we have time for me to grab our bondage gear out of the truck?"

It took everything Snow had not to crack up then. Fucking Rowe. Damn. He'd been nuts about the man within the first week of service with him. Snow worked to keep his expression fierce and leered at the guy against the wall. This idiot knew nothing—he could tell. But the look of abject terror on his face was worth the hours of bleeding eyes and shitty alcohol.

"I only had a phone number!" The guy choked out. "I swear. Take my phone. It's yours."

"What if we want something a little warmer and wetter than a phone?" Rowe asked.

Snow couldn't help it then. He lost it. The laugh came out as a loud snort first, then he let go as he bent and just let loose. "Warm and wet? Fuck, Rowe!"

The guy tried to run but Rowe slammed him back into the wall. "Give us the phone, dick wad."

Rowe had the phone in hand as the guy ran from the room. He turned and patted a still snickering Snow on the back. "You want me to find another for our raunchy threesome?"

"Oh, I want, baby. I want."

Lucas walked into the bathroom just in time to hear the last of their exchange. He grinned and walked up to a urinal. "Do I even want to know?"

Warm and wet. Snow started laughing all over again. "Yeah. Yeah, you do."

兄弟武士心

Lucas shook his head as he looked around his living room. Snow was sprawled on the couch with Ian half on his lap. The younger man had his ankles crossed on the back of the seat as he snuggled into the doctor's lap and held up bites of...Lucas didn't know what. He was five bourbons in at this point and all he knew was the warmth of family around him.

Rowe was somewhere on the floor.

Lucas laughed into his glass, the air making the liquor bubble. "Warm and wet," he repeated, sending Snow into gales of laughter hard enough to nearly shake Ian loose.

"Hey, be still. I'm comfortable." Ian held his hand up.

Snow ate whatever Ian had been holding up and sucked the younger man's finger into his mouth with loud, smacking sounds. Ian laughed and yanked his hand loose.

Lucas couldn't stop his smile. He looked at the moon, shining bright through the wall-length window, then back at his friends. These three men, were his life. They made everything worth it. But there was one more who would make this whole scene feel complete.

What was Andrei doing now? Was he in pain? Bleeding? He rubbed a hand over the sharp pain in his chest.

Lucas watched Ian, happy that the young chef was so comfortable here. It didn't take much to remember a completely different scenario—one that still scraped his gut raw. Seeing Ian, beaten and bloody...and unconscious. Watching Snow lose it. There had been so much blood. And Lucas had thought there could never be more blood than what he'd seen in the Army. He'd been wrong.

Rowe groaned somewhere in the vicinity of the couch.

"I gotta get home. Mel's gonna kill me." He sat up, proving he'd been between the couch with Snow and Ian and the coffee table. "I wonder if Gidget has had enough time to track down those numbers for us." He blinked around the room and pointed a finger at Snow. "Evil, wicked fucker. What the hell was in that last drink?"

Snow shrugged. "Ian made it."

Ian snickered. "Nobody forced you to drink it, lightweight."

Lucas couldn't stop the laughter that bubbled up from his throat. He'd needed this. Needed the people who made life worth living. Here in his home. He propped his bare feet up on the coffee table.

Snow stretched out his hand to the other side of the table and snatched the phone they'd taken from the thug in the bathrooms at the bar earlier. He squinted into it. Started touching the screen. "For someone who claimed he wasn't a fag, he sure has a lot of gay porn bookmarked on this phone."

"Ooh, lemme see," Ian drawled, snagging the phone. He frowned at the screen for a long time, then elbowed Snow hard enough to make the doctor grunt. "You need glasses. She may be flat-chested, but that's a woman."

"It's not!" Snow grabbed the phone and enlarged the photo. "Wait. Maybe it is."

"Roundest ass I've ever seen on a guy if it isn't." Ian popped something into his mouth.

"I like round asses." Rowe blinked again. His red hair was sticking up on one side of his head like he'd been smashed up against a wall. Or a floor.

Laughing, Lucas tilted his head back against his chair and closed his eyes, letting their low bickering soothe the worry eating up his insides. He wanted Andrei back. Here. Safe. He hated the idea of the man somewhere out there fighting just so he could learn who was trying to kill Lucas. Tonight's excursion to the horrible jazz bar had done only one thing. It had proved to whoever was pulling the strings that Andrei was on the up and up for them. It hadn't done anything else and frustration made Lucas want to break things.

Instead, he was here, watching the most important people in his life get loaded.

"Ian, are there more of those crab puffs in the kitchen?" Rowe staggered to his feet and lurched in that direction. "Those things are better than sex."

Ian started to answer but Snow plopped his hand over the chef's mouth. Ian's whole body was shaking as he plucked an apparent crab puff off the pan on his lap and held it over his head to Snow's mouth. The doctor ate it and nudged Ian for more.

Lucas frowned. "I didn't know those were crab puffs." He stood and dove across the coffee table, hitting the cookie sheet and sending the hors d'oeuvres flying in all directions.

"No," Rowe yelled as he ran back into the room and face-planted behind the couch.

Lucas calmly dug one of the puffs out from between Ian's legs and bit into it. They all waited as silence fell from behind the couch.

"I think he knocked himself unconscious," Snow murmured. He shrugged, nudged Ian and opened his mouth.

Lucas sat back and grinned at Ian and Snow. Later, all his fear and worry would return and keep him from sleeping just as it had every other damned night since Andrei had left. But for now, he'd enjoy them. And maybe see if Rowe had really knocked himself out.

Chapter 19

Andrei was trying not to pace, but he wasn't having much luck. It had taken him three days to find a suitable place to meet. It was only through luck that he'd stumbled across the single-story brick elementary school that had been closed down more than two years ago in Visalia, a backwater town deep in rural Kentucky. The windows were boarded up and all the landscaping was now overgrown. The cracks in the blacktop that comprised the main driveway as well as the playground were filled with weeds and crabgrass, as if nature was slowly reclaiming the area now that the children had moved on. He'd checked out the place a day prior to the meeting to find that a few people had apparently sneaked in to vandalize. There were places where kids had spray painted and others where someone had likely ripped out copper wiring and pipes, but the police had quickly closed it all up again. The electricity was even still connected. A small oversight by the city.

An uneasy feeling had inched through Andrei on his first inspection. The school had been too similar to his own elementary and middle school in his small hometown in southeastern Kentucky. While not as bad as high school, those years in his life hadn't been overly happy either. But he shook off the old ghosts and focused on the dire situation pressing down on his present day.

He'd driven for an hour to make sure he hadn't been followed here. With all the checking and sneaking, he'd be lucky to get to speak to Rowe for more than five minutes. And of course, Lucas probably wouldn't even show. It had been stupid to hope when he'd requested the first face-to-face meeting since going undercover more than two weeks ago. He'd just wanted to be further along by now.

Operating in the dark wore on his nerves. Just a quick text here and there. He liked to think if there was a major development someone would contact him. For two weeks, there had been only silence. He checked the news, waiting to hear about more attacks at nightclubs, fires, car accidents and those that happened didn't look like they could be tied to Lucas. Rowe, Snow, and Lucas would undoubtedly cover up anything, but they would tell him, right? But he'd heard nothing. Just endless, nerve-shredding silence.

Sadly, the silence wasn't the only thing that left him clenching his teeth and struggling to maintain his calm. Andrei was back in the one place he'd believed he would never see again. He thought he'd gotten it out of his system, but the rush of that first fight—landing that first punch—had been intoxicating. The blood lust, the overwhelming need to snatch back control of his life and his future, it rose up so that conscious thought slipped away and he was acting purely on instinct. The drive to survive. To conquer. He'd been brutal, letting three years of anger and frustration pour out of him, so that he'd left his first opponent unconscious in a pool of his own blood in mere seconds. For a brief moment, he thought he might be able to return to fighting. He'd been fast and agile. Maybe he had recovered enough from surgery to get back into the cage. He wasn't too old yet. Not quite thirty. He could sneak in a few years before retiring permanently.

And then the adrenaline wore off and his knee swelled. It was only through a mix of illegally acquired OxyContin and inflammation pills that he'd been able to walk the next day. Now he was getting through each fight that way and it needed to stop. He'd seen too many guys get hooked on painkillers and he didn't want to go down that road.

Headlights slipped around the edges of some boards and splashed across the wall as a car pulled into the vacant parking lot. Andrei dropped back into some of the heavier shadows and pulled his phone out of his pocket. A second later a text came asking if he wanted to see a movie tomorrow. Some of the tension eased from his shoulders. It was Rowe signaling that he hadn't been followed. Andrei typed "Sure" and put his phone in his pocket.

Moving deeper into the building, Andrei flipped on a light in a windowless room and stepped behind the door with his gun drawn. Rowe might have given the signal that he was alone, but Andrei was taking precautions until he saw it with his own eyes. Footsteps echoed through the abandoned school, crackling against broken linoleum, announcing that there were at least two people approaching.

A minute later the door pushed slowly open with a Glock entering first followed by the rest of Rowe. His boss quickly scanned the room, his eyes widening only slightly when he spotted Andrei with his weapon drawn. As he stepped farther into the room, he made a show of lifting his finger away from the trigger and putting the weapon in his holster under his arm.

Andrei's breath caught in his throat when Lucas stepped into the room a second later. Dressed all in black, he looked like death or maybe just the devil come to collect him for his sins. He turned to face Andrei and he remained absolutely expressionless, as if he'd just glanced out the window to check if it was raining. There was only a tightening of the muscles in his jaw as if he were clenching his teeth. But not a word or a smirk or a grin.

"Trouble?" Andrei demanded, breaking the silence.

"None," Rowe said with a shake of his head. "You?"

"No." He watched as Lucas paced to the opposite side of the room and leaned against the wall, crossing his arms over his chest. He said nothing and Andrei could feel the anger rising in him. No questions about how he was or if he'd been injured. Nothing to indicate that Lucas had given him even a passing thought. Just a cold, unblinking stare.

Even Rowe seemed surprised and confused, as he lifted both of his brows at his friend as if waiting for him to finally say something. Anything. The silence just stretched until it became uncomfortable.

"We're close," Andrei forced out, his voice rough and uneven.

The anger slipped from Rowe's face and his mouth popped open. "You got a name? A face?"

Andrei shook his head. "Not yet. Just another middle man. Jake Heath. A hustler and a numbers guy. He handles a lot of the bets that take place at the fights, but he's higher up the food chain. Knows about the attacks on Lucas."

Rowe groaned, shoving both of his hands through his hair. "Not the breakthrough that I was hoping for at this point, but I guess it's a step closer."

Andrei allowed a small grin. "I've been officially hired for the next job. Told them I can get them through all the security at the penthouse. Deliver them straight to Vallois asleep in his bed."

"Damn," Rowe whispered, his eyes darting to Lucas. The other man didn't flinch, his gaze still not straying from Andrei.

"We can set up a sting."

Rowe dropped his hands back to his side, a growl of frustration slipping from him. "But that's just going to catch us more thugs with no idea who hired them."

"I said I wouldn't do it unless I met the boss. And I made it very clear that I was needed to override all of your tricks." Andrei's smiled broadly, his dark eyes flashing with mischief. "They need me."

Rowe scratched the red stubble on his chin, turning over Andrei's words. "Risky but it might work."

"They're convinced I hate Vallois. That he's the reason I got canned and I'm broke." Andrei paused, his eyes pinned on Lucas. "Made it clear I'd be happy to be the one to pull the trigger."

"I'm convinced," Rowe muttered, his gaze moving between Lucas and Andrei, who continued to stare at each other as the tension built in the room.

"Anything else?" Lucas demanded in a low, business-like tone.

Andrei clenched his teeth, barely holding back a curse. What about the fact that he'd descended into hell to protect him? What happened to the 'Come back to me'? He had a sickening feeling that what he'd thought had been happening was sadly one way. He'd thought that maybe Lucas could truly see him as a friend, as someone you have a beer with on occasion and just shoot the shit for laughs. Sure, he'd never reach the elite status of Ian or Rowe—and no one would be as precious to Lucas as Snow—but at least a regular friend.

No. Lucas obviously felt nothing more than guilt. Not real concern. But then Andrei had no one to blame by himself. Ian had warned him and two weeks apart had obviously given Lucas time to come to his senses.

"No," he finally bit out.

"Rowe, leave."

Rowe's head snapped up and he grinned. "That's probably not a good idea since I'm supposed to be keeping you alive."

"Get the fuck out," Lucas repeated, his voice little more than a snarl that left no question that he would physically throw the man from the room if his order was not immediately obeyed. Andrei remained guarded, surprised by his sudden display of emotion.

Rowe hesitated another couple of seconds, obviously enjoying his ability to annoy Lucas before he shrugged and ambled out of the room. Lucas followed closely on his heels, shutting the door behind him. He paused, his hand on the back of the door as he took a deep breath as if to steady himself.

"What do you want?" Andrei demanded, unable to keep the anger out of his voice.

Lucas was on him in a flash, slamming Andrei against the wall. Andrei's grunt of pain was immediately followed by a long, deep groan of pleasure as Lucas kissed him. Two weeks of pent-up hunger and fear burned through them in a blinding flash. Lucas pressed the length of his body against Andrei's and he still wasn't close enough for Andrei. He slid one arm around Lucas's waist while the other cupped the back of his head, holding him captive as he deepened the kiss. Damn, the man could kiss. If it wasn't a slow seduction sneaking in past all of Andrei's defenses, the man was a battering ram, busting through and claiming everything as his own.

Shifting, Lucas pressed one hand against Andrei's recently damaged ribs, wringing a hiss of pain from him. Lucas broke off the kiss immediately and tried to step back, but Andrei tightened his hold, allowing barely more than an inch to separate them.

"You're hurt," Lucas ground out between clenched teeth.

"Nothing serious."

Lucas's eyes methodically swept over his face, mentally cataloguing each bruise and cut. "I want names. Everyone who touched you."

Andrei couldn't stop his grin. "Why?"

"To kill them."

Andrei laughed then winced, his head dropping back against the wall. "Stop it. It fucking hurts to laugh."

"Give me this," Lucas snapped, glaring at the other man. "I'm stuck here with my thumb up my ass, waiting to hear something and I can't do dick."

Andrei slid the hand holding the back of Lucas's head around to cup his cheek. He skimmed his thumb along his hard jaw, taking in the angry spark in his green-gray eyes. "This is a nice distraction."

A lazy grin spread across Lucas's soft lips and Andrei's heart sped up. He'd missed that smile. "Wait till this is over and I own your ass again."

"And here I thought you'd forgotten about me," Andrei teased. He instantly felt lighter, the aches and pains spread throughout his body wiped away for now.

"Fuck you," Lucas mumbled, but there was no heat to it.

"Gotten bored. Found a new ass."

"Shut up." Lucas swooped in for another rough kiss, but this time he moved his hand from Andrei's ribs to press against the wall. When he ended the kiss, he pressed his forehead to Andrei's and closed his eyes, exhaling noisily. "I'm tired of feeling useless while you take all the risks."

"You can stay safe. If you're not doing stupid shit, then I don't worry while I'm in a fight."

Lucas huffed as he pulled back. "I work. I spar with Rowe. I go home. That's it."

A slow grin grew on Andrei's lips and he dropped both of his hands to his side. "You knock the shit out of him?"

Lucas smiled, though it seemed reluctant. "Not as often as I'd like." He paced a few feet away before turning back. His long, broad body seemed looser, as if he'd shed some of the tension that had hummed through him when he walked in. "Honestly, how are you?"

Andrei shrugged, his eyes darting to the floor, unable to hold the other man's gaze. "Good. Haven't lost a fight."

"I want the truth."

"That is the truth."

"Andrei."

He sighed heavily and closed his eyes. "Don't."

"Drop the bullshit."

"It's hell!" Andrei finally shouted. "Every time I step into the ring, I'm reminded of the life that I worked so fucking hard for and can't have. I look at these desperate men and have to push down my own revulsion. It's one thing to fight someone who trains for this, who works their life for this, but these guys…it's just blood lust and desperation."

"I'm sorry."

Andrei shook his head and looked up at Lucas. "I knew what I was getting into. I knew it was going to be like this."

"It'll be over soon."

Andrei nodded, praying he was right. He was ready for this to be over so he could return to his life. Sure, it wasn't the life that he'd trained for and dreamed about, but he accepted it.

Lucas stared at the door, frowning as if he were waiting for it to suddenly open. "I need to go. Rowe's probably getting twitchy."

"You should know something," Andrei said, looking away from Lucas. "I…I went to Indianapolis with a friend recently."

"Research?"

A half smile lifted one corner of Andrei's mouth and he turned his head to watch Lucas. "Yeah, but not what you're thinking. I had a friend take me to a gay bar up there. I didn't want to do it here in Cincy. I thought it could make things...complicated."

Confusion twisted Lucas's face as he stared at Andrei. Seconds ticked by before he finally spoke. "You were doing research at a gay bar?"

Andrei nodded, fisting his hand nervously at his side. He wanted to push away from the wall. To pace the room. Something. Anything had to be better than standing there under Lucas's piercing gaze. "I had to know."

"What? If you were gay?"

Andrei nodded again.

Lucas slowly approached him, stopping when only a few inches separated them. He was so stiff, Andrei wasn't sure Lucas was breathing. "How did you research? Let men hit on you?"

"No, I kissed them."

Lucas's eyes widened and he stepped into him so that his chest brushed against Andrei's. "What?" That single word was nothing more than a low rumble of near predatory rage and possession and Andrei couldn't deny loving the rush it sent through him.

"I told them that I was there to figure out if I was gay. A number of men were happy to kiss me to help me figure it out." The words wavered as Andrei fought the sudden laughter building inside of him. Lucas was getting pissed and he wasn't even trying to hide it any longer.

"Of course they were, you fucking idiot! Sexy piece of ass like you walks in. They were probably panting to get their hands on you."

"You think I'm sexy?"

Lucas growled and Andrei could no longer hold back his laugh. It was the first time he'd truly laughed in weeks.

"How many?" Lucas asked.

"How many what?"

"How many men did you kiss, douche bag?"

Andrei grinned. "I don't kiss and tell."

"Andrei, I'm going to put my foot so far up your ass if you—"

"Four," he said with a heavy sigh as if completely put out.

Lucas completely deflated. The number obviously wasn't as high as he'd been feared. He stepped back and stared at Andrei again. He was debating whether to ask and Andrei knew it. "What did you figure out?" His voice was low and businesslike again. It was a tell for him and Andrei saw it now. When Lucas put his emotions under tight control, when he was desperate to bottle up and hide his feelings, he fell into this same tone of voice.

"That you're a damned good kisser," Andrei teased.

Lucas snorted softly, the lazy smile Andrei was addicted to sliding across his lips. "Well, I could have told you that without you whoring yourself out. Anything else?"

"That it wasn't…uncomfortable. It was…nice." Slipping his fingers in the waist of Lucas's pants, he pulled the other man closer, enjoying the feel of Lucas's hard muscles pressed against him. "I'm not saying I saw anyone that I'd let near my ass," he said with a sly grin. "Just that I've apparently got more options when it comes to the dating scene."

Lucas kissed Andrei—rough and possessive—as if Lucas were claiming him, before he pulled back, glanced at the door, then shook his head. "Fuck, Rowe." He reached down, wrapped his fingers around Andrei's wrists and put his hands on either side of his waist. "Touch me."

Andrei groaned and pulled Lucas's hips into his. He spread his legs and began a slow roll—cock to cock—rubbing against Lucas. Lucas's body felt hard and hot against his. Andrei slid his hands to Lucas's ass, dug his fingers in and kneaded the taut globes, pressing harder against him. He buried his face in Lucas's neck, licked the hint of sweat under his jaw, rubbed his face against the stubble.

It was like an inferno lit between them.

Lucas worked his hand between them, unbuttoned Andrei's jeans, and slid his hand inside his boxers. He wrapped his fingers around Andrei's cock, rough and hard. He tightened his fingers and pulled up, then pressed down.

Andrei gasped and thrust into Lucas's hand. He wedged his shaking fingers between them and opened Lucas's jeans, wrapped his fingers around Lucas's cock, amazed that he loved touching another man like this. Hot, velvet skin over a hard steel shaft. He stroked his fingers up and down, opening his mouth over Lucas's neck as the other man worked his cock.

Nothing had ever torn him down to such a basic level, had turned him into a man who felt, tasted and breathed in another's scent like he couldn't…or *wouldn't*… live without it. He pulled back enough to slant his mouth over Lucas's, swallowing the other man's groan as Lucas increased the speed of his hand.

Andrei saw stars. He wanted this to last, to go on forever, but it was building so damned fast. He gasped, then sucked Lucas's tongue into his mouth, rubbing his thumb over the gathering moisture at the head of Lucas's dick with every upward slide of his hand. Lucas thrust his hips harder, setting a faster pace as he slid up and down in his hand and Andrei realized through his own fog of lust that he'd reduced this strong, controlled man to one who couldn't seem to stop thrusting against him while he let out shaky, low moans.

Again, he pulled back. But this time it was to meet that half-glazed stare. They locked on each other and their movements slowed, became languid. Lucas's mouth dropped open, his eyes slid mostly shut and only a hint of glittering green and gray stayed on him as Lucas spilled over his hand. Andrei couldn't stop the cry that tore from his throat as he used his free hand to pull Lucas's mouth back to his. He pressed hard against him, thrusting into Lucas's hand.

Lucas pulled away, his lips skimming along his cheek to his ear. "Please baby, come for me. I need you…" he panted. Something fragile and vulnerable in Lucas's voice pierced Andrei's chest, sending him soaring toward the edge. Lucas squeezed and Andrei lost it, trying hard to hold in the noise, failing as it felt like his heart had been pulled through his cock.

He sagged against the wall, wiped his hand on it.

Lucas turned and did the same, then chuckled. "Shit, Andrei." The words were hardly more than a whisper.

He didn't speak again and Andrei was fine with that. He didn't know if this had been brought on by his bar story, and he didn't care. He'd gone to that bar to settle his own worries, but he'd known the concern had been playing in the back of Lucas's mind as well. Lucas had probably been worried that he'd coerced or forced Andrei into this arrangement. No, whatever this was, took no coercion.

Andrei shook his head. "You'd better get out of here. We don't need Rowe walking in on this shit."

Lucas gave him one more direct look then kissed him softly. The kind of kiss that made something flutter inside Andrei's chest.

"Yeah, the poor guy's got enough on his mind." He walked to the door after he arranged his clothes again.

"Lucas."

He stopped as he reached for the doorknob and looked over his shoulder at Andrei. In a low, heated voice, Andrei repeated the same bit of nonsense Romanian he'd translated for Lucas their one night together. As he'd hoped, Lucas smiled broadly at him, chuckling softly. The words meant nothing, but it was the moment they were both clinging to. A good memory in this blood and pain and fear. It wasn't just Lucas's life on the line anymore. If Andrei screwed up, if this bastard discovered his true intent, Andrei was dead.

But for now, in the broken-down abandoned school in the middle of nowhere, deep in the hills of Kentucky, they were laughing and the world could wait.

Chapter 20

Nodding briefly to George as the bodyguard finished his inspection of Lucas's office, Lucas walked to his desk, placing his briefcase on the surface. Tonight was the night of the "attack." Andrei was scheduled to have his meeting with the man pulling all the strings and then he was to lead them over to the penthouse where they would break in. Of course, Rowe and several of his people were already going to be in place to capture Lucas's would-be attacker, not allowing one of them to get near Lucas. But if all went according to their plan, it would be over tonight. The bastard would be caught and Lucas could return to his normal life.

Anxiety churned in his stomach. There were so many things that could still go wrong, but there was a different shadow in his mind. The fear of nothing going wrong and Lucas having the chance to return to the life he'd been living before he'd met Andrei. Did he really have to give up Andrei? No, that wasn't an option any longer and they both knew it. But could they just…continue as they were? Fucking. Laughing. No strings and no complications. That couldn't be hard. They both had their own lives and their own friends. They could just arrange it so that their paths crossed on occasion. That's how relationships worked, right? He was so useless when it came to this shit.

Lucas rubbed the bridge of his nose with his index finger and thumb. This was not a good line of thought. Not for eight in the morning. He jumped slightly when his cell phone vibrated in his breast pocket. It was too early in the day for Snow and Rowe to contact him and Candace was in her office. Pulling it out, he frowned at the unknown number but he answered it.

"Lucas, I'm out," announced a rough, older voice in rush.

"Thomas?" Lucas demanded, taking a moment to place the voice. "What's going on? What happened?"

"Someone broke in last night. Shot at us. He shot at Marilyn!"

"Calm down, Thomas. Tell me exactly what happened."

"I'm telling you, someone broke in and tried to kill us," the older man nearly shouted. He took a deep breath, the sound rattling over the phone. When he spoke again, it was obvious he was trying to keep his voice low and even. "After midnight, someone set off the alarm, breaking into the house. He shot our bodyguard and tried to kill us. Our bodyguard managed to shoot him as well, but he got away. The police don't think he'll survive based on all the blood that's splattered across my walls."

"I'm sorry, Thomas. What can I do?"

"Nothing. We're out. I'm calling my lawyers today and making it clear that I'm selling my property to whoever wants it. Patrick is already dead and Marilyn could have been killed last night. It's not worth it."

"I understand. Sell it to me."

"What?"

Lucas paced away from his desk to the windows looking out on the river. It was a dreary day, the sky a dull gray of thick clouds that promised a cold rain. "Sell it to me. I'll buy it for whatever you paid for it. I'll hold it untouched for six months. If this is cleared up and you find that you want it back in six months, we'll swap and pretend I never bought it."

Thomas was silent for several seconds. There was only the sound of his heavy breathing on the line. "But that will put the bastard on your tail."

"He already wants me dead and I know I'm close to nailing the son of a bitch. I've got less to lose than you."

"But—"

"When you hang up with me, call your lawyer," Lucas directed, his voice low and forceful. "Tell him to contact my lawyer, Sarah Carlston. I've already talked to her about this. She'll help speed up the paperwork. If your man is good, we can have this all filed away by close of business today."

"Are-are you sure?" Thomas's voice wavered.

"Sign the paperwork and then take Marilyn to the Seychelles for a couple of weeks. You've both earned the rest. When you get back, we'll do brunch at Orchids."

"Yes," he said slowly as if still trying to convince himself. "Yes. That is a good idea. You'll have to bring Andrei along. Marilyn would like to see him again."

Lucas smirked. Andrei was going to be amused to find that the Lyntons were anxious to see him again. Apparently the man had made an excellent impression on Marilyn. "Of course. We'll talk when you get back."

Thomas hung up and Lucas sighed, shoving his phone into his pocket. He'd warned Sarah as soon as Andrei had gone undercover at the fights that he would buy Thomas Lynton's Corryville property if his lawyer approached him. Uncovering the bastard threatening their lives was taking far too long and the Cincinnati police were proving to be useless in this matter. Sure, he could have been a little more forthcoming with information, but he'd also been unwilling to completely sacrifice his privacy so that they could dick around in his life and waste his time finding this fucker. And truthfully, after the initial attack in the alley, Lucas had been all too eager to handle this personally.

But he understood Thomas's need to get out. He was surprised the older businessman had stuck it out as long as he had after the death of his partner. No, Lucas was happy to take care of this matter alone and then hand the land back to Thomas when the man returned from his impromptu vacation with his wife.

Staring out the window, Lucas couldn't stop the smile that rose on his lips. This was his city. At times she was narrow-minded, prejudiced, frustrating, and too often years behind the trends of the rest of the country, but she was beautiful and elegant and his. He'd made his fortune here. He climbed up from nothing, worked his ass off for four years in the Army before working his way through college and then up the corporate ladder. No one was going to scare him or stop him.

Lucas walked back to his desk. He needed to get some work done before Detective Banner inevitably appeared at his office to inform him of the events at Thomas's house and try to pressure him into aiding his search for this bastard. As he dug through his briefcase, searching for a contract he wanted to review, his eye snagged on a large yellow envelope he hadn't noticed before and hadn't left on his desk since he'd last been in the office. Candace and Kevin, his other assistant, didn't place things in his office without his knowledge. They held it at their desk until he was in and they placed it in his hands.

Putting his briefcase on the floor without retrieving the contract, Lucas picked up the envelope, fighting to push down the uneasiness that was trying to overwhelm him. It was nothing. He was sure it was nothing. It was likely something he'd told Candace to drop on his desk and he'd simply forgotten. The past few weeks had been insane and his mind was not fully on work. It was just an overlooked contract or a special report that he'd requested. Inside he found only a hastily scratched letter and photo.

The piece of paper was written with what looked like a sharpie in block letters and said:

Deliver $10M to 1034 Boron at 2AM Tonight or He Dies

Lucas flipped the photo over and the air in his lungs left him in a rush. He released the photo as if it had suddenly burst into flames and he let it float down to his desk as he stumbled back a step. It was Andrei. Oh fucking Christ, it was Andrei. He couldn't tear his eyes away from the photo even while his stomach churned in horror. Andrei was slumped in a chair, his bindings the only thing holding him upright, his naked body covered in ugly bruises and gashes. What Lucas could see of his face was swollen and bloody.

They knew. The fucking bastard had somehow found out that Andrei was a spy and he'd been tortured before they decided to demand their ransom. Was he even still alive?

Lucas's chest burned and he suddenly gasped for air. He couldn't breathe. He could barely think. Every damned memory of Andrei kept flashing through his head. Andrei laughing and teasing him. Andrei shielding him from the fire, protecting him from the bullets. Andrei talking to Ian as they cooked breakfast. Andrei trusting him. And interspersed in the picture show was that damned photo of Andrei bloody and dying.

Gripping the edge of his desk, Lucas clenched his eyes shut and swallowed his need to shout. He wanted to scream while the trembling in his frame shook him to pieces. With each breath, he gathered up more of his emotions until they were wadded into a tight, hard ball in his chest. He tucked them down and locked them up. If Andrei was still alive, he needed Lucas to be in control. He needed Lucas calm and focused. And if Andrei wasn't alive…well then, Cincinnati was his city. Lucas would be the one to burn it to the ground to get his revenge.

Hiding the photo and letter in the top drawer of his desk, Lucas violently jabbed the four digits to Candace's line and summoned her into his office. He had to wait only a minute before the woman scurried in, carrying her usual assortment of reports, contracts, and emails for them to review, thinking he was ready for his usual morning meeting.

"Send everyone home now," Lucas bit out before she could cross the room to his desk.

Candace's gait immediately slowed until she stopped several feet away from the chairs positioned before his desk. "Mr. Vallois?"

"Now. Send them home now."

"But…" Her voice drifted off as if she were struggling to formulate a thought in response to his strange request. Lucas had never done this before. In fact, he preferred that all of his employees worked in the office whenever possible rather than remotely from home. Face-to-face meetings were always more effective to accomplishing tasks.

"An emergency has come up. Tell them all to pack up. Work from home. Come back tomorrow."

"Sir..."

Lucas opened his mouth to shout at the woman but stopped himself. Pressing both his fists into the top of the desk, he took a deep breath. He'd just convinced the woman to start working for him again. He didn't need her to quit because he was an asshole for what seemed like no reason.

"I haven't the time nor the inclination to explain," he said, struggling to keep his voice low. "I want everyone to work from home today. The place needs to be cleared out in fifteen minutes."

"Of course, Mr. Vallois," she said firmly, drawing Lucas's gaze back up to her. The woman stood facing him, her back and shoulders straight. "Is there anything I can do for you...off the record?"

The woman never ceased to amaze him. She knew very little of what was going on and he intended to keep her in the dark. If things went bad and the police got wind of half the shit he had in mind, he didn't want Candace dragged into any of it. But there was one thing he wanted. He stood and opened a drawer in his desk, pulling out a plain white security key card, which he handed over to her.

"After everyone leaves, use this card to access the security room. Turn off all the video and recording surveillance for this floor. Erase it for the entire day. Wipe down anything you touch and then lose the card on your way home."

Candace nodded and then left without another word. She never questioned him. Fuck, he was going to have to give her another raise if he survived this.

Alone in his office, Lucas called Rowe on his cell phone. In his rage, he could only demand for the man to pick up Snow and come immediately to his office downtown. Luckily Rowe didn't question it. He grunted in acknowledgement and hung up. They'd all known that things could go bad quickly when Andrei went undercover. Maybe they'd even been waiting for it, but the pain that threatened to swamp Lucas left him sure that he hadn't truly been prepared.

While he waited for his friends to arrive, Lucas informed George that his boss was on his way and got the man to complete a sweep for bugs in his office yet again. He couldn't be sure how the bastard had discovered the truth about Andrei. The only place in Lucas's life that saw a steady flow of people was his office, but he'd never spoken of his plans for Andrei while at the office. Could someone have gotten past the security at the penthouse and sneaked in a bug there?

Minutes before Snow and Rowe's arrival, Candace stopped in his office one last time to inform him that everyone had left. George had found nothing in his office and was checking the rest of the floor just in case. The silence that settled over the executive suite was suffocating. The sounds of the street below didn't reach him and the wind was still. There was nothing in the room but the rush of blood in his ears and his ragged breathing. Lucas closed his eyes against the cityscape beyond the window, trying to order his thoughts. They needed a plan. And considering there were only three of them against an unknown number, Lucas had to make sure it was a fucking brilliant plan.

兄弟武士心

Rowe stalked into the office twenty minutes after Lucas's call while Snow trailed behind him looking ragged and bleary eyed. The man had likely been in bed for less than an hour after his shift at the hospital when Rowe came for him. He wanted to feel bad for Snow, but he couldn't. He needed his friends if they were going to save Andrei. George poked his head into the office and gave Lucas a short nod before closing the door behind the other two men.

"What happened?" Rowe demanded.

Lucas withdrew the photo and letter from his desk, handing it to Rowe. The man cursed as he handed it to Snow. The surgeon's jaw tightened but he said nothing as he placed the items on the desktop.

"How?" Rowe snarled.

"I don't know. The office is clean." Lucas shook his head. "Maybe he was followed and didn't know it. Maybe someone got into the penthouse. I don't know and at this point, it doesn't matter."

"What's the plan?" Snow asked.

Lucas stared at his friend, allowing his emotions to harden once again before turning his cold gaze over to Rowe. "What are the chances that he's still alive?"

Rowe looked away from Lucas, his eyes darting from place to place in the office while he rubbed the top of his head with one hand. "Not good. They might keep him alive as insurance. Wait for you to show up and then put a bullet in his head before killing you."

"But it's not necessary," Snow interjected. "He's likely dead."

Lucas didn't react. Not outwardly. Something inside of him screamed but nothing broke through. His focus hardened. "Then we return the favor."

"Lucas," Snow whispered. "Have you considered going to the cops? Hand this over to them to finish?"

"This is my fight. They attacked me. Attacked Andrei. This bastard is mine."

Snow stared at him for a moment before looking over at Rowe. The other man was stone faced, looking as if he were ready to march into whatever hell Lucas led them into. "You realize we're not military anymore. We're civilians. This isn't some black op sanctioned by the government. We do this and there's no way your high-priced lawyers save our asses if the cops catch us."

Lucas felt the sneer twist his lips and he couldn't hold back his words. "You say that like this is the first time we've broken the law."

"I know you and Rowe have done things to cover up my mistakes, to pull me back from the edge."

"That wasn't the fucking edge, Snow. That was you lost in the goddamned abyss!"

"Hey!" Rowe barked. "This isn't helping!"

Snow and Lucas ignored him as they locked eyes. "I pulled us down that road," Snow said in a low, icy voice. "And Rowe has done his fair share as well. But you've always been careful to stick to the straight and narrow when it comes to your business. I just need to make sure that you've thought about this. You know what you're doing."

Lucas blinked and took a step back. He got it. There was a weight that came with this decision. It wasn't just his life that he was threatening to fuck to kingdom come. No, Snow and Rowe could die. And if they didn't, they could potentially lose everything if they were caught. And the consequences of that Lucas would have to live with on his conscience. Of course, Snow and Rowe weren't walking in blind. They knew what Lucas was asking. Blood. Chaos. Destruction. Death. Both men could walk away, but they wouldn't because of their loyalty to Lucas.

"I've had weeks to think about this," Lucas admitted. It was a struggle to unclench his jaw. His entire body was one giant tensed muscle, but then it was the only way to hold all the rage inside. "I knew this could happen. I knew..." His voice drifted off and he glared at the photo on the top of his desk. "I end this tonight with or without you."

"We go together," Rowe said.

"Someone has got to watch your slow ass," Snow added with a wicked grin.

Lucas nodded and he could feel some of the anger recede again, back under his control. "Get your Gidget on this building," he said, pointing to the address on the ransom note. "Pull up blueprints and anything she can on the place—what it was used for, who owns it, how long it's been abandoned. We'll meet tonight at Rowe's to gear up and lay out a plan of attack."

"And the good detective who has been on your heels?" Snow inquired.

"He'll be around today to tell me of the attack on Thomas Lynton's house." He paused, utterly disgusted by the thought but he knew it was the best option he had. "I'll tell him to guard Ian tonight."

Rowe leaned close, unable to hide his surprise. "Are you going to warn Ian?"

"Of course not! I'll just get the detective to spend the evening in Rialto's office and then get him to escort Ian home. Neither person needs to know the truth."

"You will properly threaten Banner ahead of time," Snow commented, but Lucas couldn't tell if his friend was asking a question or making a statement.

"If I survive tonight, I'll be more than happy to castrate the bastard on my way home."

Rowe sighed loudly. "You know, the guy is allowed to date."

"Ian? Of course he can date," Lucas replied, sounding utterly reasonable.

"He just can't date Hollis Banner," Snow added.

"What the fuck ever," Rowe said wearily, rubbing his hand over his face. Before turning toward the door, he snatched up the photo and letter from Lucas's desk. "I'll get started on the research and equipment. Gotta get some protection for Mel too. See you at nine."

Both men watched Rowe stroll out of the office. Lucas had expected Snow to go with him, but the doctor stayed behind, something obviously on his mind that he preferred no one else hear. Lucas waited, watching his friend. His usual cold, emotionless demeanor was absent, pain filling his pale blue eyes as he looked at Lucas.

"I made a mistake with you," Snow ventured after nearly a minute of silence.

Lucas flinched, surprised by Snow's words. It wasn't what he'd been expecting. "What do you mean?"

"You've pulled me out of the abyss time and again. I bounce back, in my own way," he added a bit wryly. "I'm still alive because you keep coming in after me."

He took a step toward Snow but the man stunned him by stepping backward, shaking his head. "Snow, you're my brother. My friend. I love you. I will always come for you."

"But I always thought you came back out of the abyss with me. I was wrong. You've been living in the abyss and I have no idea for how long." A sharp, bitter laugh broke through the room. "I've been so lost in my pain and my problems that I didn't see it. Not until I saw you with Andrei."

"Snow—"

"It's true. You laugh with him. You smile with him."

"I laugh with you."

"You're sarcastic and reserved with us. The rest of the time, you bitch and order us about."

"Bitching at you and ordering you around makes me happy."

"Don't, Luc. I'm sorry it took this for me to see it." Snow looked away from Lucas, shaking his head, his throat working. Seams tugged, loosening on Snow's composure. Lucas started to come around the desk, his natural instinct to comfort and protect Snow rising to the foreground, but Snow took a step back and pulled himself together. "I'm sorry I didn't try to save you like you saved me. And I'm sorry about Andrei. If he lives, I'll fix him."

Snow's promise tore through Lucas. It was on the tip of his tongue to agree, to say that Snow would save Andrei and nothing would snatch the man's life away. But he swallowed back those desperate words. He knew Snow's limitations better than the man himself. If Andrei's injuries were too extreme, no skill in the world could save his life and he couldn't put that unrealistic demand on Snow's shoulders.

Walking around his desk, he stood in front of his childhood friend and cupped his cheeks with both hands. "Go home. Sleep. I need you tonight."

Snow gripped him tight in a fierce hug for only a couple of seconds before turning and wordlessly leaving the office. Lucas stared at the closed door, trying not to think about his friend's pained words. Had he been floating in the same abyss he continually pulled his friend from over the years? No. It wasn't the same. Lucas's personal hell had become something different after they left Oklahoma for the Army. Beyond the love he allowed himself to feel for Snow, Ian, and Rowe, Lucas felt nothing. Not real joy or sorrow. There was nothing and hadn't been for so long, he'd almost become convinced that he couldn't feel.

Now there was Andrei and Lucas felt like he was drowning. Didn't matter. Tonight he was going to fix that.

Chapter 21

A bitter wind moved into the river valley with the setting sun, putting a chill in the air that tried to settle deep into Lucas's bones. The sky was clear with stars glittering bright overhead, but the moon was absent as if she approved of their endeavor, providing what darkness she could. It was just before one in the morning, approximately an hour before Lucas was supposed to arrive with a case full of money to trade for Andrei's life. If Lucas had believed for a second that Andrei would be safely released for the money, he wouldn't have hesitated to comply, but Rowe's assessment in the office was the most likely outcome if Lucas had tried. This asshole had killed Patrick and attempted to kill Thomas and Lucas. It wasn't going to stop until Lucas was dead.

"Figaro in place." Snow's voice whispered rough through the earpiece.

"Gepetto in place," Lucas answered.

"Fuck you both. Who the hell picks codes names like this?" Rowe snarled.

"I'm sorry. What was that? I didn't copy," Snow snickered.

"Blue fucking Fairy in place," Rowe grumbled.

"Eyes," Lucas snapped, bringing the two men back to the job at hand. "I count four. Two on rotation. Two by the doors, mobile."

"Confirmed," Snow replied.

"Two more are stationed at the front door."

Lucas drew in a deep breath and shifted his weight, stretching muscles that had become stiff and sore from staying still for so long. They'd taken position outside the warehouse on Boron more than an hour ago. Rowe had dropped them in a dimly lit subdivision several blocks away and they'd hoofed it through thin woods and low brush, across train tracks and around other buildings to take position in a ditch less than a hundred yards away. At the same time, Rowe had run a separate errand before slipping onto the roof of another building with a sniper rifle.

An earlier thermal sweep of the building had revealed that there were nine people inside and no one new had left or arrived in the hour since they came to the scene. One of those people was Andrei and Lucas was willing to bet that it was the person alone with the weakest thermal reading. They needed to get in there if they were going to save him. The temperature wasn't bad if you were fully dressed but Andrei had been stripped and tortured. His time was dwindling fast. Lucas didn't have high hopes of saving him, but he was going to try.

Tightening his hand on the pistol in his hand until his knuckles throbbed, Lucas pushed to his feet while remaining crouched. "Gepetto in motion."

"Figaro in motion," Snow immediately answered. From two different angles, Snow and Lucas converged on the building. Their careful footsteps through the long grass and weeds made only a soft rustling easily dismissed as the wind. As the first of the sentries came into sight, Lucas lifted his pistol, squeezing the trigger. There was no sound beyond a quiet expulsion of air as the tranquilizer dart left the gun and hit the guy's neck. He had barely time to lift his hand at what felt like a bee sting before his knees gave out and he collapsed with a muffled thud to the ground. At Rowe's request, they were using tranquilizer darts to start. Of course, all three of them were also carrying regular handguns loaded with bullets as well as several knives. They were all willing to take lives if it became necessary, but Rowe and Snow were determined to fucking protect what was left of Lucas's soul whether he wanted them to or not.

As the guard nearest to the first reacted, Lucas pegged him and they were both out. "Two down," Lucas whispered.

"My two are down." Snow's words followed seconds later.

"The front is clear," Rowe chimed in.

Lucas pressed his back against the wall beside the rear door, his pistol held up in front of him. He took a deep breath, and released it slowly. He was calm, distant from the events unfolding with each action he took. There was only the methodical plan that he and Rowe had laid out before leaving.

"Hit it," Lucas bit out.

A couple seconds later, lights around the area winked in a wave that washed over the land, deepening the darkness. One of Rowe's little errands was a well-placed charge on an area electric transformer. The tiny explosion would have thrown a few sparks as if some mechanical piece had suddenly gone bad, plunging the entire grid into darkness. It would take Duke Energy at least a half hour to get someone dispatched and another hour to fix the problem, leaving them plenty of time to slip in and out under cover.

Switching on his night vision goggles, Lucas pulled open the door and entered the building. Men were shouting and bumping into things while others had wisely pulled out their phones to use the flashlight app. Lucas, moving as soundlessly as possible, darted around large crates and stacks of busted wooden skids that had been left behind by the last owner of the warehouse. The smell of old grease and mildew filled the air following years of being closed up and neglected. The place had previously been a fiberglass manufacturer, but the owner had moved all the large equipment out so that now it held only a few crates and lots of I-beam poles holding up the roof. Snow and Lucas had entered from north and west, respectively, and were sweeping south with the goal of clearing everyone out until they reached Andrei.

"Figaro in. Two down."

Lucas squeezed off a round and ducked behind a skid. He looked to make sure no one else was close before he answered. "Gepetto in. One down."

"Blue Fairy blind. On approach."

They'd estimated that it would take Rowe three minutes to cross from his current location to the warehouse where he would enter from the front and take down any stragglers along the east wall. In that three minutes, Lucas and Snow were to get the place mostly cleared out and Andrei located.

"What the fuck?" someone shouted from the far end of the building. "Someone kick on the generator and check the guards. No one is answering."

"He ain't supposed to be here for another hour," another voice shouted back with a bit of a whine.

"Yeah, and he's survived too much so far. Go get the damned generator!"

Lucas swore under his breath and backpedaled toward the door. They had figured that the location was temporary and would be crippled if the electricity was cut. They weren't supposed to have a generator. Time was running out. Lucas had to keep everyone inside and blind to the fact that they'd been infiltrated. The only thing on their side was that it seemed like this bastard had stuck with the usual crew of thugs and fighters. No military training. They didn't realize they were already fucked.

Another man using his cell phone as a flashlight came around the corner. He spotted Lucas before he was hit with a dart in the chest. He fell heavily, his phone clattering loudly to the concrete floor, the light left shining up at the ceiling. Lucas stepped up to it and flipped it over, putting the area back into darkness in hopes that no one else would come in that direction so he could continue toward the offices at the south of the building.

"Hey! Someone knocked out Pete!" The new voice echoed through the warehouse. The voice came from farther to the north of Lucas so it was likely the prick had stumbled across one of Snow's victims. Fuck.

"Cat's out of the bag," Snow muttered over the earpiece. "Gotta move now."

"I got one more," Lucas said evenly. "Four left."

"Everyone to the office!" the boss shouted while gunfire echoed through the building. Bullets pinged off the various metal I-beams and hit the roof. Lucas ducked behind a crate and put a dart in two more men as they ran down the center of the warehouse toward the south.

They both collapsed in a heap, causing more shouts. The one man Lucas missed dove into the office and kicked the door closed.

Cursing, Lucas shoved the dart gun in a holster and pulled his 9mm. He was done with this shit. They went in quiet, picked them off, and didn't take any lives, but it wasn't working. There were at least two left—the boss and the guy who dove into the office.

"Gepetto, I've got a locked door. I think it's holding the target." Snow's low voice sent a chill down Lucas's spine, pulling him back at the last second from storming the office.

"Where?"

"Southeast corner just past the bay doors."

Lucas frowned. He was along the west wall. He'd have to cross the center of the room to get to Snow. "Go hot and get ready to cover me. Blue Fairy check in."

"Blue Fairy is one minute out. Hold positions."

"Can't," Lucas snarled. They couldn't waste any more time. "Get your ass here."

"Fuck," Rowe whispered but didn't argue further.

"Go," Snow barked and Lucas moved. He broke from cover and darted across the main floor, trying to keep an eye on the windows of the office that looked out on the warehouse and the open floor in front of him. Unfortunately, the men in the office had had enough time to adjust to the darkness. The sound of shattering glass crashed through the night followed by the deafening rattle of automatic gun fire. Lucas tripped over the body of one of the men he'd knocked out and started to go down. At the same time, pain ripped through his arm. Gritting his teeth, Lucas tucked into a roll that carried him to the opposite wall as Snow fired back at the men in the office.

"You hit?" Snow demanded as he ducked down and scuttled over to where Lucas was regaining his feet.

"Grazed. I'm fine."

Snow ignored him, inspecting Lucas's arm. Reaching inside a pocket in his cargo pants, he pulled out a wad of gauze and some tape.

He covered the wound in record time while Lucas covered his friend. "Might need a couple stitches. Nothing serious."

"That's what I said."

"Back off. I'm making sure you don't leave any easy DNA evidence behind for the cops."

"Thanks," Lucas muttered. His friend was right. They were trying to make sure they didn't drop anything that could be tied to them. "Cover me as I get to the door."

Snow led the way to the door he'd found and then took position to the side, protecting Lucas as he slid up to the door.

"Blue Fairy inside."

"Two in the office, armed. We're at the southeast wall, unlocking the door," Snow provided.

The door was large and heavy, dented and battered from years of abuse. Lucas quickly checked it and wasn't surprised to find it locked with a deadbolt. With nimble fingers, he dug out a lock-pick set and began unlocking the door as Rowe joined them.

"The warehouse is clear," Rowe murmured, his voice seeming to echo with the earpiece.

"Go take care of the two in the office and make sure Andrei isn't anywhere else. I've got this," Lucas replied, his focus completely on the lock. He knew Andrei was on the other side of the door. His heart was pounding so hard he could feel it in the back of his throat. Upon reaching the warehouse, his goal has been twofold: Get Andrei and kill the bastard behind this mess. But now that only a door separated him from Andrei, he couldn't bring himself to care about the bastard that had fucked up his life.

Snow and Rowe paused, as if weighing the wisdom of leaving his side, and then darted away, staying low as they crept toward the office. It took Lucas several tries—he was sorely out of practice when it came to picking locks, something he hadn't attempted since his teens—but he finally got it open. When the door swung open, his gaze fell on Andrei lying naked on the cold concrete. A soft, anguished cry slipped past

Lucas's lips as he fell to his knees in front of Andrei. He reached trembling hands out to him, almost afraid to touch him to see if he was alive, the man was so still. With a sharp inhale of air, he placed a hand against Andrei's throat and exhaled loudly. Andrei's pulse was weak but it was there.

Reaching into his pockets, Lucas pulled out three glow sticks. Snapping and shaking them, he dropped them around Andrei, adding a yellow glow to the room before he pulled off his night vision goggles. Snow would need the light to work, to check him before they could move him to the van Rowe had brought. He inwardly cursed that he hadn't been able to bring a spare change of clothes or anything to wrap Andrei in. The man's skin was cold to the touch and it was worrying that he wasn't even shivering.

The light scrape of a hard-sole shoe was Lucas's only warning that he wasn't alone. He reached for his gun as he turned, but it was already too late. Another gun was already in his face, bearing down on him, held by Chris Green, the man he'd spotted in Shiver a month ago. The man he'd turned down for dinner. The man...who must have placed a bug in his house on his one visit to see Lucas.

"Surprise," Chris said with a wide grin. "Fingers off the gun and hands up."

Lucas did as he asked, but remained on his knees, his body blocking as much of Andrei as possible. His stomach dropped and the world seemed to tilt off its axis just a bit. Lucas had spent weeks agonizing over who could be threatening him. He'd imagined all manner of underworld thugs, gang bosses, and even the occasional mafia head who was trying to make a name for himself. The seemingly respectable and clean-cut Christopher Green had never entered his mind. "You're not who I expected. You're not some...marketing director." Lucas tried to recall the title he'd seen on the man's business card.

"Oh, I am. But that's my day job. The side that lets me meet the city's elite and the side for the IRS," he said with a smirk. "My night job of running fights is far more lucrative. And entertaining."

"Then why the fuck go after me and Thomas Lynton? Why the hell did you kill Patrick?"

Chris motioned with the gun for Lucas to stand as he stepped to the side, moving so that his back was no longer in the open doorway where Snow or Rowe could easily sneak up on him. Lucas slowly rose, his knees aching after pressing into the frigid, hard floor. He stepped toward Chris rather than away, forcing the man to take another step backward into the small room. Empty metal shelves lined the walls.

"Patrick was an accident," Chris admitted even though there was no remorse in his tone. "The men I hired took it all a little too far. But then, what do you expect from a bunch of fighters hooked on Oxy?"

"Why?" Lucas snarled, barely controlling his temper. Patrick had been a kind man with three kids who donated his money and time to local charities and was trying to do good things for the city he loved. He hadn't deserved to die.

"OTR."

"What?"

"Before it was completely made over, early investors in Over The Rhine made millions. *Millions*."

"So?"

"I'm fucking tired of inching along, building my fortune. Being everyone's bitch. I'm smarter than most of those idiots sitting the C-Suite!" He shouted, waving his gun at Lucas as his hold on his temper snapped. But he blinked, instantly calming. He smiled at Lucas, but there wasn't an ounce of warmth in his expression. "And then I heard that you were moving into Price Hill and Lynton was in Corryville. Lynton got into OTR early and everyone knows that whenever you open a new restaurant or club, the entire area becomes hot. The next Mecca for the hipsters. I figured you two might have known where the next great investment was going to be. I wanted in."

Lucas took another step forward. "You decided to steal our property. Our investment."

"Of course not. Stealing is illegal." He chuckled. "I've got trusts set up to buy your property and Lynton's."

"And if I never wanted to sell?"

"Well, that's why we're here. But first, I think I'll take care of your boyfriend. He was incredibly loyal to you when we tortured him. He screamed a lot. Begged a little. But wouldn't say a word about you." Green's smile grew even more twisted. "That's okay. You said plenty."

Rage burned through Lucas, incinerating his own caution. His own words turned against him. He didn't want to think about what he might have said during a visit with Snow or Rowe about the man slowly dying on the floor behind him. His every instinct was to protect Andrei, to keep him safe. This was not what he'd intended.

As Chris moved the gun to aim at Andrei, Lucas lunged across the short distance separating them, knocking the gun to the far right. The pistol fired, the sound leaving a ringing in his ears. The bullet soared across the room and dug deep into the drywall and cinder blocks. Lucas struggled with the other man, delivering a hard elbow to his temple and another to his throat. Despite Chris's experience in running fights, it was obvious that he hadn't much training fighting himself. The gun discharged twice more, the bullets pinging off metal surfaces before burrowing somewhere in the darkness, before Lucas finally got it out of his hands.

Stepping back, Lucas pulled his own pistol and aimed it at Chris, his heart thudding in his ears.

The man stared at him with a bitter, mutinous expression. "It was worth it," he said, his voice rough and breathless.

"I hope so." Lucas squeezed the trigger and there was a soft puff of air. Chris winced and looked down at his abdomen. A small silver dart protruded from his light blue shirt. He lifted shocked and confused eyes to Lucas before he collapsed, unconscious, to the floor.

"You didn't kill him," Rowe stated, surprise lifting his voice an octave higher. It was only then that Lucas noticed that the warehouse was quiet again. The gunfire silenced. "Are we handing him over to the cops?"

Lucas turned to find Snow already kneeling beside Andrei, gently rolling the man onto his back to check his injuries with quick, efficient hands. Andrei's face was so swollen he was hardly recognizable and his body was covered in cuts and ugly bruises. As Snow touched him, a soft moan slipped past his parted lips and his breathing quickened under the pain, but he didn't stir otherwise.

"Go get the van. We'll load him inside and Snow will take him to the hospital," Lucas ordered as he knelt on the other side of Andrei near his head. He gently ran his hand through Andrei's blood-matted hair, wishing there was some way he could take away the pain. But there wasn't. That was Snow's job.

His eyes lifted slightly to stare across at Chris Green's limp form. There was one way that he could feel better. Something within his reach that would help to ease the guilt.

"You don't have to do this," Snow murmured. Lucas glanced back to find his friend's eyes were still locked on his patient. But then Snow always seemed to be good at guessing what Lucas was thinking. "You can just hand him over to the cops and we walk away."

There would be no walking away. Chris would give up all kinds of information on Lucas and his companions. They'd get dragged through court and it would be ugly. There could even be limited jail time involved. Snow could lose his license. But sadly, that wasn't even the first or main thought dancing through Lucas's head.

"What if it was me on this floor right now and that man was responsible?"

Snow looked up at Lucas then, the smile sliding across his lips was a twisted thing filled with gleeful malice. "He'd be awake and screaming as he watched me pull one organ after another out of his body. It would make Hannibal Lecter cringe." The smile melted away and he gave a little shrug before returning his full attention to Andrei. "But we both know I have questionable impulse control issues. Not the best role model."

True.

"How bad is he?" Lucas demanded, preferring to change the subject than go into Snow's impulses. His mind was made up about Green and he knew that Rowe wasn't going to push him on it. No, Snow was just trying to save his soul and he appreciated his friend's somewhat half-hearted effort. Lucas had no interest in doing the right thing or being a good guy in this instance. He wanted only to protect what was his. And in that moment, Andrei belonged to him.

"Hard to tell. I'll take him to St. E South," he said, using the locals' name for closest hospital to their current location. "Make sure he's stabilized there before transferring him to U.C., where I can keep a better eye on him."

Some small knot in Lucas's chest eased. Once out of the emergency room, Andrei would no longer be Snow's patient but the man was going to pull every string and work every angle to make sure that he was able to have a hand in every minute of the man's recovery.

"Thank you," Lucas whispered, letting his eyes drift shut. It was nearly over.

Chapter 22

Andrei sat on his couch, staring at the wall, weighing whether the aches and pains that filled his frame had finally grown bad enough to send him from his comfortable position in search of those damned painkillers, which he'd stupidly left on his bedside table in the next room. He was overdue for a pill. Should have taken it almost an hour ago, but it had taken him nearly that long to get comfortable on the couch and now he didn't want to get up again.

Tipping his head to the right, he looked through a part in the blackout curtains over the large window in his living room. The sun had set less than an hour ago and night was falling fast over the city, clasping her in a chilly embrace. His time in the hospital followed by a week of being trapped in his apartment due to his reduced mobility had left Andrei feeling restless and disconnected from the world. Everything just felt off.

He closed his eyes and drew in a deep breath, held it, and then slowly released it through narrowly parted lips. Three weeks. Three fucking weeks since he'd last seen Lucas and he still couldn't get the asshole out of his head.

After Snow had taken him to the hospital, he'd spent the better part of the first week unconscious, hooked up to more machines than he thought they could fit into a room. Each time he'd surfaced through all the meds, Lucas had been sitting at his bedside, looking ragged and exhausted. The man didn't talk much. He just sat there, smiling weakly and holding Andrei's hand as if it were the only place in the world that he wanted to be.

By the second week, when he'd actually been conscious and coherent, Lucas disappeared completely. That wasn't to say that Andrei had been abandoned. It seemed like someone was constantly hovering at his bedside during that week. But it was a rotating door of Ian, Rowe, Melissa, and even Hollis haunting his room. The detective had briefly attempted to get some information out of him, but Lucas had made sure that his lawyer Sarah was nipping at the detective's heels the entire time with strict orders that Andrei wasn't to answer any of Banner's direct questions. In the end, the detective would just stop by and watch Jeopardy with him every evening before shuffling along.

And now Andrei had been home for a week. Lucas still hadn't stopped by. No word. No phone call. No…well, nothing. But his new friends were still checking on him. Ian had dropped off food four times, proving that the young man was an anxious cooker. He tried to hide it, but Andrei could see the worry in Ian's eyes when he looked at Andrei. And when he was worried, he cooked. Andrei was beyond flattered to be included in the caring man's circle. Plus, the food was incredible. Rowe had stopped by twice and even Snow had dropped by once. Of course, the surgeon had couched the appearance as a "house call" and hadn't bothered to make much small talk as he checked over Andrei. He'd begun to feel as if they were working their way through the guilt over Andrei's injuries, not that he blamed any of them. Rowe had explained about the bug they'd found in Lucas's penthouse and how it had gotten there. At the end of the day, Andrei knew the risk he'd taken and he was just grateful that he'd survived.

Fuck, had he really read Lucas that poorly? Sure, the man had never hidden the fact that he didn't date. That he fucked a guy and he moved on. And that's all he'd been, right? A trick. A one-night stand. A diversion. But hadn't there been something more? He was sure he'd felt something. An intoxicating spark that seemed to take on a life of its own in his belly. Andrei had been positive that Lucas had felt it too.

Come back to me.

Those desperate words still whispered through his head. They hadn't felt hollow when they were spoken. When Lucas was sure Andrei was safe and going to make a full recovery, had he simply come to his senses, realizing that he was making more out of his feelings for the man because he'd been afraid he'd die? Guilt could be a bitch to deal with.

"Fuck," Andrei groaned and then chuckled at the irony. Was this karma coming back to kick his ass? It would be fitting. He'd never been one to lead a woman on, but there had been several in his life who had misread his intentions and desires, hoping that he was interested in more than one night of fun. It was a cruel kind of justice. The first time he took a chance on someone, actually opened himself up to trust and feel something…and it was nothing more than a quick fuck.

"Idiot," he muttered to himself, pushing to his feet with another groan. His body was stiff. Snow had warned him that his newly mended ribs would be tender and sore for at least another week or two. His knees were still giving him fits as well, forcing him to shuffle along like an old man reliant on a walker. He wanted his young, fit body back, but it was going to be a few more weeks before he could hit the gym and start building muscle again. For now, he was just trying to keep moving and pushing through the pain.

A knock at the door stopped Andrei on his way to his bedroom. His brow furrowed as he stared at it. No one was expected—not that any of the people who had been stopping by had bothered to call ahead of time. As he unlocked the door, he prayed it wasn't Ian. He liked the guy, but he was running out of room in his fridge for all the food he was dropping off.

Lucas stood in the hall, holding Andrei's garment bag in one hand and another bag in his other, looking unsure and nervous. The air was sucked out of the room, leaving Andrei breathless and unsteady. For a moment, they just stared at each other.

"Hey," Andrei said, drawing in a breath to fill his starving lungs.

"Hey. I…I brought your things from my place. I thought you might need them." Lucas dropped his gaze, seeming to prefer to look down at the bags in his hands rather than up at Andrei's face.

Andrei looked down at the bag as well. He hadn't bothered to go back to Lucas's to pack after they'd decided he'd go undercover. No, he'd gone directly back to his apartment and started contacting the few people he knew still involved in underground fights, spreading the news that he'd been canned. He'd forgotten about his clothes. Or maybe he'd hoped to use them as an excuse to go back to the penthouse. Weeks later, he wasn't so sure what his plan had been.

"Yeah, sorry about that. I'm sure you could have just sent it over with Rowe," he mumbled, shuffling back so Lucas could bring the bags in.

Lucas stepped inside, carefully moving around Andrei to place the garment bag next to couch while the plastic bag was placed on the scarred coffee table littered with magazines and water bottles. "No, I wanted to come."

"Did you?" he asked, not bothering to hide the bitterness from his voice.

Lucas's head snapped up and he held Andrei's angry gaze. "Yes." And then he looked away, his eyes sweeping over the small apartment. There wasn't much to it. Just a narrow living room with a sofa, coffee table and flat screen TV hung on the wall. At the other end of the room were the even smaller kitchen and a hall that led to the bathroom and bedroom.

Lucas's adamant tone helped Andrei push through some of the anger that was crowding close so that he could really see Lucas. He didn't look good. Not like Andrei would have expected. He remembered that Lucas had been haggard and rough while he'd been in the hospital, but that came from sleeping at Andrei's bedside and surviving on what little food his friends were likely able to force down him. But Lucas hadn't been to the hospital in two weeks. His charcoal slacks and black button-down shirt accentuated his form, but the clothes seemed to hang on him a little more as if he'd lost weight. Lucas's face was thinner and more heavily lined than he remembered with dark circles under his eyes.

"Are...are you moving?" Lucas said, waving toward a stack of boxes in one corner.

It wasn't the only stack of boxes in the apartment. But Andrei didn't think about it. It was the little pause in the question. It was the second time Lucas had done it, as if he was unsure of whether to ask. As if he was carefully weighing his words. Something was wrong. Snow and the others hadn't mentioned anything to him and it had taken every bit of Andrei's self-control not to ask about Lucas, but he was determined not to sound like some lovesick debutante left behind at the dance.

Standing there, watching the man who'd turned his life upside down in too many ways, he saw it finally. Lucas was nervous. He was twitchy and anxious, barely staying in his own skin. If he'd sneezed at that second, Lucas would have jumped fifty feet. Andrei would have bet money that he'd never see the man like that. Lucas was always the epitome of calm and collected. He was always in control, particularly of himself.

"No. I just never bothered to unpack all my shit," he replied, looking around the cluttered room. It had to appear claustrophobic to Lucas considering the open space and light he enjoyed in his penthouse. His place was dimly lit and what little furniture he had was a dark navy, sucking in what paltry light the one floor lamp produced. "I tend to move around a lot." He shrugged. "Never really settle."

Lucas's eyes jumped back to his face and for a flash there was an unreadable emotion flitting through their green-gray depths that made Andrei's heart stutter before the man looked away again, frowning. Conversation faltered and Andrei stepped closer to Lucas, peering at the bag.

"What's that?"

"Books." Lucas's voice was soft and rough, almost a caress. "The books you left at the office."

"Thanks! I've been bored out of my mind." When he looked up at Lucas, he flashed him a grin and Lucas seemed to relax a little. "Rowe says it'll be at least another two weeks before he'll consider letting me come back to work. I'll pay you back for these."

"No." The single word came out hard and angry, causing Andrei to jerk away from Lucas. He heard the other man curse under his breath softly, clearly not meaning for Andrei to hear him. "No, I don't want you to."

Andrei stared at him for a second and then nodded, stepping back. "You want something to drink? I was about to take a painkiller." He started to turn for the kitchen and grinned at Lucas. "You wanna split a Percocet?"

Lucas's lips twitched as if he couldn't decide whether to grin. "No, I'm trying to give them up. Water would be nice. Thank you."

"Would you mind taking the garment bag in the bedroom and grabbing the pill bottle off the nightstand?" he asked as he walked into the kitchen. Lucas didn't say anything, but when Andrei looked up from grabbing two bottles of water from the kitchen, the other man had disappeared. He made it back to the living room when Lucas reappeared, opening the brown bottle and pouring one pill into his palm. Andrei popped it into his mouth and then struggled to open the bottle. Between the bright orange cast on his left arm and the knuckles on his right hand still bandaged, he struggled getting a good grip on things.

Putting the cap on the pills, Lucas put the brown bottle and the second bottle of water on the table before gently taking the water bottle from Andrei's fingers. He opened it and then handed it back. Andrei accepted it with an embarrassed grunt and downed half the bottle before putting it on the table behind him. There was the strangest sense of déjà vu about the whole thing that kept Andrei wanting to smile.

"How are you?" Lucas inquired.

Andrei shrugged. "Not bad. I'm usually better about handling things," he said, waving toward the water. "I just waited too long to take that pill. Too achy. But I'm bouncing back."

"Good."

And the conversation died again. Andrei was itching to ask why he'd stopped coming to the hospital and why he'd waited so long to come to his apartment. He wanted to know why Lucas looked so bad and uncomfortable. Even that first day together, when Lucas had stepped clear of the painkiller haze, they hadn't felt this awkward and uncomfortable. This was painful, cutting deep and rattling Andrei in a way he struggled to define.

Was this how things ended? When one person wanted out, but was too guilt-ridden to finally say the words that were building uncomfortably between them…left with long, painful silences until someone finally cracked.

"So is this where you tell me that it was all fun but you know, it was just supposed to be a one-night thing and you wish me well and all that jazz? No hard feelings, of course." Andrei wished he'd kept the water bottle so he had something to do with his hands.

Lucas visibly flinched at Andrei's words and took a half-step back. "No. I…no."

Andrei stared at him, willing him to explain but Lucas just looked away from him, falling strangely silent. "Then what? You're here out of guilt?"

"No," he said louder this time, but stopped, his frown deepening before he corrected himself. "I do feel guilty but that's not why I'm here."

Andrei stepped closer and was relieved when Lucas didn't move. He wasn't steady enough to chase the man around the apartment even if it wasn't that big. "You've got to let that go. This shit wasn't your fault. I knew what I was risking."

Andrei reached up and ran his fingers lightly along Lucas's jaw. A soft moan slipped from Lucas as his eyes drifted shut. Applying more pressure, Andrei cupped his cheek and Lucas leaned his head into his palm as if he craved Andrei's touch. Andrei's heart jerked while something squeezed his chest. It was suddenly hard to draw a breath. When Lucas opened his eyes, Andrei was drowning. In those stark depths, he saw pain, confusion, and something that simply stole his breath away.

"I don't know what to do." Lucas's voice quavered when he spoke. "This…I don't know what to do about this. I—"

Andrei slid his hand around to lightly rub the pad of his thumb along Lucas's lower lip, stopping his words. "*This*? There is no *this*," he said with a grin, echoing the same words Lucas had spoken to him in the run-down warehouse in Price Hill…a little more than a month ago. Hell, it almost seemed like a lifetime had passed since that night.

With extreme care, Lucas reached up and pulled Andrei's hand away. "I'm a liar and a coward," Lucas whispered. He closed the short distance between them, his breath dancing along Andrei's lips for a second before he brushed their lips together. So gentle. An aching caress that broke a moan from Andrei. Lucas slowly built the kiss, adding pressure by small degrees. Nipping at Andrei's lips, he followed with a touch of his tongue as if to soothe the momentary pain. The hunger intensified and Lucas dipped his tongue inside Andrei's mouth, exploring every inch, memorizing his feel and taste.

Until that moment, Andrei hadn't realized that every touch, every kiss prior had been aimed to seduce, to tear down his walls and make him pliable. Or aimed to stake a claim, mark Andrei as Lucas's alone.

But this kiss. This was tenderness that neither one of them had dared before. It struck Andrei's heart and left an ache behind that he wasn't sure would ever go away. This wasn't about possession, but about Lucas being possessed. It was about surrender and absolute trust.

Lucas broke off the kiss and turned his head, rubbing his cheek along Andrei's. Both of them were breathing heavy.

"If you say the word, I'll leave," Lucas said, his breath brushing along the shell of Andrei's ear. "You won't hear from me again. We go back to our lives and spend the rest of them trying to forget about…*this*."

"And if I don't?" The question came out rough as if it had nearly been caught in the back of Andrei's throat.

Lucas straightened so he could look Andrei in the eyes. "I…I don't know. You're still figuring things out… and I…"

A smile tugged at Andrei's lips and he couldn't stop himself from kissing Lucas, though he pulled away quickly. He was right in that

Andrei was still figuring things out. He was apparently bisexual, but he wasn't sure if he was ready to tell others about this discovery and he had no desire to explore this new side with anyone else other than Lucas. And then the other man looked as if he was balancing on a razor's edge, trying to decide how much he was willing to let himself care for Andrei when being involved with a man ran against all his carefully laid plans for his life. But the fact that he was talking about it, that he wasn't running for the door, meant that he was willing to try.

"It's just sex until we say otherwise," Andrei said, his lips lightly grazing Lucas's as he spoke.

Lucas pulled back and stared at Andrei, questioning. At long last, his hand drifted up and his fingers threaded through Andrei's hair. God, how he missed that touch. "Are you sure?"

Andrei let his eyes drift shut, soaking in the affection. How could such a simple touch nearly send him to his knees? "Just sex. No strings. No complications. No expectations."

"One complication, actually," he corrected, causing Andrei's eyes to pop open. "No other men. I think I can tolerate you fucking a woman…maybe…well," Lucas paused, frowning as he thought about the words now they were out of his mouth. "Well, maybe not. But definitely no other men. I find myself oddly possessive where you're concerned." Lucas's hand tightened slightly in Andrei's hair before he caught himself and relaxed his hold.

Andrei's eyes sparkled with laughter but he swallowed it back. "Can I expect the same from you?"

Lucas nodded. "It's only fair."

Andrei snorted. "Monogamous, no strings sex. That's got to be a first."

"Shut up," Lucas muttered before roughly kissing him to stop Andrei's laugh. He pulled away just as he started to deepen the kiss and frowned. "We are going to be so bad at this."

"Monumentally bad at this." Andrei grinned broadly, feeling lighter than he had in weeks. "But I'd rather be bad at this with you than spend another minute trying to be without you."

Lucas nodded jerkily, their lips brushing. "I can't sleep without you. Can't think. Can't…breathe." The confession sounded as if it had been ripped straight from Lucas's soul, driving Andrei to capture his mouth in another rough kiss.

It didn't last nearly as long as Andrei would have liked, but he was struggling to keep his feet. His damned body was still weak and shaky and Lucas could feel it.

"I should go," Lucas whispered, breaking off the kiss.

"Can't control yourself?"

"You're still injured," he evaded, not denying the obvious. Neither one of them had much control when it came to sex, but Lucas had a point. Andrei wasn't up for much until he healed a bit more.

Lucas started for the door when Andrei stopped him.

"You got plans for tonight?"

"No."

"Ian has loaded my fridge with enough food to feed an army. You wanna stay, eat some great food, and learn about my unholy love for '80s John Candy movies?"

Lucas lifted one skeptical eyebrow at Andrei. "You have *Great Outdoors*?"

"Of course I've got *Great Outdoors*," he scoffed, dramatically rolling his eyes as if the very idea that he didn't was sacrilege. "Why?"

A slow, lazy grin spread across Lucas's lips as he leaned against the front door. "Because I've got an unholy love for '80s Dan Aykroyd movies."

His heart quickened at that smile and everything in him just felt lighter. He loved that fucking smile. With his index finger, Andrei motioned between the two of them. "You know, we might be okay."

Chuckling, Lucas returned to Andrei's side, running his fingers through his long strands before kissing him. "Yeah, you might be right."

Sneak Peek

Coming in 2016

SHATTER

Book 2 of the Unbreakable Bonds Series
By Jocelynn Drake and Rinda Elliott

Read an exclusive excerpt now:

The bar gave new definition to the word "dive".
Ashton "Snow" Frost sprawled in the most unrelentingly painful chair he'd ever sat in and tried not to look too closely at his dingy surroundings. Either the decorator had been into early seventies drug den or the place had been tucked into this corner of Covington since before he'd been born. Some nineties grunge band grumbled from a jukebox near the restrooms and the high number of college kids swilling beer at the long, battered bar and around the pool tables surprised him. *And depressed him.* He wouldn't even be able to salvage his original plan to get laid tonight—the crowd too young for his tastes.
The entire evening wasn't a bust, though. He watched his friends across the room, visible despite the crowd. They'd grabbed one of the pool tables and from the expression on Andrei's face as he pressed the cue stick against his forehead, Melissa was kicking his ass. Lucas and Ian sat on barstools on either side of a small pub table, both laughing. Probably because they all knew Rowe's wife was a shark and it seemed nobody had told the Romanian. Snow couldn't help but grin. Lucas and

Ian didn't blend despite the fact they were similarly dressed to everyone else in jeans and boots. Ian, despite his short stature, looked like he'd stepped off a runway in his untucked blue shirt and sharp, brown blazer. And Snow couldn't believe Lucas wasn't even cracking a hint of sweat in his cashmere sweater in this sweltering place.

Guess the owners didn't feel the price of air conditioning a bar in December was worth it.

He shifted in his seat and glared at Rowan Ward, who sat next to him at the large table he'd reserved near the back of the bar. "You know what, Ward?"

Rowe turned green eyes his way and frowned as he pulled at the neckline of his black sweatshirt. Sweat darkened the red hair around his temples. "What?"

"I figured out what's wrong with this bar. I'm not blind or deaf."

Rowe smirked and wiped a drip of sweat rolling down his temple with a paper napkin. "It's popular with some of my employees, so I thought we'd try it out. Come on now, doc. The place has ambiance—even you have to admit that."

Snow shot him a glare. "It has wood paneling."

"I always liked wood paneling. My granddad had this old hunting cabin in Colorado—paneling in every room. I think it gives a place a homey feel. I loved it there." He picked up his mug of beer and took a huge swallow, then tilted his glass toward Snow. "And the brew's cheap."

"That's because it's shit beer." Snow turned back to catch Andrei leaning over a pool table and chuckled when he saw Lucas watching as well, focus firmly locked on his former bodyguard's ass.

Rowe had followed Snow's gaze and shook his head. "It's wild, isn't it? Turned my straight employee gay. That's some superpower Vallois has."

"Doubt he was ever completely straight." Snow slouched back, hooking his elbow over the back of the chair. "I walked in on them a couple of weeks ago and caught a bit of their action and there was nothing holding the Romanian back. Was fucking hot." Snow waved one hand at Andrei as he straightened from his shot. "Look at him. I would have worked to turn the man fully to my side as well." Lucas didn't admit that he was exclusively sleeping with his ex-bodyguard, but it was obvious that's what was going on. There was a lot more than just sex going on there.

Rowe nudged him. "You saw them?"

Snow heard something in his friend's tone that made him look closer. "Is that something you'd like to see yourself?"

He shrugged. "I love women. Love my wife. You know that. But I'm not blind and those two are ridiculously gorgeous—so it had to be something to see." He leaned closer so he could lower his voice. "Did you see who's the top?"

Snow had been taking a drink of his beer and he sucked it in so fast, he choked. Clearing his throat, he set the mug down. "It's not always one way or the other. You do get that, right?"

"No, I don't actually. From things you and Lucas have said, I got the feeling it was one or the other. Come on, doc. Fill me in."

"Fuck no. Rent some porn. I happen to know your wife loves gay porn. Like *really* loves gay porn. You do know she asked me to film something once, right? That time we were all out at that steakhouse and I picked up that blond waiter?"

"I remember. Unfortunately. You left us with the check and started making out with him before you were even out the door. What's funny is you think I don't already know about the porn and my wife."

Snow lifted an eyebrow, intrigued. "You two watch it together?"

Green eyes rolled. "No way in hell am I giving you any wank material."

"Too late." Snow gave Rowe his most wicked, teasing grin.

"Right. You don't like sex with women."

"Oh Rowe, do we need a lesson on porn and watching versus action? I enjoy good, straight porn at times. When something is hot, it's hot."

"You're telling me…" Rowe's expression went serious. "You're telling me, you could be with a woman?"

"No. I learned a long time ago that doesn't work for me." Snow had never found himself interested in anything beyond friendship with women. He liked everything about men. Liked their harder edges, their calloused hands, and masculine scents…their ability to take rough handling. He knew there were women out there who liked the latter, but he liked dick. Always had.

Snow toyed with a bottle cap, turning it over with the tips of his fingers. "What I'm telling you is that what we like to watch doesn't always coincide with what we like to do. You watch gay porn with your wife but you don't do guys, right?"

His friend's nod was slow and contemplative. "I get it. I do. I think it's just that I can't imagine having a penis and not wanting to put it into a woman. That's where everything goes fuzzy for me."

"Fuzzy isn't a bad place to be."

"If you say so." Rowe looked up and shoved out the chair next to him.

Snow followed his gaze to find Ian pushing through the crowd toward their table. It looked like the heat in this bar was getting to him as well because he peeled off the stylish jacket and draped it over his arm. His light brown hair was gelled into a style that looked messy and probably took him twenty minutes to get right. Everything about Ian always flowed together like it was effortless and knowing Ian, it mostly was. Snow had gone shopping with him once and Ian knew exactly what would go with what before he even took it off the rack. Hell, he let Ian pick out most of his suits. It certainly saved him the trouble of staying up to date on fashion. Not that he really cared about that. He just liked to know that he looked good.

"I don't know why I thought dressing for December was a good idea," Ian said as he sat next to Rowe. "But I'm still having a good time. This place is fun!"

Rowe turned a smug look Snow's way. "Snow doesn't agree. He's a bar snob. Lucas and his fancy nightclubs have tainted his view of proper men places."

Snow's grin grew, stretching his mouth wide. "Proper men places? Do tell more."

"You know," Rowe said, closing his hands into fists for emphasis. "Man caves. Places where we don't have to dress up. Where we aren't on display or trying to pick someone up. Where we don't have to smell nice for the ladies. We can hang out with other men in our natural slob states."

Ian's mouth fell open. "There are so many things wrong with that speech."

Chuckling, Snow picked up a napkin to wipe the condensation from his beer off the table. "Ladies aren't the only ones who dislike body odor. Just how does the world look with your head stuck so far up your ass? You're the only man I know with a natural slob state—" He sucked back the laughter, cocked his head. "Wait, that's not true anymore. I just remembered Banner."

"The cop?" Rowe asked.

It didn't escape Snow's notice that Ian, who'd been looking over his shoulder instantly turned back to their conversation. Hollis Banner, an annoying local detective, had been wearing out his welcome more than usual lately and none of them were under any sort of misunderstanding as to why. The big, scruffy, hard-edged asshole was sniffing around Ian and it made Snow want to hurt things. It wasn't that he had interest in Ian himself—no, their friendship was too solid for that—it was that nobody was good enough for him. Not with Snow knowing what the kid had endured as a teenager. The young chef brought out every protective instinct Snow had. Plus, they didn't need law enforcement hanging around, not when they all had things to hide.

He wiped the napkin over another spot of condensation and when it stuck to the table top, he snatched his hand back, snarled and pointed. "Really Rowan? I prefer my real men caves to at least be clean."

"This from a man who drops to his knees in men's bathrooms all over town."

"I thought you'd been paying more attention all these years." Snow winked and Ian softly snorted a laugh. "I'm not the one usually on my knees."

"Selfish bastard." Rowe laughed, probably because he'd heard enough over their more than a decade-long friendship to know that was true. Snow sometimes marveled over how well Rowe took the frank talk among their group of four when he was the only straight man. Well, mostly straight. Snow had an inkling there was a little curiosity going on up in the scrambled mess of Rowe's brain. And Lucas occasionally jumped the fence and slept with women, but Snow had always known that was more about what Lucas felt he should want, not what he truly liked.

The others came back to the table, fresh drinks in hand and the talk turned to Melissa's prowess with hard balls. Snow half-listened, finding that despite Rowe's poor taste in drinking establishments, the company relaxed him. He let his gaze roam the bar again, hoping to see someone old enough to be interesting and frowned when a shadowy figure stepped quickly out of sight. He narrowed his eyes, tried to see who it was because he had the distinct feeling the person had been watching them.

"What do you think, Snow?"

"Huh?" He turned to Ian, realizing he'd missed the subject entirely.

"Don't you agree that grocery shopping together is like a commitment?" Ian waved his finger at Lucas and Andrei. "They go together now."

Snow pursed his lips and took in the hint of red flushing Andrei's neck. "Ian, it's just food. We get that for you, it's a religion, but it doesn't work that way for the rest of us."

"It should." Ian stared at Lucas until the older man started to glare back. But Ian gave him that smile—the sweet one that could melt the coldest of hearts and Lucas's expression softened. Ian touched Andrei's arm. "This is serious, though? You two? I'm right, aren't I?"

The poor Romanian looked poised for flight as he tried to resist Ian's questions. He glanced at Lucas, cleared his throat. "We're just having fun."

"Are we?"

Everyone went quiet with Lucas's tone. The man's expression said so much about his feelings for the Romanian and Snow was sure he wasn't the only shocked person at the table.

"Is that what we're doing?" Lucas asked, voice low.

Andrei cocked his head, his dark eyes narrowing on Lucas. As usual, the heat between the two made Snow feel like he witnessed something infinitely private. Andrei had pulled his black, curly hair into a ponytail at his nape, so his curious expression was plain for all to see as he locked his stare on Lucas. "I thought so. Thought that's what we agreed on. No strings. Are you saying you want more?"

Lucas suddenly grinned. He slowly reached into the front pocket of his jeans and pulled out a single condom and held it up between two fingers.

"Prepared much?" Rowe asked, his mouth snapping shut when his wife reached across the table to smack his arm. "Hey now!" He rubbed his arm.

Lucas kept his gaze on Andrei as he flipped the condom over his shoulder. "That answer your question?"

The two men didn't move as Snow held his breath, then Andrei abruptly lunged half out of his chair, grabbed Lucas's jaw, and kissed him right there in front of everyone.

The feelings that tore through Snow confused him and made him feel faintly ashamed. He should be thrilled for his friend, happy that the man had found someone who made him feel like that. *And he was.* But some part of him felt cloudy with fear—fear that his world was about to shift. Snow had never seen his best friend like this and it caused a pang in his heart because it had been mostly the two of them since they'd been in elementary school. He took in Lucas's relaxed slouch as he let a man kiss him in public, the way he reached up to smooth his thumb over the edge of the hand Andrei had on his face.

That tender gesture showed so very much about how things had changed. Snow looked away, not focusing on anything in particular. Lucas was rearranging his life around someone he obviously cared for and that selfish bastard part of Snow—the one Rowe had joked about— wasn't sure how to handle it. He'd always wondered if he had anything of substance inside beyond his relationship with Lucas.

Seemed he'd be finding out.

Someone once again caught Snow's eye—someone who quickly turned away when Snow's gaze landed on him. But the light hit on a swarthy face that struck a chord of instant fury inside Snow. His gut twisted, his palms started sweating. He hoped he was wrong, but the clawing, black anger spilling into him told him he wasn't.

"Uh oh, I've seen that look come over Snow's face before." Melissa stretched her neck to, obviously trying to see where Snow was looking. "Looks like Snow has zeroed in a possible target. Can anyone else see? Is he hot?"

Snow let them think what they wanted. He'd excused himself from the group many a time before and there was no way he wanted one member of their group to see who he thought that was. He had to get to the guy first. He stood, ignoring the piercing, questioning stare Lucas aimed at him, and grabbed his coat. "Sorry, but I have to leave. Early surgery tomorrow."

"Yeah, right," Rowe muttered, his smile showing he was in the least put out.

He paused long enough to let Melissa press a kiss to his cheek. "Have fun, sweetie," she murmured with a dirty chuckle.

Snow strode fast toward the spot where that figure had disappeared and saw the man trying to dodge the crowd as he hurried toward the entrance. Snow caught glimpses of his black jacket as he moved. Right before the guy reached the door, he turned slightly and the light caught his face again.

Everything in Snow froze as he saw the long scar bisecting his left cheek. A scar Snow himself was responsible for inflicting. "Oh hell no," he muttered as he pushed harder through the crowd and ran outside. His breath fogged instantly in the cold as he swung right and left, looking for a face he'd hoped never to see again.

About the Authors

Jocelynn Drake is the author of the *New York Times* bestselling Dark Days series and the Asylum Tales. When she's not working on a new novel or arguing with her characters, she can be found shouting at the TV while playing video games, lost in a warm embrace of a good book, or just concocting ways to torment her fellow D&D gamers. (She's an evil DM.) Jocelynn loves Bruce Wayne, Ezio Auditore, travel, tattoos, explosions, fast cars, and Anthony Bourdain (but only when he's feeling really cranky). For more information about Jocelynn's world, check out www.JocelynnDrake.com.

Rinda Elliott is an author who loves unusual stories and credits growing up in a family of curious life-lovers who moved all over the country. Books and movies full of fantasy, science fiction, and romance kept them amused, especially in some of the stranger places. For years, she tried to separate her darker side with her humorous and romantic one. She published short fiction, but things really started happening when she gave in and mixed it up. When not lost in fiction, she loves making wine, collecting music, gaming, and spending time with her husband and two children.

She is the author of the Beri O'Dell urban fantasy series, the YA Sister of Fate Trilogy, and the paranormal romance Brothers Bernaux Trilogy. She also writes erotic fiction as Dani Worth. She can be found at RindaElliott.com. She's represented by Miriam Kriss at the Irene Goodman Agency. For more information about Rinda's stories, go to www.RindaElliott.com.

You can get updates on the Unbreakable Bonds series, read free short stories, and more at www.DrakeandElliott.com.

For social media, Jocelynn and Rinda can be found on Twitter at @DrakeandElliott. For Facebook, they can be found at www.facebook.com/DrakeandElliott.

You can also see the many inspirations for the men of the Unbreakable Bonds series on their Tumblr page at http://drakeandelliott.tumblr.com/.

Made in the USA
San Bernardino, CA
27 November 2017